a collection of twenty stories which in 1958 helped to attract . . .

THE POST ♀♂ INFLUENTIALS

A magazine is as vital as the people who read it. *Saturday Evening Post* readers, we've discovered, are an active, gregarious, spending group—talking about and recommending to others the things they read in the *Post*—liking and approving of the advertising. (In case we've missed you somehow, we'll be happy to give you Alfred Politz's figures on that.)

These readers are responding to a unique editorial package—a free-lance, feature, text magazine. *Post* contributors include almost every famous author who writes in the English language. In this year's volume are, among others, English novelist H. E. Bates, Pulitzer Prize-winner William Saroyan, and fantasy specialist Ray Bradbury.

You'll find some new names in *Post Stories 1958* along with the familiar and honored ones. The *Post* uses fiction, in the words of Executive Editor Robert Fuoss, "for that flash of insight fact can never muster." It takes fiction to make a modern magazine complete, to keep the "editorial mix" completely contemporary. Fiction's a factor, too, in exposing readers to what *you* have to say, bringing them face to face with *your* ad page. (We've got some interesting numbers on that subject, too. Just ask!)

THE SATURDAY EVENING POST

THE SATURDAY EVENING

POST

STORIES 1958

DOUBLEDAY & COMPANY, INC., GARDEN CITY, NEW YORK, 1959

Library of Congress Catalog Card Number 37-27266
Copyright © 1958, 1959 by The Curtis Publishing Company
All Rights Reserved
Printed in the United States of America

CONTENTS

POST STORIES 1958

THE DARLING BUDS OF MAY

by H. E. Bates

After distributing the eight ice creams—they were the largest vanilla, chocolate and raspberry blocks, each in yellow, brown and
almost purple stripes—Pop Larkin climbed up into the cab of the
gentian-blue, home-painted thirty-hundredweight truck, laughing
happily.

"Perfick wevver! You kids all right at the back there? . . . Ma,
hitch up a bit!"

Ma, in her salmon jumper, was almost two yards wide.

"I said you kids all right there?"

"How do you think they can hear," Ma said, "with you revving
up all the time?"

Pop laughed again and let the engine idle. The strong May sunlight, the first hot sun of the year, made the bonnet of the truck
gleam like brilliant blue enamel. All down the road, winding
through the valley, miles of pink apple orchards were in late bloom,
showing petals like light confetti.

"Zinnia and Petunia, Primrose, Victoria, Montgomery, Mariette!" Pop unrolled the handsome ribbon of six names, but heard only five separate answers, each voice choked and clotted with ice cream.

"Where's Mariette? Ain't Mariette there?"

"I'm here, Pop."

"That's all right, then. Thought you'd fell overboard."

"No, I'm here, Pop; I'm here."

"Perfick!" Pop said. "You think I ought to get more ice creams? It's so hot Ma's is nearly melted."

Ma shook all over, laughing like a jelly. Little rivers of yellow, brown and pinkish-purple cream were running down over her huge lardy hands. In her handsome big black eyes the cloudless blue May sky was reflected, making them dance as she threw out the splendid bank of her bosom, quivering under its salmon jumper. At thirty-five she still had a head of hair like black silk, curly and thick as it fell to her fat olive shoulders. Her stomach and thighs bulged like a hop sack under the tight brown skirt, and in her remarkably small delicate cream ears her round pearl-drop earrings trembled like young white cherries.

"Hitch up a bit, I said, Ma! Give father a bit o' room." Pop Larkin, who was thin, sharp, quick-eyed, jocular and already going shining bald on top, with narrow brown side linings to make up for it, nudged against the mass of flesh like a piglet against a sow. "Can't get the clutch in."

Ma hitched up a centimeter or two, still laughing.

"Perfick!" Pop said. "No, it ain't though. Where'd I put that money?"

Ice cream in his right hand, he began to feel in the pockets of his leather jacket with the other.

"I had it when I bought the ice creams. Don't say I dropped it. . . . Here, Ma, hold my ice cream."

Ma held the ice cream, taking a neat lick at a melting edge of it.

"All right, all right. Panic over. Put it in with the crisps."

Packets of potato crisps crackled out of his pocket, together with a bundle of notes, rolled up, perhaps a hundred of them, and clasped with a thick elastic band.

"Anybody want some crisps? Don't all speak at once! Anybody——"

"Please!"

Pop leaned out of the driving cab and with two deft backhand movements threw packets of potato crisps into the back of the truck.

"Crisps, Ma?"

"Please," Ma said. "Lovely. Just what I wanted."

Pop took from his pocket a third packet of potato crisps and handed it over to Ma, taking his ice cream back.

Soon, in perfect sunlight, between orchards that lifted gentle pink branches in the lightest breath of wind, the truck was passing strawberry fields.

"Got the straw on," Pop said. "Won't be above anuvver week or two now."

In June it would be strawberries for picking, followed by cherries before the month was ended, and then more cherries through all the month of July. Sometimes, in good summers, apples began before August did, and with them early plums and pears. In August and again in September it was apples. In September also it was hops and in October potatoes.

"See that, kids?" Pop slowed down the truck, idling past the long rows of fresh yellow straw. "Anybody don't want to go strawberry picking?"

In the answering burst of voices Pop thought, for the second time, that he couldn't hear the voice of Mariette.

"What's up with Mariette, Ma?"

"Mariette? Why?"

"Ain't heard her laughing much today."

"I expect she's thinking," Ma said.

"Thinking? What's she got to think about?"

"She's going to have a baby."

"Oh?" Pop said. "Well, that don't matter. Perfick. Jolly good." Ma did not seem unduly worried either.

"Who is it?" Pop said.

"She can't make up her mind."

Ma sat happily munching crisps, staring at cherry orchards as they sailed past.

"Have to make up her mind sometime, won't she?" Pop said.

"Why?"

"Oh, I just thought," Pop said.

"She thinks it's either that Charles boy who worked at the farm," Ma said, "or else that chap who works on the railway line. Harry somebody."

"I know him," Pop said. "He's married."

"The other one's overseas now," Ma said. "Tripoli or somewhere."

"Well, he'll get leave."

"Not for a year, he won't," Ma said. "And perhaps not then if he hears."

"Ah! Well, we'll think of something," Pop said. "Like some more crisps? How about some chocolate? Let's stop and have a beer. Got a crate in the back."

"Not now," Ma said. "Wait till we get home now. We'll have a stout then and I'll warm the fish and chips up."

Pop drove happily, both hands free now, staring with pleasure at the cherries, the apples and the strawberry fields, all so lovely under the May sunlight, and thinking with pleasure, too, of his six children and the splendid, handsome names he and Ma had given them. Jolly good names, perfick, every one of them, he thought. There was a reason for them all.

Montgomery, the only boy, had been named after the general. Primrose had come in the spring. Zinnia and Petunia were twins and they were the flowers Ma liked most. Victoria, the youngest girl, had been born in plum time.

Suddenly he couldn't remember why they had called the eldest Mariette.

"Ma," he said, "trying to think why we called her Mariette. Why did we?"

"I wanted to call her after that queen," Ma said. "I always felt so sorry for that queen."

"What queen?"

"The French one. Marie Antoinette. But you said it was too long. You'd never say it, you said."

"Oh, I remember," Pop said. "I remember now. We put the two together."

Ten minutes later they were home. With pride and satisfaction, Pop gazed on home as it suddenly appeared beyond its scrubby fringe of woodland, half filled with bluebells, half with scratching red-brown hens.

"Home looks nice," he said. "Allus does, though, don't it? Perfick."

"Lovely," Ma said.

"We're all right," Pop said. "Got nothing to worry about, Ma, have we?"

"Not that I can think of," Ma said.

Pop drew the truck to a standstill in a dusty yard of nettles, old oil drums, corrugated pigsties and piles of rusty iron in which a line of white ducks, three goats and a second batch of red-brown hens set up a concerted, trembling fuss of heads and wings, as if delighted.

Letting down the back board and holding up both arms, Pop took the youngest children one by one, jumping them down to the yard, laughing and kissing them as they came.

Presently only Mariette remained on the truck, wearing jodhpurs and a pale lemon shirt, standing erect, black-haired, soft-eyed, olive-skinned and so well made in a slender and delicate way that he could not believe that Ma, at seventeen, too, had looked exactly like her.

"It's all right. I can get down myself, Pop."

Pop held up his arms, looking at her tenderly. "Ah, come on. Ma's told me."

"Let me get down myself, Pop."

He stood watching her. Her eyes roamed past him, flashing and dark as her mother's, searching the yard.

It suddenly crossed his mind that she was afraid of something, not happy, and he half opened his mouth to comment on this unlikely, disturbing, unheard-of fact when she suddenly shook her black head and startled him by saying, "Pop, there's a man in the yard. There's a man over there by the horse box. Watching us."

Pop walked across the yard toward the horse box. He owned two horses, one a young black mare for Mariette, the other a piebald pony for the other kids. Mariette, who was crazy about horses, rode in point-to-points, sometimes went hunting and even jumped at shows. She was wonderful about horses. She looked amazing on a horse. Perfick, he thought.

"Hullo, hullo, hullo," he said. "Good morning. Afternoon, rather. Looking for me?"

The man—young, spectacled, pale-faced, trilby-hatted, with a small brown toothbrush mustache—carried a black brief case under his arm.

"Mr. Sidney Larkin?"

"Larkin, that's me," Pop said. He laughed in ringing fashion. "Larkin by name. Larkin by nature. What can I do for you? Nice wevver."

"I'm from the office of the Inspector of Taxes."

Pop stood blank and innocent, staggered by the very existence of such a person.

"You must have come to the wrong house," Pop said.

"You are Mr. Sidney Larkin?" The young man snapped open the brief case, took out a paper and glanced at it.

"That's me. That's me all right," Pop said.

"According to our records," the young man said, "you have made no return of income for the past year."

"Return?" Pop said. "What return? Why? Nobody asked me."

"You should have had a form," the young man said. He took a yellow-buff sheet of paper from the brief case and held it up. "One like this."

"Form?" Pop said. "Form?"

Ma was crossing the yard with a box of groceries under one arm and a bag of fruit in the other. Three big ripe pineapples stuck cactuslike heads from the top of the huge paper bag. The twins loved pineapple. Especially fresh.

"Ma, did we have a form like this?" Pop called. "Never had no form, did we?"

"Never seen one. Sure we never."

"Come over here, Ma, a minute. This gentleman's from the Inspector of summat or other."

"I got dinner to get," Ma said, and strode blandly on with groceries and pineapples, huge as a buffalo. "You want your dinner, don't you?"

Pop turned with an air of balmy indifference to the young man, who was staring incredulously at the receding figure of Ma as if she were part of the menagerie of hens, goats, ducks and horses.

"No, never had no form. Ma says so. Ma's the one who does the paper work."

The young man opened his mouth to speak, and for a moment it was as if a strangled, startled gurgle came out. His voice choked itself back, however, and in reality the sound came from a drove of fifteen young turkeys winding down from the strip of woodland.

"Won't hurt you," Pop said. "How about a nice hen bird for Christmas? Put your name on it now."

"This form has to be returned to the inspector," the young man said. "There is a statutory obligation——"

"Can't return it if I ain't got it," Pop said. "Now can I?"

"Here's another."

As he recoiled from the buff-yellow sheet of paper Pop saw Mariette walking across the yard, slender, long-striding, on her way to the wooden, brush-roofed stable where both pony and horse were kept.

"I got no time for forms," Pop said. "I got pigs to feed. Turkeys to feed. Hens to feed. Kids to feed. I ain't had no dinner. Nobody ain't had no dinner."

Suddenly the young man was not listening. With amazement, he was following the progress of Mariette's dark, yellow-shirted figure across the yard.

"My eldest daughter," Pop said. "Crazy on horses. Mad on riding. You do any riding, Mr.—Mr. —— I never caught your name."

"Charlton."

"Like to meet her, Mr. Charlton?" Pop said. The young man was still staring, mouth partly open. Between his fingers the tax form fluttered in the breezy sunlit air.

"Mariette, come over here a jiff. Young man here's crazy on horses, like you. Wants to meet you. Comes from the Ministry of Revenue or summat."

In astonished silence the young man stared at the new celestial body, the yellow shirt, as it floated across the background of rusty iron, pigsties, abandoned oil drums, goat-chewed hawthorn bushes and dusty earth.

"Mr. Charlton, this is my eldest. Mariette. The one who's mad on horses. Rides everywhere. You've very like seen her picture in the papers."

"Hullo," Mariette said. "I spotted you first."

"That's right; she saw you," Pop said. " 'Who's that nice young feller in the yard?' she said."

"So you," Mariette said, "like riding too?"

The eyes of the young man groped at the sunlight as if still unable correctly to focus the celestial body smiling at him from three feet away.

"I say every kid should have a horse," Pop said. "Nothing like a horse."

Suddenly the young man woke from mesmerism, making a startling statement.

"I saw you riding over at Barfield," he said. "In the third race. At Easter. You came second."

"I hope you won a bob or two on her," Pop said.

Again he laughed in ringing fashion, bringing from beyond the stable an echo of goose voices as three swaggering gray-white birds emerged from a barricade of nettles, to be followed presently by the half-sleepy, dainty figures of a dozen guinea fowl.

"Pity we didn't know you was coming," Pop said. "We're killing a goose tomorrow. Always kill a goose or a turkey or a few chicken at the weekend. Or else guinea fowl. Like guinea fowl?"

If the young man had any kind of answer ready, it was snatched from him by the voice of Ma, calling suddenly from the house: "Dinner's nearly ready. Anybody coming in or am I slaving for nothing?"

"We're coming, Ma!" Pop turned with eager, tempting relish to the young man, still speechless, still struggling with his efforts to focus correctly the dark-haired girl. "Well, we got to go, Mr. Charlton. Sorry. Ma won't have no waiting."

"Now, Mr. Larkin, about this form——"

"Did you see me at Newchurch?" Mariette said. "I rode there too."

"As a matter of fact, I did—I did, yes—— But, Mr. Larkin, about this form——"

"What form?" Mariette said.

"Oh, some form—some form," Pop said. . . . "I tell you what, Mr. Charlton, you come in and have a bite o' dinner with us. No, no trouble. Tons o' grub——"

"I've eaten, thank you. I've eaten."

"Well, cuppa tea then. Cuppa coffee. Bottle o' beer. Bottle o' stout. Drop o' cider."

The entire body of the young man seemed to swirl helplessly, as if half intoxicated, out of balance, on its axis.

"Oh, yes, do," Mariette said, and by the time he had recovered he found himself being led by Pop Larkin toward the house, from which Ma was already calling a second time: "If nobody don't come in three minutes I'll give it to the cats!"

"Know anybody who wants a pure white kitten?" Pop said. "Don't want a pure white kitten, do you?"

"So you were at Newchurch too," Mariette said. "I wish I'd known."

A moment later Pop threw up his hands in a gesture of near ecstasy at the overpowering beauty, which suddenly seemed to strike him all afresh, of the May afternoon.

"Beautiful, ain't it?" he said. "Perfick. I got a beautiful place here. Don't you think I got a beautiful place here, Mr. Charlton?"

In the kitchen a radio was loudly playing jazz. In the living room next door, where the curtains were half drawn, a television set was on, giving to the nine faces crowded about the table a gray-purple, flickering glow.

"Have just what you fancy, Mr. Charlton," Pop said. "If you don't see it here, ask for it. Bottle o' beer? Glass o' sherry? . . . Pass the vinegar, Ma."

Soon the young man, arms crooked at the crowded table, was nursing a cup of tea.

"Perhaps Mr. Charlton would like a couple o' sardines with his tea?" Pop said. . . . "Montgomery, fetch the sardines."

Mr. Charlton, bemused by the name of Montgomery, protested faintly that he did not like sardines.

"Mr. Charlton saw Mariette riding at Barfield," Pop said.

"And at Newchurch," Mariette said.

"Funny we didn't see you there," Ma said; "we was all there."

"Mr. Charlton," Pop said, "loves horses."

"Turn up the contrast," Ma said; "it's getting dark."

In the television's purplish light the young man watched the faces about the table as they engulfed fish and chips, ice cream, tomato catchup and jam, becoming more and more like pallid, eyeless ghouls. Pop had placed him between Ma and Mariette, and presently he detected under the great breathing bank of Ma's bosom, now mauve-salmon in the flickering light, the shape of two white kittens somehow nestling on the bulging precipice of her lap. Occasionally the kittens miaowed prettily and Ma fed them scraps of fish and pieces of biscuit.

Above the noise of jazz, television voices, kittens, geese hawking at the kitchen door and the chattering voices of the family, he found it hard to make himself heard.

"Mr. Larkin, about this form. If you've got any difficulties, I could help you fill it in."

"All right," Pop said, "you fill it in."

"It's still too dark," Ma said. "Turn it up a bit. It never stays where you put it nowadays."

"I'll give the thing one more week to behave itself," Pop said. "And if it don't, then I'll turn it in for another."

Mr. Charlton spread the yellow-buff form on the table in front of him and then took out his fountain pen and unscrewed the cap.

"Ma, is there any more ice cream?" Primrose said.

"In the fridge," Ma said. "Big block o' strawberry mousse. Get that."

"Full name: Sidney Charles Larkin," Mr. Charlton said, and wrote it down. "Occupation? Dealer?"

"Don't you call him 'dealer,'" Ma said. "I'll give you 'dealer.' He owns land."

"Well, landowner."

"Farmer," Pop said.

"Well, farmer," Mr. Charlton said. "I'm very sorry. Farmer."

"Mariette, cut the pineapple," Ma said. . . . "Montgomery, go into the kitchen and fetch that pint jug of cream."

While Mr. Charlton filled in the form, Mariette stood up, reached for the bread knife and started to cut the pineapples, putting thick, juicy slices on plates over which Ma poured heavy yellow cream.

"Real Jersey," Ma said. "From our cow."

Every time Mariette reached over for another plate she brushed the sleeve of Mr. Charlton, who either made sketchy blobs on the tax form or could not write at all.

"How many children?" Mr. Charlton said. "Six? Is that right? No more?"

"Well, not yet, old man. Plenty o' time, though. Give us a chance," Pop said, and again laughed in ringing fashion.

"Gone again," Ma said. "You can't see a blessed thing. . . . Montgomery, Primrose, switch it off and change it for the set in our bedroom."

In the half darkness that now smothered the room Mr. Charlton felt something smooth, sinuous and slender brush against his right calf. For one shimmering, unnerving moment he sat convinced that it was Mariette's leg entwining itself about his own. As it curled toward his thigh, he felt his throat begin choking, but suddenly he looked down and discovered that already the geese were under the table, where Ma was feeding them with scraps of fish, half-cold chips and crumbled buns.

Unnerved, he found it difficult to frame his next important question. "Of course, this is confidential in every way," he said, "but at what would you estimate your income?"

"Estimate, estimate?" Pop said. "Income—what income?"

Montgomery and Primrose, who had carried one television set away, now brought in another.

"Steady there, steady!" Ma said. "Watch where you're looking. Mind the cocktail cabinet."

"Hear that, Ma?" Pop said. "Income!"

Ma, as she had done in the truck, started laughing like a jelly.

"Outcome more likely," she said. "Outcome, I should say."

"Six kids to feed and clothe," Pop said. "This place to run. Fodder to buy. Wheat as dear as gold dust. Pig food enough to frighten you to death. Living all the time going up and up. Vet's fees. Fowl pest. Foot-and-mouth. Swine fever. Birds all the time dying. Income, old man? Income? I should like some, old man."

Before Mr. Charlton could answer this, the second television set threw across the room its pallid, unreal glow, now in a curious nightmare green. The twins, Zinnia and Petunia, at the same moment demanded more pineapple. The geese made shoveling noises under the table, and Mariette, rising to cut fresh slices, suddenly turned to Mr. Charlton with modest, almost whispered apology.

"I'm awfully sorry, Mr. Charlton. I didn't offer you any pineapple. Would you like some?"

"No, thanks. I'm not allowed it. I find it too acid."

"What a shame. Won't you change your mind? They're nice ripe ones."

"Ought to be," Ma said. "Cost enough."

"I'm afraid I'm simply not allowed it," Mr. Charlton said. "I have to go very carefully. I have to manage mostly on eggs and that sort of thing."

"Eggs?" Pop said. "Eggs? Why didn't you say so? . . . Got plenty of eggs, Ma, haven't we? Give Mr. Charlton a boiled egg or two wiv his tea."

"How would you like that?" Ma said. "A couple o' boiled eggs, Mr. Charlton? What do you say?"

To the delight of Ma, Mr. Charlton confessed that that was what he really wanted.

"I'll do them," Mariette said. "Three minutes? Four? How long?"

"Very light," Mr. Charlton said. "Three."

"Nice big 'uns! Brown!" Pop called to Mariette as she went into the kitchen, where the geese presently followed her, brushing past Mr. Charlton's legs again as they passed, once more to give him that shimmering, shocking moment of unnerving ecstasy.

"About this income," Mr. Charlton said. "Can you give me an estimate? Just an estimate."

"Estimate it'll be an' all, old man," Pop said. "Lucky if we clear a fiver a week, ain't we, Ma?"

"Fiver? I'd like to see one," Ma said.

"We want boiled eggs too!" the twins said, as in one voice. "Can we have boiled eggs?"

"Give over. Can't you see I'm cutting the pineapple?" Ma said.

Everybody except Mr. Charlton had large second helpings of pineapple, with more cream. When Ma had finished ladling out the cream, she poured the remainder of it into a tablespoon and then licked the spoon with her big red tongue. After two or three spoonfuls she cleaned the spoon with her finger and fed one of the white kittens with cream.

On the television screen a posse of cowboys fired thirty revolvers into a mountainside, and Mr. Charlton said, "I'm afraid we have to know what your income is, Mr. Larkin. Supposing——"

"All right," Pop said, "that's a fair question, old man. Fair for me, fair for another. How much do you get?"

"Oh, well, me, not all that much. Civil servant, you know."

"Nice safe job, though."

"Nice safe job, yes. I suppose so."

"Nothing like a nice safe job," Pop said. "As long as you're happy. Do you reckon you're happy?"

Mr. Charlton, who did not look at all happy, said quickly, "Supposing I put down a provisional five hundred?"

"Hundred weeks in a year now, Ma," Pop said, laughing again. "Well, put it down, old man—put it down. No harm in putting it down."

"Now names of children," Mr. Charlton said.

While Pop was reciting, with customary pride, the full names of the children, beginning with the youngest, Zinnia Florence and Petunia Mary, the twins, Mariette came back with two large brown boiled eggs in violet plastic egg cups to hear Pop say, "Nightingales in them woods up there behind the house, Mr. Charlton. Singing all day."

"Do nightingales sing all day?" Mr. Charlton said. "I wasn't aware."

"All day, all night," Pop said. "Like everything else in the mating season, they go hell for leather."

The plate holding the two eggs was embroidered with slices of the thinnest white bread and butter. Mariette had cut them herself. And now Mr. Charlton looked at them, as he looked at the eggs, with reluctance and trepidation, as if not wanting to tamper with their fresh unbroken neatness.

"I've been looking at you," Ma said. "I don't think you get enough to eat by half."

"I live in lodgings," Mr. Charlton said. "It's not always——"

"We want to have some of your egg!" the twins said. "Give us some of your egg!"

"Now you've started summat," Pop said.

"It's gone dark again," Ma said. "Turn up the contrast. . . . And, Montgomery, fetch me my stout. There's a good boy."

Soon, while Ma drank stout and Pop spoke passionately again of nightingales, bluebells that clothed the copses "fick as carpets, ficker in fact," and how soon it would be the great time of the year, the time he loved most, the time of strawberry fields and cherries everywhere, Mr. Charlton found himself with a twin on each knee, dipping white fingers of bread and butter into delicious craters of warm golden egg yolk.

"I hope the eggs are done right?" Mariette said.

"Perfect."

"Perfick they will be an' all if she does 'em, you can bet you," Pop said. "Perfick!"

Mr. Charlton had given up, for the time being, all thought of the buff-yellow form. A goose brushed his legs again. Outside, somewhere in the yard, a dog barked and the drove of turkeys seemed to respond in bubbling chorus. Far beyond them, in broken, throaty tones, a cuckoo called, almost in its June voice, and when it was silent the entire afternoon simmered in a single marvelous moment of quietness, breathlessly.

"If you don't mind me saying so," Ma said, "a few days in the country'd do you a world of good."

"What are we having Sunday, Ma?" Pop said. "Turkey?"

"What you like. Just what you fancy."

"Roast pork," Montgomery said. "I like roast pork. With them brown onions."

"Or goose," Pop said. "How about goose? We ain't had goose since Easter."

In enthusiastic tones Pop went on to ask Mr. Charlton whether he preferred goose, turkey or roast pork, but Mr. Charlton, bewildered, trying to clean his misty spectacles and at the same time cut into thin fingers the last of his bread and butter, confessed he hardly knew.

"Well, I tell you what," Ma said, "we'll have goose and roast pork. Then I can do apple sauce for the two."

"Perfick," Pop said. "Perfick. . . . Primrose, pass me the tomato catchup. I've got a bit of iced bun to finish up."

"Dinner on Sunday then," Ma said. "About two o'clock."

Mr. Charlton, who was unable to decide from this whether he had been invited to dinner or not, felt fate softly brush his legs again in the shape of a goose neck. At the same time he saw Mariette smile at him with glowing eyes, almost as if she had in fact brushed his legs with her own, and he felt his limbs again begin melting.

Across the fields a cuckoo called again, and Pop echoed it with a belch that seemed to surprise him not only by its length and richness but by the fact that it was a belch at all.

"Manners," he said. "Pardon," and beat his chest in stern, suppressive apology. "Wind all of a sudden."

"What's on now?" Ma said.

On the television screen all shooting had died and two men on horses, one a piebald, were riding away up a valley, waving farewell hands.

"Nobody's birthday Sunday, is it?" Pop said.

"Nobody's birthday before August," Ma said.

"Then it's mine," Mariette said. "I'll be eighteen."

"Pity it ain't nobody's birthday," Pop said. "We might have had a few fireworks."

Suddenly all the geese were gone from the kitchen and Ma, marveling at this fact, started laughing like a jelly again, and said, "They did that once before. They heard us talking!"

"I tell you what," Pop said, "if you've had enough, Mr. Charlton, why don't you get Mariette to take you as far as the wood and hear them nightingales? I don't think you believe they sing all day, do you?"

"Oh, yes, I——"

"Shall we ride or walk?" Mariette said. "I don't mind the pony if you want to ride."

"I think I'd rather walk."

"In that case I'll run and change into a dress," she said. "It's getting a bit warm for jodhpurs."

While Mariette had gone upstairs the twins abandoned Mr. Charlton's eggless plate and fetched jam jars from the kitchen.

"Going to the stall," they said. "Think we'll put honeysuckle on today instead of bluebells."

As they ran off, Pop said, "That's the flower stall they keep at the corner of the road down there. Wild flowers. Tuppence a bunch for motorists. Everybody works here, y'know."

"I think I passed it," Mr. Charlton said, "as I walked up from the bus."

"That's the one," Pop said. "Everybody's got to work here so's we can scratch a living. . . . Montgomery, you'd better get off to your goats and start milking 'em."

Presently Ma, concerned at Mr. Charlton's air of retreat, uncertainty and fatigue, spread hands like lardy legs of pork across her salmon jumper and said with earnest kindness, "Taking your holiday soon, Mr. Charlton? Where do you usually go?"

"I hadn't——"

"You should come strawberry picking with us," Ma said. "Do you

the world of good. Else cherry picking. Best holiday in the world
if the weather's nice."

"Perfick," Pop said. "Don't cost nothing either. . . . Here's Mariette. Perfick, I tell you."

Mr. Charlton rose from the table to find himself stunned by a
new astral body, now in a lime-green dress with a broad black belt,
a flouncing skirt, loose neck and short scalloped sleeves. Her beautiful eyes were smiling at him splendidly.

"Is that your Shantung?" Ma said. "You'll be warm enough in
that, dear, will you?"

"Oh, it's hot," Mariette said. "It's nice to feel the breeze blowing
round my legs again. . . . You ready, Mr. Charlton?"

Mr. Charlton, the buff-yellow form forgotten, turned and followed Mariette, who actually stretched out a friendly hand. As they
crossed a yard noisy with hawking geese, mumbling turkeys and
braying goats being led to milking by Montgomery, Pop called,
"Remember about Sunday, Mr. Charlton, won't you? Don't forget
about Sunday."

"You really mean it?" Mr. Charlton halted and turned back,
amazed. "Are you quite sure?"

"Sure?" Pop said. "Blimey, old man, I'm going to kill the geese
any minute now."

"Thank you. Thank you very much."

"One goose or two, Ma?" Pop called. "Two geese be enough?
Or shall we have three?"

Mr. Charlton, still stunned and amazed, turned to face the waiting figure of Mariette, and saw it miraculously framed, against piles
of junk, rampant nettles and, in the near distance, deep strips of
bluebells fenced away, in the strip of woodland, from flocks of
brown marauding hens. Her legs, in pale beige silk stockings, were
surprisingly shapely and slender. Her bosom was outlined with grace
by the soft lime Shantung.

He could not believe in this figure. Nor, five minutes later, could
he believe that the yard of nettles and junk, Pop's beautiful, incredible paradise, lay only a hundred yards away, screened by thickets

of hornbeam and hazel, oaks in olive flower and May trees carrying blossoms as rich and thick as the Jersey cream Ma had poured so lavishly.

"You didn't really believe about the nightingales, did you?"

"No."

"Listen," she said. "You will."

Walking along the woodland path, Mr. Charlton could hear only a single untangled chorus of evening bird song, unseparated into species, confusing as the tuning of orchestra strings.

"Let's stand here by the gate and listen," Mariette said. "Let's stand and listen here."

Mr. Charlton, transfixed, utterly bemused, stood by the gate and listened. Patches of evening sunlight, broken gold, sprinkled down through oak branches, like delicate quivering translations in light of the bird notes themselves.

"No, not that one," Mariette said. "That's a blackbird. . . . Not the one over there either. That's a wren. . . . Now, that one. The one in the chestnut up there. The one with the long notes and then the long pause. Can you hear it now? That's a nightingale."

Mr. Charlton listened, hardly breathing, and heard for the first time in his life, in a conscious moment, the voice of a nightingale singing against a May evening sky.

Enthralled, still hardly believing it, he turned to see the deep sparkling eyes holding him in utter captivation and heard her say again, "You really didn't believe it, did you?"

"I must say I didn't."

"I tell you something else you didn't believe either."

"What was that?"

"You didn't believe about me, did you?" she said. "You didn't believe I was the same girl you saw riding at Easter, did you?"

"No," he said. "How did you know?"

"I guessed," she said. "I could see it in your eyes. I was watching you."

She lifted her hands and held them suddenly against his cheeks without either boldness or hesitation, but with a lightness of touch that woke in Mr. Charlton's legs exactly the same melting, unnerving sensation as when the geese had brushed against him under the table. A moment later he saw her lips upraised.

"Who did you think I was?"

Mr. Charlton made a startling, embarrassed confession. "I thought—well, I was actually told you were someone else, in point of fact—that you were a niece of Lady Planson-Forbes—you know, at Carrington Hall."

Mariette began laughing, in ringing tones, very much like her father. "Now you've just found I wasn't."

"Well, yes."

"You feel it makes any difference?"

"Well, in point of fact——"

"I'm just the same, aren't I?" She smiled, and he found his eyes level with her bare olive shoulder. "I'm just me. The same girl. Just me. Just the same."

Again she touched his face with her hands and Mr. Charlton took hurried refuge in a sudden recollection of the buff-yellow form.

"By the way, I mustn't forget to get your father to sign that form before I go."

"You'll have to sign it for him," she said, "or Ma will. He can't write his name."

She laughed again, and Mr. Charlton, his limbs melting once more as she lifted his hand to her bare warm shoulder, heard consciously, but dizzily, for the second time in his life, a passionate burst of song from the nightingales.

At the same moment, back in the house, Pop returned to the kitchen after wringing the necks of three fat geese and poured himself a much-needed glass of beer.

"A few days like this, Ma," he said, "'ll put a bit o' paint on the strawberries."

Ma was raking the kitchen fire, putting onto it empty ice-cream cartons, scraps of fish and chips, eggshells, pineapple tops and Mr. Charlton's buff-yellow paper.

"I don't know as I shan't get a few bottles o' port wine in for Sunday," Pop said, "so we can celebrate."

"Celebrate what?"

"Well," Pop said, "what about Mariette?"

Ma laughed again, jumper shaking like a salmon jelly.

"The only thing is," Pop said, "I hope he won't want to take her away from here." He carried his beer to the kitchen door and from there contemplated, almost with reverence, the paradisiacal scene beyond. "Ma, you know we got a beautiful place here. Paradise. I don't know what we'd do if she were took away from here."

Standing in the evening sunlight, gazing across the pile of junk, the nettles, the rusting hovels and the scratching, dusty hens, Pop sighed loudly and with such content that the sound seemed to travel with perfect definition across the surrounding fields of buttercups and may, gathering its echo at last from the mingled sounds of the remaining geese, the voices of cuckoos calling as they flew across the meadows and the small, passionate, invisible nightingales.

"Perfick," Pop said. "You couldn't wish for nothing more perfick nowhere."

JOURNEY IN THE DARK

by David Walker

A big jet rumbled over the sky. Simon saw himself: Captain Simon Hall, dials glowing, instruments ticking—the only sounds at faster than sound. Night-liner captain, one hour out and five to London, a hundred travelers in his care.

He came back from that flight, and a frog was croaking a double croak. "Not you," it croaked. The frog stopped croaking in the swamp. It was a specially quiet night, so still that he could hear the river, too hot for sleep.

He turned on the radio by his bed. When it had warmed up, Simon put his ear close to listen to far-off quiet rock 'n' roll, and then a man said, "Here is the latest on Hurricane Anna." He said that the death toll in Bermuda was at least two hundred, but Anna was headed well out to sea, no cause for alarm on the New England coast.

Simon switched off. Hurricane Anna did not seem too real in the quiet here. But it was real, all right, a few hundred miles away, much realer than Captain Simon Hall of the Douglas, or the Boeing, or the Comet, or the Convair. Simon shivered. Hurricanes were great huge winds, and he hated winds. You couldn't hear or smell or feel or anything in a wind. The winds in Anna were a hundred miles an hour, the man had said, and he said, "This first one of the season is a corker." But Anna was staying out at sea.

They were talking downstairs. He tiptoed out and sat on the top step, not hearing what they said, and not wanting to. The sound of their voices, one and the other, the quick and the slow, was like a part of the old wooden house, like company for him and the house and everything in the dark. And then the telephone rang.

Dad crossed the hall and shut the door. There was a long-distance sort of wait; and then dad talked. Simon sat out of sight from down below, ready to pop back to bed and be playing possum. Dad often took a wander up, the few nights he was here.

But his father, Col. Robert Hall, did not come up. He went to the living-room door and said, "So much for Labor Day weekend. Conference Tuesday morning on the Coast. That means I fly from La Guardia tomorrow night."

"Oh, Robert, can't they ever let you alone?"

"It's the nature of the job," he said. Dad had some very important sort of Air Force job. "They would have sent a plane for me," he said, "but no flying tomorrow."

"The hurricane?"

"Yes," he said. "It's miles away, but those things have long tentacles in weather. I'll have to take the car. I'm sorry, Mary; just one of those things."

Simon heard his mother sigh, and she said, "Just one of those things that never seem to stop. The Air Force is your family, not us."

Dad said nothing.

"I didn't mean that, Bob. I know it's not your fault. But tomorrow of all days—when you were going to talk to Simon. Who's going to do it now? Do I have to tell the truth to Simon?"

"Sh-h-h, Mary. He might be awake."

The truth to Simon. Simon stood up, his hand on the rail at the top of the stairs. He turned for bed because he wanted not to hear; but he wanted to hear, he had to hear; and so he did not go to bed; he went four steps down, his bare toes knowing the quiet places on the steps. He listened.

"Why did we build up his hopes? I never wanted to."

"Carruthers said, 'As long as there's hope, then let him hope.'"

"Do I have to tell him? Couldn't we wait till Washington, for you to do it? I may be comfort and fun and so on for him; but you're his man in trouble."

"Carruthers said, 'Tell him at Tannahac, the one place he really knows. Give him a week to adjust himself.'"

"And that boarding school—why does he have to go so soon?"

"Carruthers said——"

"If you say 'Carruthers said' just once again, I'll scream."

"He says they have to be properly taught by specialists. Simon's perfectly healthy, he says. They're very happy there, he says."

"Simon won't be. He'll hate every minute of it. Besides, haven't I learned with Simon, and taught him properly?"

"Yes, darling; of course you have." Dad's voice was slow and deep and patient. "You've been wonderful. But it's wearing you out. You can't be tied to the house forever."

"I can, I can. I never want to leave the house. Why can't you understand? Why do you have to be so hard and cruel?"

There was a pause down there; and then dad, who was a kind, uncruel man, said, "Are you thinking of yourself, or Simon?"

Simon Hall went up the stairs and into his room and closed the door without a sound, and got into bed and thought, *They've just been pretending I'd get better. They knew it all along. It isn't me she's thinking of, it's her. Dad doesn't want me home. I'm no use to anyone.*

Simon saw the things that he would never see and do: He saw the jet planes in the sky. He saw trout rising on the stream. He saw a bike. He saw many things from the time before his eyes stopped working, which was two years ago, when he was nine.

When Simon was ten, he could see a bit again, and everyone said to him, "That's great news, Simon." Then it was worse; then it was better, miles better; then it was just shapes and colors. "Be patient, Simon," they said to him. But now he was blinder than any bat, for keeps—that was what mum would try to tell him tomorrow. Well, he wouldn't let her tell him. And another thing— he wasn't going away to any school.

The frog still croaked in the quiet night. He heard the river, a small sound flowing on and on. He heard waves breaking at the shore. *The waves are like some watery clock,* he thought, *tick-break, tock-wash, on all the beaches around the world.* The waves were louder as Simon went to sleep.

"What time is it, dad?" There were five ponies in his dream, five boys on five ponies in a field.

"It's after eight, old sleepyhead. Wake up!"

"I'm awake," he said. "What kind of a morning is it?" It was a muggy, heavy-feeling morning; that was how it felt to him.

"Overcast. The glass is down to twenty-nine point two." Being a pretty famous pilot, dad always watched the weather. "Some heavy rain, they say, and thirty-mile winds in the afternoon. That's the tips of Hurricane Anna's fingers, Simon. But Anna heads east by north away from us; and that means no excuse for me to stay. I have to fly to the Coast tonight."

Then Simon Hall remembered. He remembered. *The Air Force is your family, not us;* and everything.

"Sorry, son," he heard his father say. "Just can't be helped. You'll have to look after the women for me."

He put a hand on Simon's head, and gave his hair a ruffle, but Simon shook his head away. He was thinking: *Me look after anyone?* And then he thought: *If dad would just stay today, it wouldn't be too bad; and we could practice on the buzzer, too, and——*

"Keep on with the Morse code, Simon. That's a useful thing."

It was funny how dad often seemed to think of the same things you were thinking. "What are you reading and sending now?"

"Reading ten, sending around twelve, I guess." But he said, "I'm fed up with buzzing."

"That's a useful thing," dad said again. There was a pause. Simon sensed his father standing near him, and uneasy. "You all right? No aches and pains?"

He shook his head. No aches and pains. "O.K.," he said.

"There's a man," said dad in his soldier's voice, and said good-by until next week, and went downstairs.

Simon dressed. The station wagon drove away. Fried flounder fillets was the breakfast smell. He and dad had caught twelve in the bay. Simon was as good at it as dad, except for taking out the hooks.

"Simon, you didn't brush your hair," his mother said. He did that, and came back to eat his cereal.

"Do be more careful, darling. You're slopping it around."

"No, thanks," he said about the flounder fillets. "Don't like flounder."

"Me too," said Jennifer. "I hate old flounder."

"You had three the last time," mum said to him. "Besides," she said, "you can't catch them unless you eat them. That isn't right."

"Sure can't eat 'em unless you catch 'em," Simon said. " 'T ain't right neither."

Giggles across the table. "Gosh, you're funny," Jennifer said. But mum said he wasn't funny. He had a slice of bread and strawberry jam instead of flounder. He wished he had had flounder.

"What's on this morning, darling?"

"Gotta job with Jim Kent," he said.

"All right, but be back by twelve. We'll have to—— I want to talk about plans and things this afternoon."

Plans for school and what the doctor said. He grunted.

"Please, mummy, could I go too?"

"No," she said. "One Jim Kent vocabulary in the family is

enough. Go as far as the bridge, and send her right back, Simon, and don't forget your slicker in case it rains."

"Fuss, fuss," he said. "O.K."

He and Jennifer went along the road. Jennifer was nearly six, still young enough to hold a hand. "It's a funny-feeling sort of day," she said. "The sky is sort of a muddy color everywhere all over."

The air was still, and wet-touching warm like a bathroom after you have had a bath. The smell of the sea was strong. The sounds were loud and close and hanging in the air. He heard two blue jays crying. *Blue jay on the hill, Brings water to the mill*; that was one of Jim Kent's sayings.

"Old slowpoke, why are you hanging back?"

"I was just trying it," said Jennifer. "Me with my eyes tight shut, or almost nearly, and you just take me right along. I don't see how you do it, not exactly."

"It's easy," he said. "The middle of the road is higher, like a hump; I stay on that; and I know how far to the places I know."

"You won't have to, soon, when your eyes are right again. But, gosh, Simon, even then you'll still see much better than other people in the dark."

They walked a bit. They came to the river. Jennifer saw two trout from the bridge. "Home now, funny-face," he said.

"You're a funny-face," she said.

He listened to her running back. Then he went on. The other bank of the Tannahac River was much higher. He climbed. Here was the big white pine, he knew by feel and smell and answering sound. It was easy at Tannahac Point beside the river, above the sea. It was easy because he knew it all before. They never went back to other places he had known before; flying nomads, that was what dad said about them, changing Air Force jobs and homes. But most of the summers that Simon could remember they had come to Tannahac Point in the state of Maine. The house stood alone. Jim Kent at the highway was their nearest neighbor.

Now a breeze came rushing. It came from the sea and through the spruces and across the road where Simon was walking. The squall came over and went away, and the air was still again; like one big puff to blow out all the candles on the cake, then no more puffs.

Cars passed on the highway up ahead. One stopped at the service station. Simon heard the pump motor running, and Jim Kent's voice. That was fine, Jim not off somewhere. Simon stopped to listen to a bird. It sang at treetop angle, moving about. He knew the red-eyed vireo's song, the one you might mix up with a robin's.

"Hiya, shipmate!"

"Hi, Jim!" he said. "What's cookin'?"

"I'd say a blow. Damn weatherman says not." Jim made a good round juicy-sounding spit about the weatherman. "The colonel, your dad, stopped by for gas. Off to the Coast, he says, poor fellah. Them Air Force brass, they sure do monkey around the nation."

"Sure do, Jim," he said.

"Want to work on that bike again?"

"Yeah," he said. "Back wheel and chain was next."

"O.K. then, here she is! Now listen, shipmate."

Jim told him what to undo and what to do to fit the wheel and chain. Jim had a side line making old bikes into new. Jim had about a hundred side lines. He was terrific.

Simon worked. Two cars came for gas, one old rattle-squeaker, one with a radio switched on. Hurricane still moving out and away. Heavy rain to be expected; gale warnings Eastport. That was farther up the coast. Clear of this area by six P.M.

He was pretty slow at it. "Finished, Jim," he called, and Jim came over. He said the chain was a hair too tight, and the wheel not true. "Fix that, 'n' she'll be a first-rate job."

Another car. "Portland, lady? First right, second left, and take the parkway. Set your pretty spinnakers right for lucky Portland. . . . Me? I wish I could, but momma's right up there, keepin' tabs on me from that window. 'By, then, honey! . . . Gee," said Jim. "What a dish that was! Best landin' craft I seen all summer."

"See here, Jim Kent, ah'm warnin' you. Ah won't have no flirtin' around with no loose women, you bold bad sailor you. This ain't Manila." Mrs. Kent gave a big fat scolding growl, and closed the window.

"That's fine now, shipmate; a dandy job. I gotta calm the wife, and get spruced up. Gotta drivin' job to do. You spell me at the pumps a minute?"

"Sure," he said. He sat down on the concrete place between the pumps, and he was thinking that he wished he could stay at Tannahac always. A warm damp wind blew over and died, and blew again from the east. *Go away, you damn hurricane!* he thought with a shiver; Jim Kent language.

Here came a car. "Hi!" he said. "Regular or super?"

"Super," the stranger said. "Fill her up, son." Then the man said "Oh," and showed him, and he filled her up.

"How much?" he said.

"Three-seventeen," the stranger said.

"Oil and water?"

"They're O.K." The man gave him three bills, a dime, a nickel and two pennies.

"I'll just get your windshield," Simon said, and did.

"Thanks a lot," said the man. "Top service." He drove away. He seemed like a decent guy.

"Here's the money, Jim. Three-seventeen," he said.

"That's right," said Jim. "Now let's see: Hour 'n' a half at fifty an hour is seventy-five, plus five per cent on sales makes ninety, add sea-duty pay. Here, shipmate; wages a dollar even."

"Oh, gee, I told you last time, Jim, I don't want wages. It isn't work. It's fun."

"Sure work is fun. 'T ain't the point. Point is, you earned every cent. Know what I said to your dad this mornin'?"

"What, Jim?"

" 'Colonel, sir to you,' I says, 'that boy has the mechanic's touch. I'd take him on any time.' "

"Gosh, Jim, do you think I could? I mean work here steady always?"

Pause. "Summer vacations? Why, sure you can."

"I meant——" he began to say. But here came Mrs. Kent with milk and cookies; and Jim gave him gas to clean his hands. The cookies were all right. The wind was stronger. "What's the latest on Anna?" asked Jim Kent.

"Dawdlin' along away." Mrs. Kent was a Southern girl Jim had met up with in the Navy. She was a comfortable, slow-speaking lady, decent, same as Jim.

"Thanks a lot, Mrs. Kent," he said, and he gave her back the glass.

"I'd better hoist anchor. Gotta tycoon to drive to Boston. Drop you home, shipmate?"

"I guess I'll walk," he said. "Thanks just the same."

Jim sniffed. "Better be quick, rain's coming. Y'know," he said slowly, "they may say Anna's goin' to fade away off Newfoundland, but I don't like the smell of it. Reminds me—— What do you say, honey?"

"Feels like a storm to me," Mrs. Kent said.

" 'By, Jim," he said. " 'By, Mrs. Kent."

"Shipmate!"

"Yes, Jim?" He was thinking again he just wished he could stay here always and work for Jim; but summer vacations——

"Listen now! I'm going to be away till late. The wind don't matter in that house; it's strong and no trees right near. The sea don't matter; you're forty foot up. But the river now. So say to your mum from me: If there's a helluva Noah's Ark of rain, come over quick. Old Tannahac Lake might bust her britches."

"O.K.," he said. He started for home. He was not thinking about floods or whatever it was that Jim had been saying. He was thinking: *Dad was in for gas this morning. Dad must have told about school and everything to Jim. That was why Jim sort of hesitated and then said, "Summer vacations." Jim doesn't really think I could be a mechanic. Jim was cheering me up, that's what. Jim couldn't use me either.*

The rain began as he crossed the bridge. He heard the bluejays cry again. The wind was blowing harder. The rain beat at his face and ran down his neck. It was different from ordinary rain. This rain was warmer than the wind that brought it from the east.

Simon hurried. The wind and the rain drowned everything. They drowned his private radar-sonar system. He got no echoes now from things nearby. The wind and rain muddled him. He tripped and stumbled and stood again and shivered in the warm and cruel wind and rain. This way? That way? Run! Steady, steady. Then he found the hump or crown of the road; Simon Hall walked on.

He heard a door open and shut. "Darling!" she said inside. "Wet as a codfish; you'll have to change. I watched you coming, Simon. I don't know how you do it."

"Easy," he said. And he thought, *I wasn't really scared back there; not really.* He went upstairs and dried himself and changed. The windows rattled. The rain drummed on the glass. He went downstairs again.

It was cold ham for lunch, and lemon pie. The old house shivered and shook in the wind. It had been grandfather's summer cottage —Maj. Simon Hall, United States Army, Killed in Action at Château-Thierry.

Simon dried dishes; Jennifer did the nonbreakables. "Some wind!" he said. *World's funny,* he thought. *So quiet just about an hour ago at Jim's, and now——*

"The rain is like a million bucketfuls at once," said Jennifer.

"The weatherman said it would be heavy for an hour or two," mum said. " 'High pressure,' he said, or something, and us at the edge of it or something."

"Low pressure, mum; not high. Gosh, everyone knows that."

"Not me," she said. "I'm only a dumb housewife woman. You scientists in pants—why, you're the pressure cookers."

He laughed at mum's crazy way of saying things. He hoped she was not going to talk to him about school and that. He finished his chores. The wind was stronger every minute. He escaped to switch on the radio in the living room. The static was terrible. He spun the knob along through howls and splintering cracks—a voice. He turned back to it, and heard: "Hurricane Anna has changed direction. Warnings for all." The man's voice had that same short you-get-jumping sound about it as dad's voice when dad spoke in a quiet-tearing hurry; but Simon did not hear the rest of what the man was saying. The radio went dead.

At about that time Robert Hall, Colonel U. S. Air Force, had rounded Boston on 128, four and a half hours out, halfway. He had run through heavy rain, but that had stopped. The overcast was dense; the cross-wind was troublesome at speed. The traffic was negligible for Labor Day. Robert Hall was troubled. He could not help having to fly to the Coast tonight. Such trips without notice were routine since he had taken on the A.E.C. job. What troubled him was that he had left Mary to do a thing he should have done himself—tell Simon. What troubled him was that he had said to her, "*Are you thinking of yourself or Simon?*" Psychiatrist's truth; oh, yes, possibly. But why did pain lead you to say such things? What troubled him——

"I'd better just check again," he said aloud. An hour ago, Anna was a hundred and fifty miles below Nova Scotia, moving roughly east, but slower. For these latitudes, a hurricane of small diameter and great intensity. He had placed it on his mental map, more than two hundred miles from Tannahac—the center, that was—and going away. All well, with a professional pilot's reservation that the only good hurricane was a dead one.

Boston came in strong. Hall listened. Then he cursed himself. Lucky Hall, they called him. Lucky Hall, who left his wife, blind son, and daughter——

Wheelspin on the grass dividing strip, U-turn completed, one hundred and eighty degrees. Hurricane Anna had switched direction a hundred and ten, heading fast for Augusta, Maine; and that put Tannahac in center of path.

The speedometer needle swung; the announcer spoke on: Gusts of a hundred; rainfall twenty inches or more, acute flood danger, all low-lying areas, coastal and inland. *Twenty inches*, he thought. *Or thirty. What could that do to Tannahac Lake, the reservoir?* He remembered Connecticut that other year.

The power went off just after one; and now it was four, and the wind still grew. You wouldn't believe that the wind could still be growing, but it was. It thundered and screamed and bashed the house.

Simon read a bit in Braille, but his fingers were stupid with the noise. "Why not practice on your buzzer, Simon?"

It was a battery buzzer. *What'll I send?* he thought, and he did an alphabet. And then he sent: "S-I-M-O-N H-A-L-L" about ten times; he could not think of anything else to send.

"What are you sending, darling?"

"Oh, nothing," he said. He stopped.

Mum read to Jennifer, and the wind was loud. The wind, the thunder and the rain made one huge sound together. She read a story called The Little Engine That Could, which was a small kid's story, but Simon listened; and then there was a crashing smashing of broken glass, and wind and rain in the living room. He held his handkerchief to his cheek. Mum tried to nail a board across the window where a pane was broken, but it wouldn't stay, and the wind and the rain came blasting in.

"What a carpenter!" she said. "Let's get out of the wind."

So they sat on the cellar stairs, and the storm was above them, and mum said: "What happened to your face?"

"Cut," he said.

She went away and came back, and he felt the warm beam on his cheek. "It isn't deep," she said. She put on an antiseptic and a bandage. She shook the flashlight. "Battery's almost done," she said. "How typical of Mrs. Hall."

"The cellar's all water everywhere," said Jennifer.

He heard water pouring in along the walls. "How deep?" he asked. He shivered in the darkness.

"The shoeshine table's floating," Jennifer said. "That's how deep."

"Jim said——" he began. His mouth was all dry. He tried to remember what Jim had said, but he had not been listening properly to Jim. "Jim said to say: 'If there's a helluva Noah's Ark of rain, come over quick. Old Tannahac Lake might bust her britches.'"

"Jim Kent said that? Why didn't you tell me?"

He forgot. He did not know. He didn't know anything. "Wait!" she said. Mum left the door open. This time the sound was not a clatter of glass and a roar of wind. This time the sound was a great huge hammer bashing a hole in the house, and Jennifer was crying. She held onto his legs, but he did not hold her. She was a step below him. Jennifer stopped crying.

Mum came back. "We couldn't," she said. "Not possibly."

"Water's nearly at my toes," said Jennifer.

"Upstairs we go."

Simon did not move. He couldn't. He couldn't go up to that again.

Mum shook his shoulder. She shook him hard. "Come on!" she said. He came. "Your room," she said. "It's away from the wind."

She followed with Jennifer, and pushed and prodded him from behind, and he climbed the stairs, and the noise was ten times as loud up here. He sat on his bed. Mum sat between him and Jennifer. Her arm was round him; he felt a bit better.

"What was that huge crash, mum?"

"A branch of some old tree," she said. "It came through the wall. Poor living room."

"What time is it, mum?"

"Ten after eight," she said. "Extra late-supper dividend. Ham sandwich and a banana. Here!"

"I can't see to eat," said Jennifer. "It's pitch-black dark and it's past my bedtime."

Mum laughed. "You're the character of the family," she said; and then the biggest gust, bigger than anything there had ever been, seized on the house, and Simon felt the house heave up and hang and settle back, and he clutched at the metal of his bed. "Sandwich," she said.

He shook his head. He wished dad was here. If only dad was here.

"Eat it," she said. He tried to eat the bread and ham, but he had no spit to chew it with.

"Please couldn't we have a light?" asked Jennifer.

"Our last candle—oh, we might as well."

"That's lovely," said Jennifer when mum came back, and Simon managed a half banana, and mum said: "Shall we sing that hymn?" She did not say which one, but she began to sing a hymn they knew, and Jennifer joined in, and then the three of them all sang it:

> *"Jesus bids us shine*
> *With a pure, clear light,*
> *Like a little candle*
> *Burning in the night.*
> *In this world of darkness,*
> *So let us shine—*
> *You in your small corner,*
> *And I in mine."*

"Listen!" she said. "The wind is dropping."

Simon listened. In all these hours, in all the time he ever could remember, there had been the wind, the thunder and the rain, the giants storming at him. But now the wind had dropped. Just for one moment there was no wind at all, and then it blew again, hard,

hard, hard as ever, the horrible wind. The wind wasn't dropping. Or was it now?

"It really is," she said. "I wonder, though? What do they say about hurri——"

"Sh-h, mum!"

He opened the window, and it blew again, and Simon waited, and then he heard what he thought he had heard the time before. A car horn sounded. It did not sound in one single blast, or "toot-toot" as people sound their horns to say "Thanks" or "Hi, there," like Jim Kent did to his pals along the road. This horn was sending Morse code: "S-I-M-O-N."

"Simon," he said. "That's dad." But the small horn sound was swallowed by the wind.

"How do you know? How could it be dad?"

"Everyone's different," he said. "Like writing." Clipped dots, long long dashes—dad's trade-mark on the buzzer. "It's dad, for sure."

Now again: "S-I-M-O-N." Pause. "C-O-M-E." Pause. "F-L-O-O-D-S."

" 'Come floods,' " he says.

"Why didn't he come, though? 'Come floods.' But it's pitch-dark, and the flashlight dies out each time in half a minute. How can I take you? How can I, possibly?"

He fought himself. "Wind's stopping," he said. "We can try. Come on, mum!"

Now Simon was less afraid. Now he tingled in his back, and he went downstairs, and mum and Jennifer came after him, and he thought, *Trees blown down. I'll take my stick.* He found his stick in the porch, and they went outside, and the wind was blowing. He edged along the house, and came to the corner, and put his stick out beyond the corner. The wind whipped the stick right across in his hand; that was how strong the wind was. But suddenly there

was no wind again. He heard it go roaring away through trees, and
the only sound here and now was rain.

Water up to his ankles; then a higher place, the crown of the
road? "Mum," he said. "What's the flashlight like?"

"O.K. for a few seconds now and then."

"Gosh, it's dark." Jennifer's voice was high and small and afraid
in the night.

"I'll go first," he said. "Don't use the light yet, mum." Then mum
held onto his shoulder, and she carried Jennifer, who cried a bit.

Simon walked. He held the stick in front. He stumbled, but mum
steadied him. ". . . twenty-three," he counted. Here the curve began. He followed it with his toes, left a little, left; and while he
counted, the tune was sounding in his head: *Jesus bids us shine.*
". . . thirty-eight, thirty-nine," . . . *With a pure, clear light . . .* ;
now the other way, and now the wind came blasting from the sea,
and the three of them lay together on the road, and trees were
crashing, and that gust of wind was gone, and Simon made himself get up again. The horn was sounding now again, a desperate
flicker of sound ahead: "S-I-M-O-N."

He went on. The stick struck. He put out his other hand and
felt spruce branches, prickly. "Light, mum," he said.

It was not too big a tree. She put Jennifer over, and climbed
over, and helped him over, and he led the way again. ". . . Sixty-
three, sixty-four" . . . *Like a little candle, Burning in the night.*
Now straight ahead, and halfway to the bridge, and Simon heard
the river rushing, the Tannahac, the quiet stream where dad once
taught him to fish for trout. *In this world of darkness.*

The wind came again in this world of darkness, and heaved and
plucked at them, huddled on the road. The wind went on, and
the rain was less, and the horn still hooted.

"What's happened to him? What can have happened to him?"

Mum's hand gripped hard on Simon's shoulder. The wind went
altogether now, no gust growing, no gust dying; and an old frog
croaked nearby, on as still a night as last night's frog had croaked:
"Not you," last night's frog had croaked. "Yes, you," this frog was

croaking for Simon Hall. "Yes, you." *Could be the same old frog,* he thought. "Mum!" he said.

"Yes, Simon?"

"I know about being blind," he said.

"I was thinking of it," his mother said. "Our eyes in the eye of the storm—is that being blind?"

"I see a star," said Jennifer. "Just one star straight above, and not another single speckle anywhere."

A second tree. They managed that. Simon was tired. ". . . Hundred and twenty-seven . . . twenty-eight." *So let us shine.*

"Wait, darling!" she said. "It's over the bridge."

The sound of the river was not a great sound in the middle silence of the storm. It was a rushing in the silence, another kind of power.

The bridge shuddered and trembled in the flood. Beyond these sounds, and far away upstream, a new sound had begun—the rumble-grumble of a great sound far away, quite like the sound of a big jet rolling over the sky. "S-I-M-O-N."

"Hold on to me tight," she said. They waded through the foot-plucking flood, the handrail drumming. They came through safely.

Simon led again. But the climb was steep, and he was tired, and he was stumbling. "Quick, darling! Quick!"

The rumbling grew, upriver. It was changing, swelling, filling the valley. The tune still went through Simon's head. He hummed it aloud, saying the words to himself in his mind: . . . *You in your small corner, And I in mine.*

"Robert!" she called. "Robert!"

"Mary! Have you got the kids?"

"We're all here. Are you badly hurt?"

A grunt not far ahead. Mum dropped Jennifer, and ran.

Jennifer hung on to Simon and they went together.

"Of course I'm not badly hurt. Can't you hear me?" Dad sounded very cross.

"What happened, darling?"

"Some drive, it was. . . . Finally reached . . . damned pine came

down smack on the hood of the car. I'm pinned in here, and one
leg's cracked, I guess. God knows why the horn still works. You
heard it, did you?"

"Simon heard it. He read the message when the wind was dropping; so we came."

"With that apology for a light? How the—— How?"

"Simon led us."

The noise in the valley grew, and dad said, "Simon Hall," perhaps to himself.

"Here, dad," Simon said.

"Good man," his father said.

They listened. The flood roared over flatland above Tannahac
Point, beside the river. "Good-by, dear house," said mum. Then
they were quiet, hearing the flood and thinking of the house.

"You absolutely stuck, dad?"

"Sure I'm stuck."

"Jim said he'd be late; but I could leave a message with Mrs.
Kent."

"No," said mum. "Not you."

"Here comes the wind again," said Robert Hall. "Get in back,
you three."

"But, Robert, your leg!"

"It's pinned," he said. "I'll live. Get in."

They sat in the car. The eye of the hurricane had passed.

A great wind blew now from the west, and Simon did not fear
the wind. *Old Jim will come,* thought Simon Hall; and he fell
asleep.

> *In this world of darkness,*
> *So let us shine—*
> *You in your small corner,*
> *And I in mine.*

FOR LOVE OF DAISY

by William Saroyan

"One thing about cats," a little girl named Daisy Hamilcar said to her mother. "They don't go jumping up on your new dress with muddy paws the minute they see you again."

"No, they don't," Daisy's mother said. "But they do go sneaking around. Fido loves you."

"Well, I hate him," Daisy said. "This isn't the first new dress he's muddied up with his stupid love. It's the second. I don't want Fido any more. I want a cat."

"Look at the poor fellow," Daisy's mother said. "He's all crushed by your rudeness."

"My rudeness?" Daisy said. "Mother, I don't believe I've ever known such a stupid dog."

"Fido's breed is famous for its intelligence," Mrs. Hamilcar said.

"They're notorious, I'd say, for barking when there isn't a thief for miles around, for muddying people's dresses and for whimpering with all their hearts and souls when they think everybody they know isn't madly in love with them. I am looking at the silly fellow, and I may say the silly fellow's looking at me."

"As he has been ever since you rejected his pure, steadfast, indestructible love," Mrs. Hamilcar said. "They broke the mold when they made Fido. He's a big dog with a soft heart. Red hair. A man's head, rather than a dog's. Eyes that any calf would be proud to look at wildflowers with. Ears as alert as any hare's. Tail as long as a pony's, as vibrant as a lion's. A posture like a lord's. A stance like a statue's. A walk like a boulevardier's."

"What the devil's a boulevardier?"

"Did you pick up that kind of language at camp?"

"Oh, no. They'd never let us speak intelligently there. I got it from father, of course. What is a boulevardier?"

"A boulevardier is a man who wears spats, carries a stick and always has a rosebud in his lapel. If he has a mustache, he waxes it and keeps the ends twisted up."

"I don't believe I've ever seen one of those."

"Most likely not. They do the better part of their boulevardiering in Paris."

"France?"

"Well, not Paris, Texas."

"But I was born there."

"Yes, but you were moved to New York, and then to California, when you were still very little."

"How little?"

"One year."

"That's not so little."

"Too little to enjoy watching a boulevardier walk down the Rue de la Paix."

"Why there?"

"Well, we lived on the Rue de la Paix while your father worked for the Herald Tribune, and you and I often sat at the window and watched the people in the street, including the boulevardiers."

"And you think Fido walks the way they do?"

"Exactly. I've never seen anything like it. I think you ought to know, Daisy, that you picked a great entity from the Pacific Palisades Pound when you picked Fido."

"What's an entity?"

"A whole being."

"Every dog's that."

"Not by a long shot, and I wouldn't care to think of Fido as merely a dog, because you and I know he's a good deal more. Kiss and make up."

"I will not."

"You're breaking his heart."

"I don't care if I am."

."But what's a little mud on a dress?"

"Mother, that dress was given to me last year on my eighth birthday by Miss Quillercape. Out of all of the girls of Oh-Ho Hill, Miss Quillercape gave only me a dress. What did she give the other girls on their birthdays? Little things. Little Spanish fans. Little bracelets and necklaces of Indian beads. Little handkerchiefs. But when it was my birthday, she gave me that dress, handmade by Miss Quillercape herself, bright yellow, with all kinds of little flowers sewed in."

"The dress will be as good as new just as soon as Margie comes on Thursday and does the laundry."

"My plan was to walk up to Miss Quillercape's as soon as I got home—in the dress she gave me, as I promised I would."

Mrs. Hamilcar stopped reading the galleys of her husband's third novel in order to have a good look at her daughter, for, if the truth were told—and why shouldn't it be?—she was jealous of Miss Quillercape, a little old woman of seventy who had captured the affection and admiration of every little girl in Oh-Ho Hill from the age of two to twelve. After twelve, the little girls became young women and got themselves uncaptured, only to become captured by the boys of the neighborhood who had suddenly become young men.

"As you promised you would?" Mrs. Hamilcar said.

"Yes, mother. Miss Quillercape and I are the best friends we have ever had or ever will. Why, there is no place in the whole world like her house, and no lady like Miss Quillercape."

"Well, now, I begin to understand why you're so annoyed with Fido. Perhaps we ought to have him destroyed."

"Mother, I wish you wouldn't be so insensitive and—well, vulgar!"

"I'm a little hurt," Mrs. Hamilcar said, "and when I'm hurt I'm always a little insensitive and vulgar."

"Why should you be hurt? I haven't blamed you. I've blamed Fido."

"I'm a little hurt that somebody else—another woman, at that— could mean so much to you. Why, you haven't even given me a hug since the bus let you off at the corner fifteen minutes ago."

"I didn't get a chance," Daisy said. "Wasn't Fido all over me with his big stupid muddy paws?"

"Well?" Mrs. Hamilcar said.

"Well, what?"

"Well, what's the matter with right now?"

"Golly," Daisy said. "Sometimes I'm absolutely impossible. Just get me a little mad and I think I wouldn't recognize my own mother." She ran to her mother, and they hugged and kissed.

"But I'm still mad at Fido," she said. "And I want a cat."

"Look in your closet for a nice dress, and go on up the hill to Miss Quillercape's."

"I will not."

"Why not?"

"I couldn't pay her a visit unless I had on the dress she gave me. It would be the worst manners in the world between friends like us. Oh, she wouldn't notice, of course. She'd be thrilled to see me, and we'd have hot chocolate and Scotch scones and butter and jam, and we'd talk about everything under the sun, but it wouldn't be the same, and I'd know. I'd know, and I'd die of shame because she'd know I knew, and neither of us would speak of it. We're both ladies that way all the time, and the strain of it would be more than I could bear, that's all. After two long, unbearable weeks at that goody-goody camp."

"Well, we can talk about the camp later. One thing at a time, and first things first. You promised Miss Quillercape to visit her the minute you got home from camp?"

"Yes."

"Wearing the dress she gave you?"

"That wasn't part of the promise, but, of course, I myself had planned it that way, as an expression of my gratitude and appreciation. That's why I put the dress on at camp this morning, and went to so much trouble to keep it clean all the way home—three hours of weary travel! First, we marched from the camp to where a bus was waiting. Then we got on the bus and rode to where the boat was. Then we got on the boat and sailed from Catalina to San Pedro. Then we marched again to where another bus was waiting. Then we got on that bus, and it took us to where the last bus was waiting. Then we got on that bus, and it started and stopped, letting off girls at their houses all over the whole world. And wouldn't I be the last to get off?"

"I'm sorry," Mrs. Hamilcar said.

She got up suddenly and went to the washing machine just beyond the kitchen, her daughter walking behind her, Fido lying in front of the fireplace where Mrs. Hamilcar had ordered him to lie, and stay! A request—a demand—that was now driving the dog mad with curiosity.

He had followed the conversation with anxiety and fascination, waiting desperately for the hardness to leave Daisy's voice—his Daisy, his wonderful Daisy, his beautiful Daisy, his Daisy who had been gone from Oh-Ho Hill for so long, his Daisy he had searched for everywhere, coming suddenly upon all manner of creatures, day and night, creatures he had never before even known existed—that skunk, for instance, standing stock-still and just looking at him, with its tail straight up; and that possum that waddled slowly away, stopping now and then to look back, neither a friend nor an enemy, neither scared nor eager for friendship or a fight; that garter snake that tumbled away, in and out of the tall grass, in a kind of frantic running he couldn't understand, but just had to see more of, until the poor snake was exhausted and couldn't run any more and just stopped and waited for the worst, which Fido was astonished to discover the poor fellow expected, since all Fido had been after was to study that kind of running. He went up close and looked into the little eyes, and then at the colors—why, the poor fellow was beautiful, that's what he was.

And all the little girls he'd found, instead of Daisy—the dozens he had seen from a distance and had hoped and prayed would turn out to be Daisy, but never were, some of them running into houses and hiding, others urging him on and then stroking his head and talking to him, and even asking him in to meet their people.

Well, now, here was Daisy home at last—from the other end of the world, most likely. After great trials and tribulations, great dangers, great escapes, so naturally he'd been beside himself with surprise and gratitude to heaven for bringing Daisy safely home. How was he to have remembered that his feet were muddy at a time like that?

He wanted to get up and follow them. He wanted to, but he didn't. He just stayed where his best friend in the world of adults had ordered him to stay. He just stayed and waited, and tried to go on hearing them, waiting for the hardness to leave Daisy's voice.

Mrs. Hamilcar lifted the lid of the washing machine and brought out Daisy's muddied dress, but, of course, Fido didn't see it happen, didn't, in fact, know what was happening, or why, and that was what was so difficult.

Well, now, when were they going to start talking again? He heard water running out of a faucet into a sink, but still no talk. He heard the sound of soap being rubbed into cloth, and then he heard sloshing, but still no talk. What were they up to?

At last Daisy spoke, "What are you doing, mother?"

"What am I doing?" Fido heard Mrs. Hamilcar say. Her voice

was gentle and kind; but then, it always was. It always had a touch of merry laughter in it, too, but that touch wasn't in it now. Something was going on. Something more. Something different.

"I'm trying," Fido heard Mrs. Hamilcar say, "to be your friend."

"Oh, mother, you're my mother. Mothers don't have to be friends too."

"Yes, they do," Mrs. Hamilcar said. "I almost think I'd rather be your friend than your mother. You know, you're just about all your father and I have that we really care about. You are all of our kids. All the daughters we were going to have, and all the sons too. We swore there were going to be six of each. All young husbands and wives swear the same thing, I suppose, but I think Morley really meant it, and I know I did. Well, things happen, and one of them happened to me, of all people. And so that was all for us—you. Well, you're nine now, and we know we aren't going to have very much more of you! What little time we have left, I want us to be— well, friends. Forever."

"Mother," Fido heard Daisy say, "am I going to die or are you?"

"Neither of us," Mrs. Hamilcar laughed, "except the little I die every time I notice how much more you've grown—which I'm always thrilled to notice too."

"Mother, what are you doing? Just tell me that, please."

"I'm laundering the dress Miss Quillercape gave you on your eighth birthday. After I launder it, I'm going to iron it. Then, you're going to put it on and walk up the hill and keep your promise."

"But why, mother?"

"Because I love you. Because I love your father. Because I love Miss Quillercape. Because I love everybody you know. Because I love Fido."

Fido almost sat up at the mention of his name, but not quite. This was a time for lying still, for listening, for waiting, for watching—if they'd only come back into the living room so he could watch, though.

"I'm sorry I said all those awful things about Fido."

"I knew you would be."

"I don't want a cat at all."

"You can have a cat, too, if you want one."

"Cat?" Fido thought. "Just bring a cat into this house and——"
But he cut the thought short. Suppose they did? Suppose they actually brought a cat into the house? Any kind of a cat. Not necessarily the kind he couldn't even bear to see. Not one of those
serene, snooty Angoras. Any kind at all. They'd expect him to get
along, of course. They'd expect him even to like the cat—or at any
rate to pretend to—and he'd probably try, because of love of Daisy,
but it would be criminal.

Fido prayed. "Please," he said. "Please help them to decide they
don't want a cat at all. I'm not saying cats aren't all right. They
probably are, but I don't like to have them around. I don't hate
them, maybe. I'm willing to live and let live, but I don't love them,
either. I've gone to a lot of trouble not to chase them, because Mr.
and Mrs. Hamilcar and Daisy have asked me not to, but it's never
been easy, and the cats misunderstand my control. I've actually had
them walk right up to my nose, and it's been fairly frightening, on
the whole. I don't know whether they think they're dogs or I'm a
cat, and I don't like not knowing about a thing like that, because
I know they're cats and I'm a dog. Please help them to decide for
themselves that we don't want a cat around here. There's not one
mouse in the whole house. There's several crickets, but we're all
devoted to them. Amen."

As if in answer to the prayer, Fido heard Daisy say, "But I don't
want a cat. I just said I did because I was angry."

Fido breathed easier.

"Cats and dogs get along fine these days," Mrs. Hamilcar said.

"Oh, no," Fido groaned. "Please don't say that, Mrs. Hamilcar.
Please don't believe that. Believe me, they don't get along at all.
Even when it looks as if they do, they don't. And it's always the
dog who has to do the hard work. The cat never tries to meet the
dog halfway. A cat is always a cat. But a dog, he tries to keep peace

and harmony in the house. He pretends and pretends. Pretty soon it makes him a little queer. I know three dogs in Oh-Ho Hill who have been getting along with cats for years, and every one of them is a little queer. They're confused. They don't know what happened to them. They know something did, but they're not sure what. Dogs are gentlemen. Cats may be ladies, or something like them, or something like some of them, but they aren't ladies enough. They'll watch a dog go out of his way to be courteous, but they won't go even a little out of their way to make it a little easier for a dog to go on being courteous. And that's what does the damage. Pretty soon a dog is a little off the beam. Please don't believe cats and dogs get along, Mrs. Hamilcar. It's always dogs alone putting up with cats, the same as people, if you ask me. Live and let live and all that, but a cat is a cat, and you bring one into the house and you'll soon have a different kind of place entirely—silence, silence, silence, as if they were thinking something. Well, they're thinking nothing. That's only the way they are. They walk around and look and don't say anything. They're phony, all of them, and that's what dogs hate about them. Please don't believe cats and dogs get along, Mrs. Hamilcar."

"Oh, I know cats and dogs get along fine," Fido heard Daisy say, "but what about me? I don't get along with cats."

"Bravo, Daisy!"

"I love Fido," Daisy said, "and I don't want to have any other friend from the animal world—not even another dog."

"Double bravo, Daisy!"

"Well," Mrs. Hamilcar said, "I don't like cats, either. As a matter of fact, I can't have them around."

"Triple bravo, Mrs. Hamilcar!"

Fido relaxed and listened. They talked about everything, and the laughter came back into Mrs. Hamilcar's voice, and the love into Daisy's. Fido fell asleep.

He woke up when Mrs. Hamilcar called out from the kitchen, "Stay right where you are, Fido. Don't even stand."

Fido half opened his eyes. He saw them come out of the kitchen into the living room, and they were good to see. Good to smell too. The good old Hamilcar smell of health, harmony, humor and love. Daisy was in the bright-yellow dress again, and she looked brand-new and different. Bigger, brighter and wiser.

"Don't move, Fido," Mrs. Hamilcar said. "Just look." Fido opened his eyes wider, as if to ask, "Like this?"

"Daisy's going to call on Miss Quillercape, as she promised she would."

"Don't I know?" Fido thought. Hadn't he gone along with Daisy time after time to the very door of Miss Quillercape's little house and stretched out on the little patch of lawn there, with the blossoming rose trees all around, and the lilac trees, and the honeysuckle vines all entwined around the porch railings and posts? Hadn't he waited there, breathing the perfume, until Daisy had come out?

"Fido?" Daisy said. "I apologize for being so mean. Will you walk with me to Miss Quillercape's, please?"

"Will I?" Fido thought, and almost leaped to his feet. He managed to stay put, though, waiting for the good word to come from Mrs. Hamilcar.

"Do you really want him to tag along?" Mrs. Hamilcar said.

"Mother," Daisy said, "I haven't seen poor old Fido in two long weeks. Of course I want him to come along."

"All right, Fido," Mrs. Hamilcar said. "Up, now—but take it easy."

Fido sat up slowly, and waited. Daisy went to him. She knelt and looked into his eyes. She smiled, and then she put her face alongside of his, and then she kissed him. But Fido didn't stir. Oh, it wasn't that he wasn't gone, away out there, in heaven itself. It was just that he didn't want to make any more blunders for some time to come.

Daisy stood up, embraced Mrs. Hamilcar, and then she said, "You're my best friend, mamma. My very best friend. Good-by, I'm going to visit Miss Quillercape now. Come on, Fido."

Daisy walked to the front door. Fido walked slowly and carefully

behind her, aware for the first time in years that he had four feet—
or was it five? Daisy walked out of the house, and Fido followed.
Daisy turned and Fido turned. Mrs. Hamilcar stood in the doorway. Daisy waved, and Fido watched. Mrs. Hamilcar smiled, and
then all of a sudden Fido saw tears in her eyes.

Now, what the devil were they for? Would he ever understand
people? He stood as if stuck in soft tar. He wanted to hurry to Mrs.
Hamilcar, but he wasn't sure he should. Then he heard Daisy say,
"All right, Fido, run! Run ahead!" Fido turned quickly. He was
about to bound off when he just had to have another look at Mrs.
Hamilcar. Some of the tears were rolling down her cheeks now.
Now, what should a dog do about a thing like that?

"Go on, Fido," Mrs. Hamilcar said. "Run! Run ahead!" And
there was actually merry laughter in her voice.

"I don't get it," Fido thought.

He turned quickly and bounded away. As he ran he heard them
both laugh gaily. He would have laughed, too, if he weren't sure
there must be still something more to people than he had ever before noticed. What the devil was it? Probably something human.

THE SECRET OF GUMLEY ABBEY

by Robert Standish

My interest in the Bollinger family dates from the day, some two years ago, when I met Melissa, who had just moved into a small apartment on the same floor as mine in Breadalbane Mansions, which is in the wilds of Bloomsbury.

It was January when Melissa arrived. She was a refugee from Gumley Abbey, the ancestral home of the Bollingers, a splendid Tudor pile which qualifies as one of the stately homes of England. We met on the stairs. There is no lift. Her chilblains were just beginning to heal. I told her my name was Bob Maitland.

Almost exactly a year after this first meeting, Melissa and I became engaged, and at her urgent insistence we drove down to Gumley Abbey to meet her father, Maj. Gen. Sir Henry Bollinger, K.C.M.G., C.B., D.S.O., M.C., hereinafter referred to as "the General."

"Daddy is a darling," Melissa told me in advance of the meeting, "but he is—well, a little old-fashioned and, I should warn you, doesn't like newspapermen—much."

I am a newspaperman. I don't like generals much, but it was not the time to say so.

It is essential to a proper understanding of this dauntless old man's character and personality, if he is to be made credible, to fill in as briefly as possible something of his environment, background and temptations, particularly the temptations.

Give me Gumley Abbey and a big enough income to pay and feed six indoor and six outdoor servants, as an irreducible minimum and I doubt whether I would ever want to set foot off my own land. It has everything—three hundred-odd acres of rich pasture, stabling for twenty horses, a walled garden of three acres where peaches, nectarines and even figs, ripen in the open, to say nothing of a mile of trout fishing, two big carp ponds and a stand of oaks which were mature trees at the time of the Norman Conquest.

The abbey itself, its outbuildings and walls, are built of the small Tudor bricks, warm tinted as though dipped in red wine. The site was chosen by some forgotten genius in a fold of the Surrey hills, where summer lingers and spring arrives a full month ahead of the surrounding countryside. I have gathered violets there in late January, daffodils in February, and in May, when the bluebells are blooming, the home meadows look as though a wraith of blue wood smoke lies across them.

I don't know enough about architecture to do justice to the abbey. Let it suffice to say that the old banqueting hall, with its suits of armor and half an acre of linenfold paneling, was, despite mildew, decay and cobwebs, unutterably lovely, with the afternoon sun shining through a high window onto the minstrel gallery, where a harp with burst strings spoke eloquently of bygone splendors.

The general lived in two rooms, giving the rest over to the rats and the things which go bump in the night.

Before meeting the general, I had seen a color photo of him in Melissa's living room. Wearing the full-dress uniform of his old regiment, the 29th Dragoons, he was a fine figure of a man. His silver hair and fierce spiked mustache stood out startlingly against his ruddy pink complexion.

On the day I first met him, he was wearing a green baize apron. His cheeks were no longer pink. They sagged, like the no-longer-wire-stiff white mustache, which gave him the appearance of a tired, disillusioned walrus.

It was a squalid way of living, a sorry end to a distinguished career. The general, whose only companion was his old batman, Maggs, who had followed him into retirement, had been living at Gumley Abbey for ten years when I first came upon the scene. His horse was better housed in the stables and, if lunch was a fair sample, better fed. Melissa and I were thoroughly depressed when we set off back to London in the gathering murk of a January afternoon.

It was on this drive that Melissa told me of the circumstances in which the general had retired some years in advance of expectation. I then began to understand his lack of enthusiasm for newspapermen.

One evening in his Pall Mall club the general had become embroiled in an argument with the military correspondent of the Sunday Courier. His contention was that, despite the tank and all the other mechanized refinements of warfare, the functions of the horse soldier were not, as most people believed, strictly decorative. The trouble was, of course, that the general had never ceased to be a cavalryman at heart. He loved horses, the jingle of accouterments, the smell of the stables and the rhythmic music of hooves, all of which was understandable. But he allowed himself to be carried away by his subject, and what began as a private conversation ended as a published interview in the Sunday Courier bearing his full name and rank, and titled The Role of Cavalry in Atomic Warfare.

This appeared on a Sunday. On the Monday immediately following, the general was summoned to appear at the War Office to explain why a serving officer (a) held such obsolete views and (b) was so misguided as to express them publicly. Something sar-

castic was said about bows and arrows, too, which got under the
general's skin, needling him into saying something best left unsaid.
He was forthwith dropped from the active list with a thud which,
according to a report we are not bound to accept literally, was registered upon the seismograph at Greenwich Observatory some ten
miles distant.

The decade of penurious retirement which followed, his pension
supplemented by a slender private income derived from his life
savings, both of them heavily taxed, had soured the general's dis-
position, leaving him full of resentment. It does not matter what
the rights and wrongs of the matter are; all that concerns us is that
the general was as he was.

I went to Gumley Abbey as seldom as courtesy and my devotion
to Melissa permitted. It was plain from the beginning that the general regarded me as one of his afflictions, ranking me with the leak-
ing roof, the jungle of weeds in the drive and his intermittent at-
tacks of lumbago. He practically never spoke to me, fearing—or so
I assumed—that I might quote him. I think the only bright spot on
his horizon was my admission in an unguarded moment that I was
not making enough money to marry Melissa.

Then one morning Melissa came in to see me, looking worried
and unhappy. "I think," she said sadly, "that poor daddy is going
round the bend."

Exercising all my tact, I tried to look surprised. "What makes
you think so?" I asked, wondering, as I spoke, whether it ran in the
family.

"He says he's chartering a yacht for a winter cruise in the Caribbean," replied Melissa, "and he's inviting us and several other
people."

"What's he going to use for money?"

"He's going to sell all his stocks and shares, or so he says, and
enjoy one more good holiday before he dies. It was a bad line and
I couldn't hear him very well, but there was something else about

a crowded something of glorious something. I think it was a quotation of some kind."

"Are you going with him?" I asked.

"If you'll come, Bob. Will you?"

"Yes, I'll come," I told her, "so long as he doesn't bring that damned horse."

Melissa ignored this. "I wonder," she said slowly, "whether I ought to take him to see a psychiatrist. He sounded highly peculiar on the phone."

Now I found myself on the general's side. "You're ten years too late for that," I was forced to tell her. "The time to have had his head examined, surely, was when he was making plans to sidetrack atomic bombs with a squadron of cavalry. You could have had him certified then without any trouble. But now he's behaving sensibly. He's come to the perfectly sane conclusion that 'One crowded hour of glorious life is worth an age without a name'—that is a quotation, by the way—and wants one final fling before the curtain drops, and you regard it as evidence of insanity. Mark you, if he wants to take his horse, I shall incline to your view, but otherwise, no. Let him have his fun."

We drove down to Gumley on the following Sunday, to find that there had been changes. The general's living room, which had once been the abbey library, was being spruced up a bit. It was clean—anyway, nearly as clean as the stable. Somebody had scythed the weeds in the drive. A section of collapsed roof gutter had been repaired. There was a new coir doormat and other significant evidences that money had been spent. But what really set me thinking was a snatch of dialogue Melissa and I heard while we were wiping the mud off our shoes on the new doormat in the hall. It went like this:

The general (his voice loud, resonant and confident): "It's all dashed nonsense to say that crime doesn't pay. Before we took to crime, just look how we lived. Abject squalor, that's what it was. Now look at us! No more cleaning fires, washing dirty dishes and the rest of it. Crime does pay, Maggs, and we both know it."

Maggs: "Very glad to 'ear you say so, general. Honesty's all right as far as it goes, I dessay, but it didn't never get you nowhere, nor me neither. Anyway, s'posin' we are copped, prison'd be 'eaven alongside wot you and me've gone through the last ten years. I know wot I'm talkin' about too. I did two years' 'ard labor before I joined the army. I got careless an' it served me right."

The general: "If it's all the same to you, Maggs, I think on the whole I would prefer to stay out of prison. But I would like you to know that if anything does go wrong with my plan, there isn't a man breathing I'd sooner share a cell with than you. But nothing will go wrong, Maggs, because I intend to plan this thing as I would plan a military campaign."

Melissa and I, I felt, had heard enough. To have listened to more —which was what Melissa wanted to do—would have bordered on eavesdropping. To her great annoyance, I coughed loudly and led her into the room.

The first thing I noticed about the general was that his mustache no longer drooped. It was as stiff as a cat's whiskers. His eyes were clear, his cheeks rotund and pink. There was a spring in his step and his manner was jaunty. In fact, he looked exactly what he was, a retired major general, whereas on the last occasion I had seen him he had looked like an unemployed street musician.

He was, for a change, polite to me—suspiciously polite. I began to wonder what he wanted of me. The lunch was first class. Maggs, wearing one of the general's cast-off dress suits, buttled. As the crashing of dishes in the kitchen was plainly audible while he was in the room, the clear implication was that a cook had been employed. There was a good Chablis with the grilled sole, a fine claret with the roast beef and trimmings; small things in themselves, but straws in the wind, supporting the general's own contention that crime was a paying proposition. What kind of crime, I wondered. There had been a lot of country-house burglaries in Surrey, but I doubted whether the general had the figure and that minimal agility so necessary for a quick getaway. Whatever branch of crime he had adopted, he was bound to be inexperienced, because men with marked criminal tendencies, I argued, were unlikely to rise to the rank of major general.

Melissa seemed stunned by it all, but over the port and the nuts she agreed to accept her father's invitation. I thanked him for inviting me, covering myself by saying that if my editor would give me the necessary leave of absence, there was nothing I would sooner do than spend the coming winter cruising in the Caribbean. He called it the Spanish Main, which made me suspect that he had been reading travel folders.

"I hope daddy doesn't go to prison," said Melissa dutifully on the drive back to London.

"That is what may be termed one of the occupational hazards of his new way of life," I reminded her. "But I wouldn't worry if I were you, because a first-year law student would be able to get him off the hook on a plea of insanity, by introducing into the record that famous interview of his about using cavalry to intercept atom bombs."

Melissa said I was being callous, while I insisted that I was being practical. The coolness engendered lasted for several days. This was in late September, as I remember it. Thereafter, things began to happen fast.

The general chartered an auxiliary schooner called the Pearl of Panama, then lying in Port of Spain, Trinidad. I checked on the truth of this through a friend on a Trinidad newspaper. The schooner, as reported to me, was slow, but luxuriously equipped. The general then announced that his old friend "Fruity" Bingham, a retired admiral of the Royal Navy, would take command. I had met the admiral, who lived in one of the Gumley Abbey houses as a tenant of the general's. He, too, I gathered, was finding life difficult on his pension. Another guest on the cruise was to be the dean of Chorlton-cum-Hardy, the Very Reverend Joshua Tidmarsh, a most pious man whose calculated pulpit indiscretions often found their way onto the front pages.

Then, in late November, we sailed for Trinidad in a banana boat. The admiral went ahead by air in order to see that everything was in order aboard the schooner. The dean brought his wife, and there were two other additions to the party. One was a Mrs. Makins, widow of one of the general's brother officers, who occupied rent free a cottage owned by the general at Gumley, while the other was a gloomy man named Lushington, an ex-Indian judge and an old friend of the general's. He was, latterly, justice of the peace for Gumley.

Mrs. Makins was a birdlike little woman who enjoyed—I have her word for it—poor health. She suffered from a perennial cold in the head. Dewdrops formed on the end of her nose with uncanny regularity. She carried, clenched in her left hand, a handkerchief with which, just as the dewdrop was about to fall upon her black bombazine gown, she made a lightninglike dab and saved the day. Her timing was little short of miraculous.

The voyage to Trinidad was pleasant but uneventful. The general became more expansive and genial as we approached warmer climes. He was a charming and generous host and, by popular consent, the life and soul of the ship's company. He spent at least two hours per day in the canvas swimming bath rigged on the well deck, perfecting himself in the use of his undersea diving and breathing apparatus. That there was some deep purpose behind this, I did not doubt.

The admiral met us on arrival at Port of Spain, taking us out immediately to the Pearl of Panama, which was lying in the gulf about a mile offshore. There would be, he told us, a few days' delay until the arrival from New York of some vital spare part for the auxiliary diesel engine.

The vessel was most comfortably, indeed luxuriously, equipped. My room, which was not one of the best, had an electric fan and its own shower. There was even a small desk.

The general and the admiral were now behaving in a furtive, conspiratorial manner. Most of their conversations were conducted in whispers. They spent hours poring over charts.

On the evening before we sailed they came aboard for dinner and at the table the general made an announcement. "By a most fortunate chance," he told us all, "the admiral and I have come into possession of a map, together with detailed instructions revealing the hiding place of an immensely valuable pirate treasure. We have decided, therefore, to combine pleasure and profit."

Melissa and I had been offered that one in a Port of Spain bar, complete with the pirate's dying confession as certified by the chaplain of H.M.S. Nautilus just before the pirate was hanged at the yardarm. It struck me that the general and the admiral were old enough to know that the sale of maps revealing the whereabouts of pirate treasure is one of the major industries of the Caribbean. They were run off in thousands by an enterprising Glasgow printer who specializes in that kind of thing and are on sale in every waterfront bar between Key West and the mainland of South America.

"Darling," I said to Melissa after dinner, "I'm afraid you were right. The old man is right round the bend, otherwise he couldn't have fallen for that old gag."

That is what I said. That is how it seemed. But a nagging doubt persisted. The general was pouring out large sums of money. The charter of the Pearl of Panama—I had taken steps to ascertain this —was costing him five thousand dollars a month. Fuel, wages and stores—there was a crew of ten—would come to almost as much again. Where was it all coming from?

The more I pondered the matter, the more muddled became my thinking. If he hadn't taken to some profitable form of crime, there seemed to be no other explanation.

I found him late that night, smoking a cigar on deck. "You know, my boy," he said genially, "this treasure hunt is right up your street. Wonderful story! You ought to be able to make a pot of money out of it."

It didn't ring true, because if I made a pot of money out of it, he knew darned well that I would marry Melissa, which was the last thing he wanted. But then, why had he invited me?

I went ashore early the following morning to send a cable asking whether the Argus Syndicate would be interested in a treasure-hunt story, telling them to reply to me by radio addressed to the Pearl of Panama. The reply came later in the day when we were beating our way against the trade wind with Tobago some fifteen miles distant on our starboard bow. Argus said they would pay well for a factual and "successful—repeat successful—treasure-hunt story." And somehow, against all the probabilities, I believed it was going to be just that, proving that confidence can be as catching as measles.

The ladies did not appear at dinner that evening—that is to say, the elder ladies. Melissa, who is a good sailor, was quite unruffled by the violent pitching in the short steep seas.

"Did I ever tell you, my dear," the general asked her abruptly, apropos of nothing, "that one of our ancestors, Roger Bollinger, was a pirate?"

"No, daddy, never," replied Melissa. "Tell me all about him."

"The family has never admitted that he was a pirate, of course. He sailed under a letter of marque, a device used to make piracy sound more respectable, but that's all he was—a pirate. He sailed these seas for years, with a price put on his head by the Spaniards. But they never caught him. With the loot taken from the Spaniards, he bought Gumley Abbey and settled down to the life of a well-breeched country squire. Became a most pious man toward the end. Butter wouldn't melt in his mouth, from all accounts. There's a book about him in the library. You should read it one day. Remind me to find it for you."

Was this, I wondered, the old boy's way of preparing Melissa for the shock of learning that her father was a criminal, by pointing to the existence of an earlier Bollinger who had blotted the family escutcheon? Or was he just proud of an ancestor who had probably been a conscienceless, murdering ruffian?

The next week was spent at anchor on the leeward side of Tobago, in a sheltered palm-fringed bay where, for several hours daily, the general and the admiral perfected their undersea techniques.

"I suppose," I remarked at lunch one day, "that the treasure is at the bottom of the sea?"

"How did you guess it, my boy?"

"I'm the seventh son of a seventh son," I told him. "How long has the treasure been there?"

"Since 1680—since the pirate—Smith was his name—Joe Smith put it there. No better hiding place in the world than the sea bottom. Ask the admiral."

"A lot can have happened since 1680," I continued. I wanted to make them talk. "The treasure may be under twenty feet depth of sand by now."

"I doubt it," said the general briskly. "Bill Smith was a pretty smart fellow, from all accounts, and, doubtless, he would have thought of all that."

"From what accounts?" I asked. "Besides, I thought his name was Joe."

It was no good. When I asked what the location of the treasure was, I was told, "On the bottom of the sea!" I gave it up.

From Tobago we went across to Grenada and there followed one of the most glorious months I have ever spent, cruising among the Grenadines, a chain of largely uninhabited, waterless islands, lying between Grenada and St. Vincent. Melissa and I swam, fished and lazed, listened to the radio in the evenings, went to bed early, rose with the dawn and lost all count of time. We called at St. Vincent for water and then for several days were out of sight of land. The heat of the sun was mitigated by the trade wind.

We were not a sociable ship's company. The judge ate enormous meals and hardly ever spoke. The general and the admiral spent most of their time whispering in the chart house. The dean, Mrs. Tidmarsh and Mrs. Makins—the latter, by the way, lost her dewdrop—played three-handed bridge most of the day, trying in vain to rope in Melissa or myself. It was a delightful, *dolce far niente* existence, overshadowed for me by all the apparent inconsistencies. If this was a treasure hunt, why wasn't some effort made in that direction? The only break in the idyllic monotony was when the dean conducted an Ash Wednesday service on what turned out to have been a Friday, assuming from the fact that we had pancakes for lunch on the Thursday that it was Shrove Tuesday.

At dawn one day soon after this we entered a crescent-shaped bay formed by what were virtually the arms of a sandbank, curving for about two miles. It could hardly be called an island, for at no point was it more than about six feet above sea level and its greatest width was about one hundred yards. The only vegetation was a few coconut palms, some coarse grass and stunted bushes. At one end Melissa and I found a crude hut of palm thatch, a few rusted tin cans, presumably left there by fishermen from some other island. The only evidence of our whereabouts was some faded cigarette packets printed in Spanish. From this I concluded that we were somewhere near Cuba or one of the other Spanish-speaking islands.

The general and the admiral now became more conspiratorial than ever. They spent hours swimming with goggles and examining the sea bottom. Melissa and I, swimming over the same ground one day, were able to see plainly the outlines of a wreck at a depth of around thirty feet.

One morning the general and the admiral left the schooner before dawn. When they returned for breakfast, an old oil can used as a buoy marked the spot where they had been diving. They were both jubilant.

"We think we've located it," said the general. "We need all hands to haul it to the surface. Not the crew, of course. No good giving them ideas."

The crew, by the way, were mixed-blooded men from Panama, where the schooner was registered. None of them spoke a word of English or, if they did, I did not hear it.

After breakfast the longboat was launched, and we all went across the bay to the marker buoy, and there followed—at least for me—

the most unpleasant hour of the cruise, while we men hauled to the surface a barnacle-encrusted object about the size of a small traveling trunk.

When we had hauled it into the longboat, we rowed back to the schooner, setting it out on deck to give the water time to drain out of it. Then, at the specific request of the general, Melissa and I, armed with chisels and mallets, proceeded to chip off the barnacles. In less than half an hour we had exposed to view an iron-bound wooden chest in a good state of preservation. With a heavy hammer and a chisel, it was the work of a few moments to force the lid off the chest.

The first object which came to view was a beautiful gold chalice, slightly dented. The dean, after reading the Latin inscription at the base and around the rim, gave it as his considered opinion that it was loot from a Spanish cathedral. Next was a pair of massive gold candlesticks, weighing not less than ten pounds apiece, followed by some other gold ornaments which suggested ecclesiastical use. A small box, when opened, revealed fifteen beautifully matched pearls, several of which were badly blemished. Mixed up among them were a double handful of gems, including one large rose-pink diamond and a lot of rubies, emeralds and sapphires, which had been wrenched from their settings by some vandal hand. Fragments of their gold settings still clung to them. If these were real—and it was impossible to doubt this—they were worth the proverbial king's ransom. At the bottom of the chest, to a depth of at least two inches, was a medley of gold coins, Spanish and Portuguese, most of them, and some I could not identify.

Exciting? I suppose it was, if only because something atavistic in most of us responds to the dull gleam and rich clunk of gold, something which has nothing to do with greed. There is greed, too, of course, but the two responses are not related. There wasn't enough excitement, I decided, bearing in mind that the two old men chiefly concerned, who had been feeling the pinch of poverty for years, were now rich and able to gratify every whim—at least, the kind that money satisfies.

"Come on, all of you," said the general, while we were examining the find. "Lunch is on the table. There'll be lots of time to look at that stuff later."

As we took our seats at the table in the saloon, I found myself wondering if that was what age did to all of us, acting like a late frost on the buds of enthusiasm. I hoped it would not happen to me.

Melissa and I examined the things more closely during the afternoon, but the chill of anticlimax had taken the joy out of the day, and I was quite glad to see the gold and the gems locked away in the general's cabin.

Well, I had my story, and the three days before we reached Antigua, our next port of call, were fully occupied writing it. I sent it off to London with some satisfaction. From Antigua we returned to St. Vincent and thence southward down the chain of the Grenadines. We did not hurry, and Easter was behind us when at length we dropped anchor again off Port of Spain, where we remained for some days before returning to England.

Neither the general nor the admiral would talk to the reporters who dogged our steps in Trinidad. It was left to me to keep them at bay and satisfy their curiosity. It was the same in England on our return.

All this time Melissa was a shade too thoughtful for my taste. Something, evidently, was on her mind. Something was on the general's mind, too, when Melissa and I went down to Gumley Abbey for lunch. He was ill at ease with us, which made him sensitive to Melissa's odd manner toward him.

"Something on your mind, my dear?" he asked solicitously.

"Yes, father"—she usually called him "daddy"—"there is."

"Then get it off your chest, my dear," he said heartily. "No good bottling things up. What is it?"

"I'd like to hear your explanation of a few things that have been puzzling me for some time," she replied.

"Ask me what you like, my dear," he said, with a suggestion of bluster in his manner. "Only too happy to explain anything—if I can, of course. Can't have a pretty girl like you worrying about trifles."

"Then," Melissa began, fixing her steady gaze on her father, "perhaps you can explain how you and the admiral were able to find that treasure chest so easily."

"Fruity will have to explain that to you, my dear. It's all above my head, you know. Fruity's an unerring navigator—highly complicated calculations involved—years of experience required."

"All right, we'll let that pass," said Melissa judicially, "and come to the next question. This Joe Smith, the pirate—or was he called Bill? Anyway, Joe or Bill, it doesn't matter—you say he hid that treasure chest in 1680. Was that the date?"

"If you say so, my dear."

"I don't say anything, father. He's your pirate, not mine, although there is no trace at the British Museum Library of a pirate at that time called Bill or Joe Smith. Was it 1680, or if not, when was it?"

"Yes, 1680, or thereabouts, give or take a couple of years. Why?"

"Well, I was wondering how a chest which has been lying at the bottom of the Caribbean since 1680—give or take a couple of years, of course—contained several hundred George III guineas, bearing in mind that George III didn't come to the throne until 1760, eighty years after Bill or Joe Smith put them there. Odd, isn't it?"

"Most interesting point you've raised, my dear; most interesting! Makes you think, eh? Dashed carelessness somewhere—the kind of thing that only an expert could answer. No good asking a poor old soldier like me." The general was not happy.

"There's something even odder, father," persisted Melissa, "something you'll have to find a lot of experts to explain—to me. In among those gold coins I found this"—"this" was a crown top from a bottle of Dobson's beer—"which is even more remarkable, because even if crown tops were invented in 1680, Dobson's Brewery wasn't started until 1825. Look, it says so on the top."

Lacking the necessary experts to explain this away, the general began to bluster.

"Perhaps, sir," I suggested helpfully, "some of our readers may have theories to account for it all."

From the explosion which followed this, I gathered that the general wanted no publicity. Fear took the place of anger in his eyes. "What have you got to complain about, anyway?" he snarled at me. "You had a pretty good holiday, didn't you?"

"The truth, please, daddy!" said Melissa quietly.

Without replying, the general led the way into the old banqueting hall of the abbey, which was steeped in gloom and festooned with cobwebs. Moving aside a suit of armor which hung with many others on the paneled wall, he seized a carved Tudor Rose, giving it a half turn. With slight pressure, a section of the paneling opened inward. An electric flashlight hung on a nail inside. A flight of stairs led downwards. I counted twenty-two stairs.

At the end of a short tunnel, in a vaulted chamber, a weird sight awaited us. Shackled to a ringbolt in the wall was a blackened skeleton. Beside it were pewter utensils which had once contained food and water. Then the beam of light crossed the chamber to a massive wooden table which had rotted and collapsed under the weight of a vast hoard of gold coins, which had spilled across the floor.

The general's composure was now returned. We followed him in silence the way we had come. Closing the panel, we went out into the golden afternoon sunshine.

"Roger Bollinger must have hidden it there when he turned respectable," said the general, "and then died without revealing the hiding place."

"But why all that silly business of the treasure hunt, daddy, when it was here all the time?" asked Melissa, looking utterly bewildered.

"It's perfectly simple, my dear. I will explain it to you. Maggs and I discovered that panel by accident last year. There is in England a dashed awkward law known as the law of treasure-trove, under which all that boodle could have been claimed by the Crown —by the government, which finances the welfare state and looks after everyone except old soldiers like me, who have served it faithfully. At best, if I had declared this, there would have been an inquest and years of delay before any decision was made. As I own the land where it was found, I might—might, mark you—have been allowed to keep some of it. Well, I'm tired of penny-pinching, so I didn't give them the chance. Fruity Bingham and I cooked up the treasure hunt. We bought that barnacle-encrusted chest, put some of the loot in it and, as you know, found it at the bottom of the sea. Who's going to challenge that story? Dash my buttons! It was found in the presence of a justice of the peace, to say nothing of old Tidmarsh, who's only a dean now, but is being made a bishop next week—as well as"—he gave me a dirty look—"a dashed scribbler who has spread the story far and wide.

"Let the government take it? Not me. No government is going to spend my money buying false teeth and spectacles for a lot of loafers who are better able to afford them than a pensioned major general.

"I blame myself for not spotting those George III guineas. They might have been very awkward. But that beer-bottle cap—well, that was just dashed carelessness; might have caused a very bad impression if one of those chaps from the British Museum had spotted it."

"Don't worry, daddy," said Melissa sweetly. "I invented the beer-bottle cap, just to see how you would explain it."

We left then.

"You're very silent, Bob," said Melissa, after about ten miles. "What's on your mind?"

"I'm worried, darling," I told her. "Like everyone else at some time or other, I thought your old man was round the bend. But he's a pretty smart cooky, if you ask me."

"Then what's worrying you?"

"Well, suppose there is a role for cavalry in atomic warfare," I said, "and he's the only one smart enough to realize it? It makes you think, doesn't it?"

THE CONFORMERS

by Charlotte Armstrong

The breakfast room was on the east, for the sake of the sun. The sun shone in. Bob Smite, husband and father, stabbed the yellow fluff of his scrambled eggs from the pale green plate. In his left hand, he held a section of the morning paper, folded to reveal to him a quarter of the editorial page.

Larry Smite, sixteen-year-old son, had his chin tucked in to permit him to pore down upon the sporting section. He had spilled a little cocoa on it.

Dorothy Smite, wife and mother, crunched toast in her good white teeth, and looked out the window, crinkling her eyes against the double light—the sun, and the bounce of the sunlight from the shining machinery: the pop-up toaster, the percolator, the electric frying pan. On the fourth side of the table, cords snaked into the wall.

"Not going to be late tonight, are you?" she asked in the voice she used to her husband, not the voice she used to her son.

"Six-fifteen, as usual," Bob answered. "Far as I know. Why?"

"I was thinking of a rib roast. But I guess I'll just take a steak out of the freezer."

"Nothing the matter with steak," he said.

"Hey, mom, could I use the car after school?" the boy asked.

"Why?" asked she, and did not wait for the answer. "The thing is I've got some shopping and then I am supposed to have my hair done. But if it's important——"

"No, that's O.K. I can get a ride," her son said promptly.

"Ride where?"

"Game."

"Who's playing?" the father asked, looking up with his sense of duty showing.

"Jefferson."

"Going to beat them?"

The boy shrugged.

"Well, good luck," the father said, and looked at his watch. He went up to clean his teeth. When he got down, the boy had gone. He kissed Dorothy on her temple. "By the way, can you take my gray suit to the cleaners? Tell them, on special?"

"O.K.," she said.

Such was breakfast time, at the Smites', an autumn morning.

Bob Smite, husband and father, householder, jobholder, proceeded in an easy gait, past two blocks' worth of smart little houses like his own, each just as fresh and neat on its small plot. Leaves were falling from certain slender trees. The neighborhood was too new for trees of size. The neighborhood was proudly kept up. Leaves did not linger long upon these little green rugs of barbered grass.

The bus line was certainly convenient. Nevertheless, he would soon have to have a second car. Bob's attention flickered, unfocused, through layers of consciousness—weather; money; a slight pinch of his right shoe; and, deep and far, a point in his mind from which he observed the commonplace luxury of his home, and, with a little blend of scorn and sorrow, assessed the table talk, considered his wife and her hairdo, his son and the football game, and himself moving in his groove.

When he came to the corner, he was suddenly focused and alert. Yes, there was time. If the first bus was not the one, he could wait for another and maybe—— He exchanged a placid "Good morning" with a passenger he had seen before, but he took care not to involve himself in conversation. The first bus was not the one. Bob Smite, risking some questioning looks, let it go.

Eight minutes later, on the second bus, he saw what he had been hoping to see. He climbed aboard with a sense of delight and made his way well back, where he bent over the man in the aisle seat and said firmly, "Would you mind, sir, shifting to the other side? We'd—er—like to talk."

The strange man shifted, with grace enough, and Bob thanked him and sat down with a sigh. "Well," he said to the remaining passenger, "here we are again. Now, where were we?"

The little man in the window-side seat had a face brown as a nut and wrinkled as a prune. He had pure white hair and white eyebrows as saucy as a cat's whiskers on his brown brow. A merry little blue eye peered from under. Bob Smite did not know this man's name, nor did this man know his. They took a peculiar care not to know.

The little man said, "We were in outer space, I believe. Been troubling you?"

"Oh, I've been floating around out there," said Bob genially. "Frankly, I don't understand it. Stars and stuff. Masses and gases, and everything moving. I don't see how we can ever understand. And sometimes I doubt that we ought to try."

"There's no doubt we really are trying," said the little man dryly. "If by 'we' you mean the human race. The human race keeps pushing its brains out, all the time, and proving how it has been all wrong, up to now."

"Yeah," said Bob. "Proving that, about every two weeks, these

days. It used to get proved every two or three centuries. What I
was thinking——"

"Go ahead," said the little man eagerly.

Bob plunged ahead. "Here is man, standing in the middle. Looking up and out at huge speeds and distances. Also, looking down
and in, at microscopic——"

"Submicroscopic." The little man nodded.

"Do you think we are actually in the middle?"

"Say," said the little man, gleaming, "that's an interesting question. From where man sits, of course, it would have to seem to be
the middle. Is that your point?"

Bob felt a surge of pure affection for him. "Listen," he said un-
necessarily, for this man could and did listen, "we aren't happy,
suspended in the middle, are we? You might say the suspense is
terrible. Why? Because we'd like to know, we'd like to feel satisfied.
Look at the new thoughts about space—if I dig them, which maybe
I don't. They are saying maybe space curves around on itself. And
there aren't any ends. Well, that ties it up, in a way, doesn't it?
That's a restful thought. That's a kind of unity. Also, going the
other way, man keeps trying to get to one thing. Maybe it's all one
thing. Energy, for instance. We want something simple and unified.
We want something we can throw our brains all the way around."

He didn't know what he was talking about. Maybe it was science.
He didn't know much about science. Maybe it was philosophy. He
didn't know much about philosophy, either. But Bob Smite was a
member of the human race, and within the limits of his ignorance,
he, too, took pleasure in pushing his brain out, frightening himself, humbling himself, and wondering.

He couldn't remember how he had got into this exchange with
this stranger, but every once in a while they met on the bus and
wondered together. Sometimes they wondered together without
speaking. Now the little man's head was nodding slowly and Bob's
pleasure was enormous.

"Can you," the man said, rather dreamily, after a while, "with your human brain, really imagine the true track of this bus in—well, in space? Here is this bus, going down this street westward, by our reckoning. It is also at the same time revolving with the earth on the earth's axis. It is, furthermore, moving swiftly through space as the entire solar system is moving. Now what is its true track, taking into account the speeds?"

"And such speeds," said Bob, his brain creaking.

Too soon, it seemed, Bob had to get off at his corner. He felt strangely refreshed and fortified. He always did. The day closed around him, jobholder, breadwinner. He plunged into the day.

Larry Smite slouched along to high school, achieving a split-second rendezvous with a friend as if it were nothing but a coincidence, speaking of dual pipes, overdrive, and the first-string quarterback's right knee—maintaining the necessary attitudes. Goons were goons. Squares were squares. Culture was for the birds.

He went through his first three classes, looking as if he would at any moment topple and go to sleep. Fourth period, he had English with Mrs. Blair, who was a small, thin, middle-aged black-and-white-haired woman, with thick glasses that much magnified her brown eyes. Larry Smite looked sleepier than ever. But his ears missed not one syllable this woman said.

As class was dismissed, she spoke up carelessly, "Larry, would you stay a moment?"

The boy's heart jumped, but he took care to look as stupid as possible. When the students had gone, some few bothering to give him a sympathetic grimace, Larry closed the classroom door without instruction to do so. He approached the teacher. He stood quietly beside her desk.

Mrs. Blair opened the center drawer and took out his manuscript. He recognized the smudgy typing, and also the very shape of his words, as familiar to him as if, with fingers, he had pressed them into this shape and no other. Its sudden dearness shook his heart.

"This," said Mrs. Blair, leaning back, seeming to let go and lose the tension of authority, and therefore show herself to be humanly fatigued, "is fine, on the whole. Now, I am pretty sure that your ear and your instinct are as good, and probably much better than mine, so I hesitate——"

"The seventh line and the eighth," said Larry. "I knew it! I knew it! It's too dum-de-dum. You must mean the seventh and eighth lines, don't you, Mrs. Blair?"

"Yes, I do," she said, her enlarged eyes meeting his eager eyes respectfully. "And now, if two of us notice the same thing, we can assume——"

"It's wrong," he said. "How can I fix it?"

"There are no rules I can quote to cover this," said the teacher. "You are far beyond the doggerel stage, Larry. You are handling rhythms that——" she sighed. "I had a teacher, once, myself, who compared them to the sea. The waves come in and break and you expect each breaking, but it never comes at the exact second that you expect. There is always the little surprise."

"Not dum-de-dum," said the boy. "Not bong-bong, like a drum. I know. I know. And I knew it wasn't right, just in those two lines. But, jeepers——" He rubbed the bristles on his head. He had forgotten himself, completely.

"How did you know, I wonder?" murmured Mrs. Blair.

"I don't mean I know," the boy said. "I just kinda feel. I feel around." Now he moved his fingers in the air. "Then, when it feels right to me—well, then it does. But I don't know if I really am right. That's why——"

The teacher shook her head gently. "I can help you a little more. But not much more. The best I can do is encourage you. I think this is excellent, Larry. On the whole, excellent. The music, the images." She stopped, feeling inadequate.

"It's not music, though," he said quickly. "In music, see, a note is a note. A certain sound. But this—is words."

"And words," said the teacher at once, "have other dimensions.

Associations. Meanings." She leaned forward. "Appendicitis is quite a pretty sound."

The boy grinned at her, appreciatively. "Sure," he said. He picked up his manuscript, the one sheet with the poem on it. "I got to try to fix it," he murmured.

"Yes, it's up to you," the teacher said in a humble way. "I have no rules to give out."

The boy's eyes were a greenish blue, quite brilliant, when he let them be seen, although he wasn't looking at her, but through her, now. "It's not exactly by rule——" he began.

The teacher held her breath.

"It's like the tail of a—of a——" He threw his arm out in a swinging curve. "Oh, I don't know. Not a breeze, exactly—but something that goes trailing through that we can't see, but only by the bending of the grass."

The teacher was absolutely quiet and motionless.

"Oblique," the boy said, frowning. "That gets somewhere near what I'm trying——" Then he shook his head. "But not exactly." He fell silent, with his head cocked. He seemed to be listening.

The teacher stirred in a moment. "After you fix it," she said gently, "what shall we do with it? Would you like to see it printed somewhere?"

"Oh, no," he said, flustered, and jolted back. "I just fool around with this, Mrs. Blair. I mean, I wouldn't want people to know." His young cheeks were hot. "And, anyhow, I'm not sure I can fix it."

The teacher said quietly, "You must fix it. And that has nothing to do with other people."

He met her eyes and his were intensely aware of her meaning and then they fell. He didn't answer.

"But I'm bound to tell you, again, what I think is true," said the teacher. "I think you are gifted. I think it is important."

"Well, I just—— Gee, thanks a lot, Mrs. Blair." The strangely wise, or strangely new, spirit behind the greenish eyes winked out.

This was an embarrassed high-school boy. He wadded the paper into his pocket, pretending it didn't matter much.

Mrs. Blair said, yearningly, "Tell me, do your parents——"

Larry caught his lip in his teeth and shook his head. The eyes were wary.

"I'd like to see it when you've fixed it," she said carelessly. "Just privately. If you don't mind."

"O.K." He let his breath out rather tremulously. "Well, so long, Mrs. Blair. Thanks, I mean, for what you said."

She nodded, withdrawn, as he wished her to be, and she began to shift other papers on her desk.

Larry went out into the corridor. He went, fast and swinging, toward the cafeteria, and he felt swell. That old Blairsey, she was smart and no kidding, because she spotted that bad place right away, and it made him feel good. And she knew how to keep quiet too. (While his mom was shopping. Shopping, for Pete's sake! And his pop went back and forth, back and forth, every day on the bus.) But of course he, Larry Smite, would never be a poet. A fellow doesn't want to try to be a poet. For a living, for Pete's sake? But in that seventh line he needed a different word, a word with the right feeling, soft and thick, and kinda black-dark, hanging on it like moss. And yet two syllables—ping, pong; the pong darker.

At this point in his reflections, Larry passed into the cafeteria and merged with his contemporaries. After school, he went to the game and sat in the card section and did his bit between the halves.

Dorothy Smite took the car that afternoon and made her rounds, accomplishing a lot of petty errands that she lumped under the term "shopping." Took Bob's suit to the cleaner. Bought a new plastic glass for the bathroom. A card of shirt buttons. Two pairs of nylons at a sale. The marketing.

At four o'clock she entered the beauty parlor. Edna's strong fingers felt wonderful on her scalp, so she let her neck muscles go and her head hang heavy over the washing tray. Wet-headed, she sat before the mirror in the little booth and Edna began to make pin curls. Dorothy sighed.

"I waited for you, Edna," she said. "I hope you realize that is why I was such a filthy mess."

Edna had a long, narrow face, and when she lifted her long upper lip, she revealed long, narrow teeth. "I keep remembering what you said last time. About peace."

"Yes. Yes, peace." Dorothy closed her eyes.

"It sticks in my mind."

Dorothy smiled. "What did I say?" she asked, then remembered. "I said the trouble starts when anybody gets it into his head that he is absolutely right. He knows. He's got it totally solved. His is the only way."

"Which gives him the license to beat this perfect truth into somebody else's head, with a bomb. Uh-huh. Well, I think you're absolutely right," said Edna with a certain impishness.

Dorothy beamed at Edna's image in the mirror. "I used to worry about these things when I was a child. It's funny. You're supposed to grow up. The dirty word, these days, is 'immature.' But what do they mean, 'mature'?"

Edna snorted. "These days, the thing is to go along without upsetting any apple carts at all. It's called adjusting."

Dorothy shivered. "Oh, how I hate that word! What if we see something going on that is wrong? We shouldn't adjust to it, should we?"

"Right," said Edna.

"We shouldn't change ourselves to get along with it. Figure how to live with it."

"Let the rest of the world adjust to us, eh?" said Edna cheerfully.

Dorothy closed her eyes once more. "Well, that depends. If we really knew what's wrong, and what's good. Of course we think we are sure of some things. Peace, for instance. That's good. Doesn't everyone agree?"

"I think it is good," said Edna soberly.

"Yet if people really wanted peace," said Dorothy, "it could be had. We're smart enough. We ought to be. Look at all we know already, about psychology and all? People keep talking about maturity and love and understanding. Then why aren't we peaceful and good?"

Edna's fingers went on working, while she considered. "I think everybody probably wants to be good, don't you? The thing is, what does he mean by that? A juvenile delinquent, now, he probably thinks not to be 'chicken' is a good thing. So he breaks the law to show how brave he is. Well, bravery—that's not bad, is it? I guess we all try pretty much to be good in our own way."

Dorothy opened her eyes and stared at herself. "You know what I think? I don't think we are on the track at all. Not yet. We get too mixed up. We try to do our duty, but maybe we're too quick."

"Quick?" said Edna, softly, and receptively. Her fingers, lifting the tiny strands of hair, gave feathery sensations to Dorothy's scalp.

"Well"—Dorothy lifted both hands under the bib she wore— "what I mean is, we settle too quickly for something like that. 'I got to be brave.' Or these: 'I got to be patient.' 'I got to stick up for my rights.' But those two are almost opposites. You see? Both good. But only part good."

"H'm," said Edna in quick response.

"You know," said Dorothy, "once or twice in my life I've had a—well, a funny feeling. As if, for one second, I got out of the crust of myself, as if I saw everything differently, just for one second."

Edna said, "When you get this feeling, whatever it is, you're not proud of yourself? It's not like feeling happy either?"

"No," said Dorothy, her eyes widening. Eyes met, by way of the glass.

"Did you want the back curled high?" asked Edna. "Or rolled on the neck, kinda?"

"I guess, on the neck," said Dorothy. "My husband likes it that way."

"You know what my husband says? He says he likes my hair straight!"

They laughed.

Dorothy looked at the woman in the mirror, not the one named Edna, but the other one. "Take 'love,' " she said murmuringly. "The word 'love' is all over the psychology books these days. But what it means, everybody figures that out just for himself. And it has a hundred meanings. A million meanings. Everybody settles for part of them."

Edna said, and her unhandsome face looked blind, "Does anybody know, I wonder, the whole meaning?"

Dorothy ducked her head suddenly. She said contritely, "Oh, I'm sorry. Did I jerk? I guess I don't know what I'm talking about."

"That's O.K.," said Edna, and worked silently for a while. Then she said wistfully, "We're too small, I guess. We're too busy. Trying to do the right thing and to love our neighbor. We just take it for granted we know what that means. Or else we think other people must know and so we do the way they do. We all go along."

"No, we don't," said Dorothy suddenly. "Not everybody. Not everybody, always. Couldn't have. Or nothing would ever have changed, in all the centuries. Don't you see?"

"That's so," said Edna. Dorothy saw Edna's head tilt. Then Edna said in an impulsive rush, "You always give me something to think about, Mrs. Smite."

Dorothy closed her lids, because, for some strange reason, her eyes had filled with tears.

At the dinner table that evening, Bob Smite spoke admiringly. "Say, you must have shot the works today, hon. Looks pretty nice."

"Just a shampoo and set," his wife replied. "Improvement, huh? I guess I had let it go a little too long." She cut meat. "Anything new at the office?"

"The usual," he said cheerfully. "Who won?" he asked his son.

"They clobbered us, 28 to 7," said Larry. "Hoffendorp's knee went out in the second quarter."

"Too bad." His father clicked a sympathetic tongue.

"I'm glad you're not heavy enough for football," said Larry's mother absent-mindedly. She'd said this before. Her son shot her a sharp green glance, but said nothing.

"Take my suit?" Bob asked.

"Ready Thursday."

"Well, that will do, I guess."

"Eat your salad, Larry."

"I am, mom."

Such was dinner time, at the Smites'. Pleasant people, they were. Mutually interested. Mutually kind.

Not much later, Bob Smite sat in his accustomed chair with the evening paper in his hands. He was trying to make a three-dimensional image of the track of his chair in space. Let's see. A rolling, that was more or less like a spiral bracelet, which bracelet was also in another spiral, probably. Then the single track of the chair, and its speeds which must alter the shape of the track. . . . He couldn't extract it. He bent his brain. Suddenly he got a whiff in his mind of something shining—distant, beautiful, strange. A little scary. Bob swallowed. He would like to try to describe this experience. Like to tell somebody. *Ah, nuts!* he thought. *The family would think I was nuts. And maybe I am. I better quit trying to sprain my brain on this stuff.*

Larry Smite was sprawled on the couch. The seventh line was singing in his head. He'd got it. But now he must put line eight, back-to-back, balanced, sort of reversed, like in a mirror. De-dum-dum. Couldn't get it. Missing one word that would carry what he wanted to put. Could he use the word "wonderful?" A soiled word. A spoiled word. Could he wiggle it into the line so that it would mean what it ought to mean? Wonder-filled. Nah, and besides, pretty nearly nobody was filled with wonder, for Pete's sakes, any more.

Larry let go, realizing that he was using his will, which he had already guessed was not the way. Forget it. Let the right word, meaning and sound, just come to him.

Dorothy finished the dishes and used scented soap on her hands. *We are pretty good people, as people go,* she was thinking. *Bob works faithfully to support us, and does it well. I keep this house as I ought, or I surely try. Larry gets good grades. He's not a grind; he is one of the fellows. He is doing nicely. And we love each other. We do our best.*

She thought with a pang, *Do I?*

She drifted into the living room. Bob had the paper, of course. Larry was flopped there. The day's work over, now was their time to relax, together, in their comfortable home, this loving family, these fine and decent people, nobody neurotic, nobody off the beam, all moving with their times.

Dorothy Smite suddenly, with a strong passion, wished she could take the Bible off the bookshelf. There was a passage she wanted to find. But that would be such an odd thing for her to do. She renounced this fierce and selfish desire, and sat down next to Bob and brightened her expression.

"What's on television?" she asked cheerfully.

Bob stirred. He loved her and wished to please her. He flipped the paper open to the amusement page. There was a symbol drawn there. A star.

A voice spoke in the quiet room. "Starshine," it said.

"What, dear?" Dorothy turned her face.

Bob felt his mouth to be open. He must have said it. He hadn't meant to speak. He wished he hadn't. It was the far-off glinting light he'd "seen"—still haunting his mind—that he'd been reaching to name. But there was no such word as "starshine." And what was Bob Smite, husband, father, home owner, jobholder, doing with it falling out of his mouth? "There's no such word, is there?" he said aloud and rattled the newspaper.

(If Dorothy now said, "How come you thought of such a thing? Is it in the paper?" Bob Smite would be unable to reply. What pressure, he quaked, in the loving curiosity that clamps right down on anything spontaneous, anything sweetly wild! "How did you happen to think of that?" they asked you, the ones who loved you. And you couldn't explain, because you loved them too. So you had to cover up what was wild and yet deep. You wanted to be what they needed and expected. How guarded you had to be!)

But it wasn't Dorothy, it was the boy who spoke. Sprawled on the couch, he was yet, somehow, totally alerted. "I don't think there's such a word," he said. "There's the word 'sunshine.' And the word 'moonshine.' But 'star*light*,' it would be." His mouth continued to move, as if it were tasting.

Bob looked at him curiously.

His mother did not look at him too directly. She was remembering within herself how Larry had always been so fond of words, so ready to play with them, as if he felt for them. She was taking note. He still felt for them, then, although this special interest had gone underground. She loved her son and she would not frighten him for anything.

So Dorothy said dreamily, "Maybe there should be such a word. The stars do shine. There must be such a thing. Too far, of course. Too far for us."

Her heartbeat quickened. She feared that she had said too much. If, in Bob's eyes, there should be loving amusement she did not want to see it. She did not look.

"Starshine," the boy repeated. "A mush-mouth noise." He cleared his throat and quickly reached for a more normal vocabulary. "I mean, it sounds kinda funny, you know?" he mumbled.

"Not so far," said Bob Smite slowly. "We walk around in it every day. The sun is a star."

The boy's green eyes had opened wide but neither parent saw this.

"There is starshine on us every day," said Dorothy breathlessly, "but we just don't—notice?" Her eyes met Bob's eyes.

The respectably pretty living room was still for half a moment. Then the boy squirmed restlessly.

Bob Smite moved. "What'll you have, Dot?" he said rather gruffly. "Big choice! A whodunit or a Western?"

"Doesn't matter to me," she said quickly. "Larry?"

"I don't care, mom." The boy relaxed into the couch cushions.

(*Funny*, he mused; *dad and a word that isn't a word. And an idea. And mom getting it, so fast.* Larry could have said a lot more about words. He thought about them so much, but secretly. Gosh, here at home, you didn't want to upset the people you loved with a lot of probably crazy stuff. You told yourself they wouldn't understand. But now into the boy's mind crept a question that made him uneasy: *What if they could understand?*) He squirmed.

"Meanwhile, back at the ranch," he droned, achieving youthful scorn.

Dorothy smiled at him, but she thought: *What is it around us every day that we do not notice? Dare not? Is it love? The whole thing? Is it a little bit too wonderful? Are we afraid?*

She blinked and turned her eyes to the screen.

Picture and music had begun. Bob went back and settled into his chair.

He had a feeling of deep happiness, as if they had all just escaped some unbearable glory, that was, nevertheless, there. But the room was normal now. It was just home. The evening was going to be typical. On the surface, considerately, they all conformed.

THE SHOCK

by Robert Murphy

Allen MacCormack, a personable young man, walked quickly out of the building where his office was, without paying too much attention to where he was going. He had worked late and was overdue at his brother Tom's house, where he was to spend the evening. His brother's handsome green-eyed wife, Deirdre, had made some vague mention of a girl; and, as Allen was lately back from a two-year stretch in South America with the oil company, his stock of girls was low. He was wondering, naturally, what this one would be like when he ran into someone. He pulled up, looked around in a bemused way, and saw a boy about eleven years old picking himself up off the sidewalk.

There was no one else immediately about, and Allen was rather surprised to think that the child, well dressed and apparently of a good family, would be alone in the middle of town so late. He extended a helping hand, which the child, on its feet by that time, slapped violently aside. Allen fell back a step and the boy, who appeared rather odd to him, gave him a look that was startling in its naked menace and hostility.

"Oaf!" the boy said. "Stupid barbarian!"

Allen stared at him, nonplused. "Well," he said, pulling himself together. "It was my fault. I'm sorry."

"You may be sorrier," the boy said.

"You'll be sorrier yourself," Allen said, beginning to get sore, "if I dust your breeches and send you home to your mother."

The boy's face took on an expression of rage so adult and venomous, so unchildlike, that Allen was more startled than before. "I would like you to try," the boy said, stared at him for a long moment, and with a strikingly feline movement turned and hurried into the building.

Allen stared after him, more disturbed by the encounter than he wanted to admit to himself; and his arm, now that he became aware of it, felt as though it had been hit with a club instead of a boy's hand. He flexed it several times, swore, and then walked on to the parking lot where he had left his car that morning.

He was still thinking of the boy when he turned into his brother's driveway and saw a fire-engine-red sports car parked in it. This was an interesting development, and distracted him; he parked his own sports car behind the other one and went into the house. There was no one in the living room, but he could hear the television in the other, smaller living room next door. Tom and Deirdre, like himself, watched television infrequently, and this room had been set aside for the two little girls and the "twenty-one" screen. He opened the door and looked in.

The boy he had encountered so unpleasantly was on the screen, talking, and with a feeling of malaise Allen turned away from him and looked at the family group. The two little girls were sitting on the floor, rapt; Tom and Deirdre and a strange girl, tall, black-haired and very pretty, were all standing and watching the screen with an air of fascination.

"Hey!" he said.

They all turned, except the little girls. Tom grinned, put a finger to his lips and turned back again. That was unusual, for him. The girl's dark eyes rested on Allen for a moment and she smiled slightly; the effect was unexpectedly pleasant, coming from a complete stranger. Only Deirdre moved. She came over to him, put a friendly hand on his shoulder, and whispered, "Watch this little monster. It's important, and anyhow he won't be on much longer."

"You've all betrayed me," he said, and gave her a brotherly kiss.

"We've done our best," she whispered, glanced toward the girl, and grinned. "But that's for later. Watch, now. Watch good."

She moved away again, and Allen looked back at the screen. Warned that something was afoot, that they were going to discuss the thing later, he concentrated on the boy. The fleeting impression of oddity which had struck him when he first saw the boy strengthened.

The boy was quiet for a moment—the announcer was talking about his sponsor's product—but in his quietness there was a complete muscular immobility like an adult's. There were no boy's unceasing nerve impulses to move a hand or a foot; nothing. Also, his face hadn't the soft, unformed boy's look, but an appearance of having gone through its changes and set. It may have been caused by the excitement and tension of the moment, and most people wouldn't have thought about it, but Allen saw it. It gave him a strange feeling, as though he were looking at a small but otherwise normal adult, whose growth had ended during boyhood, but who was still dressed up in boyhood's clothes.

"And now," the announcer said, "we come back to our young friend, Alexander Bovary. As we all know, Alexander, whose specialty is history, has swept the deck clear of his youthful rivals and tonight tries for his college scholarship at Harvard. This scholarship includes his Ph.D., which, in case you don't know it, folks, is a lot of scholarship. . . . Before we start the final questions, Alexander, I want you to stand up and give our audience a big, scholarly smile."

Alexander gave the man a sidewise, scathing glance. He stood up with a fluid grace most unusual for a boy. Staring at him, Allen thought at once of a cat, a weasel, some creature whose beautiful co-ordination was as smooth as flowing water. The boy smiled, or at least the corners of his mouth turned up; his look at the screen was so superior that it constituted an insult. There was a low murmur from the studio audience. The announcer hadn't seen the expression, but had seen the fluid movement; he did a double take.

"Why, you move like a ballplayer, Alexander," he said. "I didn't know you were also an athlete, boy."

A shadow of vexation flitted across the boy's face, and he stumbled and awkwardly caught himself. "I'm not," Alexander said. "I have to study too hard."

"H'm," the man said; and added quickly, "Well, sit down, son, and we'll see if our sponsor has a Ph.D. on his hands."

Alexander sat down, and it seemed to Allen that he was consciously clumsy; he slumped a little in his chair, which he hadn't done before.

"Well, folks," the announcer said, "here we go. Two final questions for that big Ph.D. . . . Now, Alexander, the temples of ancient times were built to various gods, in many architectural styles and of many materials. They varied exceedingly, but there was one thing in their design they had in common. What was it?"

"They had altars to all sorts of silly animals," Alexander said, "stars, improbable gods and other delusions, but I'm sure that isn't what you meant."

"No," the announcer said, pursing his lips, "it isn't."

"Good," Alexander said coolly. "The design, of course, would have less to do with human folly."

There was another murmur from the audience, a little louder this time. The announcer frowned. "Alexander," he said, "confine yourself to the question, please."

"As you wish," Alexander said. "The thing they had in common was orientation. They pointed to something. They all faced the rising sun on a certain day, the direction from which fertilizing floods came or something similar. This impressed the ignor——"

"Correct!" the announcer said, interrupting him. "That's abso-

lutely right, Alexander!" There was a scattering of applause, and
Alexander sneered. The applause ceased raggedly, and the announcer looked a bit haggard for a moment. He passed a hand
quickly over his brow and said, "You are now halfway to that
scholarship, my boy. Here is the final question." He paused and
held up a hand against the background murmur. "Quiet, please.
Here is the final question, and," he added, with an appearance of
satisfaction which he quickly covered by turning away, "I believe
our young friend will have to think about it for a moment. . . .
Alexander, where did the term 'proletariat' come from?"

"It is a badly misused word," Alexander said, "and has come to
be a term glossing over the fact that the entire history of man—
despite all his talk of striving for the good—is evidence that he
never wanted to do anything but enslave everyone else."

He paused for breath, and the announcer, who had begun to fidget,
said, "You must have a very happy home life, my boy, to study so
well."

Alexander gave him a sardonic stare. "My home life is probably
of less interest to you than your selfish dishonesties," he said, and
gestured toward the screen, "and those of your fellows are to me."

There was a strange and shocking air of menace about him as
he said this. Allen felt a chill go up his back, and he could hear
the rising clamor as the audience began to get out of hand.

The announcer ran back and forth, raising his hands. "Folks!
Folks! Quiet, please! Quiet! Let's get this over as decently as we
can."

The background noise quieted down, except for scattered out-
bursts. "The answer, Alexander," the announcer said desperately.
"No comments. Just the answer."

"The term came from Rome," Alexander said. "It came from
proletarius, the enrolled class who raised *proles*, offspring, citizens
for the state. They were usually sent off as colonizers."

"The answer is correct!" the announcer shouted. "Alexander has won his scholarship and will be an ornament to——"

Tom stepped forward and shut the television off. There was an immediate and concerted outcry from the two little girls. "Turn it on again, if you want," he said to them. . . . "Come on, grown folks. Let's blow."

They followed him into the other living room and shut the door. He put his back against it and spread his arms. "Go on and enjoy yourselves," he said. "I'll do my best to keep him out of here." He dropped his arms, took the strange girl by the hand and brought her over to Allen. "Allen, this is Iris Weller. She wants to take you for a ride in her sports car."

"I've been hoping this is the way it would turn out ever since I saw the car," Allen said, and they shook hands.

The arm the boy had slapped pained him as he raised it, but he forgot it at once because the girl had such a warm and friendly smile. She was even prettier in the soft light of the living room, away from the television's sepulchral glow. She was almost as tall as he; a quiet girl, but not too quiet; not too anything.

"Sit down and I'll fetch some drinks," Tom said. "We need something after that."

They sat down in front of the fireplace, and Deirdre said, "Well, give. What did you think of our boy?"

"Your boy?" Allen said. "Are you sure?"

"Yes, indeed. He's Iris' neighbor."

Allen turned to the girl. "There must be another house on the other side," he said, "full of trapdoors and bats, where Charles Addams keeps the rest of his characters."

"It was awful, wasn't it?" she asked. "I don't know what to expect now. He's been a little superior on the other broadcasts, but nothing like this. I don't know what's happened."

"I think it was me," Allen said, and told them of his encounter. When he touched his arm to show them where the boy had hit him, it was so painful that he took off his coat and rolled his shirt sleeve up. The arm was black and blue halfway to the elbow.

Tom came in, looked at the arm and passed the drinks around. He backed up to the fireplace as Allen put his coat on again. "I could hear you being lighthearted about our young friend," he said. "I wish he struck me that way. He'll obviously be a big shot and control a lot of lives someday, but I doubt I'll be here for that. I get a creepy feeling that he has something to do with now —with the present."

"Oh, come, Tom," Deirdre said. "Next you'll be saying that this little Hitler dropped from a satellite or is one of the new generation ruined by atomic fall-out."

"Tom's not going off into science fiction," Allen said. "I felt the same thing. He doesn't look like a kid, or act—or hit—like one. No eleven-year-old could have such comparatively obscure information or be so actually menacing."

"He was menacing," Tom said. "The little devil made my hair stand up. . . . Iris, what are his parents——"

"Pardon," Deirdre broke in decisively. "I know I started this, but now it's got to stop. Let's talk about something else."

When it was time to leave, Allen announced that he would follow Iris home.

"You don't have to do that," she said. "I've been out after dark before."

"I didn't know you then," Allen said. "It's different now. Something might catch you, and I don't want that."

"I'll admit," Iris said with a smile, "to being scared. Alexander will be home from his program before I am."

They said their good-bys and went out. Following the red convertible, Allen, who had a critical eye for the drivers of sports cars, was pleased by the way Iris handled it. Then she began to pull away, leading him on; he moved closer, and presently they were having a sort of swift and exhilarating progress, like a dance, through the moonlit night. He was sorry when she turned into a long and curving drive, passed the big house among the trees and came to her garage. He waited for her outside, standing in the driveway.

"You should always bring yourself," he said. "That was fun. Do you dance as well as you drive?"

"When I have as good a partner."

"We'll have to see," Allen said. "Do you have to go in quite yet?"

"I should," she said. "But let's walk down to the pool. It's nice on moonlit nights."

They went through a rather formalized garden which opened up on to a long stretch of lawn at the bottom of which a dark rectangle of tall evergreens stood. Allen judged that the pool was there, and as they started down the lawn he saw the other house several hundred yards away. He recalled that Deirdre had mentioned Alexander being Iris' neighbor. He had forgotten Alexander, and suddenly wished that he could forget him again.

"Is that where he lives?" he asked. "Alexander, I mean."

"Alexander? Yes."

"Iris," he said, "what are his parents like?"

"They're nice, but he isn't their child. They adopted him four or five years ago."

"Was he always like that?"

"I don't really know," she said. "I have quick impressions, that's all. I see very little of him. He's always reading, or going to the United Nations, or something like that. He's——" She suddenly stopped, and the look she gave Allen was startled. "Do you know," she said, "I've never thought of it before, but I'm sure he was the same size when they got him. I don't think he's grown at all."

He stared back at her, realizing with dismay that the exhilaration of the drive had gone when Alexander and this new bit of information about him had come into the conversation. He could see that she felt it too.

"I'm sorry I mentioned him," he said.

"I am too," she said a little ruefully. "The way he looked and spoke, and the talk at Tom's—— There couldn't be anything in it, of course, but——"

A slight shiver went through her, and her voice died away. They started to walk again. They came through the evergreens, and it was only then that they realized there was someone in the pool. Allen had a confused impression of the disturbed moonlit water, the white borders of the pool against the dark trees and the sinuous white body playing about with a sleekness and skill of an otter, that superlative swimmer. Nothing human, Allen thought in his confusion, could move in water with that silence and speed and flowing grace.

He watched in fascination, and felt Iris' hand tighten on his arm. He drew her back into the dense shadow, and as he did so the creature turned over on its back, swimming, and raised two white arms in the air, its joined hands cupping water. It moved back and forth, like an effortless ghost, and in the water cupped in the hands a small, bright white light like a star was born. It moved eerily, floating, and went out.

The man, creature, whatever it was, shot out of the pool and landed on its feet on the border. It was Alexander; he was too close to mistake. He dropped his arms and the water ran in little silver streams from his hands.

Then he moved, swung about, his head turned toward them and he stared for a long moment, like an animal frozen at a sound. His eyes were faintly luminous in the moonlight with a cold and feral glow.

He turned again and Allen could see, at each side of his neck near the base of it, a heavy dark line. He thought, wildly, of gills. Alexander slid into the water, which closed over him with hardly a ripple, and Allen put his arm around Iris and hurried her toward the house.

They didn't stop until they were at the side door. They faced each other, and the girl's eyes were wide. "Oh, Allen!" she said. "Did you see——"

"Yes," he said, shaken. "Don't think about it now, Iris. Take a sleeping pill. Two pills. I'm sorry I let you in for this."

"It was me," she said, in a small and shaking voice. "He didn't see us, did he?"

"No," Allen said, wondering with revulsion and even fear if he was right.

"Allen, what will we do?"

"I don't know," he said. "I'll call you. Take the pills and go to bed, for now."

"Yes," she said. "Allen?"

He moved closer to her, and took her in his arms. They kissed softly, like frightened children comforting each other, and she went into the house.

Allen got up reluctantly in the gray light of morning. He had slept badly. Memories, all too pictorial, had run endlessly through his head, and with their march had come an oppressive feeling of impending evil. There was too much that he couldn't begin to understand or appraise, no point from which to start out. He felt an almost overwhelming urge to do something, to act, and didn't know what to do. To whom could he go? He had nothing but a wild tale which would probably get him committed if he tried to tell it.

As he stood before the bathroom mirror he felt like the loneliest, most helpless man in the world, beset with inimical phantoms; and then, suddenly, he thought of Iris. The warmth and comfort of the kiss came back to him and warmed him again. He went to the phone and called her.

"Iris," he said, "did you sleep?"

"Not very well. Did you?"

"No," he said. "But I discovered one thing. If it had to be someone, I'm glad it was you."

"It's odd," she said without coquetry, "but I am too. Allen, whatever you do, let me help you."

"Thank you for that. It may be very dangerous, Iris. Do you still think, because of that——"

"Yes," she said.

"We must get some evidence, something. People will think we're raving mad without it. If only——" He was silent for a long moment, then an idea came to him. "Iris, under the pretext of having a friend who wants to adopt a child, can you get from—Alexander's mother the information about his adoption? The place, the man to see, everything you can? It may be a place to start."

"I can do it, I think."

"Then meet me for lunch at the University Club. Could you?"

"Yes," she said. "Good-by."

After they'd sat down at a table and ordered, Iris said, "Have you seen the morning paper? There was nearly a riot in the studio, and now there's a great uproar. Elizabeth Bovary, Alexander's mother, is nearly out of her mind. She never looks at television, she didn't know he'd got on the broadcasts, and people are calling up and threatening all sorts of things. He's been doing a lot of things they haven't known about lately."

"He certainly gets around, for an eleven-year-old."

"He's been doing it for nearly a year. At first they were pleased because he was precocious, and encouraged him. But something's happened to him, Allen; he's changed. I had the feeling that things have been happening that she can't understand. I think she's very frightened and lost. She cried, and talked about the little boy he was—he used to be."

Their lunch came, but neither of them felt like eating it; Alexander, with his cupped hands, his glowing eyes, lay upon them like a pall. They both pushed their food around a little with their forks, and then Iris looked up.

"I can't," she said finally. "I'm sorry, Allen."

He reached across the table and took her hand, and they stood up and walked out. They came to the Foundation, the impressive small building the address of which Iris had got from Elizabeth Bovary; and after Allen had talked with the receptionist, they were ushered into the beautifully furnished office of a man named Berringer. He seemed affable enough, but guarded. "I'd like to help you," he said, "but, as you probably know, our information is quite confidential."

"I was sure it might be," Allen said, "but could you give us a little background on the boy? I assure you it will be completely off the record. Everybody's going to do a piece on Alexander; a lot of sour things are going to be said, and we want to be fair. The more we know—even if we don't say it—the fairer we can be."

Berringer looked at him for a long moment. "Well," he said finally, "that's better than I expected from the press, particularly after this morning's paper. We don't want any more bad publicity, especially from a national magazine."

Iris looked at Allen in surprise, but he gestured and caught Berringer's eye. "Did you see the broadcast?" he asked.

"Ah," Berringer said. "Yes. Yes, I did."

Obviously he had been disturbed by it, but apparently he had decided to say as little as he could. Allen waited for a moment, then said, "Mr. Berringer, was there anything unusual in the physical records of that child?" He drew a finger lightly along the base of his neck.

Berringer started up as though an electric shock had gone through him, and stared at Allen with an expression that seemed compounded of apprehension and loathing. He opened his mouth, closed it again, and in a measure got control of himself.

"I don't know how you——" he began, and stopped. He licked his lips. "The embryonic gill slits, which never closed. We thought they would——in time. I wasn't with the Foundation when he came here, but there was——" He stopped again.

"There were other things," Allen said. "What of the records?"

"I will tell you something," Berringer said unhappily. "Because you know a fact which is unknown to anyone else now but the foster parents and myself. I must ask you to keep it entirely to yourself until after the directors meet this evening. Mr. MacCormack, our records on our children are kept in a vault, and no one but myself has access to them. Our entire file on this boy has vanished since last night."

Allen looked at Iris; her face had lost a good deal of its color. He turned to Berringer again and stood up.

"In that case," he said, "I will do nothing until I see you in the morning. It is most disturbing, and I may be able to help you later. Thank you, Mr. Berringer. Good-by."

Berringer stood up and somberly watched them leave. Allen had taken Iris' arm and hurried her down the hall. As they passed the switchboard the phone began to ring. "Hurry!" Allen said, and increased his pace. He almost ran out the door. He hailed a passing cab, fairly stuffed Iris into it, and told the driver to get him to his office as quickly as he could.

"Whew!" he said, after the cab had turned the corner. "I told them we were researchers for a news magazine, and that made us liable to arrest for impersonation. I was scared stiff that the magazine men would come in while we were there. That might have been a phone call from New York as we left." He paused. She still had some of her pallor, but her eyes were a little speculative as she looked at him from her corner. "What's the matter?" he asked.

"I'm learning about you," she said, and then gave him a little smile. "I didn't think you could be such an efficient reducer. I wouldn't have liked to be Mr. Berringer."

"I wouldn't like it either," Allen said, and took her hand. "He still knows more than he's saying. But tomorrow, I think, we can go back with the FBI."

"Allen, will you be careful? We still have nothing but intangibles, but they frighten me, and they're mounting up. Be careful, please."

"Yes," he said. "But you forget already what an efficient reducer I am. Just think of that after I get out and the cab takes you home."

After he had waved at the departing cab and turned to go into his office building, Allen dropped the cheerful manner he had put on for the girl. He was greatly disturbed, and wondered what to do. His mention of the FBI had been merely something to say, a comforting phrase for her benefit; he was well aware that he had nothing to go to the FBI with. If he told them of the scene at the pool, they would think him a crackpot; if he offered to take them there to wait, Alexander would probably not appear; and if he brought up the matter of the missing records, they would surely say that Berringer had misplaced them and was covering himself up with a fantastic tale. The local police would be worse; they would probably put him under surveillance, and he couldn't blame them.

He was helpless and alone, and, besides this feeling, there was a terrible urge upon him to act quickly. As Iris had said, the frightening intangibles were mounting up, and he didn't know what they would mount up to. The more he thought about it the more he felt like a man in a dark closet fighting an increasing mass of choking cobwebs, while a great spider coldly waited and watched from farther in the gloom. He sat at his desk thinking these things. His secretary looked in upon him once and he motioned her away. Her expression was concerned, but he didn't notice it.

Sometime later, his brother Tom came in. "Well, boy," Tom said, after a moment, "you look as though you'd seen a ghost."

Tom smiled, and Allen suddenly felt as though air and sunlight had come in with him. "I'm glad you came," he said. "But what brought you?"

"Your secretary called me. She saw a look on you that scared her, and she didn't want to go to the brass. What is it, Allen?"

As Allen told him, he listened quietly, playing absently with a pencil that he'd taken from the desk. "I didn't sleep either," he said, when Allen had finished. "Maybe you remember that I had a creepy feeling about the present. But what is he, Allen? Where did he come from?"

"Or what's he going to do?" Allen asked. "Tom, I have a feeling —a compulsion, really—that we've got to get rid of him. Quickly, before something——"

Tom dropped the pencil. "That can wait," he said. "We've got to get him figured first."

"Tom, we've got no basis. There's nothing in this world like him." His voice rose a little. "The swimming and the light in his hand. Like a way of communication with—with——"

"Forget that," Tom said. "Why did he get on that program, attract attention to himself? I'll tell you why. I talked to the president of my company about him after his last broadcast. The brass—and other brass too—is interested in him. He's extraordinarily bright. He attracts attention and worms his way in at the top. From something Iris said once, I gather he might have done the same thing at the U.N. and in Washington. He gets in, he learns, maybe he pops up with an idea, a notion that sounds good, but is disruptive. Subtle, not noticeable at first, maybe, but when all of them are added up there is a spreading confusion. He did it to us; it was—— But there's no use going into that now. But where's it going to stop?"

"Tom," Allen said. "Tom, we've got to stop it."

"How?" Tom asked.

They looked at each other for a long moment, in a sort of anguished helplessness.

"But," Tom said, "look. He's not only attracted attention to himself. Lately he's aroused hostility. That's not what he wants. I'm sure that's not what he wants. Something has happened, Allen. Something's gone haywire."

"Yes," Allen said. He had listened until now, or half listened, engrossed by his impressions—the luminous eyes, the physical strangeness. Now an excitement began to take hold of him. "Tom, Iris said that too. She talked to his mother, who is worried half out of her mind by the change in him. Ah, why didn't I think of it? You were always the level-headed one."

"I didn't see what you saw."

"Tom," Allen said as his excitement increased, "maybe there's a way. Maybe we can't hurt him or even touch him. We don't know what he's proof against. But maybe he has to have water and be out under the stars. The gills and the swimming, maybe there's a connection with the place he came from. He's in trouble; he has to—communicate and needs that. There's not much water around here. Tom——"

The excitement in him increased as he talked; he stood up quickly and began to walk around.

Tom stared at him. "Maybe you've hit on something," Tom said. "And whatever you've got in mind, count me in."

"No," Allen said. "You've got kids and Deirdre. If anything happens, you can get help then and march in."

Tom stood up. "I don't like it that way," he said. "I don't like it for a damn."

"And don't follow me," Allen said. "Don't do it, Tom."

"Allen——"

Allen put a hand on his shoulder. "Thanks," he said. "Thanks for that level head. I'll call you, kid."

They shook hands and Tom went out.

Allen had no appetite for dinner. He went to his apartment and sat looking out the window until after dark. He watched the lights of the city come on in their orderly, familiar progression, and wondered with an odd feeling of detachment whether he would ever see them again. After a while he went to the telephone, called the Bovary house and asked for Alexander.

"This is Allen MacCormack," he said. "We met in front of the studio building before your broadcast. Do you remember?"

"Yes," Alexander said.

"I'd like to meet you again. In half an hour at the pool." There was a silence, and Allen said, "Alexander?"

"Yes," Alexander said. "And if I do not find it convenient to come?"

A tightness began to gather in Allen's chest. "There aren't many pools nearby," Allen said, "and they can all be drained." The silence fell again, and sweat came out on the palms of Allen's hands.

"It's fifty miles to the nearest lake or stream of any size, and more inconvenient for you to get to any of them than for me."

The open line crackled faintly and Allen imagined that he could see the luminous eyes staring at him from the blank and shadowed wall. He wondered desperately if he had been wrong and had no hold on the boy.

"I will come," Alexander said suddenly, and hung up.

Allen took out his handkerchief and dried his hands. He stood up, and although the floor seemed to stream away and fall on all sides of him, he didn't stumble. Steadiness came to him. He left the apartment, rode the elevator down to the garage, got into his car and started toward Iris' house. He didn't turn into the drive, but parked in the road and walked across the fields.

Alexander was waiting for him, sitting on the marble bench at the end of the pool. Allen stopped several feet away, and Alexander stood up. His expression in the moonlight was unreadable, but calm.

"Greeting," he said, and it sounded curiously archaic to Allen, in view of what had happened. "You have discovered much," Alexander said, "and the fault was mine. I fell into error; I revealed myself. I allowed the different intensities of phenomena—the photons electromagnetism and radioactivity—of this planet, this earth, to affect me. If," he added, with a flash of scorn, "you know what that means."

Allen said nothing.

"We seldom destroy," Alexander said. "Our procedure is otherwise. But we will put it to the question, and see whether you have ended my usefulness or whether we will end yours." His expression changed; it became sardonic, and a touch of menace returned to it. The dark lines on his neck seemed accentuated. "However," he said, "if I go, do not be comforted. You cannot know how many we are or how we will prevail. Whenever you see a brilliant child, you will wonder. And you will never know. Zentho!" he said, in a curious, singing tone, and slid into the pool.

He moved like a playful otter; his arms came up, and the cupped hands. The light was born and moved eerily, and then turned a fiery red, as though the power that controlled and spoke through it, its far-distant and mysterious master, was bitterly displeased and wrathful. Suddenly the water of the pool was gathered up and shattered, and Alexander was gone. Allen looked above his head, into the sky. There was a wink of silvery light high above him, and that was all.

Presently he turned away, and then saw Iris standing there. She was in her stocking feet, for quietness, and held a futile shotgun in her hands. He was so moved that he couldn't speak.

"Allen," she said. "Allen. I felt something and came to be with you. But I was late; I saw you start, and followed. You shouldn't have come without me, Allen."

He moved then, and took the shotgun from her and laid it on the grass and took her in his arms. "Never," he said. "Never any more."

GIRLS ARE FOR THE ASKING

by William Holder

Eddie was a little frightened about the whole business. It was exciting, all right, going out with McCall and Ski. They were a lot older and they were both Machinist Mates 1/c—McCall had three hash marks and Ski had two. But he sure felt funny about the whole thing.

As soon as they were out of the yard, McCall waved for a cab and they got in. McCall told the driver, "Kelly's," and they settled back in their spotless, carefully pressed whites. McCall and Ski wore tailor-mades, and Eddie knew he'd have to get some. The three red stripes on his upper left arm continued to catch the corner of his eye.

Ski was big and blond. "So we go to Kelly's. The kid's gonna get a girl at Kelly's?"

"The fueling operation has precedence," McCall said. He was slim and dark and handsome. "Kelly's supplies room for thought. This is not a matter to be considered lightly. Besides, it's still too

early. Whoever heard of being social at four o'clock in the afternoon?"

"I did," Ski said. "And at ten o'clock in the morning."

"It's just your steaming Polish blood. Try to act like a civilized
human being once in a while."

"If it's all the same to you," Eddie said, "I'd just as soon go to
a movie."

Ski grunted and McCall threw up his hands. "What is the Navy
coming to? We're three weeks at sea and an able-bodied American
youth who just made Fireman comes ashore and wants to go to a
movie! Did you ever hear of anything like it?"

"No," Ski said. "Not in my born days. It wasn't like that in my
time."

McCall leaned back in his seat and shook his head. "I don't figure it at all. For almost six months we sit in the Mediterranean,
and all that lush stuff is draping itself around our shoulders, and
this new member of the United States Navy does not partake. First
there was Naples. Ah, those ravishing Napoli signorinas! And then
there was Cannes, and the magnificent bundles on the beach who
smiled and smiled and smiled. And then there was—— But it was
all there, Ski. You saw it."

Ski said, almost reverently, "Yeah, man. I saw it."

"Fireman Blake neglected it," McCall said in a flat, condem-
natory voice. "Fireman Blake used his liberties in sight-seeing, in
museum visiting, in taking pictures of ruins. The entire trip, in a
truly Navy sense, was lost on him."

"Look," Eddie said. "Everything was fine. I——"

"You're supposed to have one in every port," McCall told him.
"Having the uniform is like having a license. They're supposed to
tell you that, when you sign on."

The car stopped at Kelly's on Front Street and Ski paid the fare.
He said to Eddie, "You understand the evening is strictly on us.
All expenses paid by the Initiation Committee. After this you're
on your own."

"I've got money," Eddie said.

"Good. Hold onto it."

They went into the cool dimness of Kelly's and sat in one of the big booths. McCall told the waiter, "Ski and I'll have beer and a couple of shots, Joe. Our friend will have a beer."

"Your friend will have a beer if he's eighteen, Barney."

McCall said, "Show him the ID card, Fireman Blake."

Eddie dug his ID card from his pocket and the waiter looked at it and handed it back. "By two days," he said. "It's lucky you didn't make a fast trip."

The drinks came and McCall lifted his whisky. "To this fine town and the plentiful quail."

Ski nodded. "And they should take weeks to fix those lousy engines."

The beer tasted good. Eddie had had a glass at home quite a few times on a hot summer evening. There had even been hot toddies on two occasions, when he and his father had come in from a long cold day in the duck blind. He wondered if the ship would be in long enough so that he could get ten days' leave to go home. The fishing should be good now on Little River and on Long Lake. He wondered about the boat, if Johnny was taking care of it.

Ski waved to the waiter and indicated McCall and himself. When the drinks came, he said, "O.K., what's the scoop? Where do we go?"

"There's no rush," McCall said. "This is a thing to be carefully planned. We don't want to make a bad impression on our boy."

"The Mill," Ski said.

McCall shook his head. "Rowdy. Coarse. The Shore Patrol hits that layout every night. There's always a brawl."

"Henry's, then."

McCall said, "Not Henry's. We can do better than that."

They were names Eddie had heard on the trip back to the States. He felt himself blushing.

"Well, I sure ain't gonna sit here all night," Ski said. "You two don't do anything to me at all."

Eddie said, "We passed a good movie on the way to here. Gary Cooper. A Western."

They both looked at him, then studied their drinks. McCall raised his head with a smile. "Mamma Jo's."

Ski frowned. "That place gives me the willies. Everybody's so damned polite. You'd think you were in a soda fountain."

"So there's no sawdust on the floor. You always think a joint has to have spittoons. You're never happy unless some guy is breaking a bottle over your thick head. You have low tastes."

"It's just that I don't have to have everything fancied up."

"We'll go to Mamma Jo's," McCall said decisively. "For what it is, Mamma Jo's is a very nice place."

It was a name Eddie had heard spoken of with a certain amount of respect.

"This is gonna cost," Ski said. "You know that, don't you?"

"It won't cost you a dollar more than Henry's or The Mill, in the long run. Good whisky, no mickies, no trouble. You're the only stingy Polack I ever sailed with."

"I'm not stingy. I just wanted to call it to your attention so that when we split the bill you don't start screamin' like always and——"

"I've got money," Eddie said.

They ignored him. McCall looked at his watch. "One more and we shove off." He turned to Eddie. "You ever going to finish that beer?"

The beer was flat. Eddie wished he could have avoided this whole thing, but the way McCall and Ski had come at him about it, there hadn't been much that he could do but go along. They'd been talking about it for the last week, ever since he'd been foolish enough to answer the question. He would have hurt their feelings if he hadn't come along. Well, maybe it hadn't been only that.

The new beer was fresh and frothy, and he sipped it, wondering what Mamma Jo's would be like.

It was just an ordinary brownstone, three-story house when they got there at six o'clock. The sun was still high enough so that it was hot, but there was the feel of a breeze starting to come in from the sea. They went up the short stoop and McCall pushed the button beside the door. In a few moments it opened and a short, round woman with gleaming black hair and a dazzling white smile stood there. She slapped McCall on the arm. "Barney! It is a long time I don't see you! Where you been?"

McCall patted her plump shoulder. "As if you didn't know. I'll bet you've got the movements of the Sixth Fleet charted on a wall."

"Not back yet!" the woman said. "Not for another three months!"

"We were detached. Something wrong with the engines." They were in a hall, the door closed behind them. McCall said, "You remember Ski, Mamma."

The smile faded a little. "No fights!"

"Doves," McCall said. "We're lambs. And we brought a recruit, Mamma. This is Eddie. He's on our watch."

The woman nodded approvingly and the smile gleamed again. "A nice-looking boy."

Eddie said, "How do you do, ma'am."

She looked at him and nodded again. "Is very nice."

The ground floor of the house, Eddie saw, was mainly one large room. There were ten or twelve tables spaced along the walls, and a juke box was prominent. The lighting was subdued and everything was very clean. Two couples were dancing in a cleared space in the middle of the room and several more sat at scattered tables. It was an all-Navy gathering.

They sat at a large table and McCall told the stout woman what they were drinking. He turned to Eddie. "How do you like it?"

Eddie said, "It looks very nice. It's a nice place."

"The best," McCall said. "Nothing but the best for you this evening, my lad." He looked at Ski. "And remember, no trouble."

"Don't worry about it," Ski said. "I never start those things."

McCall snorted. "Now I've heard it all. But just keep in mind that I have a very good reputation here."

"It's a great place for it," Ski said.

A dark girl brought their drinks on a tray. McCall said, "Rosie! It's been a long time! Sit down!"

The girl sat down. She was very pretty, Eddie thought. She wore a brown dress with a white collar. She said, "You have a good cruise, Barney?"

"A tour. First-class accommodations. You know Ski?"

The girl looked at Ski and smiled. "Yes. Hello, Ski."

Ski said, "How's the girl?"

"You don't know Eddie," McCall said. "Eddie, this is Rosie."

Eddie got to his feet and said, "How do you do," and sat down.

The girl's eyes embarrassed him. Her voice was very low. "Hello, Eddie." He looked away at the couples dancing.

Soon there were two other girls at the table. Helen and Ethel. Helen was blond, and Ethel had red hair. They were very nice and they talked about movies and about fellows McCall and Ski knew. Helen sat near Eddie and asked him about the trip, and he told her about Naples and Cannes and the other places and dug some pictures out of his wallet.

The place was filling up and the air was getting heavy with smoke. One bunch in a corner was making a lot of noise and there were quite a few people dancing now. McCall was out on the floor with the girl named Rosie, and Eddie could see that he was very good. Ski was drinking quite a lot and laughing with the red-haired girl.

Helen said, "You want to dance, Eddie?"

He'd been afraid of that. "I'm not very good."

"We'll get along," the girl said. She got up and he followed her to the middle of the room.

It was very crowded and he kept bumping into other couples. The girl was close to him and she used a very heavy perfume. He looked down at her and was surprised to see that she was much older than she had seemed to be at the table. Really old. She must be twenty-three or twenty-four, he thought.

She said, "My, you're tall!"

"It runs in the family, I guess. My father's very tall and my mother's quite tall. My kid brother, Johnny, is only fifteen and he's as tall as I am."

The girl said, "You don't say."

There didn't seem to be much more to talk about. When the number finished, they went to the table again. Helen said, "Aren't you going to buy me a drink?"

"Oh, sure!" Eddie said. "I'm sorry I forgot to ask. And I'm sorry about the dancing too. I told you I wasn't very good."

She got up and patted him on the cheek. "We'll do all right. I'll be back in a minute."

He sat there and watched the rest of the people. Ski was dancing with his girl now, but he couldn't see McCall. It was getting pretty noisy, and someone dropped a glass across the room. He saw a couple of fellows from the Robinson and they yelled at him and he waved back.

He tasted the beer, but it was getting warm now, and with all the smoke and noise he was starting to get a headache. The place was all right, he guessed. It somehow wasn't like he'd expected it to be. He didn't know how he'd expected it to be, but this wasn't it. He looked again for McCall, but couldn't see him in the crowd.

Then the girl named Helen came by with a gunner's mate named Rogers, from the ship. She said, "You just hang around, Eddie. I'll be right back." They started to dance.

And suddenly he wanted to leave, and there was no one to stop him. He couldn't see either McCall or Ski. He hadn't really wanted to come with them in the first place, but the way they had arranged it, he just hadn't been able to back out. Well, maybe that wasn't all of it. But now that he was here, he didn't like it.

Leaving was simple. He just stood up, took his white hat from the back of the chair and walked out. No one seemed to notice him at all. He walked slowly down the street, feeling ashamed, somehow, but feeling good, too, to be out of the smoke and the noise and the heavy, scent-filled air. He took a deep breath. It was still plenty light, but it had cooled a bit. McCall and Ski would be sore at him, he knew. He'd just tell them he'd felt sick and had to leave. There wasn't any reason to feel bad about it, he told himself. Just as there wasn't any reason why you had to go somewhere just because someone asked you to. Maybe a person just didn't feel like going.

He walked for four blocks and suddenly discovered that he was hungry. He was almost down to Front Street again when he saw the restaurant. The sign said: JACK'S—SEAFOOD A SPECIALTY, and it looked clean and not too expensive. He crossed the street and went in.

It wasn't very big. There were maybe fifteen tables, and only four of them were occupied. He took a small table against a wall and hung his hat on a hook above the table. He figured he had never been so hungry. There were quite a few items on the menu and he studied them carefully.

Someone set a glass of water on the table and he looked up.

The girl was very slender and very pretty. Her hair and eyes were brown, and he guessed she was about medium height. She wore a light dress that flounced out somehow, and an apron, and something like a little kerchief on her head. She did not smile.

Eddie ordered clams and clam chowder, and said, "Can I have a steak?"

The girl's voice was very soft. "I guess so, but I'd better ask." She went away. Eddie liked the way she walked.

When she came back, she said, "Yes, we have steak."

Eddie said, "All right, I'll have the steak with some French-fried potatoes. Will you make the steak medium rare?"

She stood there writing it down on a little pad, and he said, "You don't seem to be very busy."

"It's a little late. Most of our customers have been and gone."

"Sure," Eddie said. "I'd forgotten about the time."

She went off to the back of the restaurant, and in a little while brought him a half dozen clams. When he had eaten them, the girl took away the shells and brought him a big bowl of chowder. It was wonderful chowder.

When she came back for the plate, he said, "That chowder is very good."

She said, "Thank you."

Eddie stretched his neck. "I'll bet you made it yourself."

She smiled for the first time. It was a very timid smile. "Oh, no. I didn't make it."

"Well, it was very good chowder."

In a little while she brought him the steak. It was a fine steak, just the way he wanted it. It didn't take him long to eat it and the potatoes and the dish of salad. He felt a lot better.

The girl came for the steak platter and he said, "Now don't tell me you didn't cook that steak. It was very good."

Her smile was not quite so timid this time. "Oh, I couldn't cook like that. My father does all the cooking."

"Is this your father's place?"

She said, "That's right."

"Well, let me tell you, it must be fine to have your father running a restaurant like this. You certainly shouldn't go hungry."

"No," she said. "I certainly never go hungry."

"You'd expect to see a big fat girl," Eddie said. "Her father running a place like this."

The girl said, "No, I don't get fat. Would you like something else?"

"Just some pie and ice cream," Eddie said. "And a glass of milk."

In a few moments she brought the pie and ice cream and the milk. Eddie said, "Do you live here? I mean, in this building?"

The girl shook her head. "We live over on Garland. It's about half a mile."

"Well, I guess it would be nice to live here. Convenient, I mean. Just have all your meals in the restaurant. All you wanted too."

The girl said, "Well, I think it's nicer to have a kitchen right in your own house."

"Well, I guess it would be," Eddie said. He couldn't think of anything else to say. He looked around. The other customers had left. The girl started to move off and he said, "Well, it looks like most of your customers have gone."

The girl nodded. "It usually gets slow around this time."

"Well, I guess you just close up then, don't you?"

"We usually close in about an hour."

She walked off and Eddie ate the ice cream and the pie. He drank the milk and asked for another glass. He tried to figure something else to eat, but he didn't think he could hold any more. The girl was near the rear of the restaurant and he waved to her. "I guess I'd like a check."

She stood there and added up the check and handed it to him. He got a bill out of his wallet and said, "Let me tell you, that was very reasonable for a meal like that."

"I'm glad you think so," the girl said. "I'll get your change."

She went to the register on the little counter near the door, made the change and came back with it on a platter. She put the platter on the table and said, "Thank you very much."

She started to walk away, and Eddie said, "You know, now that you're closing up and all, I don't guess maybe you'd want me to walk you home? Or maybe it isn't too late for a movie?"

She stopped and turned and looked at him very seriously. She said, "I don't know. I'll ask my father." She walked to the back of the restaurant and disappeared.

Eddie wondered if he should get up and walk out. He had forgotten about her father being the cook. He picked up his change, put a half dollar under the platter and took his hat from the hook. He walked around a couple of tables slowly, and then he heard a heavy voice say, "Mary, I told you. I don't want you hanging out with any Navy."

The girl said something Eddie couldn't hear, and then the man said, "All right. Let's take a look."

Eddie started for the door, then pulled up short and faced the back of the room. The girl came out first, followed by a big man, almost as tall as Eddie, but wider and heavier. He stood about five feet from Eddie and looked him up and down. "So you want to take my daughter home. Or to the movies."

Eddie said, "Yes, sir. I mean, I thought if she's all through working she might like—to have someone walk her home."

"What ship you on?"

"The Robinson. It's a destroyer. We're detached from the Sixth Fleet and came back here for engine repairs."

The big man was silent for a moment, then he said, "Lemme see your ID card."

Eddie hesitated, but only for a moment. He dug the card out of the wallet and handed it over. The big man looked at it as if he'd seen a lot of them. He muttered twice to himself, "Blake. 6462348," then handed the card back to Eddie and stared at him for what seemed a long time. Then he nodded. "O.K., Blake. She has the Saturday-night leeway. Have her home before twelve o'clock."

Eddie breathed for the first time in several minutes, it seemed to him. He said, "Yes, sir."

The big man said, "And, Blake." Then he stopped and said, "O.K. Before twelve." He turned and walked back into the kitchen.

The girl went to Eddie's table to clear the dishes. She said, "I'll be right out." Her smile was very shy.

Eddie walked to the front of the restaurant. He felt very light and very tall. He put on his hat and then took it off again. He guessed he had done everything all right.

The girl came out in a little while and he opened the screen door for her. When they were on the sidewalk, he said, "Well, here we are. I thought your father was going to be mad or something."

"He sounds pretty fierce, but he isn't, really."

They walked down the street and Eddie said, "Do you want to go straight home or go to a movie?"

"It's such a nice night. It seems a shame to waste it in a movie."

The last light was blue-green, far down in the west, and a moon two days away from full was walking up the eastern sky. They walked, and Eddie said, "I guess you come from here?"

The girl shook her head. It came just about up to his shoulder, Eddie noticed. "No, I've lived in several places. We've been here about four years. Ever since Pop opened the restaurant."

"It's a nice town. Real nice."

"We like it fine."

Eddie said, "What are all those lights? Over there?" He pointed. "Seems like just outside of town."

"Oh, those. That's Neptune Park. It's an amusement park. They have rides and things. You know."

Eddie thought for a moment. "Could we go there? I mean, it's such a nice night and all."

"We couldn't walk. We'd have to take a bus."

Eddie suddenly said, "Gosh, I don't know your name! I think I heard your father call you Mary, but that's all."

"Mary Taylor," she said. Then she smiled. "I heard my father call you Blake, but I don't know your first name."

"Eddie. Eddie Blake. I'm pleased to meet you." They both laughed. Eddie said, "Where did your father have his restaurant before you came here?"

She looked at him and started to laugh. It was more of a giggle. She said, "He retired from the Navy on twenty years five years ago."

Eddie stared at her. "He what?"

"He was a Chief Commissary Steward. He always wanted to open a restaurant of his own."

"But I heard him tell you that he didn't want you hanging around with any Navy!"

Her laughter had a nice sound. "I know!" Then she said very quietly, "He must have liked you."

"Well!" Eddie said. It was all he could think of.

The bus got them to Neptune Park in fifteen minutes. It was a nice place, right on the beach, and it wasn't crowded. There were lots of rides, a dance pavilion, eating places and game booths. They just walked around, going on this ride, then on another. The Devil's Dip was a fine roller coaster, the fastest Eddie had ever been on, and The Whip was good, and the Flying Airplanes. They talked as they walked, and Eddie learned that the girl was an only child, that she was seventeen, that she had worked in the restaurant during school vacations, this year and the year before. "Pop doesn't want me to work, but the work is easy and the tips are good." She looked at him and grinned, and he felt foolish.

They went on the Ferris Wheel, and it was wonderful swinging in the carriage high up, with the moon silvering a long path on the ocean stretched out before them. Eddie found himself talking about Hilldale, the town in Michigan he came from, and about the farm, and about graduating from high school. "And now I'm taking armed-forces courses. It's almost like going to college. Agricultural courses. Sounds funny, doesn't it? A sailor taking farming lessons?"

"I think it's very nice," the girl said.

The dance pavilion was near the Ferris Wheel, and when they came down, the girl said, "Would you like to dance, Eddie?"

It was the first time she had used his name. He liked it. "I don't dance very well, I guess."

"That's all right."

The band was playing a waltz, and Eddie was thankful. He wasn't so bad at waltzing. He held the girl gently and moved carefully, and it was just like dancing with a feather, he thought. She smiled up at him and said, "Why, you dance very well, Eddie." She smelled like the breeze coming in from the sea, fresh and clean. It was the first time he had ever really enjoyed dancing. When they walked away from the pavilion, he was surprised to find that they were holding hands.

Eddie won a small woolly dog knocking some wooden bottles off a stand with a baseball. When they walked away from the booth, Eddie stretched his neck. "There's a ride we haven't been on. I'll bet it's pretty scary." It was called Tunnel of Love.

The girl said, "Well, I guess so," and Eddie bought some tickets and they got into a small boat held by an attendant. When he let go of it, the boat drifted toward a dark cavern.

It was black as pitch in the tunnel, and every here and there frightening figures flashed at them, and once the girl squealed. Eddie moved to put his arm around her, then stopped. He remained rigid all through the ride.

When they came out into the light again, the girl looked at him. "It was certainly pretty scary."

Eddie laughed. "It sure was." He thought his voice sounded a little funny.

They had custard cones, and walked away from the lights toward the ocean. There was a boardwalk that stretched to the left and right as far as you could see in the moonlight, and they walked for quite a way until they came to an empty bench. They sat facing the sea, and Eddie told the girl about fishing on Little River with his father and Johnny, and she talked about her school and some of the cities she had lived in.

Then they were silent for a little while, and Eddie found that he had stretched his arm along the back of the bench.

The girl turned to him and started to say, "One time in——"

Eddie's arm just dropped of itself and tightened a little and he kissed her. Her lips were sweet and fresh and soft, and in a moment he felt her hand touch his face lightly. In a few moments he drew back and his arm loosened. The girl's relaxed lightness leaned against him and he drew a deep breath and looked out over the ocean. He was all a little mixed up, but he felt wonderful, and the scent of the girl's hair seemed very soft and important. She didn't move or look at him.

In a little while he said, "Well, gee, I guess we'd better get going." He looked at his watch and they had plenty of time, but he knew he wasn't going to take any chances. Not with this girl.

She said, "I guess we'd better," and they got up and walked along the boardwalk to the park and through the lights and the noise. It seemed very natural to Eddie that they were holding hands now.

There wasn't very much to say on the bus. The girl held his hand and smiled at him when they came to her stop, and they walked four blocks to her house through the soft night.

They stopped in front of a wooden house with a porch, and the girl said, "Well, this is where I live."

Eddie said, "Well, I want to thank you. I had a swell time."

"I want to thank you," the girl said. "It was lots of fun."

He noticed for the first time in an hour that she still held the little dog. He said, "Maybe you'd like to go out there again some night. Or to a movie."

"I think that would be nice."

"I mean, if your father didn't mind."

She smiled. "I don't think he'd mind."

He said, "Well, good night, Mary." He wanted to kiss her again, but he knew somehow that it wouldn't be right, here.

She said, "Good night, Eddie," and walked up the steps of the porch to the door. She turned once and waved to him, then went into the house.

He walked down the street to the bus line and was a little surprised to hear himself whistling. Then he found himself in a panic because he hadn't made a date, really, and he doubted if he could find the house again. But he certainly remembered where the restaurant was. And he guessed it would be all right about the date.

He was just going aboard the Robinson in the yard when he met McCall. McCall was weaving a little, but not bad. He said, "Well! Fireman Blake! What happened to you?"

"I didn't feel so good," Eddie said. "I didn't see you around, so I left."

"You didn't see me around, so you left. That's fine." McCall lit a cigarette. "Where you been?"

"The park," Eddie said. "Neptune Park."

"Neptune Park. I suppose you went on all the rides?"

"I guess we hit most of them."

"We? Who's 'we'?"

"I met a girl," Eddie said. "A very nice girl." He hoped McCall wouldn't say the wrong thing.

"A nice girl, eh?" McCall looked at him unsteadily for a moment. "You know, I'll bet you did, at that. Sometimes I wonder who's smart around this outfit. Who's really smart. I know it isn't me."

He went aboard the ship, and Eddie followed him. He glanced at his watch. It was just midnight. He was glad he'd got Mary home in plenty of time.

HIGH TERROR

by Brian Cleeve

He was a big, shambling boy of a man that no one in the valley ever took much notice of, for good or bad. Blue eyes under lint-pale eyebrows, that never seemed to be looking quite at what any-one else was looking at. A soft, straggling fringe of beard on his chin that somehow made him seem more of a child than if he'd shaved it off, and a mouth as gentle as a woman's who's in love. It was hard, though, to think of Bruno Holtzmann's ever being in love. He seemed too far away. Not an idiot, now. Hans Trott, the schoolmaster, said that if he'd only have applied his mind to things he'd have been as clever as any boy he ever had through his hands. But just far away.

You'd see him sometimes sitting on a fallen log at the edge of the forest, thick shoulders stooping, huge hands hanging between his knees, blue eyes gazing at nothing; at the moss under a tree, maybe, or a line of ants climbing the bark. Nothing at all. And if you asked him what he was doing he'd smile and say, "Just looking." Or else he'd be carving things with a knife. He could carve quite well, too, and the schoolmaster tried to help him, showing him how to make bottle corks with funny heads to sell to the summer visitors. But he'd never do what Hans Trott showed him— only foolish things out of his own head, or that he'd seen in the woods; things that no one would ever buy. And so even Hans left him alone after a while, and we never thought about him in connection with the real life of the village.

He drifted through his schooldays, and out of them, as aimless as a cloud in the summer sky, hardly seeming to realize that he'd become a man. He did what his mother told him about their small bit of a farm, his father being dead, God rest him. He'd chop wood for her, or dig, or draw water, or hoe the lines of vegetables behind the cottage, but never as if his heart were in it. He did these jobs only out of obedience and gentleness toward his mother, and as likely as not he'd forget what he was doing halfway through a task and stand stock-still, leaning on his hoe or the helve of his ax, staring at the sky or the mountains or a bird pecking on the ground.

Often enough as I'd pass by the door with the mailbag, his mother would come out to me and say that she didn't know what would become of him when she was gone. Although I never said so to her, I didn't know either. The patch of land they had wouldn't keep a man long the way he worked on it. And then, almost between one day and the next, it seemed, it came so suddenly, Brunnhild Winterhalder married him.

It was as if the valley had been struck by thunder. Brunnhild Winterhalder, old Gustav's only daughter! It couldn't be believed. The Winterhalders were like royalty. Half the valley belonged to them, and Brunnhild walked through it like a crown princess. She was tall and slender and full of pride, like steel mixed with gold. The other girls played in the meadows with the boys in summer, fought with snowballs in the winter, stole kisses in the cowsheds, blushed and giggled if a man spoke to them. But from the time she could walk, Brunnhild Winterhalder was different, as if she knew even then that life would belong to her.

And almost from that time it had been the common word that when she was grown enough she'd marry her second cousin, Konrad Goltz, whose father owned a bank in Neuberg. Every summer and Christmastime the Goltzes came to spend a holiday with the Winterhalders, and often enough Konrad would stay on afterward for as long as school would let him, until I suppose he was as much like a brother to Brunnhild as a cousin. Maybe that was the trouble because, as a man, you couldn't compare him with Bruno Holtzmann. Compare him? As well compare a race horse with a donkey dreaming over a clump of thistles. He was tall and dark, and wide in the shoulder, and strode down the village street like the soldier he was, with a way of smiling that set the girls following him with their eyes like sheep after a piper.

And yet one summer when Konrad was away with his regiment, Brunnhild said that she was marrying Bruno. That Sunday Father Bauer read out the banns as if he were reading a death sentence.

"Herr Bruno Holtzmann and Fräulein Brunnhild Winterhalder, both of this parish, declare their intention of joining in holy matrimony on the third Sunday from this day. If any man or woman——"

You can guess well enough what followed. The arguments and the pleadings and the threatenings. But they were of age, and where Brunnhild stood like a rock, like steel against every word that was said to her, Bruno was like water, slipping between their fingers when they tried to fasten him with arguments. He'd smile and lower his eyes, his great hands folded on his ax or hanging between his knees, and say only, "I love her."

It was like blasphemy to hear it. How? Why? When had they become close enough even to think of such things? Never, that we could see. Certainly Brunnhild had talked to him at times, looked over his shoulder at his whittling, been kind to him; but so had everyone. He had hardly seemed to notice her. Once or twice indeed he had given her his carvings. But then, he would give them to anyone who was kind enough to take them. Usually people just threw them away when they were out of his sight again. Anyway, love doesn't spring from a foolish gift. How? Why?

All Brunnhild would say was, "I have chosen him," her chin lifted as if the people talking to her were rebellious subjects instead of her elders trying to persuade her for her own good. But I can tell you, I wasn't one of them. I've enough business of my own to mind, delivering the letters round the valley and keeping the village post office in order.

I wouldn't even have seen the wedding if I hadn't had a message to deliver to Father Bauer that day. Usually weddings in our valley are great events. For weeks the women are in and out of the girl's house, helping with her dress and her trousseau, gossiping and crying over her, and heaven knows what. And the week of the wedding you'd hardly see the church for flowers and green branches. Then on the day itself there isn't an inch of space on the benches; the village children are scrubbed and starched and lined up at the church door with their hymnbooks. Hans Trott is at the organ, with the tears running down his long nose from behind his spectacles, with his gray hair on end like a bird's nest, and finally the bride comes like a queen in glory. We keep up the old ways, and she wears the crown of virtue—a thin, golden circlet so old that no one remembers when it was made. For that day she is a queen, and her man a king.

I've heard the priest say that every husband is the king of his own house, and every wife the queen. But in the grayness of the days their royalty becomes forgotten. It's only on their wedding day that one sees them as they truly are.

If that is so, there was small royalty for Brunnhild. Barely a woman of the village, except her father's servants and her own mother, went near her in the weeks before, except to scold her. Father Bauer even wanted to keep the crown from her and hold the marriage almost secretly. But she set her mouth at that. Maria, the priest's servant, told me how she down-faced him.

"I will wear the crown," she said. "And we will be married at midmorning on Sunday." She meant, "so that everyone may watch who cares to watch."

She had her way, for whatever good it did her. I don't think there were a dozen in the church. Her mother was there, looking as if it were a funeral; and her father, old Gustav, with his gray beard like an iron plowshare, and his hard, pale eyes. I think he'd have stayed away, only he wouldn't please the village to see how deeply he'd been hurt. He sat in the front row like a statue carved out of oak, his arms folded and his beard sunk on his chest. And, of course, there was Bruno's mother, frightened out of her wits, bobbing a curtsy to old Gustav whenever she caught his eye, which wasn't often, and crying into a handkerchief. Then there were a few house servants of the Winterhalders, and one or two of the people who'll stare at anything if it's free. Myself, I was only there because of the message I had for Father Bauer, as I've said.

There was no choir of children, and Hans Trott had refused to play the organ, so Maria, the priest's servant, played it. It sounded like geese being killed. Into the near-empty church came Bruno, looking like a dancing bear in his best suit. It was too small for him, and the black cloth stretched over his chest and shoulders until you'd think the buttons were going to burst, while his huge hands and wrists stuck out of the narrow sleeves like tree branches.

Then came a wailing squeal on the organ from Maria, and the bride was there in the church door. Suddenly I realized that old Gustav shouldn't have been in the church at all as yet. He should have been with his daughter, ready to give her away, but he sat like a rock, and the few of us on the benches craned round to see who was with her. It was her Uncle Kurt, a poor creature who had been wounded in the war and could barely drag himself about. Old Gustav kept him, out of charity. Now apparently he had chosen him to give Brunnhild away because he couldn't bring himself to do it.

And so with the organ wailing and Bruno shambling to his feet to wait for her, Brunnhild came up the aisle on her uncle's one arm, his left leg dragging and shuffling along the floor. It looked as if she was supporting him rather than he supporting her. She was wearing the crown, but I think it must have burned her forehead with shame. Yet she never flushed, never faltered. She walked as if the man she had chosen were a king, and there were drawn swords around her.

I thought the priest would choke before he got through the ceremony. "Do you, Bruno Holtzmann, take this woman——" I was watching old Gustav's face, and word by word the color drained out of it till it was like lichened stone. And when Brunnhild said "I do," her mother sobbed and buried her face in old Gustav's shoulder. But somehow the thing was done, and by that night Brunnhild was in her new husband's cottage, whose small, narrow windows look down the valley at her father's great, red-roofed farmhouse, with its timber stacks and spreading fields.

And still no one in the valley knew why. We only began to guess a few months later, when her cousin, Konrad Goltz, arrived, on leave from his regiment. In the meantime, I won't say we'd got used to the matter, but the first sharp edge had worn off it. Everyone recognized that it was done and couldn't be undone. It had to be accepted, although that didn't mean it had to be approved.

Somehow, I don't quite know how, we felt that Brunnhild had struck a blow at all of us. She had upset the order of things. Where once she had had the respect and admiration of everyone, she now had something that was near to hatred. And her poor shambling fool of a husband shared in it. Nobody gave them more than the curtest of good-days when they'd see them about the valley. No one called on them; no one invited them, and within a month you could see it telling in Brunnhild's face.

Before the marriage the sheer bravado of what she was doing had carried her along. The dreadfulness of her choice had seemed to give it a kind of perverse splendor. It was like suicide, and people had looked at her as you'd look at a man poised on a cliff's edge, threatening to jump. You'd go on your knees to him to stop him jumping, the way most of us had gone on our mental knees to her. But let him jump, and he's nothing but a shameful body of flesh, to be buried out of sight and mind in unhallowed ground. Brunnhild had jumped, and in these few months she found the difference between threatening and doing.

Her face grew very pale and drawn, and her mouth grew as hard as a steel trap. Everything must have rasped on her like gravel on bare skin. The coarseness of the food, the manners of her mother-in-law, like those of a frightened servant; the narrowness and poverty of the cottage, with its three rooms like boxes—she who had grown up in rooms bigger than the church. Above all, her husband must have torn her nerves in shreds, because he didn't treat her like a husband at all. Never gave her a task to do. Never gave her the feeling that someone stronger than herself had taken her destiny into his hands. How could he, poor fool? He treated her like some injured, helpless bird that he might have found in the woods, carrying it in his great hands and making a nest for it in an old shoe, to sit and stare at the softness of its feathers and the brightness of its eye for hour after hour. As for her mother-in-law's giving her work to do or a sense of belonging to the house, she could hardly bring herself to speak to Brunnhild without curtsying.

Brunnhild took to wandering in the woods, or up the mountains, going away all day with a knapsack of food and a stick, and coming back at dusk. I'd meet her sometimes on my rounds, striding with blind eyes like a lost Valkyrie, as if only by wearing herself out could she hope to stay sane. The snow came, and she'd go skiing, but always by herself. Bruno would drift through his strange, faraway days, not much differently from the way he had always done, except that now he did work harder. A wood stack grew slowly behind the cottage and, with the spring and the melting of the snow, he began to plant a kitchen garden, beds of herbs and vegetables, and even flowers, and strangely enough he did it as neatly as anyone could have done it, touching the plants with his fingers as if they were alive.

And then in the first days of summer Konrad came in a motorcar. He stopped first at the Winterhalder farm, and for an hour he was with old Gustav in his study. One of the servants told me you could hear him all over the house before the end.

"How could you let her do it?" he'd shout again and again.

The old man's voice, between sorrow and fury, answered, "Why didn't you come before it was too late?"

At the end of the hour he stormed out of the house and into his car and slammed it up the track toward the head of the valley. But halfway there it stuck in the mud, and he had to get out and trudge up to the cottage on foot. Bruno was at the kitchen garden when he came—I can tell you there were more than one or two people followed Konrad to see what would happen, and I've had every word of it from three or four of them—and for once Brunnhild was in the cottage, doing something. She was mending a dress or some such, as her father had refused to give her a pfennig of cash or a length of cloth beyond what she carried with her on her wedding night.

Bruno straightened himself up, or as much as he ever did, and smiled at Konrad as though there was nothing between them in the world. Konrad stood for a second in front of him, quivering. I don't know what he had meant to do in coming, but whatever it was, I think he forgot it in the wave of anger he felt at seeing Bruno in the flesh, seeing the creature that had dared to marry Brunnhild. Looking at the two of them together, you'd understand his anger. They were like two races of men. Of men? Of man and beast almost. Konrad slim and swift and handsome, with his hooked, arrogant nose and hard, soldier's eyes. And Bruno, his little fringe of beard like untidy wool, and his mild, foolish eyes gazing at everything as if they saw what wasn't there. His hands were dark with earth from planting, and he tried to brush them on the thighs of his trousers.

"You swine," said Konrad. "You bestial imbecile." And he struck Bruno full in the mouth with his closed fist. Bruno stared at him in bewilderment, not even lifting his hand to defend himself or to wipe away the blood running from the corner of his lips. "I should kill you," said Konrad, drawing back his fist again, and with that Brunnhild came out of the cottage in a white blaze of fury.

"We'll see who'll kill," she raged. "Hit him," she said to Bruno. When Bruno didn't move, she beat her fists against his shoulder. "Kill him!" she screamed. "Kill him! Don't just stand there, you shameful lout. Strike him back!"

For answer Bruno bent down and took up his spade, turning it in his gigantic hands as if it were a trowel, and the people who were there gasped and half turned to run, thinking that he was going to split Konrad's skull with it. Even Konrad flinched, they say, as if he suddenly realized the size of the man he had struck. But Bruno only set the blade of the spade in the earth and pressed it down.

"The poor man is in great sorrow for you," he said to Brunnhild. "He did not mean what he did."

"Is that all your answer?" Brunnhild whispered.

He just smiled at her and began to dig. For a long moment Konrad and Brunnhild stood there as if they didn't know what to do. Then Brunnhild spun on her heel and fled inside, pressing her knuckles against her mouth. Konrad hesitated, made to follow her and stopped still again. Then he, too, spun round and almost ran down the hill toward his car.

In the days that followed we found out something of what lay behind it all—gossip here, a word overheard there. It was nothing very much out of the way. Just a quarrel, really; hardly even a lovers' quarrel because, as I've said, Brunnhild and Konrad had grown up too close together to have that lovers' suddenness between them. But what they lacked in one passion they made up for in another—pride. A small quarrel had become a fierce one. He had gone back to his regiment, swearing that he wouldn't come back till she sent for him on her knees, and she had sworn that unless he came back on his own knees within three months she'd marry the village idiot before she'd marry him. He hadn't come, and she'd kept her word—or as close as it could be kept, lacking an actual idiot to marry.

It was a pathetic-enough story, almost like a fairy tale. The prince and the princess betrayed by pride, and the princess fallen into the hands of a hideous monster. Perhaps that last isn't quite an accurate description of poor Bruno, but it's the way the village began to think of him. With one of those sudden swings of opinion, everyone began to blame Bruno for the whole thing. And when Konrad didn't leave, but stayed on with the Winterhalders, there weren't too many words said against it. Heads began to nod and tongues to whisper. Konrad had been seen up at the cottage when Bruno was over in the next valley buying some seed. Brunnhild and Konrad had been seen together climbing up the Altenburg, and although a few said no good could come of it, others said that times had changed, and that in the cities and among rich people these things were done every day and thought nothing of. Day by day we expected something to happen, although I don't know what.

But thinking of it now, what did happen was stranger than the strangest thing that any of us expected. I was up delivering a letter to the herdsmen in the summer pastures, high, high up beyond the face of the Altenburg that falls like a great thousand-foot curtain of stone between our valley and the smaller Alps. It isn't a difficult path if you're used to it. In a few places the path becomes a ledge no wider than your boot sole, with the Alten River in its gorge like a ribbon of white lace eight hundred feet below. But beyond that the cliff slopes back and gradually becomes the summer pastures. The cattle come up by another, longer route, of course, but a man on foot should have no trouble crossing the cliff face if he's a mountaineer, unless there's a wind. But this day the wind was screaming off the cliff like an eagle, trying to tear me off my feet, and I can tell you I wasn't thinking of much but getting home as I came along the ledge.

Brunnhild, Bruno, Konrad—they were a thousand miles from my mind. So far from it that, once I was on the broad track leading down through the forest, I almost passed two climbers without realizing who they were. Brunnhild and Konrad Goltz together. Konrad bent down to retie his boot lace, as if hiding his face, but Brunnhild went by with her head lifted and her eyes like iron, and the thought came to me that maybe they'd been quarreling again.

"I should be careful up there," I said. "The wind is bad." They never answered me.

Half an hour later I was passing Bruno's cottage. He was digging in the garden, and really it was a wonder to see. The little plants green and trim as dancers in their rows. He had a beehive now, painted white, with the bees humming and crawling like golden pollen on its wooden step. I gave him "Grüss Gott" and was going on, because what I had seen above made me feel almost guilty toward him. Suddenly he called to me.

"Walther," he called. "Will you come into the cottage and sit down?" He leaned his spade against the fence, and I, wondering what on earth he wanted, although something in me guessed at part of it, hung my satchel on the gatepost and followed him in.

I had never delivered a letter to Bruno or his mother in all my years as postman and had never seen the inside of their house. It was very strange. Small and full of shadows, and yet also curiously light, as if the shadows themselves were luminous. There was a smell of herbs, and scrubbed wood, and everywhere there were the things that Bruno had whittled out of old pieces of timber. A table with field mice on its legs as if they were running up an ear of corn; a squirrel clinging to the branch it had been carved from; and, lying on the table, a wooden head. Even from the doorway I could see that it was meant to be Brunnhild's head.

"What do you want from me, Bruno?" I said rather roughly.

"Good advice," he answered me, smiling and looking out of the window, as if thinking of what he saw there rather than of me. "You have always been good to me," he said. "You will tell me what is best for me to do." Suddenly I felt ashamed and wanted to run down the hill and never see Bruno Holtzmann again. But I couldn't run. He had picked up the wooden head now and was looking down at it. It was not a big thing; quite small, and seeming smaller still, cradled in his hands.

"They say they want to go away together," he said softly. "And that if I say certain things the marriage we have had can be undone, as if it never was. But those things would not be true. What shall I do, Walther?"

I swallowed and tried to think. "Why did she marry you, Bruno? And why did you marry her?"

"She says now because she was mad. But then"—he smiled again, and I realized in that moment how much sadness there had always been in Bruno's smile—"but then—then she said differently. That it was because she saw something deep down inside me—the kind of thing I see in the woods and the sky. Depth on depth of things that you can't put into words, and only a little of it into carving." And he fondled the wood in his hands as if it were alive.

"And why did you marry her?"

"Because I, too, saw things in her." His voice trailed away in that disconcerting fashion he had that made people call him simple, and stayed silent for God knows how long, looking out of the window, his fingers folded over the small head. Suddenly there was the sound of running feet outside, and Brunnhild was there, her long fair hair broken loose from its braids and streaming like a golden cataract on the white shoulders of her thick wool jersey. Her face was flushed with running, and with something else—anger? shame?—I couldn't tell.

"Come," she said, "come," seizing Bruno by the arm, dragging him out of the cottage like a boy driving a bull. I followed, and we all went running up the path through the forest toward the cliff, Brunnhild running ahead and then back again to Bruno, tugging and worrying at him, and every now and then flinging a word of explanation over her shoulder.

"Konrad . . . he's on the ledge . . . the wind . . . afraid to move." The fury in her voice as she said "afraid" was like a whip hissing through the air, searching for bare flesh to strike. Down here the wind was merely ruffling our hair and cooling our foreheads, but once we were above the trees it beat against us like soft clubs.

When we reached the ledge, I saw that the wind had almost doubled its strength in the last hour. It shrieked down the naked rock gorge like a maniac, tearing flakes off the face of the cliff, tossing and thrashing at the heads of the forest far below, stopping the words in our throats and pulling us toward the nothingness of the gorge. I drew back, not even daring to look down.

"There," said Brunnhild, pointing.

I looked and saw Konrad, a hundred yards farther on, face flat to the cliff, arms spread, the wind now plastering him against the rock, now pulling him out from it. He was just beyond the narrowest part of the ledge, and beyond him the ledge narrowed once more to perhaps twelve inches wide. Apparently he was afraid, being city bred, either to go forward or come back. Glancing down for a second, I could hardly blame him. With the wind at that strength I wouldn't have tried the ledge myself.

Brunnhild had gripped her husband by the arm and was staring into his face. "Will you fetch him back for me?" she said—or rather, she screamed, because only a scream could be heard against that wind.

Very slowly Bruno nodded. He bent down to tighten his boot laces, and then his belt, so that nothing should catch against the rock and, without a word or even a look at either of us, began very slowly to walk along the ledge. Walk for a little way. Then turn with his back to the cliff and shuffle. Then inch his way fraction by fraction as the ledge grew narrower, not much wider than his boot sole was long, while the wind screamed and tore at his shoulders and blew the lamb's-wool fluff of his beard about his chin. At last he was close enough to Konrad to touch his shoulder.

Brunnhild and I had drawn back and down the path a little to where we could still see, but were a little out of the wind. "If I were Bruno I would kill him," said Brunnhild savagely. "How easy it would be."

As Konrad turned his head and saw who was touching him, you could tell that the same thought came to him. Even a hundred yards away you could tell it. The sudden shiver and start of a new terror. I thought he'd fling himself down. But Bruno was already holding him, trying to draw him back toward us. Konrad clung to the face of the rock like a child, screaming, out of his wits with terror.

"Oh, God; oh, God," said Brunnhild, and her fingers sank into my arms like steel hooks. I thought she was afraid for Konrad until I looked sideways at her face and saw the shame there, as if she were being whipped. To have had Konrad despise her husband had been bad enough; but to have her husband despise Konrad, and to know that he would have the right—it was like wormwood on her heart. If ever a proud woman brought shame on her own head through pride, it was Brunnhild. But in those minutes I had no time for thinking—only watching.

For half a minute, maybe, Bruno tried to persuade Konrad to come with him. Then, realizing that it was useless, he did a thing that gives me nightmares to this day whenever I think of it. He pulled Konrad bodily off his feet and swung him into his arms like a child—with twelve inches of stone to stand on, a sheer cliff at his back and eight hundred feet of emptiness below. The heart turned over in me to see it, and I wanted to shut my eyes. I couldn't. I think I stopped breathing. Then the deathly slowness of working his way back to us. One leg sideways—the other drawn up to it— the first leg sideways again. Foot by foot along the ledge, with Konrad in his arms held over the gorge, and the wind slamming against them like a giant door.

"Oh, Mother of God," whispered Brunnhild, and this time her voice was quite different. The shame was still there, but another kind of shame, until the worst part was over. But still Bruno carried Konrad, until he came up to us, where we were sheltering behind a low rock. He bent down and laid Konrad at Brunnhild's feet, and I saw that Konrad had fainted dead away, like a girl.

"There is your Konrad," Bruno said to her. "I will go back to the house now," and he walked away down the slope of the mountain toward the edge of the forest.

For a long, long moment Brunnhild stared after him with a most strange expression in her eyes. Then she turned her face to the rock and began to cry. I left her there and followed Bruno down. But I took care not to catch up with him.

That was the last I saw of Konrad. The next day he and his motorcar were gone, and none of us has seen him again. There were half a dozen wild stories about why he had gone, but except for Bruno and myself and Brunnhild, no one knew the truth of what had happened, and we kept silence, although sometimes when I'd hear the women gossiping and speculating in the post office it tore my heart not to tell them what I knew. But that day had given me a new feeling for Brunnhild and her strange, strange man, and I held my tongue, because I knew that they wanted me to. And the secret has made a bond between us.

Now, whenever my round takes me past their cottage I go in, and in these days Brunnhild is always there, tending the things a wife should, or doing some other thing for their son, who will one day be as tall and fair and big as his quiet father. And she has peace in her eyes. Her mother-in-law is not so afraid of her now, although still she treats her with great deference, and so does Bruno. So indeed do I. But then, she in turn treats Bruno as if he were a king. And sometimes, when she puts her hand on his arm and smiles at him, I think of what Father Bauer used to preach; that in his own house each man of us is a king, and that for every one of us there comes a day of royalty. He meant the marriage day, of course. Perhaps he is still right, even for Bruno Holtzmann and his wife.

I think that day on the ledge was their true marriage day. And curiously enough, when I looked again at the carving Bruno made of his wife's head, I saw that he had given her a crown, the same thin crown she had worn so sadly as a bride. But in the carved face

there is no sadness. Instead, there seems depth on depth of understanding in it; and, turning to Brunnhild's face from the carving,
I can see the same understanding there.

Was it always there? Waiting for Bruno to discover it? Or did
he put it there with the same quiet fingers that carve wood, and
grow flowers, as no one else in the valley can? Can a man have
that gift of magic in his hands? I don't know. But men have started
to come to Bruno for his carvings, and I saw one of them empty
his wallet onto the table trying to buy that head. Bruno only smiled
at him, and pushed the notes away.

MAVERICK BOY

by Prentiss Combs

Outside in the dusk the dog's deep-throated threats changed to wails of welcome. The boy had come home and all three of them sitting to supper knew it. Sara Macafee's plain face went soft with her joy. She chanced one flung glance at her brother, Graven Macafee, just bending his massive head for grace. He caught the glance and his face closed like a clenched fist.

Adam Threewitt, sitting at the hand's place at table end, smiled faintly and his smile deepened when from the woodpile there sounded one straight-down thud. It was not a slanted, chip-starting stroke. It was a blow. So Graven hadn't stomped out the last spark of gumption in his boy, after all, he thought. But the ax picked up the steady whick-whack rhythm of an axman making a cut, and Adam rubbed at the line calluses on his thumbs, withdrawing himself from what did not concern him.

Graven began his grace, his voice like all else about him, the deep ringing of hammered strength. Adam waited for Amen before he pushed back his chair and went to the door. Graven let him have the knob in his hand before he spoke, and then it was a boss talking to a hand.

"Leave him be, skinner," he said.

"If there's need for wood," Adam said carefully, "I'll cut it. He's likely down to the ragged edge after a week of it. He's only thirteen and a week to that age can be a year."

"I've no need for wood," Sara said quickly, and Graven would not even give his spinster sister a stature-granting glance.

"I've said what I mean," he said flatly. "Leave him be."

Adam came back to lean on the back of his chair. There was no challenge in any line of his easy body. A mild-faced, stringy length of man with puckers of wrinkles about his eyes, he was as contained as a trace chain in its leather boot.

"I don't know much about boys," he said slowly. "I know mules, though. A mule must be broken to be useful, but even a broken mule must be left something. Break him all the way and he's not worth his salt."

Graven reached for the potatoes and his eyes measured Adam. "What is it you leave a mule?" he asked.

Adam's big brown hands worked on the chair back, and there was a trace of wonder in his voice.

"Why, you leave a mule a piece of himself. A bit of his pride. When he's nearly played out, you coddle him. He feels mighty alone, then."

Graven spooned his potatoes. "Stick to your mules," he said. "I only got one boy and had him late, but I remember my own raising. A human can be beat down to the patches of nothing and scrape pride out of the dust. I know my boy. He's cutting wood to make a pile to hide his face behind. He'll come in and dump the wood noisy in the box. He'll take his hiding without crying out loud. That will be hook enough to hang his pride on. He did wrong and he needs to be punished. He ran away from the strap and he came back to the strap."

"Maybe it wasn't the strap he came back to," Adam answered, reluctant to involve himself, but driven to it by pity for Sara.

"Tend your mules," Graven said, but the ring was suddenly gone from his voice.

Adam sat down and began to eat, and Sara, looking at him sitting so withdrawn, suddenly hated the whole breed of mule men. Rootless and moody. Each feeding his life by dreaming some silly dream which he would never get. This one and his foolish gypsy cart was sillier than most. But, unwillingly, she thought of sitting, after dishes done, on the kitchen steps, with Adam telling the boy in his slow, easy voice how nice and cozy a well-made gypsy cart was, and her arm for once unnoticed across the boy's shoulders.

Halfway through the silent meal the boy pushed through the door, crossed the room and knelt at the woodbox. One chapped, blue-cold hand laid the topmost stick noiselessly in the box. The hand groped again and laid a second stick, silent as a mouse in wool.

"Stand up, boy." Graven's great voice stopped the hand in midair. "Stand up and drop that wood in the box hard as you can."

The boy's bent knee quivered under the taut cloth, but he did not rise until Sara's agonized voice pleaded in the silence.

"Ah, John Thomas, will you do as he says?"

He dropped the wood in the box, then; but he didn't look up. One sleeve came up and stayed across his mouth as he backed to the door. On the back porch he fumbled the leather strap from its hook and came back to kneel, joint by tired joint, beside Graven's thick knee. He held up the strap.

Graven knotted a big hand in the boy's jacket front and lifted him.

"You deserve a licking, don't you?"

"I'm waiting for it," John Thomas said dully.

"Then it's one you'll owe me," Graven said. "Fill his plate, Sara."

Sara flew to the range, but John Thomas flung himself out of Graven's grasp and stood, half crying.

"I'll not owe you anything. If I've got it coming, give it to me."

Graven held him and looked down at him and said in hurt wonder, "Now, son, you think I want to?"

"No, father," he said, "I don't think that." By the tone, by the hopeless twist of his body, it was a lie, and everyone knew it for a lie.

Graven's great neck swelled, hurt and furious, feeling the injustice of it; he had the boy and the strap across his back in one roaring rush.

"I will not have a liar about," he gritted, bringing down the strap.

Sara, standing stricken beside the range, made a small noise deep in her throat and it was that tiny sound that halted Adam as he backed toward the door. He pitched his voice to carry just over the sounds of the strap and the noises that leaked through the boy's clenched teeth.

"Don't you fret. Humans don't scrape their pride like Graven said. He keeps his pride close guarded in some secret place. That strap isn't touching that place. He'll be fine."

He went out the door, still seeing Sara's eyes on him in mute thanks, and the lie he'd told her troubled him a little. The boy was close to breaking.

He went out to the corral and leaned against the fence and saw that his mare mule Sheba had coaxed the colt away from its mother again and the tiny thing was nuzzling the useless dugs and jerking its head in protest against the absence of sweet flow. Sheba craned her neck to lick him. All happy and miserable at once, he knew, and as he stood watching he was shaken with how alike Sheba and Sara were. Sheba, forever tolling a colt from its rightful dam to ease the aching emptiness of her body; and Sara, an old maid with no prospects, letting Graven's boy come to be life and breath to her. Poor things, he thought. He straightened and sighed, feeling a great urge to move on, feeling himself soft iron between the hammer and anvil of the forces on the Macafee place. It was a troubling feeling.

There was a stumbling run in the yard and the hinges of the harness room squeaked. Adam told himself it was none of his business, that Graven could do with his boy as he liked, but in the end he couldn't make it stick. He gave John Thomas half an hour to sob dry his well of despair and then opened the door and stood outlined a few seconds so as not to startle the boy. He squatted beside the sack-and-husk mattress and rolled a cigarette by feel. When he struck the match he held it high to catch a glimpse of the white, tear-wet face before it turned wallward.

"What got into you to light a shuck the way you did?" he asked.

Adam waited and finally John Thomas spoke with a terrible weariness.

"I couldn't ever please him. Haying, plowing, choring; I just couldn't please him. I was slopping the hogs that night and the old boar got his head in the bucket and spilled the slop. I knew he'd find it out, someway. It just seemed like too much."

"Headed anyplace in particular?"

The boy didn't answer right away and when he did in his voice was the same quality of longing that was in Adam's when he talked of his cart.

"I always used to think about turning into a place about chore time and asking for work to pay for my supper. I'd hustle and the man would ask me to stay. I'd please him."

"And it wasn't so," Adam said, shaking his head.

"Nobody needed a hand."

"Now you always seemed like a hustler to me," Adam comforted.

"Adam Threewitt," the boy asked softly, "will you please sit down and tell me about the wagon? I got to thinking about listening to you telling about the gypsy cart and it seemed like I just had to hear it again."

"All right, John Thomas, I'll tell you about the cart. But that's not why you came back. Nobody needed a hand and you were cold and hungry, but you were alone. You ever see a stray dog out on the roads? He tucks his tail and hides in the brush. That dog is alone. He's looking for some place so as not to be alone. When he finds a home, likely he'll be kicked and starved; but, boy, he won't be alone. And someday, maybe that man that kicks him and starves him will reach down and pat his head."

"Are you going to tell about the cart?" the boy asked desperately.

"I will, but first, why do you sleep out here with the mice?"

"I like it here," John Thomas answered. "If I sleep in the house Sara is always coming in to tuck me in or kiss me good night."

"She's a good woman and she loves you."

"She can't be my mother. She tries, but she doesn't feel like her."

"You ought not to cheat her," Adam said, thinking of Sheba and the nuzzling colt.

"After my mother died," John Thomas said slowly, "one night I was out here and he came out and talked to me. Adam, he talked nice. He talked about my mother and about the place, and—about us. Him and me. He—sounded awful lonesome."

"That when you moved your bed out here?"

"About then," John Thomas answered stiffly.

"And he never came back again," Adam said.

"Oh, yes, he did," John Thomas said quickly. "One night he came to help a mare foal. Him and me, we worked all night. We saved her. Hadn't been for us he said she'd have died sure. Him and me, we did it together."

Adam thought of the boy standing beside his father and sharing in the agonizing and mysterious splendor that is birth. He began to talk about the gypsy cart. His words came deeply but easily, as a man repeats a rare poem for his own pleasure. The poem is so well known that the words have lost all fresh meaning and the deep pleasure of it is all in the run and rhythm of it and the enduring thought behind it. The tongue needs no thought to form the words and yet the words have taken on a rare clinging sweetness that is forever sweet.

"Shem and Sheba, I have. Prime young Spanish mules, and a spring wagon with springs so jouncy she rides soft as a goosedown tick. No nails in this cart I'll build on the frame. Every joint mortised and tenoned. She'll ride so light sprung that if a wind blows hard of a night—why, a man lying cozy in his bunk inside is rocked like in a baby's cradle. I'll have a stove there with a door that has glass windows, so a man can take comfort from the flames, and a swing-down table of goldy pine. I'll have a copper lamp swung by a chain from the roof. I'll eat by that lamp in the evening when the stock is cared for, and by that lamplight I'll read the Stockman's Journal. I'll listen to the stock outside stomping and snorting, sleepy-like, and I'll think, *Why, this is all mine*, and I'll say yea and nay to no man. My own man, free as an eagle."

The shucks rustled and John Thomas' voice was hollow with longing.

"Oh, Adam," he said, "will you favor me with a thing I want most? Will you tell it—oh, please—with two bunks and two chairs and two plates?"

Adam's breath went out with his shock. "I can't," he said. "It's my own cart and always has been. I can't let anybody else in."

"Oh, Adam, please, I want to lie in that bunk and watch you reading by the lamp and help tend the stock and say yea and nay to no man."

Adam lighted a match and held it high between them so the boy could see his hard face.

"I can't let you have any part of my dream, boy," he said roughly. "Don't ever ask about it again."

John Thomas stood on his knees and caught Adam's sleeve.

"Dream?" he asked, his voice high with disbelief. "Dream? Is this just one of the things you dream about? Like mine? Are you just pretending about the cart?"

Adam jerked loose and stood up. The shucks rattled again, a small hailstorm of protest as the boy turned his face to the wall. Adam went out into the dark and leaned a shoulder against the barn corner and made a mess of rolling a cigarette. He was so shaken that he didn't hear Sara until she stood beside him, a covered plate in her hands, a lighted lantern hanging from the crook of her elbow.

"I've brought him some supper. He's growing and shouldn't miss meals," she said, and Adam nodded vacantly. Sara didn't leave, but stood awkwardly arranging the cloth on the plate.

"Adam," she asked, "why must it be all struggle and strife here? Don't other people love each other? Other places you've been, don't they laugh?"

Adam was sick to find that he couldn't comfort the poor thing at all. All his life had been spent with mules and in bunkhouses with lone and moody drifters, each prisoner in the cage of his meager life.

"Sara, I just don't know. Haven't you ever loved anything?"

"I loved my father, I guess. But love was a show of weakness to him. When he died and Graven's wife passed away I came here to tend Graven and the boy. I was almost glad, because I thought it would be a chance to be a mother to the boy. He's all I ever had. Him and the baby things on the place."

"Take him his food," Adam said gently. "Fondle him."

But Sara didn't go. "It's funny. I love him beyond life's breath, but trying to fondle him is like touching a wild thing. He hunches under my hand and moves away. He—he's like he's not tame."

"Taming is nothing but trusting. It takes time. Take him his supper," Adam said, and she turned and went.

Adam stood alone and thought bleakly of Sheba and Sara, yearning and sick for love, and of himself and his suddenly empty life. He was cold in the grip of his new-found loneliness. He heard the harness-room door squeak and turned to see Sara hurrying toward him, the lantern making agitated arcs in the deepening dark. She stopped and looked up at him.

"You did something to him that Graven and his strap couldn't. What did you do?" she asked fiercely.

Adam shook his head numbly. "He just found out I'm never going to build the gypsy cart. He'll get over it, but maybe I won't. I didn't even know it myself. All these years I've been lying to myself and didn't know it. I'm never going to have that gypsy cart."

He looked down at her with the lantern glow reflecting small and lonely far back in the depths of his eyes. "Or the swing-down table or the lamp."

Sara put a hand on his arm. "Does it have to be so? I've watched you. I've seen dreams moving behind your eyes. Oh, Adam, dreams that I'm sure can be. You can dream heaven-high, and you're bound to nobody. You can do it. You can."

But Adam kept shaking his head. "Nor the stove with glass windows. He showed me I'd never have any of it."

"Oh, you fool!" Sara said harshly. "Steal the lumber if you must and shape it with your fingernails. Build a ramshackle, jerry-built cart that won't get a mile down the road. But build it and show John Thomas that a man doesn't have to die in the rut he's made for himself. A man can dream, and dreams can be."

"No," Adam said, swallowing. "I'm a mule man. I'll train mules until I die, knowing it was a job that took skill and something beyond skill. I'll hold to that."

The upward glow of the lantern made Sara's eyes look deep in her face and the downward flick of her mouth was all contempt.

"You poor thing. You are a mule man. You're worse than any of us. You're nothing."

Adam found himself pitied by someone who had even less than he, and it was that and the knowledge of having lost his dream that drove him to a rare anger.

"Where," he asked harshly, thrusting deep with the awl of his anger among her secret agonies, "are the babies you bore and the man you comforted and strengthened? What are you but an empty mare mule of a creature tending a mean man and dry-suckling a real female's colt? What are you?"

He was instantly horrified at how easily it was done. Her face sagged and one hand came up to her throat while her eyes looked at him with a vast reproach, dry with a dryness of hurt beyond tears.

"Nobody ever wanted me," she said with a strange and terrible dignity, and then began to cry like any woman in the world who was never wanted. She brought up both arms and clutched herself, and this gesture rebuked Adam like no words she could have said.

Adam moved forward to comfort her, all stricken, to humble himself and take back his words, but she turned and ran toward the black bulk of the house, bumping awkwardly into a wheelbarrow in her path and then into the closed gate.

Adam climbed wearily to his bunk in the haymow and looked up at the stars shining like ice splinters through the hay chute and felt small and empty. He turned on his side and shut his eyes, wanting sleep to come, filled with fear of the vague and formless yearning that shaped itself inside him, but it was no use, the dim longing took form. He saw Adam Threewitt all snug in his gypsy cart of an evening reading the Stockman's Journal by the light of the copper lamp over the goldy-pine table. Then another chair was sketched in on the other side of the table, and Adam moved the Journal to make room for books on ciphering, spelling and reading. John Thomas was in the chair, raising his bright head and smiling straight at Adam. Adam's whole being clutched with his longing for a son.

Adam threw back his blankets and stumbled down to the harness room. John Thomas rolled away from him, awake all in one startled piece, one arm upflung. Adam lighted a match.

"John Thomas Macafee," Adam said formally, "I'm going to need help to build that gypsy cart. I want her to be as cozy as I always said, and I'm going to have to plan her to the last splinter to make the two of us fit."

He flicked out the match, but not before he saw the smile on John Thomas' face and knew he was committed beyond back-out.

It wasn't until Graven rousted him at dawn and he sat shivering on the bunk side that he called himself a fool and felt the dry-mouthed fear that fills every man when his feet leave a well-known road and turn onto a strange one.

Going out to chore, Adam saw the colt nuzzling Sheba again, and he watched for a long minute, wondering at Sheba's strange content. When he went in to breakfast, Sara didn't turn from her place at the range and he sat down silently. He heard Graven washing noisily on the back porch.

"You were right," he said to her thin back. "I've got to build the cart now." Sara didn't turn. "I've asked the boy to go with me. I want him."

She turned and he saw the shine of tears in her eyes. "I hoped," she said simply.

"Graven will likely have me up for child stealing," Adam said sourly.

"Never!" Sara said. "His pride wouldn't let him. That boy was a week out on the roads, dead for all Graven knew. He didn't call a soul."

"You'll miss him."

"Like my breath. But he'll have a chance to live. I'll be content."

Adam went through his day, turning over the whole thing and coming to see gradually with what wisdom Sara had spoken. A wisdom springing from the deep well of her loneliness and rejection. He thought of John Thomas beside him, looking up to him, measuring himself beside him, and he was scared, seeing himself taking up the task of making a boy into a man. It was scary, but if he did it—why, he could make the dust and shadow of his life into something that flowered and grew.

Next morning he was hitching the mules to a stone sled when Sara came out to him, holding her skirts up from the muck.

"The Evanses are tearing down their old milk house," she said. "You could get lumber there, seasoned and all, for the asking."

"I might just go over there tomorrow or next day," Adam answered, fishing for a bellyband.

"I thought you'd best go today," Sara said.

"I'll build my cart in my own way and in my own time," Adam answered. "Anyway, I've got no tools."

"I'll ask Graven for the loan of the tools," Sara said mildly.

"If I want the loan of tools I'll ask, myself," Adam said harshly. Sara looked down at her hands without speaking.

"I'm going to build it!" Adam said savagely. "But I'll not be pushed."

That night when he swung the team around the barn he found a mess of scantlings and siding up against the barn side.

"Sara and I fetched them from the Evanses'," John Thomas told him. "She said father said to bring back the tools as sharp as you took them. We can start on that old cart just any time."

So Adam began to build his cart with the reluctance of fear, driven only by Sara's gentle prodding and the strength of his word given. At first he threw out this beam and that board for imperfections, delaying the building by whatever means. But, even with his slowness, the thing began to take shape under his hands and he began to discard pieces because he would have no thing in his cart that was not perfect. The fever had come on him that comes when a man hews slabs of raw wood and fits them to make a shelter, and there is no pride in all man's doing that can equal the lifting pride that rises as the shelter rises.

Sara came sometimes in the evenings, bringing cake and coffee. She sat in the lanternlight looking at them with a strange mixture of sorrow and pride. Adam, seeing her with her head leaned against a post, was moved to pity for her, thinking of how he was robbing her of someone to love.

The cart took shape as winter waned. One morning there was no ice in the horse trough and Graven began to fret over harness. He put tar on hoofs and found a million things to do, and it seemed as if he could do none of them without calling John Thomas to help him. If he did not praise him, Adam noticed, he did not find fault either.

Graven was a man who forced the land to yield, not working with the great cycles of weather and earth. He had to force the weather and crowd the land to produce by his own stubborn strength. Each spring while the fields lay sodden masses of mud Graven would stand by the barn and stare bleakly at the resting land and on the

first day that the weak sun made steam rise from the mud, Graven
would hitch a team to the greased plow and bog both mules and
plow in the first twenty feet. It was his gesture against the earth
and his neighbors, content to wait for true spring. On that day
Graven would wrestle out the plow with his ox strength and whip
the mules until their hearts went, and they would not strain in
their collars, but would only stand quivering, heads down. Only
then would Graven come home, saying that he would have been
there yet, but the mules had quit.

One raw morning Adam and John Thomas were shoveling out
the barn and John Thomas leaned on his fork and spoke.

"What do we do out there on the roads, Adam? Besides tending
stock, what work will we do?"

"As little as ever a man can do and feed himself, boy," Adam
answered lightly. "There's more to life than working."

John Thomas turned to the barn lot where Graven had brought
in sand fill and watched his great body working with a heavy
rhythm, lifting shovels of sand and spreading it.

"It's funny," he said, puzzled, "it just don't seem right. Not to
work, not to make crops grow. Oh, but it'll be good not to get up
in the cold. I'll get used to it."

He bent over his fork, loading the fork and throwing it with
Graven's very rhythm.

As the cart came closer and closer to completion, Sara came more
frequently after dishes-done to sit and watch hungrily as John
Thomas and Adam sanded and smoothed and fitted, their heads
close together, shutting her out. Her eyes went often to the boy,
who paid her not the least half mind, as if she weren't there.

"Ways," she said dreamily, one night, "I hate to see spring come.
You two out on the roads, free, and us here the same as always,
just the two of us, working and working. You don't forget us now,
John Thomas."

"No, ma'am," John Thomas answered looking directly at her, "I
won't."

"That mare mule of yours," Sara said to Adam. "I don't know

when I've seen a neuter beast so taken with a colt. Usually they hate colts."

"I pry them loose every chance I get," Adam answered absently.

"Ah, you shouldn't. You shouldn't deprive her," Sara said softly. Adam rose and looked levelly at her.

"She should face up to it," he said deliberately. "She's barren. She's never going to have a colt and should face up to it."

Sara looked up at him and her arms came up again in that gesture of rebuke and then adjusted her shawl. She got up stiffly and went to the house. Adam looked after her and wondered why he had to be forever hurting the poor thing.

The rains turned to drizzles and the drizzles stopped. The sodden ground lay waiting for the sun to dry it for plowing. Graven went into a frenzy of preparation with harness and gear, and called John Thomas to help him again and again. If he was working in the harness room of an evening John Thomas would put down the work he was doing for Adam on the cart, and go to hold straps steady for Graven to put the brass rivets in. Graven would take his help without thanks, grunting instructions shortly.

One morning the pale sun came out and shone on the wet fields, and feathers of steam came up from the land. The next day the sun was stronger and Graven could stand it no longer. He hitched four big mules to the greased and shining plow, his big muscles jerking plow and mules, impatient to take up his fight with the land and force it to yield another year to his strength and stubbornness.

"You come along," he said to John Thomas. "I'll have all I can handle with the plow. You think you can handle the mules?"

"I'll handle them." Adam spoke up quickly, but John Thomas stepped forward, his face pale.

"I'm going to try," he said.

Once in the field the mules strained and slipped and Graven heaved, using his great strength, yanking the plow clear and sinking it. Foot by foot the team moved forward and Adam saw, as he stood in the pasture, that the muck was so wet there was no furrow after the plow, that the wet mud flowed in and covered every trace of their passing.

"Now, why does he do it?" he asked Sara, who had just come up.

"He's a fighter. He's lonesome and a fighter," she said.

Adam went back to the barn, shaking his head. In midmorning John Thomas came to the barn, driving the tired mules. He was covered with mud and trembling with exhaustion.

"Harness up another span," he said.

"You're going back?" Adam asked in amazement.

"The mules quit," John Thomas said shortly. "Not us."

At noon they had made a full circle, up and back, and came in. Adam looked out at the field and saw it as level as if they had never made the struggle. They were mud to their eyebrows and Graven's bull shoulders were slumped, but there was a pleased look on his heavy face. He put one great muddy hook of a hand on John Thomas' head.

"Going to have me a skinner here," he said. John Thomas silently started stripping harness from the steaming mules. He had to stand on tiptoe to reach the hame cleft, but he managed it.

"Hold still there," he said roughly to the mule, although the mule was too tired to stir.

Two nights later Adam sat in the gypsy cart and looked around and called it done. He sat at the goldy-pine table under the lighted copper lamp, and John Thomas came on him that way.

"Sit over there," Adam said, motioning to the opposite chair. "Set a day when we light a shuck. Set a day when we start saying yea and nay to no man."

John Thomas looked around, taking in all the details and saw his hand's work, in all of it, and his heart's longing.

"It's just like you always said, Adam," he said. "Cozy as a cradle. But I reckon I'll stay."

Adam fumbled at his tobacco sack and tried to make a cigarette, needing something to steady his mind. He tried to think of something to say and was dumb.

"He needs me," John Thomas went on, very carefully. "It wouldn't be fair to leave, just when plowing's to be done. Besides, he told me I'm the only one can make those fool mules behave. He liked the way I handled that team."

Adam nodded vacantly and John Thomas got up and left quietly. Adam looked around at the cozy inside of his gypsy cart and it was a coffin. He stood up stiffly and blew out the lamp and stood looking at the glimmering glow of the wick in the dark.

Outside in the corral he saw the colt again nuzzling Sheba, and in a sudden anger he slapped the silly colt back to its mother. He went up to his bunk and lay on his blankets, looking up at the lone emptiness of the sky through the hay chute. Without any effort at all he slipped into the dream, but he saw himself sitting old and empty on the seat of his cart and the road was long and desolate ahead of him.

He thought of the dying of the wick in the lamp. After a long time he rose and went down the ladder and drew out a gallon from the coal-oil barrel.

He walked softly around the corner of the barn toward the gypsy cart and stopped dead. A light shone through the window and it was so warm and beautiful he felt his heart go empty with longing. He crept forward, his breath caught.

Sara had dredged up a rocker from somewhere and it had a silly flounce around the bottom. She was holding her arms as if they carried something, her head bent down in the ancient position of woman and child and she rocked slowly.

All the blood in Adam's body sucked back into the void of his heart. He saw in that instant that God made a mule a poor, tormented and empty creature and it was a terrible punishment. But a man—why, a man had a choice.

When Adam opened the door she looked up in panic, and then lowered her head.

"I just had to sit in it once," she said in a voice so low and shaken he could hardly hear.

He put a fumbling hand down and cupped her chin and forced her to look up at him.

"I know, now, I was building for it to be so," he said humbly.

Sara began to cry. She was plain with the touching plainness that is of all women crying, but Adam saw her beautiful. He had made a woman weep with joy, and to a lone man that was mightier than life itself. It could perhaps be equaled only by the first heard cry of a man's own son.

O MY LOVELY CAROLINE

by Hobert Skidmore

Claude Hanson stood on the upper deck of the showboat Starlight and watched the hillmen hang lanterns from the trees on the river's bank. As each lantern was lighted, more and more hill people appeared suddenly, like apparitions, out of the darkness. To Claude they were eager mourners come to watch him perish.

Though still erect, still large and handsome at sixty, Claude lowered his head. But he understood that prayers could not change the inevitable. Never before in his life had he broken a promise to his beloved Caroline, but now he knew he was going to be forced to forsake her.

His arms hung loosely at his sides, the fiddle in his left hand and the bow in his right. As each lantern was lighted, throwing a sterner glow on the wooden lacework of the showboat's decks, each one seemed to highlight a different moment of his life with Caroline. He saw again the astonishing way they had met, the immediacy of their love, the patient weeks and months during which she had taught him to read music and to learn the lines in the plays, the joyous years on the river, the night he had saved the Starlight from sinking, and Caroline's pride in him. He could hardly believe they had had twenty-five years together—forty, really, for though she had been gone fifteen years, he had never once felt she had left him.

The last picture appeared clearly before his eyes, stronger than memory, sharper and more immediate.

The Starlight, tied up at Charleroi on the Monongahela, squatted grandly in the moonlight and though the spring night was balmy, their little room behind the stage held a fearful coldness.

"I've always loved you, Carrie," Claude said, holding his wife close to him, smiling a reassurance he did not feel, for the doctor had said she would never survive the diphtheria.

Lifting her hands, she placed them on his cheeks. Though she was forty, she seemed almost a child, an eager child forever impetuous and hopeful, as though the days and years were too brief. Her eyes passed around the tiny room, seeing each memento, every small and personal reminder of their years together: tintypes, bits of costume tinsel, sheet music hung about the mirror, souvenirs from hundreds of towns along the rivers. "You love the river, don't you, Claude?"

"Yes, Carrie, honey, just like I love you."

"How many rivers there are. The Wabash and Tennessee, Kentucky, Green, Ohio, Kanawha and Arkansas. And the Mississippi. Floating down them, playing the shows—oh, it's a special kind of life. The years have passed like magic. It's gone so quickly I don't even feel like I am a woman yet."

"You are my girl."

As though she did not hear him, Caroline continued, "It's a private world. The shores separate us from other people. And inside there's another world. A world we create on the stage. It is magic. It is!"

"Of course, Carrie."

Suddenly, frenzied, she grabbed him, her eyes looking at him

with desperate beseeching. "Don't ever leave the river, Claudie.
Promise me. Whatever happens, I'll always be on the river. Don't
leave me, Claudie—don't leave me alone on the river."

"Never, my darling. Never."

And then, as simply as footlights go out, she was gone from him.

From beneath the flickering lanterns on the bank someone
shouted, "Bring your fiddler! Old John's here! Your fiddler scared,
or something?"

Only now did Claude become aware of the shouting and taunting around him. The entire company and crew of the Starlight were
lined along the deck in front of the hand-painted pictures of wild
animals, acrobats and characters from the plays of Shakespeare,
shouting at the hill people. On the shore, the women were silent,
but the men, fortified with whisky, yelled defiantly, "Old John can
outfiddle any man can lift a bow!"

Claude started slowly down the deck toward the gangplank.
When he passed the new captain, the younger man did not speak,
but only nodded, saying silently, *You had better win, Claude
Hanson.*

For years he had outfiddled anyone who challenged him—anyone from Minnesota to the bayous of the Atchafalaya. Caroline
had taught him theatrical runs and trills, double-stops and quick
changes of tempo, and even when he knew he was being bested,
he had always been able to overwhelm his opponent and the audience by a fiery display of style. But it was not going to work tonight. Glancing ashore, he saw the aged, stooped man known as
Old John of Ravens' Glen, and known, too, as the best fiddler who
ever lived. Claude's heart sank. He could not remember how many
fiddlers along the rivers had said to him, "The best of 'em all, the
fairest fiddler of all is Old John of Ravens' Glen."

At the gangplank, Emil Hausner, the temperamental cook and
female impersonator, reached out and touched his arm. "You'll win,
Claude. You'll win. I just know it."

Claude tried to smile thankfully, but he knew the captain would
fire him if he lost the contest. And there would not be another job

on the river, not for a man passing sixty, a fair fiddler, but a poor player of villains. No, there wouldn't be another job. *I'll have to leave the river and desert my Caroline,* he told himself as he walked down the gangplank, his shoulders thrown back and the fiddle swinging at his side as though it were an extension of his arm, a part of his body.

The hill people moved back as Claude strode slowly up the bank. Someone had brought two empty nail kegs, and Old John sat on one of them, his left arm bent and the base of his fiddle resting in the crotch of his elbow. He looked up and nodded, saying, "Howdy."

Claude spoke, bowing slightly, but as he took his place on the other keg he studied the aged man's face in the flickering light. Old John was small, wizened, and his cheeks were sunken inward between his toothless gums. His face was expressionless, except for his astonishingly hazel eyes, which sparkled with mischievous anticipation.

Glancing around, Claude saw the women were standing far back in the darkness, but the men were edging closer, speaking directly to Old John, but speaking words which Claude knew were aimed at his ears, "Play him right down the river, Old John. Play all the different kinds of tunes you know to mind."

Claude looked at the hillmen. They were angry and resentful. Not merely because he was going to play against Old John. No, it was something else, something he had seen happen hundreds of times. Not more than an hour before, the hill people had sat in the theater, entranced with the play, removed from their own world into a life so rich and vivid with emotion that they resented the sudden ending of the play which plunged them back into their toil-filled lives. It wasn't simply that he was the villain in The Red Dagger and during the performance the men in the audience, carried away by the play, had loudly threatened to kill him if he kidnaped the heroine. They had felt every emotion the actors portrayed and they were indignant that the performance had transported them into a dazzling world, and then, abruptly, abandoned them,

making them appear foolish. Now they were determined that Old
John should put him to shame and defeat.

"You play Rippytoe Ray!" a gaunt hillman shouted. He had his
hands folded beneath the bib of his overalls, and when he spoke,
it was like a command. "You hear me, Old John! Play Rippytoe
Ray!"

Old John did not look up. "I got to discord my fiddle to play
that," he said, as though there was no tune or style of playing which
he did not know. He quickly tuned his fiddle so the bow could
be drawn across two strings at a time and a rush of notes flew upward from the open strings.

Claude sat quietly.

The gaunt hillman began to shout out the words as the bow
sawed out the three-eighths time:

> "And *a damn good fiddler was he!*
> *But all the tune he could play*
> *Was Rippytoe Ray, oh, Rippytoe Ray!*
> *Oh, Rippytoe Ray, oh, ree-e-e!*"

Closing his eyes, Claude thought of all the contests in which he
had played. In the early days, his beloved had always stood beside
him, smiling confidence and pride, and ever since her death he
had sensed her presence. But tonight there was something angry
and violent in the air, and it seemed, as Old John's bow sped across
the strings, that he was alone for the first time since he had met
Caroline. He wondered, as he sat with his head lowered and his
eyes closed, if, with the passing of the years, his mind had become
strange. He wondered if it was only his imagination which had
made him feel she was near him. It was a thing that could happen
when a man was heartsick with loneliness.

Old John's foot was going now, beating out the rhythm on the
ground. It reminded Claude of Caroline's dancing, the quick, light
tapping of her feet in the Highland fling. Even up to her death
she had been billed as The Singing and Dancing Wonder. He im-

agined her whirling before him, wearing her short, full skirt, the bespangled bodice dazzling in the light. For a moment she seemed almost near him, smiling as she spun, and he lost himself in the reverie, remembering that always at the end of the number, when the curtain rolled down to the floor, she hurried to him, kissing him happily and crying, "Oh, Claudie, Claudie, I love to dance to your music!"

"Well, mister, you aimin' to play?"

"Maybe he's done give up already."

Claude roused himself. He had hardly been aware that Old John had finished his tune.

Awkwardly, fumbling, he tuned his violin, wondering what discorded tune he could play. The only one which came to his mind was Lost Indian. Testing the bow on the strings, he recalled the day Caroline first began teaching him the tune. It was a haunting song, filled with eerie sounds, but it was a song of river people. It was the story of a showboat tied up at a landing because the swollen river was filled with logs and driftwood. To while away the time, the company danced to a fiddler's tunes, but in the middle of the dance they heard weird shouts and looked out on the raging water to see an Indian on a large log. As they watched, the current caught the log, whirled it violently, and with a wild wail the Indian disappeared in the angry water. The fiddler became almost demented by the frightful scene, and forever after, it was said, he could play only the tune he was playing when the Indian drowned.

Caroline had asked him to play it often, for she felt there was joy and sorrow, life and death, in the haunting tune, and something of the awful cruelty which can come even to the innocent.

Catching his bow near the center because the tune was very fast and fine, Claude began to play, but each time he tried to imitate the wails and shrieks of the Indian, his bow only grated against the strings. Over and over he played the chorus, but it had neither life nor style and it revealed nothing of what he wanted to say, nothing of the awareness that life must end, violently or peacefully, but it must end.

Finally he dropped the fiddle from his shoulder and waited.

Old John began at once. He played Sally Goodin, and the hill-men shouted out the verse:

> "A *sheep and a cow*
> *Awalkin' in the pasture.*
> *The sheep said, 'Cow,*
> *Can't you walk a little faster?'* "

Claude knew that Old John and the men were taunting him because he had not played fast enough. He looked at the aged fiddler, but Old John appeared lost in his music, unaware of anything about him. Briefly he glanced at Claude, and his startlingly colored eyes were indifferent, almost defiant and scoffing.

The words of the song ran through Claude's mind: *I had a piece of pie, and I had a piece of puddin', and I gave it all away for to see my Sally Goodin.*

What had there been in life, what would there ever be, he wondered, that he wouldn't give to see his Caroline? From the day they had met, he had wanted to possess nothing except that which would give her pleasure and happiness. Now there was no reason to possess anything, except the pride and joy she had given him.

He had been twenty when they met, tall and raw and unlearned. He had come down from the hills and stood along the banks of the Arkansas River, entranced with the beauty of the boat, waiting for the show, for it was rumored that the show was for men only. He had never seen such a show and he was young, almost trembling with eagerness. But when the manager saw that the audience was made up solely of men, he told them they had the wrong idea and that all the women on the boat were ladies. "Go to the box office and get your money back," he had said from the stage.

The last to leave, Claude looked once more at the ornate tier of box seats. The acetylene-gas footlights were still glowing and the white, pale green and rust colors of the auditorium were like white clouds reflected in the water, the green of shoals and the burnished sunset on the river. As he stood, entranced and awed with the beauty, the curtain was rolled up and the prettiest girl he had ever seen walked onto the stage. Her beautiful red dress hardly reached to her knees and some pretty in her blond hair gleamed and glistened until a man could hardly believe it. Seeing him, she stopped suddenly, and then, as though she had no shame, she came down from the stage and walked up the aisle to him.

Claude was so frightened he wanted to run.

"I'm sorry there isn't going to be a show," she said in a soft, sweet voice.

"I am, too, ma'am. Sorrier than I can speak."

"You live here?"

"No, 'm. I live back in the hills. A ridge farmer is my life, but I'm alone and it ain't what you'd rightly call a real life. I thought seein' a showboat show"—he paused, blushing at what he had thought to see—"I'd have somethin' to call to mind durin' the wintertime."

Looking him directly in the eyes, she laid her hand on his arm. Claude felt that he was going over backward. The touch of her hand sent his heart to pounding so loudly he was afraid she would hear it.

"I like to ask people their names. Names interest me. What's yours?"

"Claude. Claude Hanson," he managed.

"And you're a handsome man, Claude. Now I'll never forget it. Claude Hanson."

His breath stopped. There was nothing wicked or forward in the way she talked. It was a thing she felt, and she said it honestly. And it was a thing a man could hardly bear to hear from a beautiful girl. Blushing, almost terrified, Claude turned and stumbled outside.

"Maybe next year!" she called after him. "Maybe next year, Claude Hanson!"

Next year! How could a man live so long? Reaching the bank, he leaned against a tree, hidden in the dark, and stood there for hours and hours, unable to believe what had happened to him. Inside the boat, he knew, there was such beauty and ease and joy that no other world seemed real to him. Any other life was only a burden, a thing to be endured.

Near midnight he heard the voices. Hillmen with their wives and sweethearts walked along the road and down to the gangplank, shouting happily that they had their women now and they wanted to see the show.

When the performance was over, Claude sat silently, unable to applaud or smile or shout. All his life, even before his parents died, he had been starved for beauty, and now he had found it. But it was in another world, a world which floated effortlessly through time, and he did not think he could bear to leave it.

At the top of the gangplank the beautiful girl was selling pictures of herself. He could not read well, but he saw her name, Caroline, written across the bottom of the pictures. "Car-o-line," he pronounced slowly. "It couldn't 'a' been any other name in the whole world."

And then they looked into each other's eyes. Though he was shy, even backward, he did not take his eyes from hers, for she seemed to command him. Suddenly she grabbed his broad hands and pressed them to her cheeks.

"Where do you go tomorrow?" he asked. "Where could I see the show again?"

"Moss Landing."

"I'll be there. I couldn't stand it not to see you again."

"I know, Claude. I know. I never danced as I did tonight."

Before he realized it, he was saying, "You got a work-job, here, for a man?"

"There'll be something!" she cried. "We'll find something!"

And then she embraced him.

Suddenly an older man spoke, "Caroline. Caroline, you'd better go inside."

"Yes, father," she said softly, almost like an obedient child, but she turned, and pulling Claude's head down, she gave him the first kiss he had ever had from anyone. "I'll be waiting for you."

Near dawn Claude reached his ridge farm. He gave his cow and his horse and chickens to a neighbor to keep, and started the forty-mile walk across the mountains to Moss Landing, carrying only his cash money—twenty-two dollars—and the suit he had bought when his mother had been buried at the clapboard church in Thunder Hollow.

He had never returned, but, looking at the hillmen about him, he thought it strange that they did not realize that he had been born one of them. It gave him a feeling of being stranded, of being neither a hillman nor a riverman, with no way ahead and no way back.

Old John had changed tunes and tempos and was playing Mississippi Sawyer. It was an old tune, a favorite with fiddlers everywhere. But as he listened, caught in the memory of his empty youth, Claude knew he had never heard the song played so beautifully. Through Old John's tricky bowing there could be heard the faint sound of anvils, the clinking of horseshoes and the sawing sound, drawn and easy, of sickles and scythes being whetted. It was a square-dance tune and the people began to clap hands to its rhythm.

Claude sat silently trying to recall the dreamless days of his boyhood, but his youth seemed so empty that he could hardly remember living before he met Caroline.

Living on the solitary ridge, he had grown to manhood knowing only loneliness and work, but from the moment he walked aboard the Starlight at Moss Landing, there had never been another moment of loneliness. His first job had been general handy man and bouncer, hustling ashore the drunken, pistol-waving coal miners and migrants who drifted along the rivers in shanty boats. Even at the beginning, Caroline, impetuous and determined, began to train him to become a member of the company. When she learned he had taught himself some simple fiddle tunes during the long winter evenings on the ridge, she began teaching him to read music, to play from the notes. She helped him to memorize lines from the plays and to speak them as if he were some other individual than himself. For weeks on end, drifting down the rivers or being towed up them, they sat alone on the upper deck. Though he had been slow to learn, he recalled, she had never lost patience with him.

"Don't try to hurry so," she always said, but every day she led him onto the deck and sat with him while he practiced, urging him on. And she constantly corrected his speech, showing him how to enunciate clearly, erasing from his vocabulary the words and phrases which marked him as a hillman.

"Why are you so patient with me, Caroline?" he asked.

She looked off toward the bank of the river, toward the hills, but not seeing them. He knew she was looking into the future, and it made her strangely thoughtful.

"Because I am proud of you." She turned to him, smiling intimately. "Because I love you."

"Why? I can't fathom why you do."

"I'll tell you, Claude. I'll tell you as truly as I can. I just can't help it. I guess I was made to love you."

"I couldn't ever love anybody else," he told her. "I'd be ashamed was I ever to try."

Now, sitting silently as Old John played, he knew that life on the showboat, on the river, had changed them both. Or had it been the river and the boat? Hadn't it been love, a love so total and complete that no other life existed? Had this not been the quality which made the audience adore them, and which was now missing when he stepped alone onto the stage? He remembered with happiness the first night he had been allowed to play for Caroline while she danced. It had been far down in Louisiana, far from home, but as he played both a waltz and a Highland fling, never missing a note, he felt he had found the home which life had never given him before.

He recalled, tormented by the heartbreaking reverie, the entry in the boat's log the captain had made the next day: "Stopped at Le Grand to get Caroline and Claude married. Warm rain tonight." And now it was coming to an end. He knew he could never outfiddle the aged man next to him, and since his only value to the company was playing the fiddle contests to attract people to the boat, there was no doubt the captain would discharge him. He wondered what he could do and where he could go. What was there for a man of sixty, no longer able to make a living in the hills and rejected by the life he had always held dear?

Lifting the fiddle to his chin, he wondered at the peculiar treachery of life. The one thing which had given him joy and happiness, which had caused the years to rush by like autumn leaves on the river, had left him helpless to face the desolate loneliness of the longest years.

He looked out across his fiddle at the showboat company lined along the rail of the upper deck. They were silent and distant, quiet. Already they appeared to be drifting away.

The hurt was deep in him, and yet it was not a personal hurt. That kind of hurt had long since passed from him, assuaged by his memories. The pain he felt now was a sorrow, a grief, a sense of bewilderment and loss and estrangement, as if he had lived beyond his time and was left to wander alone.

Turning slightly, he peered at Old John, trying to tell him that he knew he was beaten and that from here in he would play only the tunes which filled his heart, evoking for the last time the happiness he had known. Old John returned his gaze, and even in the pale light the aged man's oddly colored eyes seemed to change, to turn a deeper color, as though he looked inward on some ancient knowledge. Resting his arms on his crossed legs, John nodded slightly.

There was a waltz Caroline had loved: I'll Be All Smiles Tonight. While Claude played the song, unmindful of anyone about him, the words came to him in Caroline's sweet, clear voice.

> *I'll deck my brow with roses,*
> *The loved one will be there.*

It had not been only for a night that she had been all smiles, he knew. Throughout the years he had shared with her she had been gay and happy, creating an aura of joy, a sense that love could never end.

> *And even them that know me*
> *Will think my heart is light,*
> *Though my heart may break tomorrow,*
> *I'll be all smiles tonight.*

For the first time Claude wondered if Caroline knew she would die young. Perhaps she had known she must leave him and had tried to tell him that he must not mourn. But loneliness and heartbreak are different from mourning, he told himself.

Without Claude being aware of it, Old John had begun to play. Claude could not be sure whether he had just let the bow become idle on the strings or whether Old John, in a wild flourish of sound, was banishing him, subjecting him to shameful defeat.

The fiddler from Ravens' Glen was playing Bonaparte's Retreat, producing an overwhelming barrage of sounds, drumming the strings with the back of his bow, plucking them, simulating musket fire and the din of battle, and then suddenly shifting to a long and continuous use of the bow until the sound of bagpipes and fifes could be heard. Even the hillmen were suddenly silenced and a woman, taking a steel comb from her hair, stepped beside Old John and struck the strings along the fingerboard, producing a sound of drumming.

Claude could not believe any man could re-create so much of life with a fiddle and he knew there was no use to compete. Yet he could not get up and walk away like a whipped dog. There was something he had to say—say to himself and the night—he had to speak his farewell to the river.

When Old John had finished, Claude began to play, and he could not stop. One tune after another rushed through his mind like leaves whirling brightly in an eddy. He wanted to play every tune he had ever known, every song he had shared with Caroline. He wanted to play them all and regain for a brief while the life they had known together. He no longer played to be heard, but with deep longing, with yearning and with a shattering anguish, for he wondered if it would have been more fortunate if he had never loved. In his youth he had been able to bear aloneness, but now, aged and lost, he was lonely for someone, for his love, and he found that the loneliness was terrifying.

Without pausing, he began Sandy River. He did not know whether he was playing well or not, for he believed Caroline was near him and he played only for her.

Sandy River always reminded her of the time he had saved the Starlight. It had been November, almost a quarter of a century ago. They were floating down below St. Louis when suddenly the Starlight rocked and shuddered. Screaming, the actors fled to the decks, ready to abandon the boat. Claude, grabbing a lamp, ran below. The boat had struck a piling and ripped a hole in her bottom as big as his body. He stood staring at the water rushing in through the rupture. Most of the crew were asleep and his shouting would not be heard above the swift swishing of the river. The hole had to be plugged quickly, he knew, and there was only one way a single man could do it.

Bounding up the stairs, he grabbed a thick blanket from the bed he shared with Caroline and ran back below. He knew the water was freezing, but he quickly wrapped the blanket around his body and lowered himself into the hole, pushing and shoving his weight against the inrushing water until he was waist deep. His own thick body, wrapped in the blanket, plugged the hole. His outspread arms supported him upright, but his freezing body caused him to shake and he feared he would be unable to hold on.

Finally the captain appeared. Bellowing profanely, shouting for the crew as the Starlight drifted on in the dark water, he ordered them to build a box.

"Get some boards!" he shouted. "Build a box around him! Build a box to hold that hellish water out or we'll sink before morning!"

Claude had hardly been aware when Caroline came to his side. His teeth were chattering and his eyes were clenched against the icy cold.

"Here, darling. Sip this, Claudie," she urged, holding to his lips a cup of hot coffee laced with whisky. "Oh, Claudie, you're the greatest trouper on the river."

It took almost an hour for the men to build the box around the hole, and in that time she never took her free arm from around his shoulders. And never once did she weep or speak a word of idle sympathy. Instead she smiled to him, teased him for his love, laughing as though it were a lark, but there passed from her to him such a feeling of pride and love that it carried him through the following week when he lay shivering and feverish.

Days later, the captain had come to him, telling him he would always have a place on the Starlight. But as he finished Sandy River and, without pausing, started the lively Go to the Devil and Shake Yourself, Claude reminded himself that that captain was long dead. A new captain owned the boat now, and he had no regard for old promises.

All those years—the whole of his life really—seemed suddenly unreal and improbable. And yet he knew they had happened. He ached to recapture them, to live those times once more before the night was over, before the hopeless wandering began.

But he was lost and confused. He could find no talisman to lead his thoughts backward. His bow hand dropped to his side and he stared about, helpless and lost. Old John was peering at him, quietly, barely smiling. He nodded his head very slowly, almost reverently, and Claude knew the fiddler was saying, "Go ahead; I will follow."

Lifting his fiddle to his chin, Claude felt a surging strength in his arms. Through The Devil in the Canebrake and Sugar Betty Ann, Old John followed, filling in the background, giving strength and fullness to the remembered music.

Claude knew he was playing better than he ever had before. He felt as though a gentle hand guided his bowing arm and it no longer mattered about the hills and the people. It was something coming through the music, not his or John's, but the music they played together, a kind of conformation John was giving him. Once when he hesitated, wondering what tune to play, Old John took the lead, playing Darling Cory—playing it slowly, the way it sounded best. To Claude's amazement, Old John sang, flat and nasally, but directly and warmly:

> "Don't you hear the bluebirds asingin'?
> Don't you hear that mournful sound?"

And then he understood that through the music Old John of Ravens' Glen was telling him he understood—understood the heartbreak of life, the loneliness that is youth and age, understood that a man could give his life to the woman he loved, only to find that he had to remain long after she had gone.

Claude nodded to him, almost shaking with gratitude. Old John only smiled, his hazel eyes twinkling, telling him that life is not a thing that begins and ends, like a day, but flows on forever, like the river, flowing through all the days of a man's life, even the lonely and bitter ones. When the tune was finished, Old John waited.

Only Caroline had ever understood how he felt, Claude knew,

but now an aged fiddler with hazel eyes had come down from the hills, smiling as Caroline had smiled, to tell him that if a man knows real love in his lifetime, it is enough to help him endure whatever else remains.

Why didn't I think of it before? Claude wondered, recalling the words he had written long years before, a kind of poem, and the music Caroline had composed to go with them. It was *O My Lovely Caroline*, and while he had been unable to play it since her death, he lifted his bow and began.

Though he couldn't have heard the tune before, Old John followed, playing the music as if he had known it all his life, discording it, pulling the deep and trembling notes from the strings. Claude looked at him, astonished. Old John appeared ageless, quiet as a spirit in the night.

Turning back, Claude looked at the showboat and the surging river beyond. His heart rose with joy, for he was neither lonely nor fearful. Out on the river, waiting, was all the love he had ever known, and the fairest fiddler of all, Old John of Ravens' Glen, by following him, by giving him the lead, was sending him back to the river.

Now they played together. The night throbbed and hummed with their music as it spread across the river and the hills, vanishing upward. The hill people, who had been curiously quiet, as though they sensed, but did not understand what was happening, started to clap their hands, and then, hurrying to the level ground above the trees, they began to dance, whirling and spinning and stomping in the pale light, shouting joyously.

One by one, the show people came down the gangplank and joined them. Again the lives of the hill people were joined with magic as they danced with the heroine, the soubrette, the comedian and the impostor—all the characters from the play—throwing themselves into a world where happiness always won out.

Claude paused a moment, as the captain came up the bank, but

Old John urged him on, "Go ahead. Take the lead, young feller. Tonight you're acallin' the tunes."

It wasn't that Old John was implying he was the best fiddler, Claude knew. He was saying that love is a thing no man can conceal, not from a man who learned a headful of tunes by playing them a thousand times—tunes of sorrow and joy and happiness and love and loneliness, tunes learned by playing them alone in the woods, where music seems a thing caught out of the air.

The two bows began to move, darting and shooting across the strings, calling up music which first was played a hundred lifetimes ago.

NIGHT OF HORROR

by Joel Townsley Rogers

A plane was going across the big orange hunter's moon ahead when I turned off on Goodhaven Road, no more than a couple of miles from Irene and Danny at home.

One of the Southern Cross Airways' two regular evening ships, I recognized it, heading up for New York from Buenos Aires or Valparaiso at six hundred to seven hundred miles an hour. It was quite high and four or five miles away. They always flew the same course almost exactly to the quarter mile, and on schedule almost to the minute; although it was after ten o'clock now, which made it a little late.

I've never been any farther from the Eastern Shore than Wilmington and Philadelphia myself. But my father had been in the Navy Air, back in World War II. He had been killed in Brazil, in one of the old piston-engine planes of that day, when I was even younger than Danny was now. I could just barely remember him, his last time home, I guess, singing a song to me—something about

two ships, the Don and the Magdalena, that sailed to Brazil. It was
something that Kipling had written, it seemed. The two giant
S.C.A. intercontinentals were named the Don and the Magdalena,
after the ships in that old song, though which one this was I didn't
know.

A speck of tiny cloud seemed to break off from one of its wings
in the moonlight as I watched it through my station-wagon windshield. It drifted on the high night wind in this direction, while the
big plane went on. Something like a parachute, though it couldn't
have been that, of course. I lost it after a couple of moments in
the cobweb threads of the starry October night.

It showed how old-fashioned I was that I thought at times in
words like that, I checked myself as I drove along. The long thin
streaks that sometimes drift across the stars, like a few tonight,
aren't really anything like cobwebs, but just molecules of water va-
por loosely strung together, as anybody knows. There aren't any
cobwebs in the sky, and never were, except for the tiny spiders that
used to float off on their little threads when their egg pods burst;
and they were never very high. Childhood images and ideas still
stick with us, though, long after we have learned that they are completely false, and pop up from our subconscious without our realizing it. Idols of the cave, old Francis Bacon called them.

There weren't any cobwebs anywhere any more, when I got
down to it. The last of them had gone eight or ten years ago, soon
after the insects that they had been built to catch. If I should read
Danny the Mother Goose rhyme about the old lady who went to
sweep the cobwebs off the moon, it would have no associations
for him at all. No memories, when he grew up, of lacy nets spread
out on the grass in summer dawns, looking like patches of frost
with the dew on them, which a barefoot boy was careful to avoid;
nor of the geometrically perfect webs of black-and-yellow argiopid
spiders strung from bush to bush in back-yard gardens, with their
four rays of laddered silk, and of gathering around one with a gang
of other kids, thrusting out a long branch to tear the sticky threads,
then running frantically in all directions, in terror that the tiger-

striped demon of the web was after them. No memories of dusty hay barns, with cobwebs festooned down from the rafters and hanging in thick triangular sheets in the corners, where dark bloated bodies crouched in the depths of their tunnels, waiting to leap upon their prey. And I was glad he wouldn't.

Once when I had been about five myself I had gone into Grandfather Prettyman's barn at dusk, hunting for eggs which some of his wandering hens might have laid in the hay, and one of those festoons had dropped down on me, as big as a pillowcase. I would never forget stumbling and fighting my way out through the wide doorway, stifled with horror, clawing the sticky hay-wisped sheet from my eyelids and lips and hair. Even today, it was all I could do to go beneath a tree hanging with Spanish moss.

Coming that way from far-off lands and skies full of different stars, the airliner made me think of the garbled report from Brazil that had been on the kitchen radio early this morning, while I was trying a couple of shells from my new box in my shotgun, waiting for the coffee to perk, with Irene still getting Danny dressed upstairs.

It had been about a town called Iniquillos, up a tributary of the Amazon from Manaus. A small city of about four thousand people, rubber hunters, tannery workers and rivermen, Indian and white, with electricity and telephones and a radio station, which had been inexplicably cut off from communication. A plane had been sent from Manaus to investigate, with a network correspondent aboard who had phoned back a report, relayed on the radio hookup, about the town being all hidden beneath a silvery gray carpet.

His broadcast hadn't been very intelligible, fading out and getting mixed with other things; and maybe after half a minute he had been cut off, with an apology by the network commentator for the poor quality of the signal. The commentator had gone on to explain that the town was apparently hidden in morning river mist, although the reporter might have meant that it had been submerged in a flood; and they would try to have a full account later. There had been a report from Washington then about the Mars rocket, followed by a car dealer's spiel and the weather forecast. But the Manaus correspondent's thin voice had sounded excited, almost hysterical, and I wished there had been a little more of his story.

My car radio was out of commission, and I hadn't seen a newspaper all day, over at Rehoboth, Delaware, repairing the roof of the judge's beach house after Hurricane Claribel. Three hours up, and the same back, with more than ten hours of steady shingle-patching and tarring in between, wanting to get the job finished in one day.

Lights shone from the windows of the houses scattered along the road. There is something about the lights of houses in an autumn night in the country—with the day's work done and the school-age kids doing their lessons around the dining table, the little ones in bed—that is snug and homey. It makes you glad you belong to the human race, and live in a civilized age and country. Cave men had their damp rock dens to cower in from the saber-tooth, it might be, and other animals have their nests or lairs. But there is nothing like a modern man's own safe, warm, lighted home when night has come and the weather is turning cool.

The Kings' weather-beaten shingle cottage across the road from our place was all dark inside, though. Their gooseneck floodlight was on above the open doors of their old garage-shed beside the house, and their car was out. A five-gallon gasoline can was standing against one of the doors—with a potato stuck on its spout instead of a lost cap—that Lem King had brought home for their kitchen stove and been too lazy to take in. The light shone inside the shed on the oil-soaked floor, a tangle of tire chains, old gunny sacks, and the big smoked ham they had won at the raffle last week, all hanging from the center rafter. It shone on a jumble of old boxes, broken chairs, a busted baby carriage and worn-out tires piled up at the back; and over their pitted driveway and weedy lawn and broken-down picket fence in front.

Lem was a lazy mechanic, and his wife a slattern housekeeper. Irene and I, between ourselves, referred to their house as "the Kings' palace." There wasn't any need of any human beings' letting a place get all run down like that. But maybe there are individuals and families of every zoological class that are just naturally attracted to dirt and disorder and prefer it.

Their little Nancy's window up in the attic dormer was open, I saw. They had put her to bed, and left her alone again while they went out to have themselves another ball down at the Four Corners bar. The way they neglected her was a crime. She wasn't any older than Danny. Only an ordinary kid, it might be, with an ordinary hundred to hundred and twenty I.Q., but pretty as anything, with curly light brown hair and big pansy eyes and the sweetest smile. Irene thought they probably beat her, from the bruises she sometimes had, but we didn't know. We had never heard her cry.

There wasn't anything that could happen to her, of course. She wasn't the kind of kid who plays with matches. There weren't any burglars or child molesters anywhere in the county, like maybe in a city. No bear or panther was going to climb in and get her; the only wild animals we had were squirrels and rabbits, raccoons and skunks and a few possums, and maybe a deer or two over in Barnes' woods.

Still, a five-year-old kid oughtn't to be left alone in a house at night, no matter how safe. Maybe they wake up and see something stirring just outside the window, like a vine or tree branch, and they don't know what it is. Or they hear a little sound, like a stair tread that gives a creak with a change of temperature, or a water faucet dripping, and they think it's something creeping to get them, making bubbles with its breath.

I swung in our driveway and parked in front of the garage. I took my lunch box from the seat beside me as I got out. I left my ladders and stuff in the back of the wagon, having another roof job tomorrow over in Griffinsville.

Light from the downstairs windows shone out on the flagstones
to the kitchen door. Danny's window upstairs in front was dark,
I saw, and open a couple of inches from the bottom. His bedtime
was nine o'clock, and Irene always kept him to a strict schedule.
She was college-educated, with a major in child psychology, and
she thought it was even more important for him than for an ordinary kid to have everything just so. Though, as she had to admit
herself, even the smartest professors didn't know about kids like
him, and there was nothing to guide us.

From just above the fringes of my eyebrows, as I was glancing
up, I caught the movement of something dropping down on the
roof overhead, it looked like, out of the night sky. Just a kind of
sprawling shadow, blotting out the stars over the house an instant.
I stopped a couple of paces from the kitchen stoop, lifting my eyes
straight up to where the roof ridge and the square center chimney
cut the sky.

A little pale smoke was coming up out of the chimney mouth
from the oil furnace. That could have been what had caught my
eye. Or it might have been a fall of leaves from the old hundred-
foot oak, in front, that went back before the Revolution, and maybe
before Columbus, that was called the Lord Protector Oak, though
nobody knew why. It shed an awful lot of leaves. Lem King even
complained that they sometimes fell across the road onto his own
roof. Two or three times every fall I had to put a ladder up and
clean them out of our gutters. There was a bunch of them on the
roof now, so far as I could tell, in a flat pile humped up against
the chimney.

I turned the knob of the kitchen door and went in. "Hi, Irene!"
I called out as I closed it behind me.

The kitchen was filled with the smell of cooked Concord grapes.
A couple of big pots with rims of pink froth were on the sink drain-
board, with a colander full of seeds and grapeskins and a purple-
stained cheesecloth straining bag. There was an empty pan lined
with paraffin for the tops of jelly glasses. She must have made a
raft of it today. Every fall she filled the shelves of the big preserve

closet down in the basement with all kinds of things she put up.

Some man was talking on the TV in the living room, kind of low. I took off my jacket and hat, hanging them on the hook on the back of the basement door, which was standing part way open.

"Irene?" I called down the stairs.

But it was dark down there. She had taken her jelly glasses down, but had neglected to bolt the door again when she came back up, it looked like. It was likely to swing open that way unless you did. I closed it and threw the bolt.

She couldn't be watching a program so hard that she hadn't heard me. She was probably upstairs looking at Danny's thermometer by the light from the hall, deciding whether she ought to open his window another inch or close it another inch, I figured, and would be down directly.

She had set out a plate and knife and fork on the table for me, with my napkin. I opened the oven door and saw a casserole that she had put back to keep warm. I set it out on the table and got some butter and homemade bread and poured a big glass of milk. I thought I might as well get the evening paper to look at while I was eating.

On the window ledge, between the geranium pots, I caught sight of my box of shotgun shells that I had laid there this morning; and my gun still standing against the wall that I had got out from the closet under the front stairs. Irene was always petrified of guns. I was going to have an awful argument when Danny was old enough to go hunting with me.

I picked up the shells and gun to put away, and went into the living room with them. The evening paper was lying on the couch. On the TV screen a man with owlish glasses was sitting talking at a table.

"Two major mutations in one species, doctor?" I heard him say. "A great increase in size, and an even more tremendous increase in intelligence?"

They were having another one of these discussion programs, it looked like, about biology and the changes they figured were due to radiation, like they had been having for the past ten years, ever since the insects began not having eyes and died out over all the world. I sat down on the arm of the couch a minute to see if they would say anything new about the kids like Danny.

"We are very far from having any adequate data yet on the variety and extent of mutations during the past decade, doctor," a man with big ears and a bald, domelike head said, leaning on his elbows. "We can only assume that nothing is impossible in the forms that life may take. It is conceivable that mutations of one sort or another, meaningful or meaningless, infinitesimal or staggering in their proportions, beneficial or destructive to the species, may have occurred by the scores of thousands among various families and orders of all the great phyla of animals. In the ocean deeps, in the unknown jungles——"

"The human mutation is the most significant to us as men, don't you think, doctor?" someone else said.

A man with a beard, wearing a clerical collar, was on the screen. "The extraordinary increase in intellectual capacity of so many of our recent children, I mean," he said. "Seven- and even five-year-olds who think in terms of quantum variables and elementary particles, so far as their thought processes can be assayed, and are endowed with extrasensory perceptions for which we have no name. I believe that zoology regards them as a true mutation, pointing to the establishment, within the comparatively brief span of another six or ten generations, of a race of super-homo as far advanced over modern man as he is over the shaggy clam digger of the kitchen middens, or perhaps Austroanthropos."

Danny, I thought, and the others like him. He would live in a world beyond all my understanding, beyond imagination. He would be tall and shining, wonderfully clear in his thinking, a million years farther from all the scars of old dark terrors, all the idols of the cave. I would be only a flat-skulled gibbering club wielder to him, an ignorant thing of the night and the forests, who strangely had fathered him. But on me, because of him, the glory of that future world shone in a thin crack through the door.

"Quite, doctor," the big bald man was saying. "Unquestionably an incalculable intellectual leap has occurred in a proportion of the offspring of our species, increasing at a geometric rate each year. The first primitive human intelligence itself, which according to the best evidence developed suddenly in various scattered groups of small-brained, insect-eating, lemurlike mammals hunted as prey by the great saurian carnivores, in all likelihood was such a mutation, occurring in an era of great genetic whirlpool such as ours seems also to be, caused possibly by an unprecedented flood of cosmic radiation."

"Man is always most significant to himself," said the man with owlish glasses. "The question before us, however, doctor, is whether a species of another order, of a quite different class and phylum, an invertebrate, whose members have disappeared completely in our own country due to lack of sustenance, may have survived in other parts of the world and have developed a vastly larger size, with an intelligence comparable at least to man's early tribal intelligence in communication and co-operative effort in the hunt. And with unknown prospects of possibly surpassing even our own super-homo at some not too distant date."

I didn't know what they were talking about. They weren't talking about Danny though, any more. I felt a little weak.

The big man was back again. He picked up a pencil and broke it in his hands.

"The conclusion seems inescapable, doctor," he said. "Certainly not all members of the order were comparatively minuscule in size, nor solely dependent on insects for their food, like those we knew. There were, specifically, the much larger so-called birdeaters and other lesser-known giant species of the equatorial jungles. Undeniably they would have had time to establish through several generations their own mutations, if such have occurred, including an increase in size, an adaptability to changed environment and conceivably a high humanlike intelligence. At times over the past several years we have had the apparently fantastic stories from the interior of Brazil about solitary Indian hunters, and even whole jungle families in their huts, who have been overwhelmed by groups of the fabled Tigre Aranha working in concert——"

I turned to lay my gun and shells down on the couch beside me.

"——stories heretofore all completely discounted by science," the big man's voice was going on. "However, today we have been confronted by the reports of the tragedy of Iniquillos, and the crash of the airliner from Manaus less than three hours ago——"

The black headlines of the paper on the couch were beneath my eyes. And I was stumbling out of grandfather's barn again, clawing at my hair and face.

"Giant Spiders——"

Somewhere in the house there was a faint thudding which was not the thudding of my heart.

"Dan! Dan!"

From the kitchen! I threw two shells into my gun. Don't ask me why. I went back out there at a stumbling run. "Irene! Where are you?"

"Dan! Oh, please!"

I threw the bolt of the basement door and jerked it open. I caught her against me as she sprawled forward from the top step, with her dark hair matted and blood trickling down her face.

"The chair I was standing on! It tilted beneath me, Dan!" she said in gasps. "I grabbed the preserve closet, and it toppled forward on me as I fell. I think a corner of it must have hit my head and given me a concussion. It must have smashed the light bulb too. I was lying down there on the floor in the dark, everything around me all sharp and squashy! I had a terrible time finding the steps! Oh, Dan! What a dreadful day!"

Her scalp had a deep cut back of the hairline, and her palms and the knees of her brown corduroy slacks were covered with pieces of glass smeared with jelly. She had hurt her right leg too. I couldn't tell how badly.

"How long ago did it happen, girl?"

"I don't know. They were about to have a program with a lot of important scientists discussing the ghastly thing down in Brazil. I thought I'd just have time to take the last load down before it began. I guess I was in too much of a rush."

"It must have been only a minute or two before I got back," I said. "I thought you were upstairs with Danny."

"I put him to bed a little before his regular time," she said, still dazed. "I tried to keep him from hearing the news all day. He's so intelligent, but in so many ways he's even more helpless, and a baby, and needs even more to be protected from fear and shock. What are you doing with your gun, Dan?"

"I was just putting it away."

I helped her over to the sink and ran lukewarm water for her to hold her hands under, to rinse off as much as possible of the glass. There wasn't any doctor who would come out so far, so late, for anything short of death. I might have to wake up Danny and take him along in to the hospital. I mopped the blood and muck from her face with wet paper towels, and tried to get some of it out of her hair.

"It's still bleeding," I said. "Let me get you on the couch in the living room while I see how bad your knee and ankle are. I haven't heard anything, Irene, all day. Just something over the radio this morning about a gray carpet."

"A whole town!" she gasped. "They must have planned it a long time, all working together. Thousands of them, as big as the biggest octopuses! It's believed to have happened two nights ago. There's no human life left beneath the carpet—only shadows moving. The government is sending army planes over to drop gas and fragmentation bombs. They say it's the only thing to do. Thousands of them now! Soon there may be millions, covering the whole earth! You know the way they breed."

"It's a terrible thing," I told her, feeling the sickness still and

the remembrance of the film over my face. "But don't let yourself
go to pieces. Terrible things have happened since the world began.
The great scaly dinosaurs in the giant reeds beside the river, when
we had to go down to drink, and nine-tenths of us would die. The
tigers' bloody jaws seizing our parents and our brothers and sisters,
and only we were left deep in the cave. But we have survived. They
aren't going to cover the whole earth with their filthy cities and
feed on us like flies. They can be destroyed, and all their nests and
lairs, now that we know they exist, before they multiply too much
or become still more intelligent and evil, even if a million square
miles of living green hell have to be mushroom-bombed as dead
as the moon. It's natural for everybody everywhere to be horrified,
I know, but there's no reason for us to go to pieces. Get hold of
yourself, Irene. They are all a long way away."

"The Magdalena!" she said. "The big S.C.A. liner that took off
today from Manaus. Down, in the Everglades!"

"Down?" I said. "I saw one of the big regular evening S.C.A.
liners heading up for New York when I was turning onto Goodhaven Road only a little while ago. They're safer than a railroad
train. There's nothing that could get one down."

"That must have been the Don, from Buenos Aires," she said.
"The Magdalena! A hundred and eighty passengers aboard it, and
all the crew! Oh, Dan!"

I had got her into the living room, to the couch. I snatched the
newspaper off and dropped it over the back, out of sight, as I helped
her to ease down. There was a wirephoto on it that I didn't want
to look at.

On the TV screen they were still having their discussion, talking
about arthropods and arachnids and araneids, phyla and classes and
orders, about genes and biomolecules and some kind of nucleic
acid that was maybe the key to life and intelligence. I knelt and
took her shoe off, rolled up the leg of her slacks above her swollen
knee, with my gun on the floor at my feet.

"No broken bones, I don't think," I said. "When you've rested,
maybe I can get you upstairs and into a hot tub, after I've band-

aged up your head. What about the Magdalena in the Everglades?"

"We are interrupting our panel discussion," said an announcer on the TV, "to bring you a special interview from Idlewild Airport in New York City with Captain Mackland of the Southern Cross airship Don, just landed from South America, who was in communication with the Magdalena, a sister ship, for a half hour before it went down in the Everglades, and who flew low over it after its crash."

A tall lean man, with a drawn face beneath an officer's peaked cap, and a short hatless man with rumpled hair, holding a mike, were standing in the foreground of the screen then. There was a great confusion of voices and other sounds. Behind them, and at the edges of the floodlit scene, policemen were pushing back a crowd. In the background were the landing ramp and passenger doorway of a giant plane; and at the top of the screen, above the two men, was the tip of one of its wings, with the shadow of a thin rope swaying as it hung down.

It was the plane that I had seen in the bright moonlight. It had landed up there, two hundred miles away, in little more time than it had taken me to putter a couple of miles home.

"You saw the Magdalena crash, I understand, captain," said the man with the rumpled hair. "Will you tell us about it?"

The tall lean man wet his lips, bending to the mike which the rumpled man thrust at him.

"We took off from Buenos Aires," he said. "A stop at Rio. A normal flight. Over the Caribbean I was talking to the Magdalena, which had taken off from Valparaiso and put down at Manaus on the way, and was then about a hundred miles, about ten minutes, behind us. Bill—Captain Norjac, her skipper—told me about all the hysteria at Manaus, and how swarms of army planes had been taking off for Iniquillos up at the edge of the jungle, which these Tigres Aranhas were supposed to have enwrapped. I don't think he quite believed it had happened. He joked about how he had been radioed by the tower after he left there that a swarm of giant striped things had been seen leaping from the treetops as he cleared the end of the field, and that a bunch of them had fastened on his wings. They advised him to put down at the nearest field if he couldn't shake them off. He thought they were nuts at Manaus. Or if there had been such things, that they must have been frozen and swept off at his altitude and speed. He kidded me that if he could only bring one back alive, maybe he could sell it to the Bronx Zoo for a million bucks. Right afterward——"

The lean man wet his lips again.

"Go on, captain!" the rumpled man urged. "A hundred million people want to know."

"Right afterward I heard him report that a gray curtain had suddenly been dropped over all his windows, and he had lost all visibility. He was going down in a vertical sideslip, trying to shake it off. I heard him report then that he had straightened out, having been unable to get rid of it after a succession of half-rolls and other maneuvers, and was proceeding blind on instruments. I was up off Fort Lauderdale. I hauled around to rendezvous with him and see him home. I sighted him as he came in over the Everglades, down to eight thousand feet. He was calling then that his controls were jammed or cut. I saw him going down in a wide, loose, left spin, all tangled——"

"Go on, captain."

"I flew over, low," the lean man said. "Not more than fifty feet. The terrain was all swamp hummocks and silver water. It was like a gray fallen tent, with things leaping. I made another pass over, but there couldn't have been any survivors of the crash itself. I had my own passengers and ship that I was responsible for. I zoomed up, reporting it, and headed on home."

"Weren't you concerned that some of those things might leap up and fasten on your own wings, captain, while you were flying over?"

"I thought of it with the second pass I made," the lean man said. "That was why I pulled the wheel back against my belt and blasted the hell up out of there. But I guess none of them were quick enough to make it."

The long shadowy rope swaying from the end of the wing above him floated down across the center of the screen.

"Look out!" somebody yelled.

The crowd beyond the police were tumbling back. The lean airman and the man with the mike disappeared from the screen. The sound went off. Distorted faces and running figures jerked and bobbed around in silence. After a moment the scene changed back to the studio announcer.

"We have a report from Idlewild," he said. "The Don is being gone over foot by foot. But there seems to be nothing except the single thread which you may have seen on your screens. One of them apparently did succeed in fastening on temporarily, but couldn't do anything alone. It was either swept off or launched itself off again. Navy planes from Key West have located the site of the Magdalena's crash, and preparations are being made to reach it with ducks and swamp boats at the earliest possible moment. We will keep you informed of any new developments. We are now returning you to our panel discus——"

Upstairs I heard Danny cry out, "Daddy!"

"Danny!" Irene said frantically, struggling to get up. "He called me!"

She was the one he always called to do all the things a mother has to do. I wasn't home all the time either. But he had called me now. I had my shotgun in my hands as I went up, four steps at a time. I put my foot against his door beside the knob, and it burst open. I went in. The window facing me across the room was wide open.

Danny was sitting up in his slat-sided bed in the corner, in his blue woolly pajamas. He looked at me with his wide grave eyes beneath his broad shining brow. There was nothing in the room that I could see.

"It's just outside the window, daddy," he said.

"What?" I said. "You must have just seen a vine or something like that against the moonlight, boy."

"It had arms and hands," he said.

"Look," I said. "See the shadow on the wall." I lifted my left hand for an instant from the gun, waggling my fingers. "We used to make all kinds of funny shadows that way when I was a boy. That was a spider. I'll make you a rabbit in a moment."

My finger was hooked on the trigger, watching the window.

"It had eight arms, daddy," he said. "I counted them. It opened the window wide. Is it bad?"

"Yes," I said. "I won't try to lie to you, boy. You've got to have your own fears too. There are bad things. And best to know them."

I moved inch by inch toward the window. There was the whisper of a soft bubbling out there, just below the ledge.

"You're a cave man, aren't you, daddy?" Danny said.

"That's right," I said. "I'm an old cave man, boy. I'm a Neanderthaler."

Downstairs on the TV they were still talking back and forth, I could imagine, about their zoology and anthropology and mutations and the chemistry of life, and how man must have happened just by chance, and might someday be wiped out of existence by the development of a more intelligent order of animal. But man's life was more than genes and biomolecules, I knew. It was more than all his own intelligence. It was something in his fiber, call it heart or soul or guts or spark, that no other kind of living thing ever would have or could have, no matter how intelligent. It was love and tenderness and sympathy and dreams, and individual self-sacrifice and hope of heaven and God. So that, when the saber-tooth came screaming into his cave, he had dropped the ochered sticks with which he was painting his beautiful pictures on the wall, and grabbed the firebrand and thrust it in the tiger's face, standing his ground to give his family and fellows time to scramble back beyond reach, even though he must die.

"Come in, tiger!" I said. "Come in, Tigre Aranha! I know you're poison and quick with nets. Come in, and I'll smash you with my rock! I'll club you down! I'll smash your great squashy body!"

There was the whisper of that bubbling, like a crab's jaws, just below the ledge. Again I felt the horror of that fetid curtain clinging to my lips and eyes and hair. My knees were water, but I kept the gun steady. I inched toward the window.

"Come on in!" I said. "This is my cave! I'm only a man, your meat. Are you afraid, tiger?"

Something swept up fast over the window ledge. I fired. A branch full of dead leaves, that tore to tatters in the blast, some in, some out. It was smart.

"Come on in!" I said. "Come flying, tiger!"

I inched forward. The whisper of that bubbling sound had ceased. I moved to the window on numb feet. Outside, the moonlight, filtering through the sere leaves and half-bare branches of the Lord Protector Oak, lay full of stripes and shadows over the yard, the hedge, and the Kings' place across, where the garage floodlight had gone out.

Beneath the window, on the house wall, nothing. Only the dark foundation planting a dozen feet below.

"You're brave, daddy," Danny said bravely. "I wasn't the least bit afraid, after you came."

"Of course not," I said. "We've never been afraid. We've always been brave, Danny, through a million years. And your sons and your sons' sons, too, no matter how all-wise they are, must continue to be brave and to be men."

Shadows of the tree and hedge and bushes. Across the road at the Kings' place there was no light at all except the moon. The Kings' palace. A line from The Proverbs was suddenly in my mind —"The spider takes hold with her hands, and is in kings' palaces."

Beyond the open dormer window in the attic, in the house alone. Maybe only an ordinary human kid, but as sweet and beautiful as they grow. Younger even than Danny. We had never heard her cry at all. But from her window across there I heard her whimpering cry.

"Danny! Dan!" Irene was sobbing from the doorway behind me. "Oh, my God! Little Nancy!"

"Close and brace the door behind you!" I said. "Close and lock the window after me. Grab Danny's baseball bat. Nancy! Nancy!" I shouted out the window. "Uncle Dan is coming!"

It was terribly much harder to leave my own cave—to go out into the shadowy lurking night, among webs that I could not see. I grabbed the window ledge, with my gun clamped downward between my thighs, and dropped into the shadows of the bushes on the spongy ground below. I picked the gun up, and I was running.

No time to turn aside and haul one of my aluminum ladders out from the back of my station wagon, and carry it across to climb with it up to her window. I would have to go in the front door and up the stairs, in blackness if I couldn't find a light. With that thing waiting! And perhaps already, in the instant, having spun and thrown its threads and cobweb sheets and dirty sticky tunnels.

"Nancy!" I was shouting. "All right, Nancy! Uncle Dan is coming! Don't be afraid!"

But it wasn't inside the Kings' house yet. It hadn't taken hold with its hands yet in their palace. It was in the littered garage-shed at the side. It was hanging from the center rafter, among the old gunny sacks and tire chains, its legs wrapped around the prize smoked ham, I saw in the moonlight shadows. Perhaps it liked pig meat best, or maybe the wide doorway had been the quickest place for it to dart into when it saw me come running across the road, shouting. But there, anyway, it was.

"Tiger!" I shouted when I saw it.

I swept my gun to my shoulder. The Thing leaped and scuttled to the back of the shed, among the crates and broken chairs and boxes. It was invisible in the trash, but deep back there I could hear it bubbling.

"Come on!" I said. "Cast your nets at me! Try flying at me, tiger!"

There was only one shell in my gun. I inched toward the left-hand open door. With eyes watchful on the tangled nest of shadows at the back, my finger on the trigger, I half stooped and grabbed the potato that Lem King had stuck on his fuel-can spout, standing there. I heaved the potato left-handedly at the back of the shed. I kicked the can over on its side, and kicked it rolling toward the back. I smelled and heard it gurgling and spouting out over the oil-soaked floor.

I backed a foot. I fumbled out a box of matches with my left hand and opened it, pulling one out. I dropped the box on the gravel, putting my foot on it. Watching, trigger-tense, ready in the instant for the flying leap or scuttling rush, I crouched, and struck the match on the box. I held it till it was burning, and dropped it inward on the floor. In that instant I leaped backward and slammed both doors shut, one and the other.

I don't know why frying pans are sometimes called spiders, or why I should have thought of it just at that moment. I don't know if the tiger screamed, or if it was just the roaring of the heat. The frying pan in the fire.

SWEET CHARIOT

by Paul Darcy Boles

When the large new car stopped, it surprised Journey slightly. As a rule they didn't stop this early in the morning. Behind him light was burning its way down the mountain path. It flamed far below through bull pines and freckled the shake-shingle roof in the hollow, but you couldn't see the rest of his house and yard for blue shadow. At the slamming of brakes Journey straightened, checked a yawn, and arranged his face into the lines it wore toward all customers.

They were affable lines, but not concerned over a sale. At thirty-eight Journey had a fawnlike expression; his eyes held hints of wildness and rushing away. He was a tall man. Only seeing him in motion—swinging down the path or squirrel hunting with his rifle easy in the curve of his arm—could you appreciate the happiness in his muscles. Rare tourists who studied him sometimes put him down as an innocent. Or called him dumb.

Arms folded on the smooth-boarded pine counter, he waited.

The car had pitched to a halt thirty yards along the blacktop road. Now it came hurtling backward. Reverse gear whined. Bulbous chrome around the taillights blinked. More chrome followed the lines of the car, then widened to spray out over the entire sweep of door and hood. Behind the wrap-around windshield the eyes of the man driving and the woman beside him appeared as remote as the eyes of Martians. This illusion was strengthened because both wore dark glasses. In the sharp morning air the engine hummed. The sound was a big bumblebee, droning metallic noise. With a scornful hissing the push-button window on the driver's side came down. Journey lifted his head a trifle and waited.

"Open for business?"

"Am." Journey nodded. His voice held astounding freshness. It was as if he agreed with all the world outside these mountains in its freedom to live and let live. And yet it was also as if he reserved the right to judge for himself and to live his own life as a rock or a tree lived.

Urged off the road, the bulging car rested in the grass. The man got out, saying something to the woman, who answered casually. He was dressed in mouse-gray pants and a brilliant orange sweater that looked as soft as a gopher's belly, and a white motoring cap of the kind worn by early motorists—Journey remembered seeing such when he himself was a child and his father had taken him the twenty-four miles to town to see the sights.

The man appeared to be one who would wear whatever happened to be most expensive. He removed his dark glasses, swung them by one of the bows as he crossed the road. His face was heavy-set; for a shake of a second it reminded Journey of the Harlins' bull, which had occupied an upcountry pasture Journey'd had to pass through every morning while going to school. But that had been long ago, the bull was long expired of sheer meanness. Journey's schooling had been cut off pretty sharply too, soon as he could get out of it. With the glasses off, there was a touch of mole-blindness around the man's pale blue eyes. He stood in front of

Journey. Splinters of brightness flickered from the jars ranged along the counter on either side of Journey's elbows.

"How much?"

"Ha'f dollar apiece. 'Less you want sourwood."

"Well, is sourwood any better?" He made a motion with the hand holding the glasses, and nearly dropped them. Journey figured that they must have cost a mint. Frames elegantly polished, bows trimmed with gold. "Ought to have a sign giving the prices!"

Lacing his fingers, Journey stared around at the darker honey jars. "Sourwood's a mite harder to git, that's all, mister. Price is a nickel extra." Mildly he added: "I figger folks'll stop and ask if they're interested. If they ain't they won't, so paintin' up the price wouldn't make no difference."

"M'm'um," the man said. He leaned over the counter, made a crablike motion with his fingers. "Let's see the sourwood."

Reaching behind, Journey fished up two jars. He held a certain pride in the product. Basswood was good all right; there wasn't another stand that sold better. But sourwood was heritage and home; the finest, surely, in the whole country. Both jars in his big hands gleamed like amber wine of choice. He set them on the counter with small clicks. "Fifty-five cents," he said—again mildly. "Per jar," he added.

The man nodded, a troutlike glazed look in his eyes. It was an expression Journey had noted once in a while in men and women who stopped. Thought they were getting the best of him. It would be easy to raise prices, even to stick up a sign saying one dollar each. And maybe two dollars for the sourwood. For the moment, the man's eyes were saying that Journey was the strange fool of the world for selling so low.

"I'll take four. That's two dollars and twenty cents. Tax?"

Journey was just reaching around to scoop up two more when the man's hand and pigskin wallet stopped in mid-air. "No," Journey said. "Tax is fer down-the-mountain. It don't affect me none, I reckon." He set down the additional jars and followed the other's eyes.

Sun had shafted back into the hollow. It was gilding more than the roof of Journey's house. It ringed his ramshackle barn and touched his sugarbushes.

Linda came to the door to throw out the slops, and the curve of water made a sluice of pure silver. The dogs Tige and Mallow went bounding toward her. Linda and the dogs were all miniatures. Journey felt pride fill him. He didn't mind the stranger watching.

"Purty, ain't it?"

The eyes facing his were wider. Something leaped in them; Journey widened his own, and waited.

"That—that car down there." Something had put itself in this man's voice too. It was husky; there was respect, even awe in it. "Who owns it?"

Journey could see the effort it was for the man to be casual. The Adam's apple worked. Striations like those in stone appeared in the jaw muscles. There was a silence filled with tension while Journey wheeled again. Staring down, he saw the scene as it had forever been, this time of morning, this season of the year. There was the house. Linda had gone in now. There was the whacking log with chips surrounding it. There was the barn behind. *Have to paint it someday,* Journey mused; *else it'll fall down of its own accord and ruin them cows some night.*

Once, twice, his eyes swept around. They even took in the Whittles' cottage, upslope a way; the Ambridges', hooded by the canopy of kudzu leaves over its doorway. In no place could he see a car wonderful enough to have riveted attention and turned a voice funny. Journey looked back, across the road. His eye flicked to the bechromed automobile; then once more he turned to the lighted hollow. This time he saw. The ash tree, going up sixty feet before its boughs began, partially obscured the machine from here. Only its brass radiator and part of one giant front wheel were visible. All the same, this man had seen it. Once again Journey blinked. There was wonder in his eyes also.

"You mean that ol' red-painted thing in my yard?"

For one more moment Journey could read war in the face thrust next to his. Shrewdness fought eagerness. For the whisper of a second, shrewdness almost won. The man's eyes said, *Good Lord, man, you don't even know what you have!* Then eagerness, in the long run, won out.

Huskily, the man said, "Yes. Yours?" Journey nodded. "Yes. It's yours then. Sure it's yours, belongs to you?" Journey nodded. "All right." He was talking much softer than he had. It was as if in the side flick of a look he gave toward the slope of the mountain, he saw spies. As if he sensed competition at his shirttails. "I'll buy it. I'll——" The Adam's apple again; another war. Angels won this one too. "——pay you. A decent price. Come on, let's go down there. Let's"—he fought for calm and practically achieved it—"just take a look at it, shall we?"

You could humor the man or you could reach and drag him, babbling, back to his own car. But Journey held up a finger. "One. That there car's about a nineteen-twelve, mister. Was bought 'fore I was born. My daddy brought it home. Was a time he'd had luck —there was a man came lookin' fer ginseng, and payin' high prices, and so happened daddy was the best ginseng hunter in these parts. So I've heard it tell. Now, she runs." He cast another glance down; yes, she ran, though it was bad as getting into frosted britches to start her on cold morns. "Yet that's the most you c'n say fer 'er. Two." He held up another finger. "I got to mind the stand. You're early, but traffic'll hype up through here in a bit. I——"

"L-listen!" the man said. His eyebrows worked; the heavy face, still reminding Journey of the Harlins' old bull, creased and darkened. A hand clutched Journey's shoulder. "Said I'd pay! I mean real pay! Don't have to worry—about what you'd lose here. I'll make it all up to you! Look, look here——" Journey moved, glad he hadn't been forced to lift the hand off. The hand was fumbling in the wallet. Cards shot forth, mica-encased. "Now, here." With politeness Journey gazed down at the name duplicated on the shining cards. "C. J. Adams," he read, out loud. Maybe the name was supposed to mean something. Journey felt just a whit ashamed that he couldn't place it. The other wanted him to—badly.

"Yes, that's right. Adams Motors; all of it." But a moth-wing flutter of apprehension stayed. "You've heard of——? Even up here, you——"

Journey didn't have the heart to shake his head. But he didn't nod either. His brown eyes were assessing. While he waited to decide, Adams slapped the counter boards. "Let's go, then. Right now, I mean. I'm waiting."

It wasn't the voice—used to having orders acted on as if the rest of the world happened to be well-trained hounds—that swayed Journey now. It was Adams' eagerness. He felt his own curiosity expanding as the sun widened over the highway down at the granite-walled curve. He lifted his head.

"Reckon I might go down there a minute. Reckon, too, you best pull your automobile over farther inta shade. Time that sun clears the gumwood top it'll git fierce. You didn't pay me," he pointed out quietly, "f'r th' four sourwood." He raked up the jars, stepped out of the stand's roof shadow. Straightened, he appeared quite a bit taller than Adams. "Show me where at to put 'em in your automobile and I'll do 'er. Then we c'n go on down." He spoke over his shoulder to Adams, who came along behind him across the blacktop.

Sun was already heating the tar. Journey reckoned when he got back from this wild-goose chase down the hollow, he'd bring some vinegar-water to drink. Be a sizzler. "Reckon y'r wife better not come down. Path's too tough f'r women-folk when they ain't used to it."

Adams nodded and flapped a hand toward the trunk. Journey noted the insigne on the hood. *Adams. Guess he makes cars like this one.*

Stationed at the rear of the trunk he waited. Adams was speaking to the woman. His voice was a rasp cutting through lesser metal. The woman said something Journey couldn't hear, only the one thing, then was quiet. Adams reached inside this flashing car; the trunk lid came up and nearly hit Journey on the chin. Journey stowed the jars with care. They'd ride well. He pushed the lid back down, and there was a click.

Against strengthening sun Adams had replaced his dark glasses. He stood beside Journey. Heaving his chest full of air under the orange sweater he said, "You claim it runs!"

"It runs. I said that."

"Let's go."

"Didn't pull inta shade. Wife's goin' t' git awful hot in yonder."

"Air-conditioned." Adams was already halfway back across the blacktop. "Push a button. That's all. You like a car like that? If yours is in any shape I'll give you one for it. Two!" All his shrewdness was leaving. He was moving ahead of Journey—in the pokeweeds, past the stand. Journey caught up to him, started past; Adams held out a five-dollar bill. "Keep change; for the honey."

Journey thrust it into a side pocket. His denims were washed just to the point where they felt like extra skin. "I'll git change." He went on. In back of him Adams' feet crushed through burdock leaves; Journey narrowed his eyes at the blazing path. Above on the road a car hummed in the distance, grew closer, shot past, hum diminishing. People were not usually such sneak thieves they'd steal from a honey stand. Maybe Miz Adams would keep an eye on it for him anyhow. "I got the change down at the house," Journey explained. The bittersweet dusty smell of the weeds and the long grasses climbed around them. "Watch where I'm steppin' and step the same. Hear a whir in the grass, stand stock-still and pertend you're a rock. Ain't as near as it looks nor as easy to git to, even goin' down. This time o' year the snakes is out." Unseen to Adams he smiled. Movement had stopped behind him. Then it started again, Adams coming doggedly, grainy bronze-leather shoes skidding on shale. *He wants what I got. And I want to know what it is myself for true,* Journey thought.

He felt conversational. But he couldn't tell Adams what was on his mind—how in the freshness of morning at the start of the honey season he never took change with him. How if people didn't have right change he'd risk a loss; tell them to drop by later to pay. Some did, some didn't. Either way, he wouldn't take tips. Daddy'd been that way, so he had to be. He wanted to say it, but Adams wouldn't have understood.

They were almost down to the Whittles'; a spring boiled from white stones in sand at the curve of the thorn-tree-ringed yard. For a glint of a moment he wished to be wholly friendly with Adams. And knew sorrow that it was impossible.

He pointed. Adams' breath came heavier. "Down so; through them trees."

"You let her stand out in the weather." Adams' eyes were bulging; they accused Journey.

Then Adams looked back at the car through the leaves. He polished his steamed glasses on a pinch of sweater.

"Reckon," Journey said. "Car ain't a cow nor yet a kid. Want to ketch wind a spell?"

Out of the corner of his eye he saw Methan Whittle and his four sons, and his oldest daughter, who was nursing a baby, go angling down through thorn trees. They had seen the stranger, were about to take a longer look. Journey caught the glimmer of Methan's oak staff, which helped the old man scurry almost as quick as a lizard. Then he saw his own children through brush, parting leaves as they gazed upward. Marla Jean's face was like a white leaf among green ones; Ferdy's freckled, thin-boned as a bird. Adams plowed on; Journey held back a bough to keep it from whiplashing. "Yond's my chaps. Them coming up through the laurel. Can't rightly see 'less you squinch your gaze."

Adams grunted. So Journey didn't mention the Whittles, twenty yards off. And when the Ambridges—young Toll; old Toll; grandmother, with hair frost-white above brown-green linsey dress—joined the watchers, Journey didn't mention them. Excitement could bring out the whole settlement. There were a dozen houses, some small farmhouses, some lean-tos, no road but instinct leading to their doors. Pride of community you could not tell to an outlander; how a man's legends upheld him in the sight of friends. Young Toll Ambridge—two years older than Journey, and they'd fought side by side in the Army overseas, but everybody called him young Toll—had his great-granddad's rifle. More than a play pretty, a thing reverenced. Men came to see it, lay hands on it. Methan Whittle had his oak staff. In whispers stronger than trumpets it was said the staff blossomed in dark of the moon. Grew leaves of moony white. An honor to touch it, a pleasure to discuss it.

As he paused for Adams to catch up, Journey mourned. He possessed no legend. Good honey was commonplace. Likely better than anyone else's, but no legend. It was an old wish to have a true legend.

They were almost on the valley floor. From both eye corners Journey could glimpse neighbors. More of them seeped down this path. They came around oak and gum tree and laurel and ash and elm with the curiousness of soft rain. Joners, Applewoods, Marlins and Peaveys. All moving where Journey and Adams were bound.

Light fell to the clearing ahead as though from a great lamp. Linda stood on the front steps, clinking lime from the black pot with a ball-peen hammer. She was fair, thin as Journey, tall with his tallness. Her hair looked to be a gold banner glinting. Pride jumped like a young minnow in Journey's chest. It was always so when he saw her after not seeing her for even a little time.

Tige and Mallow—one gingerbread colored, the other coal black —had caught the scent of the stranger. They rose, came charging down the path. They paid no attention to the neighbors. Adams had the sense to stand still.

"Sho, now," Journey told the dogs. "He's a guest." Tige sniffed at Adams' pants cuff, and Journey gave the dog a gentle slap on the muzzle. Tige looked faintly hurt and walked away stiff-legged. "You c'n walk," Journey told Adams.

Adams went arrow-straight to the car. Beyond the path the beehives took leaf-filtered sunlight. Linda was coming down the steps. A cabbage-leaf butterfly played around her hair, zigzagged away. Linda looked around to the neighbors at the edges of the clearing.

Old man Methan Whittle lifted his staff in salute. Linda nodded to him. Her daughter and son came running across bough-shadowed grass. No one was talking, even breathing much. Marla Jean's eyes slid to Adams where he stood rooted in front of the red car, and like Linda's, went back to Journey. Ferdy's mouth hung open several inches. He breathed through it. All looked at Journey.

Journey said, "Spied th' ol' thing from the road. Naught'd do but he'd see it close."

"Why?" Linda's fingers shut over a string of her apron, opened again. Her voice came as low as Journey's. "Reckon we ought to got a license?"

He shook his head. When he lucked into money he might get her perfume in molten-shining bottles, a new dress. But even with those, she couldn't smell or look finer.

"Ain't drove it 'cept summer before last up the log road t' the lake. Nobody seen us then. It was night," he said.

He let air out of his chest in a sigh. It contained his wish to explain the outside world—the nation that fled past on the road above the hollow. Shaking his head, he looked back to the orange-sweatered, white-capped man. Linda also sighed. A flicker of understanding passed like amiable current between them. Ferdy stared toward Adams. Ferdy's hand clapped like a brown starfish over his mouth. The corners of his lips curled up. Journey gave him a warning look. The boy stifled laughter and, motioning Marla Jean to come, stole across the grass toward the stranger.

Made bold, five other children—Taggart Lofting, Ked Joner, Sarah and Gradon Applewood, and the smallest Marlin boy still in flour-sack didies—crept like intent mice from the rim of the clearing, and stood behind Adams. Tige and Mallow followed and lay couchant, heads up.

Adams' neck was scarlet. He had not changed his position before the radiator of the red car. Its paint wasn't the brilliance Journey could recall from youth. But it had weathered all right. About three shades duller than a fire engine. Its temperature gauge rose from the brass radiator. The steering wheel, on the right, was for a Titan. For a moment Journey was able to see through the eyes of Adams. Tires were good, engine nobody could wear out. Magneto, electric system, battery good. The brass headlamps, eyes of heraldic owls, just about perfect. Maybe he ought to tell Adams he kept her covered with a tarp in really bad weather. But that was another point he might as well keep shut about. He did it because his daddy'd had some pride in the car, and it had been in the family a long while.

But the ability to see as Adams did was gone. Journey could not understand. Almost without knowing it, he had strolled up behind Ked Joner and Taggart Lofting. As though this called for one more to join the ballet, young Toll Ambridge hulked at his side. Neither looked at the other. Like the children, the dogs, and the rest of the adults, they studied the giant car and the well-dressed man.

When Adams moved at last, a sigh went through the watchers. As he stepped back, nearly on the toes of the youngest Marlin boy, Adams saw that he was watched. Annoyance puffed his face, then went away. His glance caught Journey.

"Ah." Adams smiled sternly.

Another sigh, wind through wheat, went through the audience.

Adams might have been calling orders to an army. "Looks perfect! Perfect. You can't tell; you can't tell, but I'd still buy on sight. On sight."

Young Toll Ambridge raised black eyebrows and gave Journey a look. Journey returned it with a sidelong flutter of eyelids. Toll had no yearning, a high place of his own, his great-granddad's rifle. All men needed a mystery. This car was that to Adams. He took another step back. The children made a Red Sea to his Moses. Scuffing at grass with one shoe toe, Adams said, muffled so those on the rim of the clearing came in farther to hear, "Wonder—you'd mind—would you start her up?"

Once more Toll Ambridge's eyes fixed on Journey's. Journey gave a nod.

"Heehap," Toll said. "All chirren stand aside." He and Journey walked toward the car. At the radiator they bent together. Toll gripped the crank handle. His eyes interrogated, urged Journey to know his luck. Journey's slid away.

Toll whirled the crank. Cords whipped out on his brown arms. His back muscles lifted. The engine turned, and again; there was a ruffling noise, a hen with iron wing feathers. Sweat laced down Journey's face. Something was happening to him. Going to make a fool of himself. He wanted to cling to something; wanted it unchanged. He bent beside the right front wheel; through wooden spokes varnished long ago, each big as his wrist, he could see Linda's legs. He had Linda, and Marla Jean, and Ferdy. Wife and daughter and son and dogs, and a middling farm. And good honey. A man wanted to keep all he had, no matter how unshiny.

He shouldered Toll. "Let a man in." He had his hand on the crank handle. This time the engine caught, and Toll ran around to set the spark. Sweat dripping as though he had run miles at noonday, Journey leaned against the radiator. Through warming brass he felt the vibrations. Air swarmed with sound. Power went through his finger tips as though he touched a hurricane. The yard was full of neighbors. They were listening, crowding, not speaking. Old man Methan Whittle hunched over, eyes glittering like a crow's. His staff—maybe it wasn't a true legend, didn't bloom in the moon's dark, but Journey couldn't believe it didn't—supported his hand, knuckles hard as ivory.

Adams was shouting right at Journey's ear. Waving a green slip of paper. He stopped, wrote on the paper, waved it, shouting again. His glasses hung from an ear. Journey brushed around the car; was on the step, had reached in, turned off the ignition, all in one motion.

In the silence a bird called from high up. Anyone could hear a drop of sweat roll from Journey's nose, splash on the once fire-red paint of the hood. Anyone could hear the scratch of the fountain pen while Adams finished writing. He was using a fender for desk. He poked the check under Journey's eyes. "There. Two thousand dollars. Stand willing to make it more."

But Journey's fingers stayed where they were. He heard himself speaking, and marveled. Paint a barn! Get a new barn for that money. Have enough left over to buy a horse. Perfumes and dresses for Linda. For the chaps play pretties, easing of their lives all round. Yet he said the words. "Reckon not. Won't sell 'er. Won't do you no good t' ask me no more." After a moment: "I'm purely sorry," he added.

He could tell from Adams' eyes; Adams believed him. And not able to look at Linda, or his children, or even Toll, Journey slid down from the car, went walking toward his house. *Shouldn't hate Adams. Only man to blame is named Journey.* He went in, slamming the door.

His hand found the coffee can on the high shelf and brought it down. He counted bills. Two dollars. And silver: eighty cents.

Outside again in sun he couldn't see well for a moment. Then the green spots lifted and all the neighbors were still there. Some looked toward him, then others. Close by on the path, Linda waited; with her were the chaps. Marla Jean smiled up, a way girl-children had; he couldn't tell anything from Linda's face. She had a right to say whatever she would. He wouldn't stop her. Ferdy stepped forward.

"Yay, pa—pa, he started back up. Reckon I'd ought to go after him? I c'd steer him over t' the old trail. Longer but easier goin'. Daresome climb fer a fat man, where he is now." Ferdy's lips quivered as if he'd like to laugh but shouldn't. Excitement; strangeness.

Journey nodded. "You do that. Here, though. Take this here with you. Give it to 'im." As Ferdy turned in a bony-jawed flash, lump of money tight in his fist, Journey called: "Certain sure he takes it! I owe it to 'im! Sure now!"

The boy streaked away, was gone under tangles of gumwood shadow. Journey went down the path. He put a hand on Linda's shoulder. It felt cool through the cloth. But he couldn't look at her eyes. He would later. They went along together. Marla Jean danced ahead, then stopped, kept back by the ring of people around the car. They had all knotted in now, standing close.

Puzzlement showed in Journey's eyes. Here was young Toll Ambridge, old Toll; both stooping beside the car. Very little noise; rustle of a garment from time to time; snip of plug tobacco sheared off by a thin knife. There was Methan Whittle, quartet of sons surrounding him, on a basswood stump close to the headlamps. His eyes were points of fire staring at Journey. His hands were knobbed around his oak stick.

But Journey didn't know what it was about. Not until old Whittle lifted a hand to point. His voice was a breeze through thorns, but packed with power.

"There she stands. A bag o' gold, he offered, an' promised to go higher. There she stands, the miracle car."

Young Toll on the other side of the circle took it up in his rumbling bass. His eyes were star-struck like the eyes of the rest. The hounds stood alert, only the tips of their tails alive and motioning. "Ain't no other car that old in history wu'th it. Hits the one and only."

"Ah, ah, ah," sang Mag Whittle, old Methan's oldest daughter. She lifted her baby, its face full of sun, the better to show it this thing. "Look on it, feast on it, honey. Look on Journey's miracle car, handed him by his daddy."

"Only one in the world today," somebody said. "Now it is proved and settled."

"Owned by our Journey. A wonder and a glory."

Then he knew. He would always have it now. Dimly, past the passion of wonder and ownership that controlled him as he walked to lay a finger on the brass radiator, he felt a wish that all men alive could have a mystery. He now had his. Sun bounced from the radiator and got lost in Linda's hair and when he looked full at her she was smiling with pride like his own.

I CAN TAKE CARE OF MYSELF

by Fred McMorrow

Georgia wasn't there when Bert walked in at nine-thirty, but he didn't say anything about it. He just walked to the bar and had a black coffee and a brandy.

At nine forty-five he took his seat at the piano to begin his fifteen-minute set, just like any other night, just as if Georgia would come right in on cue at ten o'clock as she always had.

Joey Palermo, the owner, looked at Bert anxiously, then he looked at the clock over the bar, then back at Bert again. But Bert did not return his glance.

It was still early, but Bert could feel the kind of crowd it was. It was a Miss Otis crowd, the kind that does not bother you with stupid requests, does not ask you to let Cousin Charlie here play your piano, and does not just sit there and drink either.

They were there only for Georgia and Bert. Of course, Joey would be worrying. The room had been dying when they had come to him for a tryout and now, three months later, they were in Winchell and Lyons and The New Yorker.

There were eight minutes to go and Bert was going through a second chorus of I Concentrate when Joey came up and stood in front of him. Bert's touch lightened and his foot moved over on the soft pedal so Joey could talk.

"What happened?" Joey said.

"I don't know what happened," Bert said. It was not entirely true because he had a pretty good idea what had happened.

"Well, is she going to be here or isn't she?" Joey said.

"Don't worry about it," Bert said.

"I'll try, I'll try," Joey said, and walked away.

Four minutes.

Bert went into Blues in Three, the special material he had worked out for Georgia's opener. He would just ball a blues in three flats and she would come on, singing her way through the tables and end it on her perch in front of his piano.

When he hit the B-flat chord that was her cue, nothing happened. The electrician pulled the rheostats down gently, not so anybody but Georgia would notice, but still nothing happened. Quickly, Bert cut into a key change and a chipper fingering of Nice Work and the lights subtly went all the way up again.

He could feel them getting nervous. He looked up and down the room. Near the door a big, beefy guy who had to be a cop was talking to Joey. Joey ushered the man to a table and came toward Bert. Bert wound up the number and arose. The applause was mild and just a little edgy.

"Bert," Joey said miserably, "you better go talk to that guy."

"What's he want?" Bert said.

"I don't know," Joey said. "He wouldn't tell me. But I know it's going to be something bad, real bad. I can feel it, Bert. You know?"

"Listen, Joey," Bert said. "Now listen carefully. I don't care how you feel. Stop showing it, Joey, if you know what's good for you and me and Georgia. I mean it, Joey. You know how *they* are."

"They? Who's *they*?" Joey said, paling.

"I don't have to draw you a picture," Bert said. "And look—

you've got to have somebody to cover for us. I know Andy and Alice are looking for work and I know you can get them."

"Now? Right now?" Joey said.

"Right now," Bert said. "Here"—and he fished his address book out of his wallet—"you'll find them in here. Give them a call."

"Gee, I don't know," Joey said.

"They'll be all right," Bert said. "They can get here in fifteen minutes. It's the only thing you can do."

"Aw, cheese, this is going to kill me," Joey said.

"Get on the phone," Bert said. "Don't worry about it. They'll be all right."

The big man did not get up when Bert went to his table. "Are you Bert Haber?"

"Maybe. Who are you?"

"Detective Jack Burton. Manhattan East. Are you acquainted with——"

"Let's see a badge or something, first, chief. Not that way! Hand it to me under the table."

Bert felt the detective's sunburst on the little badge, without looking at it. He passed it back.

"All right," he said. "I'm Bert Haber."

"Are you acquainted"—and the detective pulled a little folder with a photograph in it from his breast pocket—"with that woman?"

Bert looked at it and shut his eyes tight and threw it back as if it were something to be loathed.

"Yes," he said finally. "Did you have to do it that way?"

"There wasn't any other way," the detective said. "We haven't made any positive identification yet and all we could do under the circumstances was to photograph the face, right there."

"Where?" Bert said. "Where!"

Burton consulted a notebook. "An alleyway between two multiple dwellings of tenement residence, on West 55th Street between Ninth and Tenth avenues. Did she live in that neighborhood?"

"No," Bert said. "When was she found?"

"Now that's a good question," the detective said.

"What do you mean by that?"

"I don't know," the detective said expressionlessly. "Maybe you know. What do I mean, Mr. Haber?"

"Oh," Bert said. "I see. Look. I know I seem to be taking all this just as if I knew it would happen. Well, I did, but I didn't know when, or where, or—how."

"You can account for your movements, then, between the time you left here last night and when I came in just now?"

"Yes, I can. From here, I took Georgia home——"

"Did you usually do that? Where did she live? When was it, exactly, when you saw her last?"

"I had to do it the last couple of weeks," Bert said. "Somebody had to do it. She lived on East 61st, just two blocks north of here. I last saw her at four-oh-one A.M. I remember by the clock in the lobby of her building."

"That's kind of early, isn't it? I mean, these places don't close until four and it would take you more than a minute to——"

"Yes, it was early," Bert said. "But I felt kind of responsible for her. The last couple of weeks, I always got her out of here long before Joey closed so it wouldn't be conspicuous. There's always a lot of business just before closing and nobody notices somebody leaving."

The detective sat back and folded his arms and nodded. Joey came over. "It's all right," he said. "They were home. They said they'll be right over. They said to thank you."

"They're welcome," Bert said. He noted with annoyance that now that another girl and another piano player were coming, Joey seemed relieved, as if nothing had happened to Georgia. But then, Joey didn't know. Well, let him read the papers.

"Can I offer you gentlemen a drink, anything?" Joey said.

The detective shook his head.

"Ask Bill to give me a double rye on the rocks," Bert said. Georgia's drink. He thought of playing Make It Another Old-

Fashioned for her. Leave out the orange, leave out the cherry——

"No," Bert said. "Just make it a straight rye."

"Sure, Bert, sure," Joey said, and hurried to the bar.

"Listen," Bert said to the detective, "I went straight home from her place and I slept until six tonight, and then I tried to get her on the phone. It just kept ringing."

"That was at six o'clock?" the detective said, putting it down in the notebook.

"I wish you wouldn't do that," Bert said.

"Do what?"

Bert leaned forward and took the big man's arm.

"They know what happened because *they* did it. Now don't you think *they're* around here, keeping an eye on me, what do I know about it?"

The detective studied him, then folded up the notebook and put it away.

"I guess you're clean," Burton said. "Tell me about this—this feeling responsible for her. When did all that start?"

"Well, actually, I always feel responsible for a girl I'm working with," Bert said. "You don't know what it's like, playing these joints and watching these jerks get three drinks into them and turn into Rock Hudson. They think they're paying for it, the girl's their property."

"There's something you'll have to tell me," Burton said. "Did you ever have relations with this woman?"

Bert smiled. "In a way nobody else ever could," he said. "When I sat at that piano and she really sang it out, and they all shut up to listen, and she looked at me and I looked at her—yes, I guess you'd say there was a relationship there. But that's all it was. All music. Am I making any sense?"

"I mean, you weren't sleeping with her?"

"No."

"Did you ever want to?"

"Don't be silly. Who wouldn't want to?"

"Did you ever try?"

6

"No."

"Why not?"

"Well, I'm funny about those things. There's only one of the Aesop's Fables I ever remembered and that was the one about the goose that laid the golden egg. Or was that in Mother Goose?"

"Mr. Haber," Burton said, "we have reason to believe it was Little Sammy."

"What reason?"

"The way she looked. What they did to her."

"Yes. I saw that in the picture. Yes. God!"

"Did she know Little Sammy?"

"Doesn't everybody?"

"Well, I mean, did she——"

"I know what you mean! No."

The waiter brought the drink and Bert let half of it sear away the hell that was rising in his throat. He toyed with the muddler and thought, *Poor, regimented Bill. Some bartender. He'd put a muddler in a drink even when there was nothing to stir but pure whisky. Poor Bill.*

"Did she ever meet Little Sammy?"

"Yes."

"You want to tell me about it?"

"No. But I have to, don't I?"

"Yes."

"All right. I told you, it was a couple of weeks ago. We had just started this room really going. Did you ever hear her sing?"

"No. Specifically what night was it she met Little Sammy?"

"The eleventh. I remember I bought a paper on the way home and it was the first time we were in Winchell. May I never forget that miserable night as long as I live."

"What was so miserable about it?"

"Sammy was here all night. As soon as I started my first set I saw him and his gorillas sitting right over there. I went into Blues in Three. That's her opener—that *was* her opener—and right away, when she made her entrance, I could see him sweating from the eyeballs."

"Did he do anything wrong?"

"Oh, no, not right away," Bert said. "He was a perfect doll. He kept sending drinks over to us all night. The next day she got this big basket of flowers at her apartment. I don't know how he got the address."

"They have ways," the detective said.

"And that night he was there again, only then he started moving in."

"And you felt responsible for her?"

"Yes," Bert said. "Look. If she liked the guy I couldn't care less, but she couldn't stand the crumb. In this business you learn all kinds of gimmicks to stop guys like that, but nothing stopped him. At the end, there she was openly insulting him. And then there was last night."

"And?"

"And everything," Bert said. "She was passing his table to go and change. He grabbed her arm like she was one of his tomatoes. She took his drink and poured it down his shirt."

"I see," the detective said. "Yes, that would start him off. He's a bedbug about his clothes."

"I didn't help any, I guess," Bert said. "You know what I did? I started playing By a Waterfall. What a laugh it got. Everybody saw it. I don't think Bert Lahr ever got a laugh like that, trying. They were still laughing when Sammy and his apes got up and got out of here."

"It all stacks up," the detective said. "One thing this guy can never forgive, it's being laughed at. So you took her right home?"

"Not right away," Bert said. "I was feeling pretty good. Proud of us, you know. I went to the bar and had a drink. There was this guy sitting next to me, just minding his own business. Nice-looking guy, like an insurance man or something. He started talking to me.

"'Are you enjoying yourself?' he said.

" 'Sure, like mad,' I said.

" 'I'm very glad,' the insurance man said. 'That pleases me very much.'

" 'I'm happy for you,' I said. 'Now what'll we talk about?'

" 'There's nothing to make a long conversation about,' the insurance man said. 'You don't have to when you know somebody.'

" 'Buster, I don't know you and right now I don't want to,' I said.

" 'But I know you,' he said. 'You're Bert Haber.'

" 'So?' I said.

" 'And you live on the fourth floor of a walkup on East 54th, and you're only home in the daytime, isn't that right?' the guy said.

" 'What's this all about?' I said. 'I'm not buying any insurance this year, Buster.'

" 'Aren't you?' the guy said. 'I would, if I were you.' And then he reaches out quickly and shakes my hand before I can pull it away. 'I think we understand each other, don't we, Mr. Haber?' he says. Then he leaves. That's how *they* operate, isn't it?"

"Yes," the detective said.

"They don't warn you or threaten you or anything like that."

"They don't have to."

Bert signaled to Bill for another.

"I took her home," he said. "I told her I thought I ought to stay there with her, or maybe she ought to spend the night with me, or call the cops—do something. But she just kissed me good night— oh, God, a real, sweet kiss—and she said, 'Don't you worry, baby. Mamma's a big girl.' "

The detective buttoned his jacket, preparing to go. "I think that gives us a lot to go on, Mr. Haber," he said. "I think we can clean it up pretty quick. One thing. Is there anything we can do for you?"

"Anything like what?"

"Protection."

"No, I don't think so."

"We'll need you as a material witness when we put the arm on him."

"I'll be around."

"Well, we'd like to be sure of that. The case may depend on you."

"Don't worry about it," Bert said. The waiter brought the second drink and he poured it all down at once.

"Mr. Haber," the detective said, "I think you'd better come with me. Seriously, a lot of things could happen and you're very valuable to us."

"Well, for how long?" Bert said.

"I think there's a good chance we can clean it up by morning."

"That fast?" Bert said. "All right, I will."

Andy and Alice were coming in as they were going. Burton waited politely while Andy and Alice thanked Bert for the job. He didn't tell them what had really happened. They could read the papers too.

The detective led Bert to a gray, hard-top car.

"Get in back with my partner," Burton said.

Bert got in without looking at the other man. Burton got into the driver's seat and gunned the car toward the East River Drive. They were moving pretty fast. Bert turned to look at the man in the back seat with him.

"Hello," the insurance man said.

THE DISPLACED MISSILE

by Jacob Hay

"All contact lost," said the bulkhead loudspeaker in the Firing Control Center, its tone detached. "Over and out." There was a silence fraught, as they say, with finality.

"Well," said one of the stricken group standing before the Final Firing Command console, "back to the old drawing board, eh? Looks like Aggie's gone down at sea, poor girl." There was a murmur of assent. At least, Aggie had left the ground, which was, after all, no more than Jupiter C had done. Slowly, gloomily, the stricken group reached for their hats. Aggie was missing, presumed lost, somewhere in the broad Atlantic.

In this presumption the group was in grievous error. At precisely 3:52 A.M., Eastern Standard Time, Sgt. Jere Emspacher, of the Dexter, Pennsylvania, City Police, became the first man in history to see at close range the Agamemnon Mark XI Intercontinental Ballistic Missile perform an emergency landing.

"All of a sudden," Sergeant Emspacher later told the Dexter Dispatch, "there was this real bright light, oncet, and then come this wonderful big noise, like it was one of them jet planes; still, only much louder; so I looked up, and that's when I run."

It is as well that Sergeant Emspacher ran when he did, finding refuge in the concrete staircase leading to the Crystal Lunch, in the basement of the Bauer Building on the southwest corner of Continental Square, Dexter's hub. As he cringed there, a titanic cylinder settled slowly down from the heavens upon a roaring, white-hot pillar of fire to sink its huge tail fins gently into the boiling, bubbling pool of asphalt which had, until seconds before, been the surface of the square. Abruptly, the great gush of flame which spread thunderously out around it like the train of some monstrous ball gown died, to be replaced by a tremendous cloud of thick gray smoke. Then slowly, very slowly, as one of the giant fins found a softer subsurface than its fellows, the cylinder inclined its towering bulk six degrees in the general direction of Harrisburg. And stopped, its polished white shell gleaming eerily in the pale glow of the smoke-shrouded street lights, its nose cone ten stories up in the air and roughly on a level with the top floor of the Hotel Phineas Dexter, the tallest building in town. Aggie, her poor brain a hash of electronic hysteria, had arrived. In this wise began the ordeal of Dexter, Pennsylvania.

It was purest chance which made Mike Brewer, city editor of the Dexter Dispatch, the second man on the scene. He'd been wandering, lonely as a cloud and wretched as a wet hen, ever since Miss Betsy Watkins had told him firmly, just before she kissed him good night, that she would positively refuse to marry him if he persisted in his mad plan to assail New York, rather than stay on in Dexter and take over her father's newspaper. His first reaction to Aggie was, in consequence, to wonder if he was not unhinged by love. He took a second long, long look and reason returned. Then he headed for the Dispatch city room as fast as his rangy legs could run.

At which moment Dexter's air-raid-warning system went into action. Sergeant Emspacher had seen his duty and done it. And all hell broke loose.

It reflects no discredit upon the municipal administration of Dexter to state that thereafter chaos reigned. It is your rare third-class city which is prepared to cope with a ten-story missile set squarely in its center. Within minutes, roughly one half of Dexter's population was attempting to reach the square to see what went on, while the other, equally determined half sought refuge in the hills. Suffice it to say that by 5:00 A.M., the city had taken what steps it could to protect itself, although from what was not entirely clear.

It was at 5:04 A.M., that Aggie began the first of what was to become a series of nerve-rasping gurgles. Aggie went: "Blurp." And from high up her polished flank there wisped a thin jet of what might have been condensing oxygen or something no one cared to think about too deeply.

The Hotel Phineas Dexter was now evacuated right down to old Mrs. Whittigham, who had to be bundled into her electric wheelchair by force.

"The hell with the Kaiser!" Mrs. Whittigham kept yelling, with great bitterness.

And in the Dispatch city room, Mike Brewer was repeating, almost hopelessly, into his telephone, "I have not been drinking, confound it! As soon as I can get a decent print developed, I'll put it on the wire and you can see for yourself!"

"Ha!" replied the Amalgamated Press bureau chief in Harrisburg sternly. "What's all that racket?"

"The Red Cross Motor Corps!" Mike cried above the cacophony of horns which now arose from the street below. "They're conducting an emergency mobilization, only I think the Boy Scouts are in the way. Or maybe it's the Girl Scouts."

"Boy Scouts!" the bureau chief roared. "Girl Scouts!"

"Maybe it's the Loyal Order of Moose," Mike said irritably, "but somebody's setting up a field hospital." And hung up. He decided to return to Continental Square.

There he found the Hon. Leon Gladfelter, mayor of Dexter, who was in a pitiable state. "I just called the governor," he told Mike. "He told me to go home and sober up. What are we going to do, Mike? Stand around and wait for that thing to fall over or blow up? This is somebody's missile. We've got to find out whose, and then make them come and take it away."

"There ought to be some sort of night duty officer at the Pentagon," Mike suggested, peering down at his rotund honor.

"We'll use my office," the mayor said. "If I'm going to be blasted to bits, I want to be at my post."

"Graackkk," Aggie rattled briskly. "Gurk."

"Maybe," Mike said, "we'd better hurry."

"Major Nurney here," said the night duty officer at the Pentagon some minutes later. "You say your name is Brewer and you're calling from where?" Briefly, Mike outlined the situation and heard with dismay the major's muffled aside: "Some of these crank U.F.O. calls sure make you wonder, don't they, corporal?" Then, in soothing tones, the major advised Mike to put the pertinent details in a letter, noting times and compass directions, with names of other witnesses, if any. Then the major hung up.

At 5:45 A.M., the first wire photos from the Dispatch reached Harrisburg, and Mike found time to call Miss Betsy Watkins. "You're not to come in to work today," he ordered firmly, picturing her blond hair still tousled from sleep. "We've got enough women's features to make up your page, so stay home. In fact, stay down in the cellar."

"I'll be with you in fifteen minutes," Miss Watkins told him with like firmness.

Mike grinned and shrugged; Miss Betsy Watkins had a mind of her own, which was probably why he loved her, now he came to think of it. He went back once more to the square.

By now, most of the central portion of the city had been evacuated, and the square was almost deserted, except for a cluster of city officials gathered by the stairs to the Crystal Lunch.

"We've got to find out who owns it," Mayor Gladfelter was saying as Mike approached. "The city solicitor's on the phone to Washington right now, trying to get some action. But nobody's up yet."

At 6:15 A.M., the world learned of Dexter's plight. The Harrisburg bureau chief had seen the pictures and acted in the highest tradition of his news service. And Betsy Watkins arrived, storming past the police barricades in a flurry of flying skirts, blond hair and press passes. At the South George Street entrance to the square she stopped in her tracks, her sea-green eyes appalled at the spectacle which greeted them. For while she had seen Aggie from afar, the bulk of the Colonial Insurance Building had concealed the Dexter Fire Department's proudest possession, its extention-ladder truck, ladder erect and fully extended, and leaning within inches of Aggie's gleaming shell. Perched at the very top was the lank figure of Mike Brewer, horn-rimmed glasses glinting in the sun.

"It says here," Mike called from his dizzy altitude, " 'Keep Away From Fire'! And that's all it says, except 'Handle With Care'!" He began the long climb down to street level.

"H'm'm'm," Aggie murmured restively. "Zisk. Tic-tic."

"Oh, no," Betsy Watkins prayed. "Please, heaven, not now."

"I just don't get it," Mike said, when he'd rejoined the band of officials by the stairs. "You'd think there'd be some sign as to who owns it: Army, Navy or Air Force."

"I think I can answer that one," said City Solicitor Walter deHoff, joining the group. "And I think we're in worse trouble than we figured. I've just been on the phone to the Pentagon, and they've finally admitted that a missile was fired from a secret Navy testing ground—just where they won't say. But here's the rub: It was a new missile, ultra-top secret, developed by the Air Force. But get this: The actual firing was done by a highly specialized Army team."

"So?" inquired Mayor Gladfelter.

"So," replied Solicitor deHoff wearily, "nobody will admit anything. In fact, they absolutely refuse to acknowledge that this one —our missile, that is—is the one they fired this morning. But assuming that it is, the Navy says it's the Air Force's baby, and the Air Force says the Army fired it, so it's the Army's problem. That was after I told them we were only thirty-odd miles from Gettysburg as the crow flies."

"But weren't they even the least little bit curious to know if this mightn't really be their rocket?" Betsy Watkins asked tentatively from her position just behind Mike.

"This close to Gettysburg?" Solicitor deHoff laughed harshly.

Mike's dark eyes were thoughtful behind his glasses. "It may take them days to untangle the security regulations. Meantime, we may all get blown to smithereens. We've got to jolt those people loose, and fast. And maybe I've got the answer. . . . Your honor, will you and Solicitor deHoff join me in a slight conference?"

And bowing courteously, the three men withdrew in the direction of City Hall, leaving Miss Betsy Watkins staring, more than slightly annoyed, at a poster affixed to the door of the Crystal Lunch announcing that the Dexter Little Theater Workshop would present An Evening With Chekhov in the auditorium of the William Penn Senior High School the following Tuesday night.

By 8:00 A.M. nearly every available extra room in the suburbs of Dexter had been rented by the swiftly gathering horde of newsmen, and by 9:00 A.M., the first of the foreign military observers had arrived. Emergency feeding stations had been set up in the basements of four suburban churches to accommodate *évacués* from the central-city area, and Dexter's two radio stations were transmitting disaster instructions at regular intervals.

The state police had begun rerouting traffic via back roads completely around the threatened city, and the governor had twice called the mayor to demand just what the devil was going on. Told, the governor had replied coldly that the Federal Government had got itself into this mess and the Federal Government would have to get itself out.

Mayor Gladfelter called a conference of the press for that afternoon in City Hall.

And Aggie was now producing a noise that sounded like "Thunktik," every fifteen minutes. The tiny feather of escaping gas had vanished, to be replaced by a thin trickle of pinkish liquid which ran down her slanting side and formed an ominous, slowly widening pool in the seared and buckled asphalt of the square.

Over Miss Betsy Watkins' strenuous protests, Mike Brewer isolated himself in his office and made a number of mysterious phone calls. In response to Betsy's questions, the Dispatch's switchboard operator could say only that most of the calls were to various of the city's undertakers. "Looks like he's getting set for the worst," the operator declared morosely.

At 1:00 p.m., in the basement of City Hall, the press assembled in the brilliantly lighted, tile-walled chamber that normally did duty as the Police Department's drunk tank. News cameras whirred, flash bulbs flared and cameramen leaped nimbly here and there, the correspondents muttering irritably at their antics. Mayor Gladfelter rapped for order. This was his finest hour.

In brisk, businesslike tones, his honor informed the press and the world that since the Department of Defense refused to acknowledge ownership of the object in Continental Square, he, Leon Gladfelter, acting on the advice of his city solicitor, did now declare said object to be the property of the city of Dexter. Further, the mayor continued, by virtue of the authority vested in his office, he had appointed Michael Brewer, a resident of the city, as agent for the municipality in the matter of disposing of the aforesaid object. Already, the mayor concluded, Mr. Brewer had received interested queries from several foreign governments.

There was an instant's stunned silence, and then a great hoot of incredulous laughter as the press corps broke ranks and stampeded for the nearest exits to report the first word of what was quickly to become known as Gladfelter's Glorious Goof, thanks to an unknown metropolitan headline writer.

In all fairness, it must be stated that the Department of Defense had not been inactive meanwhile. Four separate boards had been established to ascertain the circumstances surrounding the firing of the Agamemnon Mark XI ICBM. The Secretary of the Air Force had spoken bluntly to the Secretary of the Navy, who had just finished a rather distant conversation with the Secretary of the Army. The Secretary of Defense, for his part, had simply said: "I want action, and I want it fast." But his decision had to be delivered through the proper channels, and this, as it is widely known, takes time.

So, all through the first long day, an anxious world waited edgily for word that Dexter had gone to glory in one titanic burst of flaming rocket fuel and exploding steel. The Chicago Star-Times was first on the streets with the news that Aggie was now going "Tik-thunk" instead of "Thunk-tik." The Kansas City Eagle through its staff correspondent on the scene, estimated that some fifty gallons of the pinkish liquid seeping from Aggie's innards now lay in the puddle in the square. A thin, unwholesome mist appeared to be rising from the puddle, the Eagle's man reported, and it had an aroma not unlike that of salted peanuts.

Only the late editions of the afternoon papers carried the story of Dexter's plan to sell its unwanted missile. The tone of their stories was generally snide. The city's agent, a man named Brewer, could not even be located to say which foreign governments were interested. The Department of Defense had no comment.

A White House spokesman hinted that the whole thing was a hoax, and later redefined this statement to indicate that, while it might not be a hoax, the incident was not in very good taste. A still later statement repudiated the first two and declared that the matter was under study, pending a full report from all agencies.

And Dexter became a beleaguered city as the curious, heedless of the potential danger, came in their legions to camp on lawns, in farmyards, in garages and in the fields, and waited, palms sweaty and eyes gleaming, for Aggie to blow up. Hawkers of plastic space helmets for children did a thriving trade, and bookmakers profited briskly as the betting on Dexter's survival fluctuated.

From Dexter that night there moved separately and by various routes a number of large, black, highly polished limousines, to assemble in the darkened streets of a village some twenty-odd miles to the south and away from the main highways. There, in the pleasantly old-fashioned lobby of The Merchants' House, their occupants were addressed by Mike Brewer, who'd spent the afternoon and evening dodging the press.

"Come straight in from the south," Mike told his listeners. "As if you were coming up from Washington. The city police will give you an escort at the edge of town. Drive straight into the square. Drivers remain by your cars and look mean."

"You're sure that thing won't blow up, Mike?" asked Mr. Stephen Littleton, professional director of the Dexter Little Theater Workshop.

"I'm not sure of anything," Mike replied, shoving an angry hand through his crew-cut black hair. "But we've got to get some action before something does happen. You gents are the bait, I hope. I figure something will happen when the Pentagon sees pictures of you characters fiddling around one of their top-secret babies."

"Don't fiddle too hard," cautioned Mr. Albert Small, senior partner of Small & Horn, Morticians. "That kind of business I don't want, believe me."

"That's it, then, gents," Mike concluded. "Now let's have a beer, relax and get a good night's rest."

After which he headed back to the city to spend the remainder of the night at the Watkins residence, where the guest bedroom offered sanctuary of a sort from the searching newspapermen.

The next day broke sparkling clear, the sun's rays flashed blindingly off Aggie's metal sheathing, and a man in Mt. View, Pennsylvania, a few miles to the north, reported that he could plainly see the giant missile's nose cone towering prominently in the skyline, as tall as the steeple of the First Presbyterian Church.

From the roof of the Hotel Phineas Dexter, by special permit of the mayor, television cameras brought the day's first view of Aggie into the homes of countless millions of Americans at their breakfast.

At his own hasty breakfast, shared with Miss Betsy Watkins, Mike wondered for the thousandth time whether the volunteers from the Dexter Little Theater Workshop were up to the tasks he had imposed upon them. Those faked license plates, for example; they must be absolutely perfect.

At 9:30 A.M., of that second day, Police Chief Amos Koons personally arrested the newly arrived correspondent of the Soviet news agency, Tass, a gentleman named Urbanov, on a charge of violating Dexter City Ordinance No. 112, as passed by the selectmen of Dextertowne and approved by the Honorable Proprietors of His Britannic Majesty's Colony of Pennsylvania in June of 1742, which expressly "forbyds anye person from smokynge a tobaccoe pype or seegar within four-score yards of anye house of worshype." Mr. Urbanov was confined, and a hearing set for late that afternoon. His presence anywhere near the square, Mike had felt, would be most undesirable, if not indeed fatal to his scheme.

At 9:45 A.M., Mike stood with Betsy near the steps leading down to the Crystal Lunch, which had become Dexter's forward command post. He held her hand in a grip of iron. Across the square, a gaggle of correspondents spotted them and, skirting swiftly around Aggie's fins, headed in their direction. Seconds later, the two were surrounded by the press, bellowing questions.

"Gentlemen, please!" Mike shouted over the uproar, which died sullenly. "I've nothing to say at this time, but I'm expecting, almost any minute now, a development which may clear up this whole ugly mess! In the meantime, I must ask you to clear the square!"

"That is, git," said Police Chief Amos Koons, approaching meaningfully. "I got ordinances I ain't used in years, if you follow my meaning. You guys are supposed to be up on the roof of the Phineas Dexter, anyhow."

The square was cleared, but not without some strongly worded protests, and for at least one edition, the Montreal Commercial carried the headline: HICK EDITOR TERRORIZES STRICKEN CITY.

At precisely 10:00 A.M., a cortege of six black limousines drove into Dexter from the south, passed smoothly up South George Street behind a Dexter City police escort, sirens screaming, and swept splendidly into Continental Square to dispose itself in a kind of phalanx facing Aggie's southernmost fin. As one engine, the engines of all stopped, and from each limousine sprang a uniformed chauffeur. From the limousines there then emerged a company of men garbed in drab gray and solid black ankle-length overcoats. Some wore broad-brimmed black fedoras, while others affected shaggy fur caps of that style so popular in Moscow, Leningrad, Kiev and points east. The entire company of An Evening With Chekhov had arrived.

Mike walked slowly across the square and gravely shook hands with the tallest of the new arrivals. "Nice timing, Steve," he told the director of the Dexter Little Theater Workshop, magnificent in a crepe beard. "We've got the press corps watching us like hawks. The bait's in the trap, so let's put the show on the road."

Immediately, the group broke up. From the trunk of one limousine were produced a surveyor's tripod and transit, and, this being set up, several of the company began making rapid but precise measurements of Aggie's dimensions. Others produced cameras, while still others flashed slide rules and other engineering instruments. Some merely made notes. Steve Littleton and Mike continued in deep conversation, occasionally nodding enthusiastic agreement.

On the roof of the Hotel Phineas Dexter there was general agreement that the District of Columbia Diplomatic Corps license plates —as reproduced by Steve Littleton's scenery-and-properties committee—could only belong to the Russian embassy, although there were those who held out for the Czechs or Poles. So engrossed were one and all by the scene, such was the whir of newsreel cameras and the uproar of conversation that what then ensued came as something of a surprise.

Mike's scheme was working better than he realized. Even as he and Steve Littleton went through their elaborate pantomime, a thunderous roaring filled the morning skies over Dexter, growing and growing until the city seemed buried beneath a flood of sheer, overpowering noise.

At exactly 10:21 A.M., Dexter, Pennsylvania, became the first city in the United States to experience a successful vertical envelopment by helicopter. Combat Command Williamson, United States Marine Corps, had the situation well in hand.

The drunk tank in the basement of City Hall was packed to bursting with various members of the Dexter Little Theater Workshop and the city's mortuary profession. Mike Brewer was in solitary, and Betsy Watkins was in hysterics in the Mayor's office upstairs. Continental Square bristled with machine guns, mortars, recoilless artillery and assorted marines, led by Col. Henry (Bulldog) Williamson, liberator of Pingo-Pango and other islands too numerous to mention.

Not until 11:15 A.M., was Betsy permitted to visit Mike, who looked somewhat rumpled in consequence of his having attempted to reason with a number of purposeful marines. "I'll wait for you, Mike, darling," were her first tearful words as she flung herself against the bars which confined her fiancé. They embraced tenderly, albeit with difficulty and to the unconcealed dismay of the marine corporal on guard, who said, "Hey!"

From an adjacent cell, City Solicitor Walter deHoff and Mayor Leon Gladfelter watched tolerantly. "Nice youngsters, Leon," said the city solicitor. "At least, we gave it the old college try."

"You wait, Walter," Mayor Gladfelter sputtered. "I'll take this incident right up to the Supreme Court."

"And I, for one, wouldn't blame you, gentlemen." An imposing

figure in the uniform of a fleet admiral had appeared in the basement. . . . "Corporal, release these people at once. . . . And
please accept my apologies, all of you. Colonel Williamson was
only doing his job as he saw it, you understand."

The admiral walked to stand before Mike's cell. "Ahem," he
coughed tactfully as the two young people faced him. "A very cred-
itable and ingenious scheme, young man, very. We tend to overdo
this security business every now and then, and maybe you've taught
us a lesson. Your announcement that you'd found a buyer for Aggie
brought more action than I've seen around the Pentagon in years.
But now, let's go upstairs and perhaps the mayor can find us all a
nice, hot cup of coffee, eh? Been quite a morning, all in all." And
the admiral chuckled jovially. "We'll have Aggie out of your hair,
or should I say square, by midnight tonight."

Barely a week later, Mike and Betsy stood by the stairs to the Crystal Lunch, gazing out across the newly repaved surface of the area
where Aggie had reared her monstrous, beautiful and deadly bulk.
A yellow moon shone down upon a scene of near-perfect peace:
A group of youthful motorcyclists preparing for a wild ride through
the moonlit countryside; Sgt. Jere Emspacher preparing to arrest
them; a hopelessly lost motorist cursing helplessly at the lack of
directional signs and bidding his wife shut up. Dexter had returned
to normal.

"I'm so proud of you, Mike," Betsy murmured. "All those New
York papers calling you the editor who licked the Space Age." And
she hugged his arm tighter than before, which was no small achievement.

"This isn't a bad town," Mike said quietly. "I'm kind of proud
of it, in fact. I think I'll stick around. Forever, I hope."

"You know," said Mayor Leon Gladfelter, who had approached
without their being aware of him, "I'm kind of going to miss the
old girl. She put Dexter to the test, and Dexter did pretty well, I
think. And she sure put us on the map, didn't she?"

"It could have been the other way around," Mike grinned. "But I guess that's progress of a sort."

And far, far away to the south, at an isolated and secret naval missile-testing station on the Carolina coast, stood a giant shape, bathed in the harsh glare of floodlights. In the concrete Final Firing Control blockhouse, a tense group listened to the loud-speaker on the bulkhead as the final count-down for the launching of the Agamemnon Mark XII Intercontinental Ballistic Missile reached zero. Their fingers were neatly crossed.

THE PELICAN THAT
HATED TO DIVE

by Don Tracy

Pomeroy sat on a buoy, feeling sorry for himself. It was a new frame of mind for Pomeroy; until very recently he had been one of the brashest, most obnoxious personalities on the west coast of Florida. He had started being difficult the moment he had found out what he had been christened.

"Why ain't my name Pete?" he had squawked shrilly, at the time. "Every other pelican in the world is named Pete, man, woman or child, and what do I get hung on me? Pom-er-oooy!"

"It," said his momma, "is distinctive."

"You ain't just whistlin' Dixie," Pomeroy said rudely.

"Well, it could have been worse," his father offered in consolation. "I, personally, put my foot down on Percival, not to mention Philemon."

"But why anything but Pete?" Pomeroy moaned.

"It's this way," poppa had explained. "Your mother happens to be the first pelicaness since the dawn of history who had so much time on her hands——"

"No such thing," his momma had said.

"——that she could lie around the nest dreaming up pretty names for you. Your mother's a romanticist, my boy, and there's nothing that can be done about it. I know; I've tried. So I'm afraid you're stuck with Pomeroy."

And indeed he was. During his pinfeather days on Spindrift Key he tried to convince his young pals that his real name was Pete like everybody else's, that this crazy Pomeroy thing was a mother's fancy. He got nowhere. After all, a bird could beat up on his playmates just so long before he had to quit from sheer wing weariness and, invariably, as soon as he took a breather there came again the yodeling cry of "Yoo-hoo, Pom-er-oooy!" and another fight was on.

The young pelicans on the other keys got into the act. Let Pomeroy try to escape the hard time at home by sneaking next door and he would be greeted by a storm of yoo-hoos and a flurry of mincing wing flaps that required satisfaction. He grew up to be a battle-scarred boy, but the name stuck.

And take the matter of fishing. The first time Pomeroy was taken on a community fishing trip, he and the other youngsters were told to watch how it was done. So Pomeroy watched as poppa, cruising at a hundred feet, unaccountably folded his wings and plummeted straight down. Horrified, the boy bird watched the Old Man hit the water with a horrendous splash.

"Did he complain of feelin' bad?" the lad hollered to momma. "Did he ever have his blood pressure——"

"Don't be alarmed, dear," momma said. "Poppa is merely having lunch."

"This is havin' lunch?" Pomeroy gulped.

The sight of poppa emerging from beneath the waves with a mackerel in his bill failed to reassure Pomeroy. Nor did the fact that other pelicans—momma, the neighbors and even his own dear little playmates—made similar high dives for fish make him feel any better. He noticed that all the pelicans, young and old, shook their heads dazedly when they surfaced. That didn't look good.

"Merely to tenderize the fish," momma explained.

"It looks like they're punchy," Pomeroy muttered.

"Nonsense," momma said briskly. "Of course, at the very first you might feel a slight jar when you strike the water, but it's nothing, really. There's a school of fish. Try it."

"I have to?"

"It's customary," poppa smiled. "Especially among those of us who like to eat."

Pomeroy looked down at the fish far below, swallowed hard, shut his eyes and dived. Three or four hours passed while the wind whistled past his ears, almost drowning out the joined juvenile jeer of "There goes Pom-er-oooy!"

Then—whammo!

Momma had mentioned a "slight jar"; to Pomeroy it was as though somebody had brought a baseball bat down on his skull. There was water up his nose and down his throat, but no fish in his bill—and who would be interested in fish, anyway, a second after taking a mule's hind hoof in the face? He rose groggily to the surface and shook his head, trying to tone down the carillon that was pealing in his ears.

"You arched your back a little too much," poppa commented, coming alongside, "but on the whole it was a very passable dive."

"I'm glad you liked it," Pomeroy said bitterly, "because it's the last time I'll ever get conned into a stunt like that. Slight jar!"

Of course they argued with him, taunted him, coaxed and caviled, momma, poppa, the hoary oldsters of the Spindrift Key colony, but it did no good.

"But all pelicans dive for fish!" they cried.

"All pelicans are named Pete, too," Pomeroy returned. "Except one. Me."

He looked shoreward, toward the pier where fishermen from all the forty-eight states and Canada's twelve provinces jostled for elbow-room. "Besides," he added, "those old guys look like they're doin' all right and they ain't goin' off the high board for it either."

Momma and poppa and the others turned their eyes toward the pier and the seven well-fed pelicans that perched on the pilings there, stealing hooked fish. A note of respect approaching awe came into poppa's voice.

"That," he explained, "is The Club."

"So I join The Club," Pomeroy shrugged. "It's that simple."

"Join The Club?" momma asked, aghast. "You don't join The Club, dear. It's very exclusive. You have to be invited, don't you, poppa?"

"Of course," poppa nodded. "The way I understand it, a committee picks one pelican from each colony in the Boca Ciega Bay area every three or four years to stand for membership."

"Every ten years," interjected an elder. "Or is it twenty?"

"Anyway, after the committee looks into the background——"

"It's not that way at all," somebody broke in. "The way I heard it, so many names are put in a hat and——"

"Where do they get the hat?" poppa asked coldly. "And if all the names are Pete what good would that do, anyway?"

An argument developed. At its height, Pomeroy snorted and headed for the pier. Those old boys seemed to have something pretty nice going for them and he wanted in, club or no club.

He was about a hundred yards from the end of the pier when the first clubman raised his head and stared with disbelieving eyes. When Pomeroy was fifty yards away, all seven members of The Club were fixing him with stony glares.

Our hero landed on a piling a bit removed from the overcrowded fishing dock. For the record, he did try to be friendly.

"Hi," he said to the nearest clubman. "Nice place you've got here."

The seven members of the elite exchanged glances. So grave was this intrusion that a tourist was allowed to land a seven-inch grunt, unmolested.

"Yup," said Pomeroy into the silence. "Mighty nice place."

"And private," creaked one of the clubmen, barely parting his bill. "For members only."

Pomeroy looked about him with exaggerated care before meeting the withering stare again. "I don't see no signs," he smiled.

"No signs are necessary," another clubman said icily.

"Well, I——" Pomeroy began, and broke off. One of the tourists had snagged a fine mangrove snapper which was beating the water to a froth in its struggle. Pomeroy slid off the piling and swooped on the fish, disengaged the hook, swallowed the snapper. He did this expertly even though it was his first experience; taking fish from hooks is as much a part of a pelican's heritage as the ability to fly.

The human who had been robbed set up a cursing, and Pomeroy returned to the piling, grinning. "This is living," he told the silent seven. "Out there"—with a derisive nod toward his parents and neighbors—"those dopes are knockin' themselves out doin' high dives while here all we have to do——"

"Young man," interrupted a clubman harshly, "go away."

Pomeroy widened his eyes. "Pardon?"

"I said, go away. This is a private preserve, the property of The Club since the first tourist cast a line from that pier into this gulf. No visitors. Posted. Keep out."

Pomeroy thrust his lower bill forward. "And if I don't?" he asked.

"Then," said the oldest of the clubmen heavily, "we shall be forced to eject you, distasteful as a brawl might be to us."

Pomeroy eyed the clubmen. Along in years, they were, and not in the best of shape by reason of their sedentary life, but there were seven of them and they were large; he was only a stripling. Still, a beating was only a beating while an unanswered challenge somehow was the most shameful thing in life to Pomeroy; so the young pelican dug his bill into his chest and said, "I take considerable ejectin'."

He got it too. While the fishermen with feverish joy pulled in mackerel, snapper, sheepshead, sailor's choices, grouper, catfish, trout, eels, crevalle jack and even one pompano without a single hook being burglarized, the seven clubmen gave Pomeroy a going-over. But good.

"Must be the mating season," observed one tourist learnedly when the ejection proceedings were at their most riotous. "I read somewhere that they turn savage then."

At the moment, Pomeroy was under water with three or four clubmen dispassionately bashing him over the head, sending him down again each time he came up. He was about ready to quit trying when there was a considerable commotion overhead and he sloshed up to blessed air to find, miraculously, that no sledgehammer bill was poised to let him have it. When he got his eyes uncrossed he discovered the reason for the surcease; his father was laying about him, and poppa was better than fair at handling himself in a fight.

The clubmen drew off in a body, outraged beyond repair and with more than one sporting a swelling eye. They scowled at poppa in concert.

"Of course," the oldest said finally in the voice of doom, "you realize what this does to your chances of becoming a member."

"I don't care," poppa panted. "You've got no call to rough up a kid like that, no matter what he did."

"They jumped me, poppa!" Pomeroy cried. "I wasn't doin' a thing and these guys just started pushin' me around."

"Come, Pomeroy," poppa said, and led the boy away. He did not wait until they got home to administer disciplinary measures; he gave Pomeroy a walloping out on the fishing grounds, in full view of the neighbors. Which, as any child psychologist will agree, is always a mistake.

"Ruin my chances of making The Club, will you?" poppa growled. *Whap!* "Put me on the black list by acting like a drape, will you?" *Whap-whap!*

"Poppa," momma protested, "not on the head."

Back home, Pomeroy got off by himself and brooded. This was one crazy world. Being a pelican was bad enough, if pelicans were expected to knock themselves silly every time they wanted a bite to eat, but to be a pelican named Pomeroy with an old man who walloped him in public just for standing up for his rights—how could it be worse? And those old creeps in The Club, where did they get off? This was a free country, wasn't it? If he wanted to, he bet he could take it up with the right people and make those guys let him feed off the tourists' fish.

If this Spindrift bunch had any backbone, forgot the exclusiveness bit, they could push The Club off the pilings, take over and feed easy. But would they? No, they'd rather yessir The Club and hope for a bid to join some day, meanwhile going bald pounding the water with their heads in hundred-foot drops.

Well, he wasn't going to take this lying down; not Pomeroy. If the old folks wouldn't back him up, he'd go it alone. Just wait.

He waited while he got a few more pounds on him, and during that time he became the biggest juvenile problem ever known to Spindrift Key. He refused to fish and when poppa ordered momma to quit feeding the big loafer as though he were just out of the egg, he went hungry until his father had to break down, fearing for the boy's health.

Came the day when momma and poppa started thinking about another little one and Pomeroy flatly refused to leave the nest. Tearfully on momma's part and grimly on poppa's, he was dumped out bodily. Pomeroy climbed back five times, but after the sixth splash his aversion to diving overcame his stubbornness and he left home. Poppa had to hold momma to keep her from going after her boy as he flapped away into the sunset.

"It'll be the making of him," Pomeroy's father said, with a couple of wing feathers firmly crossed, out of sight.

"But Pomeroy will starve!" momma wailed. "He won't dive."

"When he gets hungry enough he'll dive," poppa promised. "Through concrete, if necessary."

Poppa's prophesy, however, was not fulfilled immediately. Pomeroy went hungry for a while, but he did not dive; instead he joined up with a disreputable gang of gulls that hung around Mooney's Fish House and fed off the leavings that came down the slops chute. If he knew he was lowering himself on the social scale by several hundred notches, he convinced himself that he didn't care. Besides, Gilly, the gull gang leader, and his boys at least didn't go around screeching "Yoo-hoo, Pom-er-oooy!" in falsetto voices.

He continued this disgraceful existence until the day when, flexing his muscles, he decided he was ready to get things straight with The Club, fix it so he could eat whole, fresh-hooked fish instead of the bits and oddments at Mooney's. He made his way down to the pier, muttering what he was going to do to the first clubman that tried to stop him. He arrived and was promptly set upon by all seven members, who, it would seem, had spent the intervening weeks doing pushups in anticipation of his return.

This time there was no poppa to come to the rescue. Pomeroy finally escaped, looking as though he had been caught in a propeller.

"And stay out!" they told him, but he didn't.

Now, anyone would think that a pelican that had twice been thrown out of a place so definitely would admit he'd had it. The ordinary pelican might have, but there was only one Pomeroy. He did concede that as things stood his chances of getting those tourists' fish looked mighty dim, but he met this admission with the vow that so long as he could not dine at The Club, no other pelican would.

The next time he returned to the pier, therefore, it was not to the pilings where the clubmen held forth. Instead, he flew down the shore, picked up the pier at its land end and flew, fast and low, out its entire length, buzzing the tourists.

As has been mentioned, the fishing folk were tightly packed. Between January first and June first, railing space at the wharf was at a premium from dawn on, regardless of conditions of tide or weather. This churning mob was a perfect setup for a holocaust. Put a tourist on a pier, struggling for breathing room, already enraged by having some of the biggest fish he ever hooked in his life swiped by pelicans, one after the other, and then send a modern pterodactyl avalanching upon him, uttering weird noises, knocking off his hat and sunglasses, and you have a highly emotional individual. Multiply this by two or three hundred and you have an explosive potential that is frightening.

As Pomeroy zigzagged out the pier, uproar spread ahead of him, utter chaos followed in his wake. Some fishermen who saw him coming tried to fend him off with their rods and succeeded only in thrashing their neighbors about the head and shoulders. This brought retaliation, and the sounds of splintering tackle formed a jagged obbligato to the cries of terror and outrage. Somebody flung a can of live bait at Pomeroy and missed the pelican, but not anybody else within a twenty-foot radius. Several fist fights broke out, a large woman went into keening hysterics, the kids whooped ecstatically and the beach cops converged on the scene.

Pomeroy sailed out over the end of the pier, banked sharply, turned and made another run.

"Here he comes again!" squalled the tourists, and the second act of the panic was on. Most of those in the target area hit the deck, a few stood their ground and swatted futilely at Pomeroy. Kicked overboard in the scramble were scores of tackle boxes, vacuum bottles, picnic lunches, camp stools, bait buckets and suntan-lotion bottles. A beach cop plunging into the maelstrom was flattened by a wild swing thrown by a lady from Wisconsin. The children threw back their heads and squealed in pure rapture. Pomeroy banked again, surveyed the scene of carnage and flapped away.

"Now let's see how it goes with those old jerks and their club," he told Gilly and the other gulls who had come along to see the fun.

The clubmen had drawn off during the riot, frozen in shocked disapproval. As relative quiet descended again they went back to their pilings and prepared to take up where they had left off. They got their first inkling that something was very wrong when the most venerable of their sacrosanct number took a pop bottle beside the head.

The blow itself was not too bad, but its significance was colossal. Previously, the pelicans had been cursed despairingly in every accent known to the United States, but that was all. Now, thanks to Pomeroy, the tourists were taking to violence. Another missile, this one a bait can, grazed another clubman.

"Throw the rascals out!" sounded a hoarse voice, and that triggered a barrage of objects ranging from a child's sand pail to a brand-new sixty-dollar reel. Several clubmen were hit hard; one was knocked plumb off his piling.

"Hey!" a beach cop protested anxiously. "You can't do that! They're protected by law!"

"This for a law that protects the buzzard that busted my glasses!" cried a senior citizen from New Hampshire, and bunged a heavy sinker at the nearest pelican.

"It wasn't their fault," cried the cop. "It was that other screwball."

"A pelican is a pelican," panted the oldster, and followed the sinker with a scaling knife.

The clubmen fled, their dignity demolished. They came as close to scurrying as a pelican can and they did not stop until they were out of range of the lethal fire.

They did not return until the following dawn and they might have been slightly apprehensive about their reception, but not too much; after all, a pier fisherman lost his frustrated docility only once in a thousand years and yesterday had been that day. Today he would be his old self again, eyes glued on his bobber while his elbows fended off his compatriots and he rent the air with impotent oaths as the pelicans stole his fish from his hook.

And, indeed, this was how it was. The fires of revolt had died overnight. The beach cops who had assembled nervously at daybreak breathed a collective sigh of relief; things were back to normal. They returned to the tiresome chore of judging which Bikini encased the most admirable contents.

Then Pomeroy came back with Gilly and his gull gang from Mooney's, there to watch the fun. They saw plenty. This time Pomeroy made four runs over the pier before he was satisfied with the shambles and led his sycophants off, convulsed by jeering laughter.

Hardly had the last piercing scream died away over the Gulf of Mexico before the tourists turned their attentions on The Club. The day before, the senior citizen from New Hampshire had said that a pelican was a pelican and this was the view of all; to them it was plain that one of them damn birds roosted there on the pilings was to blame for all this. Hands reached for things to throw.

This time, The Club fled at the first volley, appealing over their shoulders for police protection. The cops were there by that time and trying to soothe the people; they did fine, too, until somebody announced that on the morrow he was bringing a shotgun with him and then those pelicans would get what was coming to them, by dogies.

"You shoot one of those pelicans and we'll have to lock you up," warned a cop.

"Lock up a winter visitor?" gasped a tourist. "Blasphemy!"

"Well, uh," said the cop. "Anyway, you can't shoot a pelican."

"We'll see if I can't," said the fisherman, and next morning, sure enough, he carried a pump gun onto the pier with him. He brought it up to his shoulder as the clubmen edged into view and so there was no meeting that day. Nor the next. On the third day the shotgun wielder was missing, gone back to Iowa, but Pomeroy was not; Gilly reported that The Club was in session again and so Pomeroy made a run over the pier and got things back to what they had been, chaotic. After that, a week passed without The Club convening.

"Those old guys must be gettin' pretty hungry by now," Pomeroy chuckled. "They must be about ready to come around invitin' me to join their dopey club."

"Sure they are," the gulls chorused, and laughed out of the side of their bills at the idea. They knew full well that a clubman would starve before he'd be pressured into making an equal of a bum from Mooney's.

Pomeroy waited and no clubman appeared, bearing a humble invitation. He checked the pier constantly from a distance, and saw no sign of The Club; all that was there were delighted tourists, snatching fish from the gulf without a single burgled hook.

"They must've found another pier," Pomeroy said finally. "They couldn't go this long without eatin'."

"Naw, they ain't found another pier," Gilly told him. "There's a club at every fishing dock and them stuffed shirts wouldn't dream of crashin' a place where they wasn't wanted. Naw, they're out in the gulf, divin' for fish like ordinary workin' stiffs."

"Then the pier they used to have is open to all," Pomeroy grinned. "What are we waitin' for?"

"You go ahead," said Gilly. "It's all yours; you earned it. Me and the boys will just come along to watch."

Pomeroy lit out, triumph high in his heart. Approaching the dock, he licked his lips; the fish were biting like crazy and they looked like blues, his favorite. And they were all his, as Gilly had said. He'd take it slow, not stuffing himself right off the bat. He'd stretch out his pleasure, dawdle over dinner, and when he'd had his fill maybe he'd hang around awhile and swipe fish off the hooks just for kicks. He'd——

"They're trying to move in again!" boomed a voice on the pier. "Battle stations!"

Pomeroy braked with his wings and stared in astonishment. Something had happened to the tourists. All these days free from pelican suzerainty had given them the will to resist; they had become bold on the heady stuff of actually keeping the fish they caught. And every man jack of them was armed with something throwable which he proceeded to hurl at Pomeroy.

The young pelican ducked and dodged, but even so he caught plenty. Something cracked him in the head, dizzying him, sending him into a spin from which he barely recovered before he crashed. Another missile stung him in the tail-feather region as he frantically winged over and tried to get out of there.

"Police!" he squawked. "Us pelicans are protected!"

The cops were elsewhere; they had determinedly avoided the fishing pier ever since the horrid possibility of having to arrest a winter visitor had been raised. Pomeroy's cries went unanswered except by gibbering laughter sent up by the gang from Mooney's, who had come to watch the fun.

The debris pelted Pomeroy, but he finally escaped, considerably beat up, and made for a buoy offshore. There he perched, the laughter of Gilly and his gang still ringing in his ears. It was a low moment.

"Fine thing," he told himself, aloud. "You were goin' to fix things and you did, all right. You spoiled it for The Club, sure, and when you did you spoiled it for every pelican that flies. That, my pointy-headed friend, includes you."

He gloomily looked out toward the fishing grounds where the pelicans who dived for a living were dropping from the skies, snagging fish, chatting with friends, laughing over little jokes, never thinking of Pomeroy these days.

He turned his sad eyes shoreward, toward the pier. Gilly and his gang had moved in and now they cluttered the pilings that had once been reserved for the most elite of pelicans, The Club members.

The tourists did not bother them—no gull could unhook a fish —and the Mooney's Fish House crowd were doing all right on dead bait, scraps of leftover lunch and other titbits.

"My pals," Pomeroy said bitterly. "Split their sides laughin' while I was gettin' that going-over. They knew what I was goin' to get and they let me stick my neck out. And I thought they were my friends."

Friends? He had no friends. The world was against him.

He peered out into the gulf again and saw that the people of Spindrift Key were starting home, the morning's fishing finished. Yes, there went momma and poppa, too, and he half raised a wing to wave to them, folded it again. No use; they were through with him.

"And I can't go back to Mooney's," he muttered. "That gang would ride the tail feathers off me. Gilly said every other pier on the West Coast had a club, so what would be the use of tryin' someplace else? All it would do would burn up the tourists wherever I went, if I tried that dive-bombin' stuff."

Burn up the tourists—for a moment Pomeroy was tempted to do just that, out of meanness, but he shook his banged-up head; somehow it seemed a pretty lousy trick, spoiling everything for everybody just because he'd goofed off completely with his own life.

"Hey," he told himself, "stop thinkin' like a square. What do you care about anybody else, any more than they care about you? It'd serve 'em right if you started up at Cedar Key and went right on down the coast to Cape Sable, makin' tourists hate pelicans. Maybe then they'd be sorry they picked on you. Maybe then they'd wish they'd never yelled 'Yoo-hoo, Pom-er-oooy' at you."

But no pelican had yoo-hooed Pom-er-oooy at him in a long, long time and no pelican would, ever again. He was alone, an outcast, a pariah, and he was only a little boy, after all. It was awful. The more he thought of it, the worse it got, and pretty soon it became too much for him to bear. He began to weep, the tears coursing down his cheeks.

How long he sat there, weeping, the buoy's bell tolling a mournful accompaniment, he never knew; but it seemed forever before a wing was thrown over his shoulder and poppa cleared his throat and said huskily, "There, there, son. It'll be all right."

Pomeroy turned and buried his face in his father's breast. "It'll never be all right," he sobbed. "I've been a stupid jerk. I've spoiled everything."

"Maybe you're a little mixed up," poppa conceded, "but there's not a vicious feather on your body. You got off on the wrong foot with that name your mother—well, never mind about that. Let's go back to Spindrift Key and start all over again. Why, you haven't even met your baby sister. Name of Pete."

"Go back? But they'd throw me out," Pomeroy cried.

"No, they won't," poppa said. "They'll welcome you home, even the fellows who were in The Club."

"Them?" Pomeroy asked, drawing back in horror. "They'll murder me."

"Unh-unh," his father smiled. "Y'see, while they may have wanted to wring your neck when they lost their gravy train, they don't now. Seems that having to get out and dive for fish did things for them. Took off all that excess weight; gave them some muscle tone. They all swear they feel twenty years younger; wouldn't go back to The Club if they could."

And that was the way it was when Pomeroy went back to Spindrift Key. Maybe the ex-clubmen were a bit cool at first, but they accepted him eventually and so did all the other pelicans when they saw how Pomeroy had changed. If you're down that way, you'll see them all getting along very buddy-buddy, at Spindrift Key and out on the fishing grounds.

And at the latter place, if you look sharp, you might notice that one of the pelicans, when he dives, hits the water tail-first, an agonized expression on his face, one wing tightly clenched over his beaked nose.

That's Pomeroy. He is firmly resolved to do everything he's supposed to do, even high-dive for fish, but that doesn't mean he has to like it.

MOON SHOT

by Frank Harvey

The wash of the surf on Cocoa Beach, Florida, did not lull Maj. Norman Gibney tonight. He had been lying in the hot motel bedroom for three hours with his eyes shut. But he hadn't slept. He hadn't even relaxed. His mind had kept going around, slowly and sickeningly, in a great grooved circle, and when it came to those last terrible seconds of decision, when the Titan intercontinental ballistic missile was rising from its launch pad, his fingers had tightened in his palms until his hands were straining fists.

Forget it, he told himself urgently, angrily. *It's done. It's over. Think of something else.*

And maybe for a minute or two he did think of something else: his gang back in the Wherry apartment at Carswell Air Force Base, Texas—Helen, Emmy and Hank—the people who depended on him, who looked to him for whatever good or bad would come in the future. They were sure it would be good. Particularly Hank. Hank thought his daddy ran the Titan program at Cape Canaveral, with a little help, from time to time, from a few thousand other people. Helen had said as much on the long-distance phone: "You better hurry up and get home, honey. Or be prepared to fly up the street on your own personal wings. Hank's starting to speak of that big monster you're working on as 'My daddy's Titan.'"

Gibney had laughed, but his lips had been stiff and his eyes, looking at the coin slots of the pay phone, had been bleak. He hadn't mentioned the trouble. Helen couldn't help. No use worrying her about it now. There'd be time enough later—when he was sent home, or to Thule, Greenland, or God knew where.

Abruptly, Gibney's mind jerked back to the Titan blockhouse, five weeks ago. He was sitting in front of his safety console with the hooded eyepiece of the observation periscope within easy reach. They'd gone through eleven hours of count-down. It was T-zero, the moment before firing.

"Watch it now, Gib," big Wes Kirby's voice said sharply over the intercom. "She's lighting."

There'd been a heartbeat of nothing. Then steam exploded out of the flame bucket in a huge white boil as the Titan's exhaust roared through the jets of cooling water. A sullen muted sound came through ten feet of sand and ten feet of reinforced concrete into the blockhouse. Gibney's gaze flicked along his console. The needles were fine—tilted beautifully in one direction, a perfect "Go reading"—and he ducked back to the scope. The Titan was now at full fury. The powerful steel arms which held it tightly on the pad, until the boosters could stabilize at max power, were partly blotted out by the glare of the flames. As Gibney watched, the hold-downs flipped free, there was an instant of hesitation, and the three-stage bird began to rise slowly, eerily, as if it were being lifted by an overhead crane. It cleared the concrete pier. A butterfly cloud of fire from the gas generators floated about the vicious white-hot stabs of the boosters.

Then the Titan was gone in a billowing caldron of flame-lit steam and Gibney was back with the needles. They were erect in a neat row, quivering slightly. It was going to be fine—an O.K. shot, a Green Bird, as they said in pad lingo.

Then the azimuth needle went crazy. It veered sharply to the extreme left—held there, quivering like a captive insect—zoomed back to vertical. Gibney hunched close, staring. The needle tilted again to the far left and held as if glued down.

Punch it, his mind screamed. *Quick, before it hits the beach.*

The rest he analyzed later. The agonizing part—the thing his eyes had seen just as his thumb mashed down irrevocably on the Air-Destruct button. That last thing had been a flick—sudden as light, but distinct as if carved in stone. The azimuth needle had freed itself from the glued-down position and erected in an even line with the rest—meaning that the Titan had cleared its trouble somehow, had turned into a Green Bird, safe to let loose into the starry blackness of outer space. But it hadn't gone there. It had disintegrated forty-five thousand feet in the cloudless sky, buckling and falling, dropping its high-energy exotic fuel in cascades of molten fire that could be seen all over the Cape—all over America, really, because the long-range TV cameras had been grinding.

Gibney hadn't gone to pieces. As a matter of fact, he'd felt almost normal for a little while. Big Wes Kirby, who was his friend as well as Martin's launch director, had talked to him in that easygoing Southern accent, had asked what had happened, what he'd seen. He'd told Wes about the azimuth needle—how it had suddenly reversed—and how he'd thought the missile was going to smash into Cocoa Beach; and Wes had listened and nodded.

"Funny none of the other consoles showed it," somebody said then. Not a condemnation, actually; just a statement. And he had looked around the blockhouse and it was perfectly quiet and nobody was meeting his eyes. That was when Major Gibney's private nightmare had begun.

Now, in his motel room, he sat up in bed and turned on the lamp. No use reliving the nightmare now. He'd lived it constantly for the past five weeks. There'd been a day—no, two days—when everything had seemed calm. He'd gone to the Cape, and the Martin guys had been great—too great, really. It would have been easier if they'd been rough instead of trying to act as if the air-abort didn't mean anything. It meant something, all right—hundreds and hundreds of hours of sweat and hope for every one of them; and he'd blown the works in half a second because he'd been too quick— Was panicky the word?—about hitting the red button.

On the morning of the third day an Air Force colonel had arrived from headquarters, Air Research and Development Command—a tall man with pale eyes which did not blink when he looked at Gibney and asked questions. What, exactly, had the needle indication been? . . . A sudden sharp deflection, eh? . . . No, two of them. . . . Was Gibney sure of that? . . . He was. . . . All right, now what had the duration of the deflections been? . . .

Finally, the colonel had said, "Do you know how much that test missile was worth, major?"

"Yes, sir. I've heard them say around two million dollars."

"You heard them correctly," the colonel said. "Look, Gibney, I'm not going to beat around the bush. We're replacing you. It's not a punishment, understand. Anybody can make a mistake."

"But, colonel, sir——"

"All right, Gibney. Maybe you saw these needles flutter—or thought you did. That's not the point. This missile program is more important than one man or a thousand men. What we do here in the next months can influence foreign policy, alliances—can swing the balance of power in the free world. I'm sure you understand that, Gibney."

Gibney nodded. He made no further defense—did not mention the Saturdays, Sundays and nights he'd spent out on the launching pad with the Martin gang, learning the details, the tools, trying to make himself expert in every phase of a launch. That didn't matter now. He'd blown up a Green Bird, worth $2,000,000, before it could give any data they hadn't already taped on previous tests.

With a mark like that on his service record, he'd never make another promotion if he lived to be a hundred. He'd seen old majors before—men who'd goofed somewhere along the line, bitter, red-faced from too much drink, waiting for twenty to get out. He'd seen them sweat, too, when the Air Force had a reduction in force. A major was not immune to the RIF. Norm Gibney knew one personally who'd been flying jets a couple of months back. Now he was an airman first class, checking schedules on the jets he'd flown, saluting the same men who'd saluted him before he lost his oak leaves. They gave you two choices in a RIF: re-enlist as an airman, or get out.

The clock beside the bed showed ten minutes to ten. That was good. Gibney could get up and dress for his last count-down. Not that he was really needed. His replacement, Maj. Dick O'Brien, was thoroughly checked out. Dick was a good man. He could handle the job perfectly alone.

Norm Gibney wasn't kidding himself. He knew why Wes Kirby had asked him to stand by a periscope and be on hand in case the new Safety Officer needed him. Kirby was a friend. He liked Gibney and wanted to give him a chance to be in on the Big One. You couldn't refuse a guy like Wes, even though you'd rather do almost anything than face those guys in the blockhouse even one more time.

It was cool and clear when Gibney left the motel. Oceanward the sky was dark, except for the sickle edge of a shadowed moon. The main drag of Cocoa Beach—a bumper-to-bumper avalanche of traffic when the Canaveral Caravan got rolling in the morning—was relatively quiet now. Gibney walked to the edge of the road and waited for Maj. Dick O'Brien to pick him up. He felt numb—numb and bitter. He'd be glad when the shot was over and he could pack up and leave this place forever. Even if they transferred him to Thule, Greenland.

But Major O'Brien, when he picked Gibney up, was both excited and nervous. He'd been on the telephone to the Cape five minutes ago, he said, and it looked good—very good. The Titan was fully checked—all three hundred thousand parts of it—and the warhead was installed inside the nose cone.

"Hydrogen?" Gibney asked.

"Hydrogen," Major O'Brien said, and his voice was hushed, as if he somehow felt that even in the car, rushing through the empty night, ears might be listening. "A full megaton."

"If it hits," Gibney said, "it ought to show."

"It'll show," Major O'Brien said. "It won't be any little pinprick either. They're using those big ROTI cameras—the ones that can photograph detail on a golf ball at ten miles. They'll get a front-page shot that'll make those Sputniks look sick."

They were not the first to reach the launching pad. The place was swarming. The missile had been erected and its handling tower had been rolled back out of the way. It stood alone under the floods, a massive towering shape cinched tightly to the concrete pier by the steel hold-down mechanism. When they parked, Major Gibney saw the staff cars with stars on them—general officers' cars—thick as cabs at a hack stand. This wasn't just one more of those low-power shots down range across the South Atlantic. It was the most powerful shot ever attempted in American rocketry. The Titan was a specially modified four-stage version, using new secret fuel of vastly superior energy. The huge missile would build up velocity as it shed stages, until the hydrogen warhead reached 26,000 miles an hour. The flight path would bend part way around the earth, in a semiorbit; then run off into space toward the moving moon. Guidance must be nearly perfect. An error of a microscopic .2 degree in path angle could mean a miss. The warhead would vary its speed in space—slowing from 26,000 m.p.h. after leaving the earth, and gaining back some speed as it entered the gravitational pull of the moon. But if all went well, the warhead would impact on the moon about twenty hours after firing.

Big Wes Kirby, the launch director, was sitting at the main control panel in the blockhouse when Gibney and O'Brien entered. He looked at them, but did not see them. He was speaking into his lip mike, and his face, in the cool air-conditioned room, was glistening with sweat. This was the first time a live warhead had ever been fired at the Cape. The warhead wasn't armed now. That would take place automatically when the final stage separated. But this detail was not wholly reassuring. The warhead was designed to go off on impact. If the Titan got away and headed back in, the destruct would have to be very quick and very certain.

"We are taking a certain risk, of course," the briefing officer had said, when they first heard of the Moon Shot. "But our stakes are the highest. This is no circus stunt. We want to hit the moon first. We want to do it positively, visibly—beyond the power of any propaganda to dispute. A high-yield hydrogen warhead is the best way."

Maj. Dick O'Brien took his place at the safety panel, put on his earphones and mike, and began making his checks. Major Gibney sat behind him, where he could see the gauges easily, and could also use the periscope. The blockhouse was now fully manned. Engineers sat in rows behind their consoles. In a sound-proofed room, behind double glass, sat the visiting dignitaries: generals, congressmen, presidents of several great corporations.

"Pad to Safety," a familiar voice said over the intercom, which Gibney was monitoring with a set of earphones. "Major O'Brien, this is Jim Hunter. Do you read me?"

"Loud and clear, Jim," O'Brien's voice said. "Go ahead."

"I have slightly low hydraulic pressure on the right hold-down cylinder. If I can't fix it in a hurry, I may have to call a hold."

"Roger," O'Brien said. "Understand."

Gibney peered into the periscope and turned the lens system to ten magnifications. Jim Hunter and his men, clustered at the base of the four-stage missile, came so close he had the illusion he could reach out and touch them. Hunter had climbed up on the right hold-down arm and was standing on tiptoe, opening an access hatch in the wall of the Titan. Two men were holding his legs, steadying him. He reached into a small, dark recess and did something with a screwdriver. Then he closed the hatch and the men helped him down.

Wes Kirby's voice cut sharply over the intercom, "Launch to Pad! What's the trouble out there, Jim?"

"No trouble now," Jim Hunter's voice said cheerfully. "Had a sticky valve in the hold-down. All she needed was a touch of the screwdriver. We're in business."

The night wore on into the dark predawn. Ash trays filled with mashed butts. Paper cups of coffee were drained and crushed. In the soundproofed room, the generals and congressmen shifted wearily in their padded seats. The count-down was plodding slowly and carefully through its technical labyrinth—through two short holds for minor reasons—and then the sickle moon paled and the sky began to get light. Gibney watched the crimson sun rise out of the sea, and heard the voices on the intercom grow thinner and sharper as the count-down moved out of its humdrum detail and into the last critical items—the tense approach to T-zero.

"T minus eight minutes," Wes Kirby's voice said. "All personnel clear the launch area!"

Gibney licked his lips. He saw two men scuttle out of the concrete utility room under the massive launching pier, run past the blockhouse and vanish. The missile glittered in the early sunshine like some giant toy. A flock of pelicans, flying in line-astern formation, flapped low along the dunes, stopped flapping as one bird, and soared. It was seven o'clock in the morning.

"T minus six minutes," Wes Kirby said. "O'Brien, check your board for proper indications and report."

Over O'Brien's shoulder, Gibney swept the console carefully. All was well. Needles steady, in line, no problem. O'Brien's voice said tautly, "Roger across the board, Wes."

Kirby did not acknowledge. He wasn't supposed to. In these last moments of the count-down he saved his attention for the big, critical things, the signs of danger. "T minus five minutes," Kirby said. "Cape radars on. Master telemeters on." The sites rogered in. Gibney waited. Presently Kirby spoke again, "T minus four minutes. I'm starting the firing sequencer now. I say again, I'm starting the firing sequencer now. Stand by for lift-off!"

Gibney saw green dots of light flicker across the big board as the automatic firing mechanism took over. It was out of human hands now. The big board would do the rest, more smoothly, more precisely than the coolest human operator could hope to duplicate.

A voice—sudden, shocking—tore across the intercom, "Safety! Safety! Check the bird! The right hold-down! Quick!"

Gibney ducked to the scope. The right hold-down arm was on his side of the missile. He stared at it. It was a steel bar eight feet long. It was supposed to be tightly socketed in a grip hole in the wall of the Titan. A moment ago it had been. Now it dangled free, loose, inoperative. Unhesitatingly, Gibney reached over O'Brien's shoulder and mashed the Hold Fire button flat.

He spoke into his lip mike, "Gibney to Launch. Right hold-down is inoperative. I'm stopping the lift-off."

Only, nightmarishly, he wasn't. The green lights on the big board had not turned red. The master warning over the automatic sequencer had not begun to glow. The Hold Fire button hadn't worked. The firing sequence was still going on.

"Safety to Launch!" Gibney snapped. "Stopcock it, Wes! My button's out! Use the emergency over-ride, quick!"

He twisted. Wes Kirby was standing up, scrabbling frantically at a panel which was a mass of electric fire and swirling smoke. A short. A big one. Wes had no emergency over-ride. Everything was gone, including the destruct button—and that big H-bomb was cooking out there with one hold-down completely free. In four minutes—in less—those main-stage rockets would cut in and shove the bird off. Not straight up toward the safety of outer space. At an angle—toward Jacksonville, New York—God knew where—with a punch equal to 1,000,000 tons of T.N.T. that could trigger automatically in flight.

Somebody screamed—a high, terrified sound, like a woman. Gibney whirled, ran through the white, shocked faces at the consoles, and wrenched the handle of the steel blockhouse door. The metal fingers which dogged it tight all around retracted with oily clicks. He crouched low and slung his weight against the door, inched it open ponderously, like a bank vault on its ball-bearing hinges, and slipped through.

The concrete launching pier was seven hundred and fifty feet away. Gibney was forty years old, out of shape. He sprinted across the open area, climbed the steel steps beside the pier, and reached the base of the Titan. The loose arm hung back in the air many feet above him. Under his feet was the intricate maze of snouts which would, in seconds, hurl high-pressure cooling water into the flame bucket. He was taking air in tortured gulps. His thighs and knees quivered uncontrollably from the furious run.

The tool he needed—had to have—was shaped like a giant wrench. It took him five seconds to locate it inside the locker. It took him another fifteen seconds to shinny up the steel framework to where he could bring the tool into action. Then, in his desperate hurry, he missed the slot.

Below him, something exploded and the air was full of stinging spray: cooling water on. He fought his way higher, gripping the framework with his knees, and jammed the tool in place. The holddown arm sagged inward. The locking pin inched toward its socket, touched delicately, and refused to enter. Gibney had one chance, and he took it. He let go with his knees and swung into space on the haft of the locking tool, like a man swinging on a horizontal bar. He felt the pin go in hard, with a definite snap, let go his hold and sprawled heavily on the concrete pier.

The boosters ignited as he reached the iron steps. The shock wave hurled him forward, and he fell, tumbling and lurching, grabbing at the railing, buried in molten light and whirling steam. It was the pier itself—a chunk of concrete as big as a warehouse—which saved him. He could not run. Something was wrong with one of his legs. But he could crawl. He made it to the underpass, dragged his body frantically into it and fell flat with his arms over his head.

The main stage of the Titan cut in. The pier quivered. The sound rose until it was no longer sound, but wrenching, pounding agony. The big four-stage bird was holding, was building up to maximum lift-off power. Then, mercifully, the sound was rising away—slowly, in steady, incandescent fury—was lessening minutely—was lessening quickly—was gone—and there was nothing but a ringing roar in Gibney's head.

Nearly twenty hours later, somewhat before three in the morning, the moon was above the horizon to seaward, a shadowed globe with a sickle edge at its bottom which the Floridians called a South Moon Under. There had been a cloud deck in the evening, but the wind had swept it away, and now the sky was dark and clear, sprinkled with faint stars.

Major Gibney was propped up in a tilting bed on the roof of the hospital at Patrick Air Force Base, twenty miles south of the Cape. His right leg, broken in the fall down the iron steps, was splinted and the flash burns from the Titan exhaust were treated with gentian violet. He had been in severe pain for the last three hours, since the morphine had worn off, but he did not want more morphine now—not until they knew for sure that the moon rocket had missed.

"She's past due," Wes Kirby's voice said beside him in the darkness. "Eight minutes and twelve seconds, to be exact."

"Radar lost it?"

"Two hours ago," Kirby said. "There's too much junk flying around out there—meteors, space dust, heaven knows what. When

you turn your gain up high enough to track your missile, you bring
in a whole howling wilderness of blips."

Gibney took a look through the powerful telescope they'd set up
beside his bed. The moon looked awesomely close through the
lenses, a huge shadowed globe pocked with dark craters and striated
with ridges and mysterious patches. The thin sickle edge was so
bright in magnification that it made him squint a little. He was
in strong pain now. The burns were on fire and the broken leg
throbbed sharply every time his heart beat. He tried to put his
mind on something else.

"What caused the hold-down failure, Wes?"

Wes Kirby chuckled. "A twenty-cent hydraulic line," he said.
"The little rascal broke and pulled all the pressure out of the locking pin. Then the hydraulic fluid drained down into a main junc-
tion box and shorted the whole works. It's real crazy. You rig up
five thousand safety checks and one little hunk of tubing blows the
ball game."

Twenty cents' worth of tubing, Gibney thought. *Four minutes
of time.* They could change a man's life. He could hack it now. He
knew that. No problem. No banishment to Thule. No RIF. He
closed his eyes. He was very tired.

And then, beside him, Wes Kirby spoke in a tight, almost savage
whisper, "Gib—quick—the moon."

He brought it to him, close and clear, through the telescope.
A spot, bright and vivid as the sun, had burned itself starkly in
the dark lower quadrant of the moon, rather close to the sickle
edge. The spot held, pure white, for perhaps ten seconds. Then
it faded gradually through yellow and orange, glowed like a dying
cigarette ember, and went out. The surface of the moon, riding se-
renely across the void of space, was dark again.

SUDDEN AFFAIR

by Margaret Bonham

They met at a sherry party in someone's house off Knightsbridge. William, the young man who took Harriet along, told her whose party it was, but Harriet was very bad at names and she instantly forgot.

She was not much interested in parties; she was there because William was interested in her, and he had talked her into it with great eloquence. Ten minutes after they arrived, pinned in a corner by a man with enormous eyebrows who talked about satellites, she stood bemusedly holding a glass and saying, "Yes. . . . No. . . . I suppose it might. . . . How fascinating," while her mind wandered irrepressibly back to her flat and the book she was halfway through.

The man with the eyebrows, loudly but almost inaudibly said, "Question of whether gravitational compensation . . . fuel injection . . . stratospheric pressure, you see." Or something of the kind.

"Oh, yes," said Harriet. "Of course. Are you a scientist?"

"Lord, no. I'm a stockbroker."

"Excuse me," said Harriet, feeling a pressure applied to her elbow.

It proved to be William. "Sorry," he said, removing her. "Was he a bore?"

"Yes."

"I am sorry; I got caught up. Let's find someone amusing. You must—— Good Lord!"

"What?"

"There's Dion Davis."

"Who's he?"

William paused and looked at her closely. He said, "Harriet, I know you have brains, you must surely read the newspapers."

"Not those newspapers. Football?"

"Or are you being an intellectual snob?"

"No, wait a minute. I do seem to—— Is it motor racing?"

"It is indeed motor racing, and not only that, he's simply the greatest."

"Oh," said Harriet. She followed William's gaze and saw a man of about twenty-eight, two or three years older than herself, talking emphatically to a middle-aged couple. He had a round brown face, a long and clearly modeled mouth and dark hair. Though his features were compelling rather than attractive, he was at least an improvement on the scientific stockbroker.

"Do you know him?" she said.

"Well, sort of. I met him once, but I shouldn't think he'd know me. Shall we have a go?"

"Why not?"

William, who was not lacking in self-confidence, did an expert shuffle that brought them face to face with Davis at a moment when conversation with the middle-aged couple died. The couple, defeated, faded away.

Davis, meeting William's ardent stare, returned it seriously, and after an agonizing moment he said, surprisingly, "A small world."

"You wouldn't remember me," said William, for once flustered.

"Oh, yes, I would. You were in the pits at Silverstone with Andrew Black."

"Yes, I was, but I didn't think——"

"The time he ran off at Stowe. I'm afraid I never heard your name."

"Knight. William Knight."

"And this is Mrs. Knight?"

"No, no, I'm sorry. I should have—— Mr. Davis, Miss Denzil."

"How do you do?" said Harriet sedately.

"The prospective Mrs. Knight, perhaps?"

"No," said Harriet.

"Then if you'll forgive us, Knight, Miss Denzil and I will go and find a drink and talk over the time when Black ran off at Stowe."

"That was me," said William, stupefied. "I mean, Miss Denzil wasn't——" His voice was engulfed in the general roar.

Davis found an angle of wall and two drinks, and arranged himself with his back to the room where no one could cut Harriet off from him. "Not very kind," he said, "but suffering purifies. What's your first name?"

"Harriet."

"How nice. Mine is Dion. Dion the Track, they call me in Pontypridd. They think I will."

"Is that where you come from?"

"It's where I was born. What do you do?"

"I work for an archaeologist."

"What? Dig things up, do you mean?"

"Help dig things up, help put them together, take notes, type lectures, make appointments, keep an eye on the petrol gauge, look up trains and retrieve gold-mounted umbrellas from all the Lost Property Offices in Britain."

"Ah, an absent-minded genius. Look, let's go and have dinner somewhere. Parties are intolerable, I can't think how I got into this one."

"But William——"

"Oh, curse William. I'll go and tell him."

In the taxi, Dion sat moodily on the edge of the seat. He said, "I hate being driven."

"Was William cross?"

"He wasn't exactly pleased, but he was too polite to show it. Anyway, he promised to bring you down to Goodwood on Saturday."

"What on earth for?"

"To see me race."

"Suppose," said Harriet carefully, "I have an engagement on Saturday? Suppose I don't want to watch motor racing? Suppose I loathe the sight of it?"

"Do you?"

"I've never seen it. Which implies I can't be very keen."

"All it implies is, you don't know what you're talking about." Dion turned toward her; his eyes shone anxiously in the moving lights. He said, "Do come. I like you very much. You calm me down."

"Do you need calming down?"

"Except when I'm racing."

Even after Goodwood, Harriet was not sure whether she liked it or not. It was something quite different; it repelled and fascinated. She drove down with William, who owned a small and noisy red sports car some years past its prime, not because he couldn't afford a new one, but because he was one of those who consider nobody can make real motorcars these days. He was torn between despair about Harriet and elation at being asked to the meeting by the great Davis, an achievement about which he would be able to boast to all his car-minded friends for months to come.

On the way down, despair won; Harriet's curling hair, dark red-brown and cut short, blew distractingly in the gale; her normally pale cheeks were stung to carnation-pink.

Passing a van and changing into top gear, he said darkly, "You don't want to get mixed up with these racing boys, you know. If motorcars were banned, they'd shrivel up like leeches and die.

You'd never be more than a shoulder to lean on, between Syracuse and Le Mans."

"I thought you liked it."

"Oh, I'm a spectator. I like driving, I like motorcars, but I haven't got a throttle growing out of my right foot. They're not human."

"He seems to me quite human, in a sort of way."

"Didn't he? Where did you go?"

"Some obscure little pub round the back somewhere, because he doesn't like taxis. It was nice, though; the food was heavenly." Remembering her qualms about whether Dion's idea of going out to dinner would be Claridge's or the Savoy, and how far Claridge's or the Savoy would raise their eyebrows at her three-year-old taffeta dress, she smiled. William saw and misinterpreted the smile. Closing his lips on another question, he drove gloomily and too fast round the next bend.

It was a clear day; white clouds rolled high above the downs. Harriet's impressions afterward were not clear at all, for she understood little of what was going on. She carried back a memory of crowds and noise and colors, and how small and menacing and brilliant the cars looked; and how she must keep in mind the green one, No. 9, which was Dion's. But soon she became confused.

"What's happening?" she said to William, who was gripping the rail.

"He's taken the Ferraris."

"He's winning, do you mean?"

"O Lord, girl, nobody's winning. They've only done ten."

Loudly, malevolently, the cars passed and repassed. After a time, Harriet said, "William, why is he so good?"

William tore himself from the track and looked at her. He said, "It isn't easy to explain, if you don't know about driving. It's just an art and he's just a master of it."

"He drives as if he were asleep."

"Yes; relaxed. The others, you see, are men in cars; he's a car and a man in one piece."

After the race, there was a great crowd and a great deal of confusion. Harriet stood hemmed in by people, wondering how to retrieve William, who had got separated from her. After some time, a stir and scuffle in the crowd materialized into Davis, who fought his way through disregarded back slaps to her side. He had taken his helmet off; his face was dark with grime except for two lighter ovals round his eyes, which made him look no longer half asleep, as when he was driving, but like a very alert owl.

He said, "Just let me get clear of this lot. I'll drive you back to London."

"But William——" said Harriet. *Whenever I see him,* she thought, *I say that. It's got to stop.* She said, "No."

"I've got a nice girl for William, all lined up. William will love her."

"No."

"Look, if you must be so strong-minded, we'll meet them for dinner, blast it! Will that do? Tell him you want to see life on the road with Dion the Track. I'll be twenty minutes. Will you wait here?"

"I don't know," said Harriet, but he had gone.

Buffeted by the crowd, she stood conscious of several layers of exasperated thoughts. *I don't know,* she said to herself. *I don't know how to cope with it; he makes me the sort of person I am not. But then, if I really didn't want to go, I wouldn't stay here. If I do want to go, it must be subconscious; I hate the thought of it. William drives fast enough, and goodness knows what—— Anyway, it isn't fair to William. If he got furious, it wouldn't be so bad, but he is too nice and he won't.*

She was still standing there, frowning, hands in pockets, when William came on her. His blond, rather monkeyish face was screwed up as if against the light.

He said, "Well, it was a nice drive."

"You've seen him?"

"He saw me."

"William, why do you put up with it?" said Harriet, suddenly angry.

"What else can I do?"

"If I were you, I think I'd knock him down and slap my face."

"That would be crude," said William. "Besides, you want to go. Best get it out of the system, I tell myself."

"I'm not sure I do want to go."

"I think you do, really, Harriet. After all, he hasn't got a gun."

"No, but he behaves as if he had."

"Well, they are very tiring, those types," said William hopefully.

"I don't deserve you."

Being driven back to London by Dion turned out to be not, in every way, what Harriet had expected. He kept her waiting half an hour, which she and William and the girl lined up for William spent drinking cardboard cups of tea and talking with a kind of cautious impersonal animation about motor racing. The girl ("William will love her") proved to have green eyes and a black crew cut and tough but expensive clothes, and seemed to understand compression ratios. Harriet relaxed a little. William liked green eyes, and appeared, though slightly wistful, not dissatisfied. He went off, when Dion turned up, quite happily with the crew cut, who looked well able to take all the fresh air she was certainly going to get; Dion had shown sense in not finding him an orchid.

Harriet also was prepared for fresh air and something about two feet high with a number painted on the side, and was surprised at being led to a small sports saloon in darkest olive green, thoroughbred and of classically orthodox design.

"Did you expect a Maserati?" said Dion, seeing her face as he got in.

He started off and apparently relapsed into a coma; soon they turned into a lane climbing the downs, away from the stream of cars.

"Does this go to London?" said Harriet mildly.

"It's the way I go to London. There's always a better route than the main road."

"I only wondered."

"You needn't. I said we'd meet them for dinner."

" 'We'll meet them for dinner, blast it,' you said; and you seem a pretty unscrupulous type to me; that's why I wondered."

Harriet, always—she now realized—slightly edgy in a car with William, had a feeling of such rocklike security with Dion driving that she could give her whole attention to talk; they seemed to progress with leisured smoothness. When she glanced at the speedometer she didn't believe what she saw.

"Do I?" said Dion. Passive in the seat beside her, his head tilted to one side, he nevertheless sounded a note of injured astonishment. "Do you mean William?" he said. "Can't William look after his own interests? And after all, if you want to be with William instead of me, you have only to say so."

"I keep saying I ought to go with William. You never take any notice."

"I kidnap you, do you mean, when you ought to go with William, because you have a conscience, but not the strength of mind to walk off?"

"Not exactly that; I know it's mostly my fault. Only William has a nice character and you do take advantage of it."

"That's William's lookout and yours. You don't have to come with me when I ask you."

"It's very difficult saying no, the way you go about it."

She glanced at Dion and was alarmed to see him turn perceptibly paler. He raised his eyes automatically to the driving mirror and drew off the lane and switched off the engine.

He said, "Perhaps that makes this easier, if it's true. I can't say it while I'm driving. How would you feel about marrying me?"

The silence, in the pause that followed, seemed to increase till it was unbearable.

"You must be mad," Harriet said.

"So you can say no. Or is that no or just shock? You don't have to answer, if you want to think." He sat half turned toward her, his eyes on her face. He said, "I know I rush at things—things like this, I mean. I'm sorry. I have to."

Harriet said almost under her breath, "Why?"

"Why do I want to marry you?"

"Why do you have to rush at things?"

"I suppose, in case there isn't much time. When I'm there, when I'm racing, I feel I'm indestructible, nothing can touch me, but afterward I wonder. I've seen people die in front of me through no fault of their own; anything can happen. When there is something you need, you feel the pressure behind you. I said, you don't have to answer now. Or if you can, and it's no, tell me."

"It's—how can I tell you? I don't even know you. It's fantastic."

"Look, Harriet, it may sound fantastic from your side. Perhaps it does, but not to me. I have a feeling of absolute certainty about you. That it has to be you, I mean, or nobody. I knew it from the start. It would be an odd sort of marriage, are you thinking?"

"A shoulder to lean on," Harriet said half to herself, "between Syracuse and Le Mans."

"As well as having a nice character," said Dion, "William is perceptive."

"Oh."

"You can't, surely, have imagined I'd take that as one of your remarks? So he's been warning you about me?"

"Not about you in particular. He just told me not to get mixed up with racing boys. They aren't human, William thinks."

"What do you think?" Dion asked.

He had not touched her and had not even moved; yet he seemed disconcertingly close. He returned her gaze with no expression but a serious concentration; she saw him as a confusion of minute details, a dilated pupil in a shining brown iris, an edge of thick short lashes, the smooth curve of cheek from cheekbone, all magnified into some kind of yet-ungrasped significance.

"I don't know," she said. "I must think."

"Very well," said Dion. He kept his eyes on her for a moment, and then, still without touching her, pressed the starter and drove on.

At half-past ten, William's car, with William and Harriet in it, stopped outside Harriet's flat. It was a bright clear night, and still warm enough to have the top down; traffic passed along the distant King's Road, but the small street where they sat under a lamp was deserted. Dion had not offered to take her home; this, it seemed, was to be William's privilege. They had dined, all four of them, at a place chosen by Dion, which turned out to be a small Russian restaurant hidden somewhere off St. Martin's Lane.

"It's one of the countries we don't yet race in; it makes a change of food. Also," he said, "Russian food is romantic, I think. They have a genius with beetroot."

Harriet admitted that the Russians did things with beetroot and with sour cream and other odd ingredients that the English did not, and with unexpectedly pleasing results; she saw as well that the restaurant was quiet and that few people seemed to recognize Dion, and after the last part of the drive to London, when heads had turned in traffic queues or from the pavement, she wondered if this was another reason for his choice.

Considering the whole situation, the dinner had not been unsuccessful. William and the crew cut, whose name was Nicolette, had begun by discussing racing, and Dion had headed them off. On other subjects the talk had been lively and intelligent, and Harriet, though with a dreamlike feeling of unreality—especially when she looked covertly at Dion or raised her eyes from her plate to find his gaze austerely fixed on her—took part and enjoyed herself. Now, sitting in the aging little red car outside her flat, she could see trouble ahead. Relations with William, though not far advanced, had a directness which she valued; and he was, as Dion said, perceptive.

"Well," he said, "you seem to be putting a face on a state of blankness. What happened? Why am I allowed to drive you home?

Did Davis," he added lightly, as Harriet did not answer, "make an attempt on your honor?"

"On the contrary," said Harriet. "He didn't even hold my hand."

"How very extraordinary," said William, taking hers in a warm clasp, but with the air of one who feels everything is not yet clear. "What did he do instead?"

"He asked me to marry him."

After a silence, still not letting go of her hand, William said, "You don't say."

Harriet looked at him mutely, with sudden depression—the whole thing loomed over her, but seemed absurd. "Are you going to?" he said.

"Oh, how on earth do I know? I've hardly taken it in."

"At least you didn't turn him down flat. It's like driving off with him, isn't it? You say you don't want to, but you do it."

"I don't mean to; I've never behaved like this before. It isn't as if I'm in love with him. It just happens, somehow."

"Oh, he's a compelling personality, all right," said William drearily. "And in a tortuous way, maddening as it is, he's rather a nice one too. You might be good for him. But it's you I was thinking of."

The previous afternoon a seventeen-year-old Welsh boy, in a remote field on his father's farm, had been digging a hole in a stony earth bank for a new gatepost, and turned up several objects that he examined for a moment and then threw aside. It was a warm day and his mind was on other things, and it was not till he stopped to cool off and was sitting on the bank beside his collie and drinking lemonade out of a beer bottle, that one of these objects caught his eye and started him wondering. He wondered why an old bedspring should be buried on a steep hillside a mile from the nearest house. He picked the bedspring up and had another look at it; after that he collected the other objects and put them in his haversack with the empty beer bottle and went back to his digging. At half-past five he returned to the farm, washed, took out his bicycle and rode down to the village to see the schoolmaster.

The schoolmaster scraped some caked mud off the bedspring and saw a fleck of rich pale gold. He put all the objects in a paper bag and carried them round to the minister's house. The minister had to go to a meeting in Aberystwyth the next day, and when he saw the bag's contents he left in the morning instead of in the afternoon. Within a few hours of his arrival the telephone rang in a study in Cheyne Walk, where the acknowledged expert on early Celtic art lived who happened to be Harriet's professor; and twenty-four hours later Harriet found herself being driven out of London again—this time by the professor and on the road to Wales.

Dion rang up before she left. "I thought we might meet to-night or tomorrow," he said despondently. "The day after that I have to go to France, and then Italy."

"I can't get out of it. It's one of those finds-of-the-century things, from the sound of it; I had a job talking him out of leaving at dawn. Probably it won't take long; it's only a reconnaissance."

"Well, if you have to think, Wales is a good place. Quiet like," he said, suddenly relapsing into purest Pontypridd. "I'll be back by the middle of next week. Shall I telephone then?"

"Yes. I will try to think, in Wales."

"And William," said Dion. "Has William thought already?"

"How do you know I have told William?"

"William doesn't need telling. What did he say?"

"For heaven's sake," said Harriet, exasperated, "I'm not engaged to William. Does it matter what he said?"

"It matters to me. William is my rival and a nice character and perceptive; I respect his judgment."

"He said you were a nice character, too, if you must know."

"And?"

"He thought I might be good for you."

"He's right enough there; it's you he worries about. It's his strength as a rival that he is so kind to me. But don't listen to William, or to me, or to anyone. I'll see you when I get back."

Harriet had been working with the professor for nearly three

years, and in that time she had traveled in his four-year-old car over
most of Britain, an indifferently acquiescing passenger. It was not
until they were leaving London on the way to Wales that she realized how much one drive with Dion had subconsciously taught her.
"It's just an art," William had said; "he's just a master of it; he's a
car and a man in one piece." Harriet had only half understood, but
she now saw that the professor and his car, far from being in one
piece, were so remote from each other that it was a miracle either
of them or herself had up till then survived.

The only thing that Dion and the professor had in common was
that both seemed to drive in a trance; the professor's trance, however, was in no way connected with driving. After Beaconsfield, he
unwrapped his thoughts from early Celtic art, blew his nose—his
catarrh was in full bloom—and said politely, "Did you have a pleasant weekend?"

"It was interesting. I went to watch motor racing."

"Really? And did you enjoy it?"

"I'm not sure."

"It must be very fascinating," said the professor, "if you like that
sort of thing. I'm told it's widely followed. The appeal, I imagine,"
he said, snuffling gently and accelerating up to thirty-three miles an
hour to cut in between a lorry and an approaching Aston Martin
with an inch to spare, "is that it's so dangerous."

Harriet was in Wales for four days, and there were moments,
though not many of them, when she had time to think, but thinking is not so straightforward. She caught herself brooding over
Dion while she was taking notes in a museum, because the profile
of an assistant reminded her that Dion was a Celt too. Later, sitting on an earth bank while the professor delicately prodded the
hillside, in remote peace, ideal for thinking, her mind stayed on
what had been found by accident in that earth, ornaments so as-
sured, important and beautiful that Dion did not seem to matter.

Then again in the primitive village inn, as she lay on a lumpy

bed listening to the cries of sheep on the hillside, Dion came between her and sleep till the early hours of the morning. What
would it be like, she thought, crowds and cameras and always traveling or waiting? She could not imagine herself marrying him, and
yet sometimes it seemed as if not marrying him would be nearly
as unbearable as the alternative. *It's crazy,* she said. *I don't love
him, but there's never been anything like this before. I don't know
what to do.*

When they returned to London at the end of the week, Dion was
still abroad. A letter from him was waiting at the flat. His writing
was black and angular; the style was not flowery: "There is a hot
wind blowing dust about and it's intolerable here—all the people
and the details and the flap. I can only get away when I'm driving.
I wish I could have come to Wales and sat on a hill without a car
in sight. Will that ever happen? Have you had time to think?"

Too much time, thought Harriet. She rang up William and said,
"I'm thinking too much."

"That's bad; you know what happened to Cassius. Shall we go
out tonight?"

"I'd love to, if it's all right with you."

"Dinner and dancing or a nice leg show to take the mind off?"

"No, I'd like to see a madly good film. Preferably French, and
depressing."

After the film, they had supper. Harriet said, "It does put life
into perspective. When I watch a piece like that, nothing real seems
so important."

"I know, Harriet, but you can't spend your married life in Continental cinemas. There aren't enough good French films, to begin with."

"I didn't say anything about married life."

"Don't be defensive. Are you going to marry him?"

"I don't know. I can't visualize what it would be like."

"Well, it wouldn't be curling up in a cottage and growing peas, would it? Cameras, pressmen, aeroplanes; Rheims, Aintree, Argentina, Le Mans, Monaco—disruptive, but a chance to travel. And watching—would you want to watch him race?"

"I wouldn't have to."

"Or not watching—waiting at home or in a hotel—wouldn't that be as bad?"

"You said he was so good, no one drives as he does. I don't think I should worry about that."

"Perhaps if you fell in love with him," said William gently, "you might find you worried, after all." When she looked at her plate without answering, he added, "Or do you love him?"

"No," she said. "But I can't get him out of my mind."

"He's that sort," said William. "Nor can I."

Dion telephoned two days later. "Back," he said. "The usual perishing rush. I've got to go down to Silverstone tomorrow. Can I see you tonight?"

"Yes."

"Or sooner? Why aren't you digging things up today?"

"He's gone off to see another prof about torques—he's in a kind of early Celtic daze. I tidied his papers up this morning and I'm not wanted any more."

"That's what you think. Can I come and fetch you now?"

"Yes."

He arrived twenty minutes later in the dark-green sports saloon. Uncertain of his plans—whether he was contemplating tea at Fortnum's, a drive to Hampton Court or a soul-to-soul conversation in her flat—Harriet wondered what to wear. She looked through her inadequate wardrobe and decided a gray suit and a white blouse would do for any emergency. In case it should be Fortnum's, though this seemed unlikely, she put a string of pearls in her pocket, brushed her hair hard, and went down when she heard his ring. Instead of getting out, he leaned over and opened the nearside door.

"Where are we going?" she said.

"Wales."

Harriet was speechless.

"Do you mind?" said Dion.

"No, but I haven't——"

"You'll be back tonight."

It took the professor five hours to get from Chelsea to the border. Finding herself speeding apparently gently along a dual carriageway at the moment when the professor would have been negotiating Hammersmith Broadway, Harriet revised her timetable and sat back.

She said, "Do you never get tired of driving?"

"Never. If I did, I'd hire a helicopter; I'd still want to go to Wales with you."

"Why?" she said.

"Partly because I didn't think I wanted to go back, but I do. Partly because I want to see where a boy dug up a bracelet, and then you sat on a hillside wondering whether to marry me or not."

"Is that where we're going?"

"You will have to tell me the way."

By six o'clock, in the warm sun of early evening, they were sitting on the hill above the farm. The opposite slope was in shadow, veined with bluebells in the thin grass; sheep moved on the sky line, a pair of buzzards wheeled into the light. Dion took off his jacket and lay down on the turf.

"Dion," said Harriet, "you look exhausted."

"I can't sleep in aeroplanes. Do you know that's the first time you've called me by my name?"

"Go to sleep now."

"This is better than sleep. What happened when you sat here and wondered?"

"When I sat here I was thinking mostly about the things the boy found."

"Were they very good?"

"They were lovely. But I did think about you as well. I didn't come to any conclusion."

"Never mind." He put an arm over his eyes and went to sleep. Harriet sat clasping her knees, watching the buzzards leaning and circling in air clear as water. She listened to the sheep, the distant fall of a stream, the sound of Dion's breathing beside her. The sun touched the hilltop; she turned and met his eyes.

He said, "I'm sorry I slept. I thought it might be easier, talking about it here."

"I suppose it might," she said. "I'm glad you did sleep. It's wonderful getting away from things. But it would hardly ever be like this, would it?"

"Not often. It's a hell of a life really; I wish I were good at something else. But I have to do it."

"I know that. There would never be any question."

"We have one great advantage; we don't try to persuade each other. Harriet, if I took your hand I should be persuading you, and I shouldn't stop at that, either. I should persuade you till you hadn't any breath to say no. You'll say no to me of your own free will. Or yes, whatever it is. Let's walk down to the pub and have a beer."

Crossing the stile, Harriet was conscious of something bulky in her pocket. She could not help laughing, producing, like a conjuror, a string of pearls that swung ludicrously in the solitude of the evening.

She said, "Shall I tell you why these were there?"

"Because you don't trust me. You've got your diamonds in your stocking tops, I expect. Why?"

"I never have the right sort of clothes, and I thought you might want to take me to tea at Fortnum's."

From the other side of the stile Dion looked at her; he was smiling, but very pale. He said, "If you thought that, Harriet, you do need more time."

"I forgot you were famous."

"That's a lousy remark too."

"I'm sorry. It's not the way I meant it."

"No, I see that now—only it touches me off. Look, will you tell me, one way or the other, on Saturday? Tell me after the race at Silverstone; I don't want to know before I drive. William will bring you down."

"All right. But do you think William will want to, if you take me back again?"

"William likes racing. And at least he'll know his fate."

It seemed a long cold afternoon, with a drizzle of rain falling, the track flat and shining and the crowd muffled and more colorless than before. Where William and Harriet sat in the stand a loudspeaker was very close to them and they had to raise their voices. It was so loud that Harriet could not take in what was happening; she listened for a name.

"What did he say?" she asked William, and William answered, "He's in the lead," and later, "Half a lap clear." He looked down at her short damp hair and the way she watched, not the cars passing but the distant track down which they approached.

"How much longer?" she said.

"About twenty-five minutes. Shall we go and walk about behind the stand?"

"All right, for a bit; my feet are cold."

The drizzle had stopped, but the grass in the field was rough and wet. They wandered among ropes and litter, behind the wall of people lining the track, around the scaffolding underneath the stand.

She said, "It's endless. Why do they have to go on so long?"

"Harriet," said William, "I told you he was a master. You weren't going to worry about that. Is it different already?"

"I don't know; it's different today. Perhaps I'm not used to watching it."

"Perhaps you're not, but if you feel like that about it, it won't get easier. It's today you're going to tell him, isn't it?"

"Yes," she said. From where they stood, the loud-speaker was more distant and easier to hear.

"Davis," it said, and as she was about to speak, she stopped and listened. "Davis should be coming down the straight. I can't see him. Davis should be in sight by now; he's overdue. Davis is overdue, with the race in his pocket."

William took hold of her wrists as she put her hands over her ears.

"Listen," he said. "Listen, will you? It could be anything. It could be gearbox, or throttle linkage, or a valve, or brakes, or a tire. Anything, do you hear?"

Against his shoulder he felt her shake her head. They stood in the damp grass by the girders, with the stand between them and the column of smoke that rose, thin and distant, from the far end of the track.

FAIR YOUNG GHOST

by Kenneth Kay

Brockden James scarcely remembered the name of the village. He knew it was somewhere in Westmoreland, hours south of Carlisle, but travel time in the dimmed-out train that was forever stopping mysteriously on the dark moors or being shunted aside at unlighted stations to let higher-priority traffic go crashing through meant nothing in terms of distance. He first saw the village when they were backed for the dozenth time into a siding and left standing. Peering glumly through the soot-and-rain-smeared train window, Brock saw narrow stone houses along a wet, cobblestoned street.

Alison, in her Wren's topcoat, was warm and solid against him. There were no seats in the packed compartments and they sat on his duffel bag in the corridor. Outside, a drizzling rain fell, interminably as the settling of time over the stalled coaches. Brock muttered irascibly and heard Alison's easygoing chuckle. She was Scots with four war years behind her and had learned to endure, but he had an American's fretting impatience with delay.

With his sleeve he scrubbed a clean patch on the smeared window. At the top of the street, higher than the cramped houses, rose a stone inn with a yellow light shining feebly on a wind-racked sign. Long watches on the dark bridge of an LST had sharpened Brock's night vision and, squinting, he read the sign. GEORGE AND DRAGON. Brock snorted. There must be scores of George and Dragon pubs in England, he thought, as many as there were Red Lions or Green Men. More pubs than names to go around, but that was the English for you, clinging to old ways and old names. Not that it was any business of a U.S.N.R. lieutenant (j.g.) from Rahway, New Jersey, what the English did in their own country. But wouldn't you think one of them would break with tradition? Would call his pub Joe's Bar—Biggest Pint of Beer in the County? Brock laughed aloud.

"Got another smoke?" asked Alison, lazily. "What's funny, darling?"

"Split one with you." Brock's cigarette supply was low after a three-day visit with Alison's parents in their Isle of Arran home and he would get no more this side of the ship's store in Portsmouth.

She drew on the cigarette he lighted for her. Her snub-nosed face with its direct blue gaze smiled at him in the ruddy glow. "What was funny?"

"The inn up there—the George and Dragon. Just hit me how funny it would look if the sign said 'Joe's Place' instead."

She looked at him blankly.

He patted her knee. "New Jersey type joke, honey. You'll understand after we've lived there a few years."

Time wore on. Once a trainman walked under the window with a lantern and another time two men in cloth caps came out of the station and stared thoughtfully at the train. But still it did not move.

"Are we spending the night here?" groaned Brock.

"There's a war on, darling," said Alison. "Relax. This is the reason I thought we should leave Lamlash early."

"Early! Rate this thing's moving we should have left last week."

"Oh, it's not that bad. There are still two days to get to Portsmouth."

"Faster if we walked," growled Brock and, ashamed of his irritation, patted her knee again.

She was an ensign in the Royal Navy office in Portsmouth to which he was attached as American liaison officer. He had known her less than ninety days, but, without a quiver of doubt, he now knew she was the girl for the rest of his life. It was not merely her looks. There were prettier girls around than Alison MacLaren. Indeed, compared to the blond, long-limbed English beauties, she was a shade stocky, a little square-hewn in a sturdy Scots pattern; and he had found under her comradely, casual manner a stanch Scots Presbyterian conscience.

She made this abundantly clear the night she finally yielded to his badgering and consented to dine in an American officers' mess. She had stood there on the green lawn between an ornamental pyramid of round cannon balls and a scowling figurehead off one of Nelson's ships of the line and looked at him squarely.

"Mr. James," she had said, a trace of the Scottish "r" in her lilting speech, "I've agreed to come out with you, and I shall. But to be fair I must say that if you're expecting what young Americans generally want, you'll take another girl in my place."

He blinked, a little embarrassed, because, of course, that was what he did want. But naturally he denied it.

She heard him out gravely. "Then it's all right," she said, "if you're telling the truth. But if you're not, then it will be better for both of us if you make another arrangement for the evening."

Her smile was kindly. "You'll have no trouble doing it, Mr. James. I know a dozen Wrens would give anything to go out with a handsome young American officer. Some are watching from the windows now." She pointed with her chin at the brick women officers' quarters. "I shouldn't mind, truly. I'd just go on to the pictures alone and in a bit some of the girls will come out as if to ask who you're waiting for and you can take your pick."

"But, my God!" he had expostulated, and "Look here!" and

"What do you take me for?" and in the end they went to his mess on her terms and had a splendid evening; and after a dozen more splendid evenings in the next three weeks, in which he was cross a few times and utterly outraged once and learned that she had a straight punch with solid Scotch muscle behind it, Brock found himself hopelessly and eternally in love.

And Alison was, too, and they began talking of marriage for after the war, and Brock meant marriage and was astonished to discover that where it came to Alison he, too, had suddenly developed an old-fashioned moral code.

So now, sitting on his duffel bag in the stranded train, everything was settled and excellent between Brockden James and his Alison MacLaren. All that waited was the success of the Overlord invasion, a quick end to Hitler's war and after that the Japanese one, and then Brock meant to take his bonny, bonny bride from the bonny banks of Clyde home to Rahway, where his father manufactured radio sets, and live there forever.

The two men in cloth caps vanished inside the station. Long minutes dragged and Brock's impatience mounted. Nothing to eat since breakfast, he thought; nothing to eat this side of London; and they could sit on this forsaken siding the rest of the night!

"This is ridiculous," he said disgustedly. "Come on, let's get off this Toonerville Trolley."

"Let's do what?"

"Get off!" he snapped. "Bail out! Abandon ship!"

"Why, what ever for?"

He gestured irritably. "To get something to eat, if nothing else."

"But suppose the train leaves?"

"It's never going to leave. And even if it does there'll be another one along someday. Come on!"

Alison shrugged. "Och," she said, laughing, "you're daft."

On a damp spring evening Brockden James, the thirty-eight-year-old vice president of the James Television Corporation of Rahway,

New Jersey, was driving a rented car east across Westmoreland. There were two bedrooms reserved in a Windermere hotel, but in some stupid fashion he had taken a wrong turning and was now miles off his course to the Lake District on this black road that meandered across the lonely moors.

If anything had been needed to heighten his annoyed frustration, getting lost in Westmoreland would have done it. He had never wanted to see the place again, had never wanted to see the U.K. again, though he could not explain why to his wife. He had tried to take Rosalind to the Continent for their European vacation, but she had this thing in her head about seeing Scotland and he couldn't talk her out of it. In ten years of marriage Brock had rarely talked Roz out of anything.

He drove in sulky silence, ignoring her bright chatter that found every flock of grazing sheep remarkable, every gorse patch, every monotonous lift of moorland, every crooked stone fence, worthy of exclamation. She was, he thought wearily, the most irritatingly cheerful traveler, the most tediously enthusiastic, he had ever known. Until their month-long holiday together he had never appreciated the blessing it was to have an office to go to each morning.

One bleak hill succeeded another. Overhead, gray clouds rolled toward the Irish Sea. A raw, warm wind buffeted the small car, and Brockden James bowed his neck and drove.

The road bent south and railroad tracks out of the north came curving beside it. At once Brock sensed an uneasy familiarity in the loom of the moors—a shape as of a land he might have visited once in a dream. He fidgeted uncomfortably. The black road lifted and the railway dropped, running level through a cut. From the hilltop Brock saw stone houses clustered in a notch beside a small railroad station where the angling train tracks bisected the road. A long way off he read the station sign: Scragsdale.

Something seemed to explode in his brain. He coasted into the cobbled single street of the moor village, stopped the car and under a sudden, insupportable weight of anguish bent his head.

"Why, Brock!" said Roz. "What's the matter?"

He blinked at the polite concern on her dark and vivid face. "What did you say?"

"I asked what's the matter. Are you ill? What is it, Brock?"

"Look up the street," he said huskily, not daring to raise his eyes. "Is there an inn up there? An old stone inn called the George and Dragon?"

"Why, Brock!" she exclaimed. "This is amazing. I didn't know you knew this part of England."

"I don't," he said unsteadily. "I spent a night here once, that's all. I—I don't want to talk about it."

He put the car in gear, but a weakness assailed him. He shut his eyes. *O Alison, Alison, my lost love; Alison.* "Look, Roz," he said with difficulty, "I want to stay here tonight. At that inn."

She stared. "Here? With reservations at Windermere?"

He struggled for calmness. "Roz. Please. I said I want to stay here."

Rosalind shrugged her fine shoulders. She was of vaguely Scottish descent four generations back and had dragged Brock through half the kirkyards between Dumbarton and Inverness, hunting fancied ancestors. From an Inveraray hotel chambermaid she had acquired this locution she liked. "Och," said Roz disdainfully, "you're daft."

Brock shuddered. "For God's sake, don't use that expression!"

She was affronted. "What is this?" she asked coldly. "Is this something to do with that girl? The one you knew over here in the war?"

He did not answer. Doggedly, with stony eyes, Brock drove into the courtyard of the George and Dragon and left Roz in the car while he went to find the manager.

"Och," said Alison, laughing, "you're daft." She rose docilely, slung her musette and followed Brock when he opened the train door and leaped out into darkness and misting rain.

They were halfway up the cobbled street when the locomotive whistled derisively, coughed up a plume of smoke and lurched out of the station.

"Well, this is nice, I must say. What was that you mentioned about walking to Portsmouth?"

Brock grinned sheepishly. "Just shows to go you. My life's a history of bad guesses. Well, let's see what they can do for us at the inn."

Under the swinging sign of the George and Dragon he rang the bell a long time before the door opened. An old woman with her hands under her apron eyed them distastefully. "And what would you be wantin' this time of night?"

"Supper," said Brock, good-naturedly. "We're famished."

She sniffed. "Supper, is it? Ah well, it's a public house."

"When's the next train for London?"

"Six in the morning, if it's on time, which it hasna been for two years."

"Then I guess you'll have to put us up for the night," said Brock.

"You're a Yank," said the old woman accusingly, and swept Alison with a contemptuous, inventorying glance. "You're no wed?"

"No," began Alison, "but——"

"There'll be no hanky-panky under my roof," said the woman sternly. "I'll give you beds, but in separate rooms on separate floors, and I'll have no tippytoeing oop and down stairs after."

Brock flushed angrily, but before he could speak Alison had faced the old woman calmly and in a broader Scots than he had heard her use before explained that they were pledged, but not yet wed, and certainly they wanted separate rooms if the lady would be so kind.

The woman cocked her head. "Ah, now. You're a Scottish lassie."

"Aye," said Alison, smiling. "Of Arran."

"My mister was Ayrshire, rest his bones. Well, come along in then." Surprisingly, the old woman smiled at Alison. "I'll serve you upstairs, though what there is to give you, with this wicked war and the rationing and all, the dear Lord only knows."

They ate in a chilly second-floor lounge. There seemed to be no other guests at the George and Dragon. The woman brought bread, cheese, half a cold pie and a tankard of beer for Brock. In front of Alison she put a glass of hot milk. "There," she said approvingly, "that will warm you this wild, bitter night."

"This is lovely," said Alison.

Brock grinned with his mouth full of bread and cheese, and raised his tankard in salute. "Glad now that train ran off and left us. This is all right, huh?"

The old woman beamed at Alison. "So you'll be going to the States to live?"

"Aye," said Alison. "When the war is over."

"In its day," said the woman, staring past them at the shadowy corner of the lounge, "this was a great house for young lovers. It's no so far, you see, from Gretna Green. In those times just a good run by posting coach." She cocked her head again, her eye bright as a robin's. "You're certain you'll be wantin' two rooms?"

"Quite certain," said Alison, blushing.

"Ah well," said the old woman, almost regretfully, "you know what's best for you, of course. Well, I'll say good night."

When she was gone Brock laughed. "Why, that old—romanticist! What happened to that stuff she gave us at the door about hanky-panky?"

"Hush," said Alison reprovingly. "She's sweet."

Brock's bed was lumpy and damply chill in a room cold as any funeral vault. He lay a long time listening to groaning creaks and ghostly whispers from the wainscoting as the wind beat at the old inn. Once he got up, smoked two cigarettes he did not want and should have saved, staring out his mullioned window at the moon-shadowed moors. The rain had stopped. Shivering, he returned to bed and at last fell asleep.

The creak of his door latch waked him with a start. A pale figure crossed the room and a warm palm covered his lips. "Brock," said

Alison in a voice of deepest sorrow. "Brock, darling. My poor, poor Brock."

He was alarmed and perplexed. "Alison! What are you doing here?"

She sobbed suddenly and clung to him, spilling hot tears on his face.

"Alison! Alison, baby! What is it?"

"I'm going to die," she said brokenly. "I'm fey. I waked in that cold, black room and knew it. I'm fey."

"You're what?"

"Fey." She shuddered and burrowed into his arms. "Marked for dying. It's a thing the island Scots know. I never believed in it. My old nurse told me, but I never believed in it. Only it's true, Brock; horribly, dreadfully true. I'm to die. Soon. I felt the ice clutch my heart. I'm going to die and we're never to marry." The bitter tears rained down.

"Now, now," said Brock bewilderedly, soothing and petting her. "Go back to bed. You had a bad dream, that's all. Go back to bed, honey, before you take cold."

She shook her head obstinately and pushed under the bed covers, straining against him frantically, shaking, weeping. Baffled, Brock smoothed her hair and shoulders. Slowly the shivering and sobbing ceased. Alison lay still, staring with dull eyes at the shadowed ceiling.

"This is all we're to have," she said in a doomed, dead voice. "Tonight is all. Tonight is the only marriage we will have."

"This is all wrong," he protested. "You'll feel differently in the morning. It's just this old inn, just the timbers creaking and the wind blowing. You dreamed it, darling. Go back to bed. You'll be fine tomorrow."

"Don't deny me," she said stubbornly. "Tonight is all there will ever be." Then she seized him frenziedly and overbore his weakening protests with wild, wet kisses.

When the old woman waked Brock with tea in a five o'clock blackness Alison was gone. On the long trip south that day she did not mention the night, scarcely spoke at all. A detached calmness possessed her, a remoteness. By the time they reached Portsmouth, Brock was wild with perplexity and frustration, and it was Alison who soothed him. With a slight, tranquil smile she said that they should be grateful for the warning that had given them all they would have of each other. She said that in the years ahead he was not to let her memory divide him from the living world. She stopped his agonized pleading with chaste, cool lips and said that he was to be happy. That if he was unhappy she would know it and be unhappy too.

The next day orders detached Brock to a destroyer in the Mediterranean. He never returned to England. An early V-1 found Alison in its path, and her mother wrote that there was not even a grave he could have visited.

"I wonder if we could have two rooms," said Brock hesitantly. "My wife's a little—not too well just now, and needs privacy."

"Nothing serious, I hope," said the owner of the George and Dragon politely. He was a man named Milbank, about Brock's age, but older-looking with a brown, close-trimmed navy-style beard.

"Just a nervous condition," said Brock, despising the lie. Roz and he had planned their vacation with the tacit, unacknowledged purpose of trying to find where they had strayed from each other, of recovering the brief, lost happiness of their first marriage year. But something had angered her early and, since Edinburgh, Roz had insisted on separate rooms. It was intended as punishment for an offense Brock could not remember giving, but now he thought of it as nightly respite from her sharp, ceaseless tongue.

"If you're staying the one night only I can accommodate you," said Milbank. "Starting tomorrow, however, I'm booked through the weekend, all but one room."

"That's all right. We're going to Windermere in the morning. Could I send a telegram to my hotel there?"

"Of course, Mr. James. Perhaps first, though, you'd like to bring your lady in."

Milbank walked out to the car with him, Brock already beginning to regret his inexplicable impulse. This was not the George and Dragon he remembered. Oh, it was the same old stone building in the same moor village, but bright now with new paint and beds of spring flowers. He recalled a dank, haunted mausoleum of an inn on a bitter, blustering night. This George and Dragon was cheerful and pretty and characterless.

What made him stop? he thought glumly. Bad as an old woman, hugging an ancient sorrow. What did he expect to find—Alison's ghost? His own ghost? The ghost of that twenty-three-year-old boy? The ghost of happiness?

Milbank's cheery voice startled him. "Hope you don't mind ghosts, Mrs. James. Your husband said you were feeling a bit nervy."

"Nervy?" said Roz, frowning at Brock. "Ghosts?" she asked delightedly.

"Well, one ghost," said Milbank, smiling. "Of a young girl."

Brock closed his eyes. "A young girl?" he said faintly. "How young?"

"Never seen her myself," said Milbank dryly. "But I can't keep chambermaids. They're country girls and a superstitious lot—forever spotting her as she flits down the corridors at night, a fair young ghost, wringing her hands, weeping bitterly. A nuisance, but, even so, I'm rather proud of her. Perhaps you know how we feel about ghosts in England. Cherish them, rather, like heirlooms. Ghosts are snobbish sorts, generally. Stick to castles. Not often found in an ordinary inn."

Brock swallowed dryly. "Someone who stopped here once, you think? Who died here or—or died shortly after being here and—and had reason to come back?"

Milbank shrugged. "Really, don't take this as seriously as I make it sound. I'm sure it's nothing but the moor winds sobbing under the eaves. This is an old house, full of creaks and rustlings. The chambermaids hear them, see patches of moonlight or reflections of car headlights passing at night. I'm sure it's nothing more."

"But I want to take it seriously," said Rosalind. "I'm fascinated. Who do they think she is?"

They were at the reception desk and Brock was registering their names in the guest book. His hand shook slightly. It was ridiculous, totally absurd, but once before in this old house he had witnessed a thing that common sense rejected.

"Who do they think she is, Mrs. James?" Milbank smiled. "No one very original, I fear. Just another poor girl betrayed by a faithless lover. All nonsense, of course. My old aunt, from whom I got this place when she died, never said anything about ghosts. Of course there are people on the moors would tell you Aunt Cathy was in league with dark forces herself. This story's developed since the war—about the young girl, I mean. Abandoned here by her lover en route to Gretna Green. Hanged herself, or some such. Chap walked off from her without sanctifying the relationship. I beg your pardon, Mrs. James."

"Don't mind me," said Roz. "I think it's a marvelous story. Imagine a girl nowadays hanging herself over something like that!"

Milbank seemed amused. "Well, they're very moral in these parts as well as superstitious. A morality tale, I suppose you could call it, intended to warn young women against straying from the strait and narrow. . . . Would you like to see your rooms now?"

They dined silently in a room bright with burnished copper, and after coffee Roz smiled mockingly. "I think you're utterly asinine," she said, "and I'm sure you'll never tell me why you chose to stop here. But if it was to annoy me, you failed. It's a lovely old place and I'll sleep extremely well. Good night, dear." She rose. "By the way, Brock, I'm not in the least afraid of ghosts."

"Aren't you?" said Brock wearily. "Aren't you, Roz? Well, I am."

After she went up, he walked through the village by twilight, thinking of the rainy night with Alison, thinking of what it had been to be happy and young and in love. How transient we are, he thought moodily. How slight and insubstantial the things which

stand tallest in our memories. Who except him now knew or cared
that Alison MacLaren and he had been happy here once?

He returned to the inn in a dreary mood, wanting a drink. There
was no servant in the lounge and he could not find a bell. While
he was hunting along the paneled walls, Milbank entered, wearing
gray slacks and a corduroy jacket. "I've a feeling about you, Mr.
James," he said. "A strong feeling that we've met before."

"In the States?"

"Never been there. Been in Canada, but not the States. It's something about the war, I fancy."

"Well, I had liaison duty with one of your admirals' staffs in
Portsmouth."

"There!" said Milbank. "I knew you'd been a sailor. When you
came in this evening I said to myself, 'There's a chap who's walked
a quarterdeck.' Navy myself. Not the wavy navy. Not the regulars.
Wartime only. It wasn't Portsmouth I saw you, though. Were you
ever in the Med?"

"Matter of fact, I was," said Brock slowly. "They posted me there
from Portsmouth. To destroyer duty. The Massingale."

Milbank clapped his hands sharply. "The Massingale! Oh, by
heaven, this is too much! Tell me, do you recollect hauling a poor,
oil-soaked sod of a leftenant commander over your sides one morning, fellow off a torpedoed corvette?"

Brock stared. "Was that you? Are you the guy we put aboard that
RN hospital ship?"

"As ever was," said Milbank, grinning hugely. "My good friend
and onetime rescuer, this calls for a drink. Did you ever taste Navy-
issue rum—Nelson's blood?"

"Sure did," said Brock, grinning too. "In some of you fellows'
wardrooms. You'll remember," he added apologetically, "ours was
a prohibition navy."

Milbank grimaced. "So I understand. Heroism above the highest
call of duty, I always thought it. Fancy going to sea without a tot
of grog! Well, now. This is quite an occasion we have here. Excuse
me a moment." He went to the cellar and, returning with a white

stone crock, poured rum into pewter tankards. "Cheers, friend James. And may I say belatedly, many thanks. Except for your smart seamanship that morning, Aunt Cathy would have had to leave the George and Dragon to my snivel-nosed half brother."

The quiet lounge became the most cheerful room, it seemed to Brock, that he had known since the war. For a long time after Alison's death he had hated with cold fury the war that took her from him, ignoring the corollary that the war had given her to him in the first place. Under the influence of rum and Milbank's pleasant company, however, and after the worse than solitary month with Rosalind, he found himself reminiscing about the war, ships and sea fights and liberty ports.

The hours passed and the rum crock grew lighter. Brock heard himself propounding with the insistent positiveness of mild intoxication a just-discovered conviction that in some ways the war had been the best thing that would ever occur in the lives of men who were in it.

"Not the ones," he said, squinting owlishly, "who got all shot up, of course, but guys like you and me who came out of it all right." He gestured, spilling rum on his cuff. "For me, at least, it was a fine time, looking back now. Being young, having everything so simple. Work your ship, fight your ship, go ashore when you could and frolic. Everything simple. Everything crys'l, I mean crystal-clear."

Milbank stroked his brown beard.

"People weren't in it don't know," said Brock argumentatively. "Don't un'erstand how things were. Take my wife—well, never mind. But they don't un'erstand, people weren't in it."

Milbank stared into his tankard. "Perhaps. Thought so myself for a while. But you can't just shut them out because of it. Not their fault, you know. It's not that they don't want to understand. I've a young wife too. Excuse me. Ought not bring up personal affairs. Home now, visiting. Montreal. Mavis, now. Well, she didn't understand about the war either. Too young, too far away from it. But I learned—— Well, you see, Brock, old boy"—they had achieved first names with the fourth rum—"had to learn it was wrong, closing her out from that important part of my life. Made her feel inferior. If it's a fair show, marriage—well, you must, you know, absolutely must take your wife into all you've done and been. They want it, old boy. Really. We went on the rocks, nearly, before I learned that. Excluding them, you see, letting them feel left out—well, it just won't do."

Brock scowled. "Never thought of it—not like that." The syllables sounded thick as he spoke them. "Worth thinking about." He stood up, a shade unsteadily, told Milbank good night and went thoughtfully to bed.

He lay there, unable to sleep, pondering murkily what Milbank had said. He supposed he had closed Roz out. Hadn't meant to, exactly, but when it came to the war he hadn't wanted to talk to her. The pain of Alison's loss, he'd never told her that. He'd mentioned once about there having been a girl; once and never again, but Roz hadn't forgotten. Nor forgiven, he suspected.

He stared at the mullioned window. It was a windless night, but he could sense the old house settling and whispering about him. What time was it? It must be late. He'd feel that rum in the morning. Roz was going to laugh sarcastically when he turned up with a hang-over. Hang Roz.

Whatever he did now, it was finished for them. It was too late. They'd just keep going through the dreary motions of a marriage that was all dry rot inside. The vacation trip had not only failed in its purpose, it had worsened matters. Contemplating the future dismally, Brock finally fell asleep.

He waked to a sensation of acutest sorrow. The room was black dark except for the pale shape of the window. What had he been dreaming? What had he heard in his sleep to induce this deep melancholy, this grief beyond hope?

Then he heard it again and shuddered. Heard it and remembered now hearing it in his dream.

Somewhere outside his door, a woman was weeping. He had never heard a sound so pathetic, so heartbroken, so utterly hopeless. He listened and they came again, endless, racking sobs, the weeping of uttermost despair. But not quite human. . . . Suddenly Brock's scalp prickled. Nonsense, he told himself sternly. Superstitious nonsense. It was the wind.

But it was a windless night. Through his window he could see the stars of a still, fine night.

The weeping rose higher, might have been just beyond his door. He sat upright in bed and, noiselessly, his door swung open.

"My God," Brock whispered as a pale, feminine figure formed in his doorway.

"Oh, Brock!" cried Rosalind in a pitying voice, "did you hear it? Did you hear her crying, that poor, lost creature?"

She ran across the room, in her nightgown, and clung to him. She began sobbing, the self-possessed Rosalind, sobbing. "Did you hear her? That poor, brokenhearted girl?" Her arms tightened about him. "I'm ashamed," said Rosalind. "Deeply ashamed. It's wicked of me not to be happy, to let you be unhappy, with all that we have. In a world that can hold that kind of sorrow, her sorrow, it's wicked, Brock. Sorrow such as I never dreamed anyone could feel."

The agonized sound of weeping in the corridor outside faltered, died out. Uncertainly, Brock began stroking Rosalind's hair. "It was just the wind," he said unsteadily. "It wasn't anything, Roz. You mustn't let it upset you."

"It wasn't wind," she said, burrowing into his arms. "You know it wasn't. You know what it was as well as I do. And it shamed me, Brock. Shamed me because with all our reasons for happiness I've let us be unhappy. Brock, I never stopped loving you, not really. Brock, can we try to be happy again?"

The sound of weeping in the corridor had ceased completely. Brock had a curious notion they would not hear it again.

"We can try," he said shakily, and drew Roz to him. "I'd like to try. It's been my fault, all of it. I haven't been fair——"

She closed his mouth with her lips. "No. It's my fault. All of it. Brock, will you let me come to bed with you?"

In the morning, Milbank looked pale about the gills, but his smile was cheerful as ever. "Well, you people still planning to leave us this morning?"

Roz colored slightly under Milbank's knowledgeable regard. She guessed that the maid who brought their morning tea had communicated to the whole household the intelligence of where Mrs. James had spent the night. "It's such a lovely old inn," she said. "Could we stay on a day or two?"

Milbank fondled his beard. "I've only the one room, you know."

Roz blushed. "That will be quite all right. I'm not—nervous any more."

Brock grinned and squeezed her hand. "Say, Alan," he said to Milbank, "did we leave anything in that crock of yours last night? I'd like Roz to get a taste tonight of the sort of hell-fire the Royal Navy drinks."

"Hell-fire!" said Milbank rebukingly. "I'll have you know that's the finest hundred-and-twenty-proof rum this side of Jamaica. Let me mix up a bit for her in a fruit cup after tea. Can't expect a lady to knock the stuff back neat the way we old tars do." Then he winked. "Letting her in on some of the horrors of our war, are you?"

In the following February, Brockden James received a letter from Alan Milbank confirming his requested reservation for two bedrooms at the George and Dragon the last week of April.

. . . *putting a fine old rosewood baby crib for the little one*," wrote Milbank, "*in the room with her Nanny and are looking forward with delight to seeing the three of you.*

Things here are much as you left them with one rather startling difference. Don't want to be annoyed with a man who saved my life, Brock, but it does seem to me you went too far. We're accustomed in England to rich Yankees making off with our household treasures, but when it comes to stealing ghosts, really, this is too much. The point is, I haven't lost a chambermaid since your visit. Fact! I don't know what happened, but the ghost has vanished. Swallowed up into—well, where do ghosts go?

                                                              Yours cordially.

Brock grinned and put the letter in his pocket to show Roz at the hospital. He glanced at his watch and rose hurriedly. It was just twenty minutes before visiting hours at the maternity ward and he was anxious to see Roz and little Alison MacLaren James. He thought that was a fine name for a newborn baby girl. Being of vaguely Scottish descent herself, Roz thought it was a fine name too. Anyway, she wasn't in the least jealous of any girl Brock had known in the war.

She hadn't any reason to be either.

THE MAGIC WHITE SUIT

by Ray Bradbury

It was summer twilight in the city, and out front of the quiet-clicking poolhall three young Mexican-American men breathed the warm air and looked around at the world. Sometimes they talked and sometimes they said nothing at all, but watched the cars glide by like black panthers on the hot asphalt or saw trolleys loom up like thunderstorms, scatter lightning, and rumble away into silence.

"Hey," sighed Martinez, at last. He was the youngest, the most sweetly sad of the three. "It's a swell night, huh? Swell."

As he observed the world it moved very close and then drifted away and then came close again. People, brushing by, were suddenly across the street. Buildings five miles away suddenly leaned over him. But most of the time everything—people, cars and buildings—stayed way out on the edge of the world and could not be touched. On this quiet warm summer evening, Martinez' face was cold.

"Nights like this you wish—lots of things."

"Wishing," said the second man, Villanazul, a man who shouted books out loud in his room, but spoke only in whispers on the street, "is the useless pastime of the unemployed."

"Unemployed?" cried Vamenos, the unshaven. "Listen to him! We got no jobs, no money!"

"So," said Martinez, "we got no friends."

"True." Villanazul gazed off toward the green plaza where the palm trees swayed in the soft night wind. "Do you know what I wish? I wish to go into that plaza and speak among the businessmen who gather there nights to talk big talk. But dressed as I am, poor as I am, who would listen? So, Martinez, we have each other. The friendship of the poor is real friendship. We——"

But now a handsome young Mexican with a fine thin mustache strolled by. And on each of his careless arms hung a laughing woman.

"*Madre mía!*" Martinez slapped his own brow. "How does that one rate two friends?"

"It's his nice new white suit." Vamenos chewed a black thumbnail. "He looks sharp."

Martinez leaned out to watch the three people moving away, and then at the tenement across the street, in one fourth-floor window of which, far above, a beautiful girl looked out, her dark hair faintly stirred by the wind. She had been there forever, which was to say, for six weeks. He had nodded, he had raised a hand, he had smiled, he had blinked rapidly; he had even bowed to her, on the street, in the hall when visiting friends, in the park, downtown. Even now, he put his hand up from his waist and moved his fingers. But all the lovely girl did was let the summer wind stir her dark hair. He did not exist. He was nothing.

"*Madre mía!*" He looked away and down the street where the man walked his two friends around a corner. "Oh, if just I had one suit, one! I wouldn't need money if I looked O.K."

"I hesitate to suggest," said Villanazul, "that you see Gomez. But he's been talking some crazy talk for a month now, about clothes. I keep on saying I'll be in on it to make him go away. That Gomez."

"Friend," said a quiet voice.

"Gomez!" Everyone turned to stare.

Smiling strangely, Gomez pulled forth an endless thin yellow ribbon which fluttered and swirled on the summer air.

"Gomez," said Martinez, "what you doing with that tape measure?"

Gomez beamed. "Measuring people's skeletons."

"Skeletons!"

"Hold on." Gomez squinted at Martinez. "Caramba! Where you been all my life! Let's try you!"

Martinez saw his arm seized and taped, his leg measured, his chest encircled.

"Hold still!" cried Gomez. "Arm—perfect. Leg—chest—*perfecto*! Now, quick, the height! There! Yes! Five-foot-five! You're in! Shake!" Pumping Martinez' hand he stopped suddenly. "Wait. You got—ten bucks?"

"*I* have!" Vamenos waved some grimy bills. "Gomez, measure me!"

"All I got left in the world is nine dollars and ninety-two cents." Martinez searched his pockets. "That's enough for a new suit? Why?"

"Why? Because you got the right skeleton, that's why!"

"Señor Gomez, I don't hardly know you——"

"Know me? You're going to live with me! Come on!"

Gomez vanished into the poolroom. Martinez, escorted by the polite Villanazul, pushed by an eager Vamenos, found himself inside.

"Dominguez!" said Gomez.

Dominguez, at a wall telephone, winked at them. A woman's voice squeaked on the receiver.

"Manulo!" said Gomez.

Manulo, a wine bottle tilted bubbling to his mouth, turned.

Gomez pointed at Martinez. "At last we found our fifth volunteer!"

Dominguez said, "I got a date, don't bother me——" and stopped. The receiver slipped from his fingers. His little black telephone book full of fine names and numbers went quickly back into his pocket. "Gomez, you——"

"Yes, yes! Your money, now! *Vamos!*"

The woman's voice sizzled on the dangling phone. Dominguez glanced at it uneasily.

Manulo considered the empty wine bottle in his hand and the liquor-store sign across the street.

Then, very reluctantly, both men laid ten dollars each on the green-velvet pool table.

Villanazul, amazed, did likewise, as did Gomez, nudging Martinez. Martinez counted out his wrinkled bills and change. Gomez flourished the money like a royal flush.

"Fifty bucks! The suit costs sixty! All we need is ten bucks!"

"Wait," said Martinez. "Gomez, are we talking about one suit? *Uno?*"

"*Uno!*" Gomez raised a finger. "One wonderful white ice-cream summer suit! White, white as the August moon!"

"But who will own this one suit?"

"Men," said Gomez, "let's show him. Line up!"

Villanazul, Manulo, Dominguez and Gomez rushed to plant their backs against the poolroom wall.

"Martinez, you, too, the other end, line up! Now, Vamenos, lay that billiard cue across our heads!"

"Sure, Gomez; sure!"

The cue lay flat on all their heads, with no rise or fall, as Vamenos slid it, grinning, along.

"We're all the same height!" said Martinez.

"The same!" Everyone laughed.

"Sure!" Gomez said. "It took a month—four weeks, mind you —to find four guys the same size. But now, five of us, same shoulders, chests, waists, arms; and as for weight? Men!"

Manulo, Dominguez, Villanazul, Gomez and, at last, Martinez stepped onto the scales which flipped ink-stamped cards at them as Vamenos, still smiling, wildly fed pennies.

Heart pounding, Martinez read the cards.

"One hundred thirty-five pounds; one thirty-six; one thirty-three; one thirty-four; one thirty-seven. A miracle!"

"No," said Villanazul simply; "Gomez."

They all smiled upon that genius, who now circled them with his arms.

"Are we not fine?" he wondered. "All the same size, all the same dream—the suit. So each of us will look beautiful at least one night each week, eh?"

"I haven't looked beautiful in years," said Martinez. "The girls run away."

"They will run no more, they will freeze," said Gomez, "when they see you in the cool white summer ice-cream suit."

"Gomez," said Villanazul, "just let me ask one thing."

"Of course, *compadre*."

"When we get this nice new white ice-cream summer suit, some night you're not going to put it on and walk down to the bus in it and go live in El Paso for a year in it, are you?"

"Villanazul, how can you say that?"

"My eye sees and my tongue moves," said Villanazul. "How about the Everybody Wins! Punchboard Lotteries you ran and you kept running when nobody won? How about the United Chili Con Carne and Frijole Company you were going to organize and all that ever happened was the rent ran out on a two-by-four office?"

"The errors of a child now grown," said Gomez. "Enough! In this hot weather, someone may buy the special suit that is made just for us that stands waiting in the window of SHUMWAY's SUN-SHINE SUITS! We have fifty dollars. Now we need just one more skeleton!"

Martinez saw the men peer around the poolhall. He looked where they looked. He felt his eyes hurry past Vamenos, then come reluctantly back to examine his dirty shirt, his huge nicotined fingers.

"Me!" Vamenos burst out, at last. "My skeleton, measure it, it's great! Sure, my hands are big, and my arms, from digging ditches! But——"

Just then Martinez heard passing on the sidewalk outside, that same terrible man with his two girls, all laughing and yelling together. He saw anguish move like the shadow of a summer cloud on the faces of the other men in this poolroom.

Slowly, Vamenos stepped onto the scales and dropped his penny. Eyes closed, he breathed a prayer.

"*Madre mía*, please."

The machinery whirred, the card fell out. Vamenos opened his eyes.

"Look! One hundred thirty-five pounds! Another miracle!"

The men stared at his right hand and the card; at his left hand and a soiled ten-dollar bill.

Gomez swayed. Sweating, he licked his lips. Then his hand shot out, seized the money.

"The clothing store! The suit! *Vamos!*"

Mr. Shumway, of SHUMWAY'S SUNSHINE SUITS, paused while adjusting a tie rack, aware of some subtle atmospheric change outside his establishment.

"Leo," he whispered to his assistant. "Look."

Outside, one man, Gomez, strolled by, looking in. Two men, Manulo and Dominguez, hurried by, staring in. Three men, Villanazul, Martinez, and Vamenos, jostling shoulders, did the same.

"Leo." Mr. Shumway swallowed. "Call the police!"

Suddenly, six men filled the doorway.

Martinez, crushed among them, his stomach slightly upset, his face feeling feverish, smiled so wildly at Leo that Leo let go the telephone.

"Hey," breathed Martinez, eyes wide. "There's a great suit, over there!"

"No." Manulo touched a lapel. "This one!"

"There is only one suit in all the world!" said Gomez coldly. "Mr. Shumway, the ice-cream white, size thirty-four, was in your window just an hour ago! It's gone! You didn't——"

"Sell it?" Mr. Shumway exhaled. "No, no. In the dressing room. It's still on the dummy. This way, gents. Now which of you——"

"All for one, one for all!" Martinez heard himself say, and laughed wildly. "We'll all try it on!"

"All?" Mr. Shumway stared.

That's it, thought Martinez, *look at our smiles. Now, look at the skeletons behind our smiles! Measure here, there; up, down; yes, do you see?*

Mr. Shumway saw. He nodded. He shrugged.

"All!" He jerked the curtain. "There! Buy it, and I'll throw in the dummy, free!"

Martinez peered quietly into the booth, his motion drawing the others to peer too. The suit was there. And it was white.

Martinez took a great trembling breath and exhaled, whispering, "Ai. Ai, *caramba!*"

"It puts out my eyes," murmured Gomez.

"Mr. Shumway." Martinez heard Leo hissing. "Ain't it dangerous precedent, to sell it? I mean, what if everybody bought one suit for six people?"

"Leo," said Mr. Shumway, "you ever hear one single fifty-nine-dollar suit make so many people happy at the same time before?"

"Angel's wings," murmured Martinez. "The wings of white angels."

Martinez felt Mr. Shumway peering over his shoulder into the booth. The pale glow filled his eyes.

"You know something, Leo?" he said, in awe. "That's a suit!"

Gomez, shouting, whistling, ran up to the third-floor landing and turned to wave on the others, who staggered, laughed, stopped and had to sit down on the steps below.

"Tonight!" cried Gomez. "Tonight you move in with me, eh?

Save rent as well as clothes, eh? Sure! Martinez, you got the suit?"

"Have I?" Martinez lifted the white gift-wrapped box high. "From us to us! Ai-hah!"

"Vamenos, you got the dummy?"

"Here!"

Vamenos, chewing an old cigar, scattering sparks, slipped. The dummy, falling, toppled, turned over twice, and banged down the stairs.

"Vamenos! Dumb! Clumsy!"

They seized the dummy from him. Stricken, Vamenos looked about as if he'd lost something.

Manulo snapped his fingers. "Hey, Vamenos, we got to celebrate! Go borrow some wine!"

Vamenos plunged downstairs in a whirl of sparks.

The others moved into the room with the suit, leaving Martinez in the hall to study Gomez' face.

"Gomez, you look sick."

"I am," said Gomez. "For what have I done?" He nodded to the shadows in the room working about the dummy. "I pick Dominguez, a devil with the women. All right. I pick Manulo, who drinks, yes, but who sings as sweet as a girl, eh? O.K. Villanazul reads books. You, you wash behind your ears. But *then* what do I do? Can I wait? No! I got to buy that suit! So the last guy I pick is a clumsy slob who has the right to wear my suit——" He stopped, confused. "Who gets to wear *our* suit one night a week, fall down in it, or not come in out of the rain in it! Why, why, why did I do it!"

"Gomez," whispered Villanazul from the room, "the suit is ready. Come, see if it looks as good using your light bulb."

Gomez and Martinez entered. And there on the dummy in the center of the room was the phosphorescent, the miraculously white-fired ghost with the incredible lapels, the precise stitching, the neat buttonholes. Standing with the white illumination of the suit upon his cheeks, Martinez suddenly felt he was in church. White! White! It was white as the whitest vanilla ice cream, as the bottled milk in tenement halls at dawn. White as a winter cloud all alone in the moonlit sky late at night.

"White," murmured Villanazul. "White as the snow on that mountain near our town in Mexico which is called the Sleeping Woman."

"Say that again," said Gomez.

Villanazul, proud yet humble, was glad to repeat his tribute: "White as the snow on the mountain called——"

"I'm back!"

Shocked, the men whirled to see Vamenos in the door, wine bottles in each hand.

"A party! Here! Now tell us, who wears the suit first tonight? Me?"

"It's too late!" said Gomez.

"Late! It's only nine-fifteen!"

"Late?" said everyone, bristling. "Late?"

Gomez edged away from these men who glared from him to the suit to the open window.

Outside and below, it was, after all, thought Martinez, a fine Saturday night in a summer month, and through the calm warm darkness the women drifted like flowers on a quiet stream. The men made a mournful sound.

"Gomez, a suggestion." Villanazul licked his pencil and drew a chart on a pad. "You wear the suit from nine-thirty to ten, Manulo till ten-thirty, Dominguez till eleven, myself till eleven-thirty, Martinez till midnight, and——"

"Why me last?" demanded Vamenos, scowling.

Martinez thought quickly and smiled. "After midnight is the best time, friend."

"Hey," said Vamenos, "that's right. I never thought of that. O.K."

Gomez sighed. "All right. A half hour each. But from now on, remember, we each wear the suit just one night a week. Sundays we draw straws for who wears the suit the extra night."

"Me!" laughed Vamenos. "I'm lucky!"

Gomez held onto Martinez, tight.

"Gomez," urged Martinez, "you first. Dress."

Gomez could not tear his eyes from that disreputable Vamenos. At last, impulsively, he yanked his shirt off over his head. "Ai-yeah!" he howled. "Ai-yeee!"

Whisper, rustle—the clean shirt.

"Ah!"

How clean the new clothes felt, thought Martinez, holding the coat ready. How clean they sounded; how clean they smelled!

Whisper—the pants, the tie; rustle—the suspenders. Whisper. Now Martinez let loose the coat, which fell in place on flexing shoulders.

"*Olé!*"

Gomez turned like a matador in his wondrous suit-of-lights.

"*Olé*, Gomez; *olé!*"

Gomez bowed and went out the door.

Martinez fixed his eyes on his watch. At ten sharp he heard someone wandering about in the hall as if he had forgotten where to go. Martinez pulled the door open and looked out. Gomez was there, heading for nowhere.

He looks sick, thought Martinez. *No; stunned, shook up, surprised, many things.*

"Gomez! This is the place!"

Gomez turned around and found his way through the door.

"Oh, friends, friends," he said. "Friends, what an experience! This suit! This suit!"

"Tell us, Gomez!" said Martinez.

"I can't; how can I say it!" He gazed at the heavens, arms spread, palms up.

"Tell us, Gomez!"

"I have no words, no words. You must see, yourself! Yes, you must see." And here he lapsed into silence, shaking his head until at last he remembered they all stood watching him. "Who's next? Manulo?"

Manulo, stripped to his shorts, leaped forward.

"Ready!"

All laughed, shouted, whistled.

Manulo, ready, went out the door. He was gone twenty-nine minutes and thirty seconds. He came back holding to doorknobs, touching the wall, feeling his own elbows, putting the flat of his hand to his face.

"Oh, let me tell you," he said. "*Compadres*, I went to the bar, eh, to have a drink? But no, I did not go in the bar, do you hear? I did not drink. For as I walked I began to laugh and sing. Why, why? I listened to myself and asked this. Because. The suit made me feel better than wine ever did. The suit made me drunk, drunk! So I went to the *Guadalajara Refritería* instead and played the guitar and sang four songs, very high! The suit, ah, the suit!"

Dominguez, next to be dressed, moved out through the world, came back from the world.

The black telephone book! thought Martinez. He had it in his hands when he left! Now he returns, hands empty! What? What?

"On the street," said Dominguez, seeing it all again, eyes wide, "on the street I walked, a woman cried, 'Dominguez, is that you?' Another said, 'Dominguez? No, Quetzalcoatl, the Great White God come from the East,' do you hear? And suddenly I didn't want to go with six women or eight, no. One, I thought. One! And to this one, who knows what I would say? 'Be mine!' Or 'Marry me!' *Caramba!* This suit is dangerous! But I did not care! I live, I live! Gomez, did it happen this way with you?"

Gomez, still dazed by the events of the evening, shook his head. "No, no talk. It's too much. Later. Villanazul?"

Villanazul moved shyly forward.

Villanazul went shyly out.

Villanazul came shyly home.

"Picture it," he said, not looking at them, looking at the floor, talking to the floor. "The Green Plaza, a group of elderly businessmen gathered under the stars and they are talking, nodding, talking. Now one of them whispers. All turn to stare. They move aside, they make a channel through which a white-hot light burns its way as through ice. At the center of the great light is this person. I take a deep breath. My stomach is jelly. My voice is very small, but it grows louder. And what do I say? I say, 'Friends. Do you know Carlyle's Sartor Resartus? In that book we find *his* Philosophy of Suits.' "

And at last it was time for Martinez to let the suit float him out to haunt the darkness.

Four times he walked around the block. Four times he paused beneath the tenement porches, looking up at the window where the light was lit, a shadow moved, the beautiful girl was there, not there, away and gone, and on the fifth time, there she was, on the porch above, driven out by the summer heat, taking the cooler air. She glanced down. She made a gesture.

At first he thought she was waving to him. He felt like a white explosion that had riveted her attention. But she was not waving. Her hand gestured, and the next moment a pair of framed glasses sat upon her nose. She gazed at him.

Ah, ah, he thought, *so that's it! So! Even the blind may see this suit!* He smiled up at her. He did not have to wave. And at last, she smiled back. She did not have to wave either. Then, because he did not know what else to do, and he could not get rid of this smile that had fastened itself to his cheeks, he hurried, almost ran around the corner, feeling her stare after him.

When he looked back, she had taken off her glasses and gazed now with the look of the nearsighted at what, at most, must be a moving blob of light in the great darkness here. Then, for good measure he went around the block again, through a city so suddenly beautiful he wanted to yell, then laugh, then yell again.

Returning, he drifted, oblivious, eyes half-closed, and seeing him in the door the others saw not Martinez, but themselves, come home. In that moment, they sensed that something had happened to them all.

"You're late!" cried Vamenos, but stopped. The spell could not be broken.

"Somebody tell me," said Martinez. "Who am I?"

He moved in a slow circle through the room.

Yes, he thought, yes, it was the suit; yes, it had to do with the suit and them all together in that store on this fine Saturday night and then here, laughing and feeling more drunk without drinking, as Manulo said himself, as the night ran and each slipped on the pants and held, toppling, to the others and, balanced, let the feeling get bigger and warmer and finer as each man departed and the next took his place in the suit until now here stood Martinez all splendid and white as one who gives orders and the world grows quiet and moves aside.

"Martinez, we borrowed three mirrors while you were gone. Look!"

The mirrors, set up as in the store, angled to reflect three Martinezes and the echoes and memories of those who had occupied this suit with him and known the bright world inside this thread and cloth. Now, in the shimmering mirror, Martinez saw the enormity of this thing they were living together, and his eyes grew wet. The others blinked. Martinez touched the mirrors. They shifted. He saw a thousand, a million white-armored Martinezes march off into eternity, reflected, re-reflected forever, indomitable, and unending.

He held the white coat out on the air. In a trance, the others did not at first recognize the dirty hand that reached to take the coat. Then:

"Vamenos!"

"Pig!"

"You didn't wash!" cried Gomez. "Or even shave, while you waited! *Compadres*, the bath!"

"The bath!" said everyone.

"No!" Vamenos flailed. "The night air! I'm dead!"

They hustled him, yelling, out and down the hall.

Now here stood Vamenos, unbelievable in white suit, beard shaved, hair combed, nails scrubbed.

His friends scowled darkly at him. For was it not true, thought

Martinez, that when Vamenos passed by, avalanches itched on mountain tops. If he walked under windows, people spat, dumped garbage, or worse. Tonight now, this night, he would stroll beneath ten thousand wide-opened windows, near balconies, past alleys. Suddenly the world absolutely sizzled with flies. And here was Vamenos, a fresh-frosted cake.

"You sure look keen in that suit, Vamenos," said Manulo sadly.

"Thanks." Vamenos twitched, trying to make his skeleton comfortable where all their skeletons had so recently been. In a small voice, Vamenos said, "Can I go now?"

"Villanazul!" said Gomez. "Copy down these rules."

Villanazul licked his pencil.

"First," said Gomez, "don't fall down in that suit, Vamenos!"

"I won't."

"Don't lean against buildings in that suit."

"No buildings."

"Don't walk under trees with birds in them, in that suit. Don't smoke. Don't drink——"

"Please," said Vamenos, "can I sit down in this suit?"

"When in doubt, take the pants off, fold them over a chair."

"Wish me luck," said Vamenos.

"Go with God, Vamenos."

He went out. He shut the door. There was a ripping sound.

"Vamenos!" cried Martinez. He whipped the door open.

Vamenos stood with two halves of a handkerchief torn in his hands, laughing.

"R-r-rip! Look at your faces! R-r-rip!" He tore the cloth again. "Oh, oh, your faces, your faces! Ha!"

Roaring, Vamenos slammed the door, leaving them stunned and alone.

Gomez put both hands on top of his head and turned away. "Stone me. Kill me. I have sold our souls to a demon!"

Villanazul dug in his pockets, took out a silver coin and studied it for a long while.

"Here is my last fifty cents. Who else will help me buy back Vamenos' share of the suit?"

"It's no use." Manulo showed them ten cents. "We got only enough to buy the lapels and the buttonholes."

Gomez, at the open window, suddenly leaned out and yelled, "Vamenos! No!"

Below on the street, Vamenos, shocked, blew out a match, and threw away an old cigar butt he had found somewhere. He made a strange gesture to all the men in the window above, then waved airily and sauntered on.

Somehow, the five men could not move away from the window. They were crushed together there.

"I bet he eats a hamburger in that suit," mused Villanazul. "I'm thinking of the mustard."

"Don't!" cried Gomez. "No, no!"

Manulo was suddenly at the door. "I need a drink, bad."

"Manulo, there's wine here, that bottle, on the floor."

Manulo went out and shut the door.

A moment later, Villanazul stretched with great exaggeration and strolled about the room.

"I think I'll walk down to the plaza, friends."

He was not gone a minute when Dominguez turned the door-knob.

"Dominguez," said Gomez.

"Yes?"

"If you see Vamenos, by accident," said Gomez, "warn him away from Mickey Murillo's Red Rooster Café. They got fights not only *on* TV but out front of the TV too."

"He wouldn't go into Murillo's," said Dominguez. "That suit means too much to Vamenos. He wouldn't do anything to hurt it."

"He'd shoot his mother first," said Martinez.

"Sure he would."

Martinez and Gomez, alone, listened to Dominguez' footsteps hurry away down the stairs. They circled the undressed window dummy.

For a long while, biting his lips, Gomez stood at the window, looking out. He touched his shirt pocket twice, pulled his hand away, and then at last pulled something from the pocket. Without looking at it, he handed it to Martinez.

"Martinez, take this."

"What is it?"

Martinez looked at the piece of folded pink paper with print on it, with names and numbers. His eyes widened.

"A ticket on the bus to El Paso, three weeks from now!"

Gomez nodded. He couldn't look at Martinez. He stared out into the summer night.

"Turn it in. Get the money," he said. "Buy us a nice white panama hat and a pale blue tie to go with the white ice-cream suit, Martinez. Do that."

Mickey Murillo's Red Rooster Café and Cocktail Lounge was squashed between two big brick buildings and, being narrow, had to be deep. Outside, serpents of red and sulphur-green neon fizzed and snapped. Inside, dim shapes loomed and swam away to lose themselves in a swarming night sea.

Martinez, on tiptoe, peeked through a flaked place on the red-painted front window. He felt a presence on his left, heard breathing on his right. He glanced in both directions.

"Manulo! Villanazul!"

"I decided I wasn't thirsty," said Manulo. "So I took a walk."

"I was just on my way to the plaza," said Villanazul, "and decided to go the long way around."

As if by agreement the three men shut up now and turned together to peer on tiptoe through various flaked spots on the window.

A moment later, all three felt a new very warm presence behind them and heard still faster breathing.

"Is our white suit in there?" asked Gomez' voice.

"Gomez!" said everybody, surprised. "Hi!"

"Yes!" cried Dominguez, having just arrived to find his own peephole. "There's the suit! And, praise God, Vamenos is still in it!"

"I can't see!" Gomez squinted, shielding his eyes. "What's he doing?"

Martinez peered. Yes! There, way back in the shadows, was a big chunk of snow, and the idiot smile of Vamenos winking above it, wreathed in smoke.

"He's smoking!" said Martinez.

"He's drinking!" said Dominguez.

"He's eating a taco!" reported Villanazul.

"A juicy taco," added Manulo.

"No," said Gomez. "No, no, no."

"Ruby Escuadrillo's with him!"

"Let me see that!" Gomez pushed Martinez aside.

Yes, there was Ruby! Two hundred pounds of glittering sequins and tight black satin on the hoof, her scarlet fingernails clutching Vamenos' shoulder. Her cowlike face, floured with powder, greasy with lipstick, hung over him!

"That hippo!" said Dominguez. "She's crushing the shoulder pads. Look, she's going to sit on his lap!"

"No, no; not with all that powder and lipstick!" said Gomez. "Manulo, inside! Grab that drink! Villanazul, the cigar, the taco! Dominguez, date Ruby Escuadrillo, get her away. V*amos*, men!"

The three vanished, leaving Gomez and Martinez to stare, gasping, through the peephole.

"Manulo, he's got the drink; he's drinking it!"

"*Olé!* There's Villanazul, he's got the cigar; he's eating the taco!"

"Hey, Dominguez, he's got Ruby! What a brave one!"

A shadow bulked through Murillo's front door, traveling fast.

"Gomez!" Martinez clutched Gomez' arm. "That was Ruby Escuadrillo's boy friend, Toro Ruiz. If he finds her with Vamenos, the ice-cream suit will be covered with blood, covered with blood——"

"Don't make me nervous," said Gomez. "Quickly!"

Both ran. Inside, they reached Vamenos just as Toro Ruiz

grabbed about two feet of the lapels of that wonderful ice-cream suit.

"Let go of Vamenos!" said Martinez.

"Let go that suit!" corrected Gomez.

Toro Ruiz, tap-dancing Vamenos, leered at these intruders.

Villanazul stepped up shyly. Villanazul smiled. "Don't hit him. Hit me."

Toro Ruiz hit Villanazul on the nose.

Villanazul, holding his nose, tears stinging his eyes, wandered off.

Gomez grabbed one of Toro Ruiz's arms, Martinez the other.

"Drop him, let go, *coyote, vaca!*"

Toro Ruiz twisted the ice-cream-suit material until all six men screamed in mortal agony. Grunting, sweating, Toro Ruiz dislodged as many as climbed on. He was winding up to hit Vamenos when Villanazul wandered back, eyes streaming.

"Don't hit him. Hit me!"

As Toro Ruiz hit Villanazul on the nose, a chair crashed on Toro's head. A moment later Toro was ruins at their feet.

"*Compadres,* this way!"

They ran Vamenos outside and set him down, where he freed himself of their hands with injured dignity.

"O.K., O.K. My time ain't up. I still got two minutes and—ten seconds."

"What!" said everybody.

"Vamenos," said Gomez, "you let a Guadalajara cow climb on you, you pick fights, you smoke, you drink, you eat tacos, and now you have the nerve to say your time ain't up?"

"I got two minutes and one second left!"

"Hey, Vamenos, you sure look sharp!" Distantly, a woman's voice called from across the street.

Vamenos smiled and buttoned the coat. "It's Ramona Alvarez! Ramona, wait!" Vamenos stepped off the curb.

"Vamenos," pleaded Gomez, "what can you do in one minute and"—he checked his watch—"forty seconds!"

"Watch! Hey, Ramona!" Vamenos loped.

"Vamenos, look out!"

Vamenos, surprised, whirled, saw a car, heard the shriek of brakes.

"No," said all five men on the sidewalk.

Martinez heard the impact and flinched. His head moved up. Vamenos looked like white laundry, he thought, flying through the air. His head came down.

"I don't want to live," said Gomez quietly. "Kill me, someone."

Then, shuffling, Martinez looked down and told his feet to walk, stagger, follow one after the other. He collided with other men. Now they were trying to run. They ran at last and somehow crossed a street like a deep river through which they could only wade, to look down at Vamenos.

"Vamenos!" said Martinez. "You're alive!"

Strewn on his back, mouth open, eyes squeezed tight, tight, Vamenos motioned his head back and forth, back and forth, moaning.

"Tell me, tell me; oh, tell me, tell me."

"Tell you what, Vamenos?"

Vamenos clenched his fists, ground his teeth. "The suit, what have I done to the suit, the suit, the suit!"

The men crouched lower.

"Vamenos, it's—— Why, it's O.K.!"

"You lie!" said Vamenos. "It's torn, it must be, it must be, it's torn, all around, underneath?"

"No." Martinez knelt and touched here and there. "Vamenos, all around, underneath even, it's O.K.!"

Vamenos opened his eyes to let the tears run free at last. "A miracle," he sobbed. "Praise the saints!" He quieted at last. "The car?"

"Hit and run." Gomez suddenly remembered and glared at the empty street. "It's good he didn't stop. We'd have——"

Everyone listened. Distantly, a siren wailed.

"Someone phoned for an ambulance."

"Quick!" said Vamenos, eyes rolling. "Set me up! Take off our coat!"

"Vamenos——"

"Shut up, idiots!" cried Vamenos. "The coat, that's it! Now, the pants; the pants, quick, quick, *peons!* Those doctors! You seen movies? They rip the pants with razors to get them off! They don't care! They're maniacs! Ah, quick, quick!"

The siren screamed. The men, panicking, all handled Vamenos at once.

"Right leg, easy; hurry, cows! Good! Left leg, now; left, you hear! There, easy, easy! Quick! Martinez, your pants, take them off!"

"What?" Martinez froze.

The siren shrieked.

"Fool!" wailed Vamenos. "All is lost! Your pants! Give me!"

Martinez jerked at his belt buckle.

"Close in, make a circle!"

Dark pants, light pants, flourished on the air.

"Quick, here come the maniacs with the razors! Right leg on, left leg, there!"

"The zipper, cows, zip my zipper!" babbled Vamenos.

The siren died.

"*Madre mía,* yes, just in time! They arrive." Vamenos lay back down and shut his eyes. "*Gracias.*"

Martinez turned, nonchalantly buckling on the white pants as the interns brushed past.

"Broken leg," said one intern as they moved Vamenos onto a stretcher.

"*Compadres,*" said Vamenos, "don't be mad with me."

Gomez snorted. "Who's mad?"

In the ambulance, head tilted back, looking out at them upside down, Vamenos faltered.

"*Compadres,* when—when I come from the hospital, am I still in the bunch? You won't kick me out? Look, I'll give up smoking, keep away from Murillo's, swear off women——"

"Vamenos," said Martinez gently, "don't promise nothing."

Vamenos, upside down, eyes brimming wet, saw Martinez there, all white now against the stars.

"Oh, Martinez, you sure look great in that suit. *Compadres,* don't he look beautiful?"

Villanazul climbed in beside Vamenos. The door slammed. The four remaining men watched the ambulance drive away. Then, surrounded by his friends, inside the white suit, Martinez was carefully escorted back to the curb.

In the tenement, Martinez got out the cleaning fluid and the others stood around, telling him how to clean the suit and, later, how not to have the iron too hot and how to work the lapels and the crease and all. When the suit was cleaned and pressed so it looked like a fresh gardenia just opened, they fitted it to the dummy.

"Two o'clock," murmured Villanazul. "I hope Vamenos sleeps well. When I left him, he looked good."

Manulo cleared his throat. "Nobody else is going out with that suit tonight, huh?"

The others glared at him.

Manulo flushed. "I mean—it's late. We're tired. Maybe no one will use the suit for forty-eight hours, huh? Give it a rest. Sure. Well. Where do we sleep?"

The night being still hot and the room unbearable, they carried the suit on its dummy out and down the hall. They brought with them also some pillows and blankets. They climbed the stairs toward the roof of the tenement. There, thought Martinez, was the cooler wind, and sleep.

On the way, they passed a dozen doors that stood open, people still perspiring and awake, playing cards, drinking pop, fanning themselves with movie magazines.

I wonder, thought Martinez. *I wonder if—yes!*

On the fourth floor, a certain door stood open. The beautiful girl looked up as the five men passed. She wore glasses and when she saw Martinez she snatched them off and hid them under her book.

The others went on, not knowing they had lost Martinez, who seemed stuck fast in the open door.

For a long moment he could say nothing. Then he said: "José Martinez."

And she said: "Celia Obregon."

And then both said nothing.

He heard the men moving up on the tenement roof. He moved to follow.

She said, quickly, "I saw you tonight!"

He came back. "The suit," he said.

"The suit," she said, and paused. "But not the suit."

"Eh?" he said.

She lifted the book to show the glasses lying in her lap. She touched the glasses.

"I do not see well. You would think I would wear my glasses, but no. I walk around for years now, hiding them, seeing nothing. But tonight, even without the glasses, I see. A great whiteness passes below in the dark. So white! And I put on my glasses quickly!"

"The suit, as I said," said Martinez.

"The suit for a little moment, yes; but there is another whiteness above the suit."

"Another?"

"Your teeth! Oh, such white teeth, and so many!"

Martinez put his hand over his mouth.

"So happy, Mr. Martinez," she said. "I have not often seen such a happy face and such a smile."

"Ah," he said, not able to look at her, his face flushing now.

"So, you see," she said quietly, "the suit caught my eye, yes, the whiteness filled the night, below. But the teeth were much whiter. Now, I have forgotten the suit."

Martinez flushed again. She, too, was overcome with what she had said. She looked at her hands and at the door above his head.

"May I——" he said, at last.

"May you——"

"May I call for you," he asked, "when next the suit is mine to wear?"

"You do not need the suit," she said.

"But——"

"If it were just the suit," she said, "anyone would be fine in it. But no, I watched. I saw many men in that suit, all different, this night. So again I say, you do not need to wait for the suit."

"*Madre mía, madre mía!*" he cried happily. And then, quieter, "I will need the suit for a little while. A month, six months, a year. I am uncertain. I am fearful of many things. I am young. The suit changes me, makes me strong."

"That is as it should be," she said.

"Good night, Miss——"

"Celia Obregon."

"Celia Obregon," he said, and was gone from the door.

The others were waiting on the roof of the tenement. A cooler night wind was blowing here, up in the sky.

Martinez stood alone by the white suit, smoothing the lapels, talking half to himself.

"Ai, *caramba*, what a night! Seems ten years since seven o'clock, when it all started and I had no friends. Two in the morning, I got all kinds of friends." He paused and thought, *Celia Obregon, Celia Obregon.* "All kinds of friends," he went on. "I got a room, I got clothes. You tell me. You know what?" He looked around at the men lying on the rooftop, surrounding the dummy and himself. "It's funny. When I wear this suit, I know I will win at pool, like Gomez. A woman will look at me like Dominguez. I will be able to sing like Manulo, sweetly. I will talk fine politics like Villanazul. I'm strong as Vamenos. So? So, tonight, I am more than Martinez. I am Gomez, Manulo, Dominguez, Villanazul, Vamenos. I am everyone. Ai. Ai." He stood a moment longer by this suit which could save all the ways they sat or stood or walked. This suit which could move fast and nervous like Gomez or slow and thoughtfully like Villanazul or drift like Dominguez who never touched ground, who always found a wind to take him somewhere. This suit which belonged to them, but which also owned them all. This suit that was—what? A parade.

"Martinez," said Gomez. "You going to sleep?"

"Sure. I'm just thinking."

"What?"

"If we ever get rich," said Martinez softly, "it'll be kind of sad. Then we'll all have suits. And there won't be no more nights like tonight. It'll break up the old gang. It'll never be the same, after that."

The men lay thinking of what had just been said.

Gomez nodded gently. "Yeah. It'll never be the same, after that."

Martinez lay down on his blanket. In darkness, with the others, he faced the middle of the roof and the dummy, which was the center of their lives.

And their eyes were bright, shining, and good to see in the dark as the neon lights from nearby buildings flicked on, flicked off, flicked on, flicked off, revealing and then vanishing, revealing and then vanishing, their wonderful white vanilla-ice-cream summer suit.

FRAME-UP ON THE HIGHWAY

by John and Ward Hawkins

Jimmy Franklin didn't know how the accident happened. He was driving carefully. A seventeen-year-old with two minor accidents charged to him had to drive carefully. Too, he had just passed the scene of a crash on Lake Boulevard—police cars, an ambulance, a swirling crowd—and the memory of that held his speed down and sharpened his awareness.

The night was clear, the gentle curves of Dutch Hill Road were dry, there was little traffic. He came up on a new and expensive car going about twenty-five. "Mrs. Murphy," he said. He knew the car, knew the driver. She was married to pop's best customer. He followed her for a time, wondering why she was just poking along. Then he pulled out and passed her, alert for any danger that might come around an approaching curve. He swung back in good time toward the right-hand lane.

Her headlights were on the high beam. They hit his rear-view mirror and blinded him for a moment, but not long enough to

322 Post Stories 1958

cause him any trouble. There was no car approaching, no reason to hurry the turn back. He had done everything right, everything safely, and yet he was no more than across the center stripe when something struck his car a giant blow.

He yelled, a hoarse, wordless sound of fear. His car went out of control, tires squalling across dry pavement, the steering wheel twisting in his hands. Jimmy could not think in his panic; he could only fight instinctively and desperately, and he fought with considerable skill.

The careening car almost overturned; somehow he managed to hold it upright. Then it began to fishtail, the rear end whipping back and forth, the front end seeking the ditch on either side of the road like a thing possessed.

He was aware that headlights had flashed crazily across the trees on the right of the road, and now he heard a second crash behind him. He was sickened, as if he'd been struck again, but he was fighting too hard to give it thought.

The fishtailing stopped at last. With the car rolling straight, he used the brake—not hard, pumping it carefully—and brought the car to a stop two hundred feet down the road from the point of collision. Shaking, weak with shock, he could not move for a moment. Then awareness came back to him suddenly.

"Mrs. Murphy," he said hoarsely.

He hammered the door of his car open, lunged through it, stumbling, to the road. The road back of him was dark and empty. He yelled the name of the woman again and ran that way—seventeen, a lanky, gangling boy in desperate haste.

The woman's car had left the road on the right side, plunged down a small incline and into a grove of trees. It had struck two trees hard. The chrome-laden front end was crushed, the long and shining hood stood open to the sky. The headlights were out, smashed, but the dash lights glowed. Looking down from the shoulder of the road, Jimmy saw that a man had reached the car before him.

"Is she hurt?" he called fearfully.

The man was leaning into the car. He straightened and looked at Jimmy. "Yeah, she's hurt." He turned to the car again.

Jimmy went down the bank in clumsy, great strides. There was enough light from the interior of the car, the stars and the newly risen half moon to see the man who had preceded him. He was wearing overalls, a vest, a short-sleeved shirt—a stringy wisp of a man, near fifty. He was trying to pull the inert body of the woman from the car. Jimmy caught his shoulder.

"Don't move her!" He'd had first aid in high school; he knew that much. "You can hurt her bad!"

"She's hurt bad now! She——"

Jimmy pushed past the man and leaned into the car. What he saw filled him with nausea and turned his bones to rubber. Mrs. Murphy had been a very pretty woman, twenty-five or six, long blond hair, dark blue eyes. She'd been an actress or something, and there'd been talk about her after she'd married Mr. Murphy. Jimmy hadn't listened much to the things people said, they sure didn't matter now.

Her face had hit the steering wheel. She was half lying on the seat, unconscious, breathing heavily. There was quite a lot of blood on the seat, in her hair, on her face, and she was still bleeding. Jimmy fumbled helplessly, mind numb with shock, almost blank. Then, suddenly, he found his senses. He backed out of the car and turned on the thin wisp of a man.

"Call a doctor!" he said. "Get an ambulance!"

"Why me? I——"

"Because I can't leave!" Jimmy yelled at him. "There's plenty of houses on the other side of the road! Get up there and get to a phone! Tell 'em Dutch Hill Road near Forty-seventh. And for gosh sakes, hurry!"

The man stared at Jimmy, openmouthed, then wheeled and scrambled up the bank. He reached the road and began to run. Jimmy turned back to the injured woman. He tried desperately to control his panic, to think clearly. Arterial bleeding—look for that first. There was none. Jimmy tore off his warm-up jacket and covered her. He ripped his white shirt apart, made pads and applied them gently to the woman's face.

Cars passed on the road above, driven by people too preoccupied to read the story the skid marks had to tell. But others stopped. Jimmy was aware of men's voices, excited, questioning. He answered briefly, if at all. He resisted one hand that tried to pull him away from the little he was able to do for the woman. Presently, sirens moaned to a stop on the road above, doors slammed and uniformed men came down the slope. A hand touched Jimmy's bare shoulder.

"We'll take over, son," a quiet voice said. "Stand aside."

The police and the ambulance crew took care of Mrs. Murphy, giving her emergency treatment. They lifted her gently to a stretcher and took her away, bandaged, blanket-wrapped and still unconscious. Jimmy watched it, sitting in the police car, as he'd been told to do. He tried to ignore the curious who peered in at him, he tried not to hear their voices.

"Damn kid! Wouldn't you know?"

"A hot-rodder!"

"Look at that car of his. Flames painted on the fenders! You see a wreck, you see one of those, practically every time! They oughta rule 'em off the road!"

Jimmy held his head in his hands. A hot rod—that was a laugh! Roy Wyatt had painted those fenders when he'd owned the car, trying to make it look sharp. A hot rod! A beat-up, worn-out oil hog was more like it. Fifty miles an hour, down a steep hill with a tail wind, was the best you could get. Buying the car, paying for insurance, feeding it oil—he couldn't afford to repaint the fenders. But if you were seventeen and had a car you were a hot-rodder—a dirty word.

The police cleared the road. There were two of them, sober and frowning. They came back to the car where Jimmy waited. One of them had Jimmy's warm-up jacket in his hand. "You better put this on, son." Jimmy got out of the car, so shaken he could barely stand.

"How is she?" he asked. "Will she be all right?"

The officer with the jacket, Sam Riggio, was a lean-hipped, heavy-shouldered man with a fighter's dark, tough face. Mark Bradford, his partner, was tall and wore glasses. Neither man was a stranger to blood and broken bodies, both knew the damage youngsters can do. Bradford resented teen-age drivers, sometimes to the point of hate, but Bradford had no children of his own. Sam Riggio had a son, fifteen.

Riggio decided that whatever else this skinny, man-tall boy was, he was not a hot-rodder. Where was the long hair, the tight jeans, the boots? This kid was crew-cut; he wore cords. He had a homely good-looking face, with brown eyes that looked at Sam Riggio, pleading.

"She'll make it," Riggio said gruffly.

Grimly, Bradford said, "How about her face?"

"Hold your lip," Sam Riggio said.

The two officers left Jimmy in the car while they took measurements and made sketches. Then they came back to get Jimmy's statement for their reports.

"We're short the name of the guy in overalls," Riggio said. "That's a must—get the name of anybody who might be a witness."

"How could I?" Jimmy asked. "He never came back!"

"Who needs witnesses?" Bradford asked. "The facts speak for themselves. The kid cut back too fast, jammed her wheel."

Riggio scratched his cheek. "At least he didn't make it a hit-and-run like the guy on Lake Boulevard a little while ago. That one left a woman in tough shape. It's ten to one against her."

"I didn't cut back too fast," Jimmy said.

Bradford made a soft sound of ridicule.

Riggio got out of the car suddenly. "Come on, son," he said. When Jimmy was beside him, he shut the door and spoke through the window to his partner, "I'll ride home with the boy in his jalopy. You follow us. And wait outside, will you?"

"I'll be glad to," Bradford said.

The right rear door of Jimmy's car was smashed, the glass broken, the right rear fender was crumpled against the wheel. Officer Riggio pulled the metal away from the tire and checked the running gear.

"Looks all right," he said. "Let's go."

He got into the front seat on the right side. Jimmy had to get behind the wheel. His hands were shaking, his legs were weak. He didn't want to drive.

"I—I don't know if I can," he said.

Riggio got a cigarette from his blouse pocket and took his time lighting it. "This isn't the end," he said. "You've got a lot of years to go, a lot of cars to drive. The time to try again is now. I think you can do it."

Jimmy's eyes watered and his throat hurt—kindness always did that to him. Then he set his jaws. The man said drive, so he'd drive! He got the car going and felt his confidence return.

"I didn't know there were cops like you."

"Only a million of them," Riggio said.

Jimmy kept his eyes on the road. "A couple of things I didn't tell you," he said. "I went past that accident on Lake Boulevard after it happened. It scared me—y'know, a guy thinks how easy it could happen to him. That's one reason I was being careful. The other reason, I recognized Mrs. Murphy's car before I pulled out to pass it. Her husband is a contractor. My father sells heavy equipment. He sells a lot to Mr. Murphy."

Riggio sighed. "How tough can it get?"

"That's one car I wouldn't want to scratch," Jimmy said. "I gave her plenty of room. You can see why I would."

Riggio shook his head. It was a gentle lie—a gesture that spoke of equal puzzlement, when there was no question in his mind as to the cause of the accident.

"Your father buy this car for you?"

"No," Jimmy said. "Pop told me I could have a car when I could pay for it and the insurance and the gas and oil. I saved my money since I was fourteen. I work at Keefer's Supermarket after school. That's where I was tonight. I just came from there."

Where, Riggio wondered tiredly, was the reward for virtue he'd always been hearing about? The hit-and-run driver who had left the elderly woman broken and bleeding on Lake Boulevard would probably never pay for that piece of dirty work. The chance of finding him was slim. But this lad—he'd stayed at the scene, done all he could, seen the blood and felt the pain—this lad and his family would pay dearly.

Jimmy turned into the driveway of the house where he lived —a comfortable home, white siding, white brick, green shutters, trimmed hedges and green lawn. Suddenly it didn't matter who was to blame. He had to tell his mother and father he'd had another accident, had to watch what hearing it would do to them. This was a prospect that brought him sickness almost beyond bearing. Officer Riggio knew what was in his mind.

"I'll be with you, son," he said.

They went up the walk together. Jimmy opened the front door. There were voices in the living room. The TV was going. Pop was in there, resting after a day at the plant and three hours in the garden. Pop grew the best flowers of anybody in the neighborhood.

"Jimmy," his mother said as they walked into the hall, "you're late."

She came into the hall. She saw Officer Riggio and stopped. She was small and slim, she had brown hair and brown eyes. Her name was Ann, but pop called her Cricket, because she was never still. She took care of her house and her people at a dead run. Pop had a joke about that. "If she thinks she's going to get double time," he'd say, "she's got a busted sprocket." Pop didn't like his Cricket very much, he was pure crazy about her.

"Jimmy," Cricket whispered, "where's your shirt?"

"I had an accident," Jimmy said.

Cricket closed her eyes. Her mouth got the pinched look it had when she was scared or hurt. Pop came out of the living room then. He was a big man, heavily muscled, deeply tanned. He had thick, dark hair, dark brows, gray eyes. A laborer at fourteen, a construction superintendent at twenty-five. At forty, he was close to being a partner in Western Machinery, selling heavy equipment to highway contractors. Jimmy had always thought he'd be satisfied if he turned out to be half the man pop was.

"This's Officer Riggio," Jimmy said.

"Come in," pop said.

He led them into the living room, switched the TV off. Officer Riggio sat on the davenport. Cricket would not let Jimmy beyond the reach of her hands. She made him sit in a chair, then sat on the arm of it beside him.

"Was anyone hurt?" pop asked.

"A woman," Riggio said. "The driver of the other car."

Jimmy tried to swallow the lump in his throat—tried and failed. "It was Mrs. Murphy, pop."

Twenty years of construction work had given Roger Franklin a tough face. His thick brows came down in a scowl. The scowl didn't scare Jimmy, though it made him feel immeasurably worse. Pop looked like that only when he'd been hit cruelly.

"Hurt bad?" pop asked.

Riggio glanced briefly at Jimmy, then gave the boy's father a look of warning. "Too early to say," he said. "Facial cuts—cheeks, lips, forehead. Concussion, but I don't think a skull fracture. An ambulance took her to Mercy Hospital."

"I'll be right back," pop said quietly.

He used the telephone in the hall, listening more than he talked. His face had lost color when he returned.

"Still in emergency surgery," he said. He looked at Jimmy. "Maybe you'd better fill us in."

Jimmy told them what had happened, trying to straighten it out in his head. He did it badly, because each part of the memory frightened and sickened him again—the crash, fighting to keep his car under control, the second crash, the woman's ruined car, her bleeding face. He was shaking and sweating when he finished.

"I see," pop said. He looked at Cricket. "Clean him up, will you?

Get him a shirt, try to get some food in him—not that he'll eat. Some milk, maybe."

Cricket touched Jimmy's arm. "Come on, son."

"Pop," Jimmy said, "you'll call the hospital again?"

"In a little while," pop said.

He waited until Cricket and Jimmy were beyond hearing behind the swinging door, then turned to Officer Riggio, his tough face softened with concern.

"Is it as bad as it sounds?"

Officer Riggio took a deep breath. "I like to call on parents after accidents, y'know? When the youngster's committed a crime—speeding, squirreling, drinking, reckless driving—I warn the parents so they can take a hand. A lot of kids need a whipping." His eyes came up to meet pop's. "Your son's not like that. He's a good boy."

"I know that well," pop said. "But both his mother and I thank you for saying it."

"The hospital told you about the woman's face? That it could be disfigured?" Riggio waited for pop's nod; then went on, "I didn't think it was time to hit the boy with that. He'll have to know, but why not a little at a time?"

"Thanks again," pop said.

"The accident——" Riggio said. He got his notebook from his pocket. "Weather clear, road dry. The woman was driving at a moderate speed. The boy passed her, going about forty-five. No visibility problem, no oncoming traffic. The cars collided in the right-hand lane—the tire marks, glass, mud on the pavement show that, beyond doubt. The woman was taken to the hospital unconscious. I couldn't get a statement from her. The boy honestly believes he did everything according to the book, safely. The facts say something else."

Pop said, "He cut back too fast."

"He's seventeen," Riggio said. "He's got a right to drive, a right to learn. But how long does it take to learn? And who pays for the mistakes kids make while they're learning?"

"A tough question," pop said. "I don't want to answer it now—not for the record."

"I know—they don't give kids much insurance."

"And I'm not a rich man," pop said.

He walked to the front door with Officer Riggio, thanked him again and let him out. Then he called the hospital. Mrs. Murphy was off the critical list, sleeping under sedation. No, there had been no skull fracture. Yes, her face had been damaged. Broken nose, broken cheekbone, severe lacerations. Pop put the telephone down, a very sober man. He went into the kitchen to face two very worried people.

"Off the critical list," he said, "but her face took a real beating."

"I knew it!" Jimmy said. "I saw her." He slammed a fist into a cupped palm. "She was so pretty."

Cricket whispered, "The poor woman."

"One of us has to call Charlie Stern," pop said. "The insurance company is going to get hit hard on this one; they'd better know."

"It's my insurance," Jimmy said. "I'll call him."

Pop and Cricket waited in the kitchen. They listened to the one-sided conversation, anguish in their faces. They expected him to be heartbroken and utterly defeated when he came back, but his round face was tight and there was anger in his eyes.

"He didn't believe me either!" he said.

"Believe what?" pop said.

"That I didn't cut back too fast. I told him how the accident happened. He didn't say it right out—he said, 'Don't admit the blame to anybody'—but he might as well have said it."

"Jimmy——"

"I had two other accidents," Jimmy said. "An old lady with thick glasses and a dog jumping around in her car; a fat guy who smelled like a brewery. His fender—the one that got nicked—had dents so old they had rust in them. I'm a teen-ager, I'm wrong all the way. He gets a new fender and I get the blame. The old lady——"

"The facts say this one's your fault."

"The cop's facts." Jimmy was pacing the kitchen. "While you were in there talking to Riggio, telling each other what lousy drivers kids are, I was out here, thinking about my facts. I'd like to have somebody listen while I tell 'em."

Pop's voice was firm. "Whoa, Jimmy."

Jimmy paused in mid-stride, dropped his hands. "I was yelling. I'm sorry," he said. "But I was driving with extra care because I'd passed where there'd been a hit-and-run accident—cops all over, ambulance, crowds."

Pop said, "On Lake Boulevard. We heard about it on TV."

"Yeah," Jimmy said. "Accidents scare me, so I was driving carefully. And I recognized Mrs. Murphy's car. Mr. Murphy's one of your best customers. I'd run in the ditch before I scratched that car. Wouldn't I?"

"If you had a choice," pop said.

"I tell you I gave her plenty of room."

"The collision was in the right-hand lane."

"Does that mean it was my fault?"

Pop said, "I'm afraid it does."

"What if she ran into me?" Jimmy said. "What if she hit the gas? With all the horses she's got in that car, she'd be up my back before I knew it."

Pop stared at the boy. "Jimmy, for the love of Mike!"

"It could happen," Jimmy said.

"How fantastic can you get?"

Cricket said, "Please, pop. He's upset. Let's don't talk about it now."

Jimmy looked at her. "You don't believe me either."

"I didn't say that, son. I——"

"You don't have to say it." He looked at his father. "Or you, pop. You both think I'm trying to alibi, trying to chicken out of my responsibility. You both think I'm a liar."

"I do not!" Cricket said.

"Honestly mistaken," pop said. "I don't doubt for a moment you believe you were driving safely. You may have been thinking too much about the accident you'd seen and not enough about your driving. You may have misjudged speed and distance. Face it, Jimmy; no one would overtake a passing car deliberately or by accident. You can't sell it to me or anyone. Don't try to sell it to yourself."

Jimmy's face was tight. "That's the last word?"

"That's it." Pop stood up. "I've got to go and talk to Ben Murphy and tell him how I feel about his wife being hurt." He looked at his son. "You don't have to go."

Cricket said, "Not tonight! Jimmy's——"

"I'm all right," Jimmy said. "I'll go."

Pop and Jimmy reached Ben Murphy's gate at ten o'clock. The yard lights were on, a dozen or more scattered over an acre of table-land bulldozed out of the hillside. A brick wall paralleled the road. "High enough to discourage outsiders," pop had once said, "low enough to let them see what they're missing." The house, ablaze with lights, was long and low, white brick and glass and red roof tile. Pop parked the family station wagon beside a bullet-nosed sports car in the drive.

"Pop," Jimmy said, his face still tight, "no matter what you think or I think, I can't take the blame. Charlie Stern told me not to."

"We're not here to take the blame," pop said. "We're here to show we're responsible people, that we're as sorry as people can be that Mrs. Murphy was hurt."

They got out of the car and followed a white walk around the house to the front door. Ben Murphy answered their ring. He was wearing a light topcoat and a hat and held a drink in one hand. He was a stocky bull of a man. His face was round and flushed, his mouth full-lipped. His eyes were hard, flat chips of glass that caught and held the light.

"Franklin," he said, "what do you want?"

Pop said, "This is my son, Jimmy. He was——"

"Sure!" Murphy's voice was harsh. "James Franklin! That was the name they gave me, but I didn't tie it to you." He looked at Jimmy, sudden fury clouding his face. "You lousy little punk! Do you know what you did to my wife? You damned near killed her, that's what you did. You tore her face all to hell!"

Jimmy said, "I'm sorry, Mr. Murphy. I——"

"Sorry! You should see her! I just came from the hospital, and I tell you it tore me apart. A beautiful face—in shambles. Nose smashed, eyes closed, deep cuts." He lifted his glass and swore. "You're sorry! You're gonna be worse than sorry!"

Pop eased his big bulk in front of Jimmy. "Slow down, Ben." His voice was soft, but it held an edge. "We came to tell you we couldn't feel worse about it and that we're standing by. Don't rough the lad; he's feeling bad enough."

"Let him talk," Jimmy said.

"What's that?" Murphy's voice was sharp. He tried to see past pop. "You smart-talking me, kid?"

"No, sir, I'm not," Jimmy said. "I know how you feel about Mrs. Murphy. Take it out on me if you want to. I saw her after the accident—I took care of her. And I wish I had somebody to take it out on."

Murphy stared at Jimmy a moment. Then, to pop, he said, "Get this kid outta here!" His voice was hoarse, shaking. "I don't trust myself. That murdering brat of yours—I'd like to use my hands on him. Run my wife off the road——" His mouth jerked. "You'll hear from me, Franklin. You'll hear from me!"

Pop turned and took Jimmy's arm. "Come on, lad."

Pop and Cricket sat in the kitchen, facing each other across the kitchen table, after Jimmy had gone to bed. They didn't joke as they usually did, hunting light words to make a serious moment less painful. Cricket's hands were locked together. Pop rubbed his face.

"Ben Murphy is not what you'd call a kind man," he said. "He's rough and at times he can be as ugly as sin. I think he'll be ugly about this. A second wife, twenty-five years younger than he is, a beautiful woman—to a man like Ben, a woman like that is more than a wife. She's a prize possession, proof he's a success as a man and as a businessman."

Cricket said, "She's no better than she——"

"Hey, now!"

Cricket caught a lip in her teeth. She was silent a long moment, struggling with herself. Then her eyes came up to meet pop's. "Can I take that back?"

"Sure, hon," pop said gently. "I thought the same thing; I had to take it back too. No matter what she is, she's suffering now. Calling her names won't help us or Jimmy."

Cricket nodded miserably. "I know."

"Ben would sue his grandmother for a scratched fender," pop said. "For a personal injury—this kind of personal injury—he'll be downright savage."

"Jimmy has public-liability insurance."

"Ten thousand." Pop got up from the table to pace the kitchen slowly. "How much is a woman's face worth, Cricket? Any woman, and a beautiful woman in particular?"

Wearily, Cricket said, "Whatever you can get."

"Right," pop said. "And anything over the insurance will come out of us. Fifty thousand, a hundred thousand—what's the difference? We've done all right, but it wouldn't take a big judgment to clean us out. Jimmy's insurance company will fight the suit and we'll fight it. But we might as well take the truth by the nose—Jimmy was to blame. We haven't got a chance."

"Don't tell Jimmy—please!"

Pop went to her, put his hands on her shoulders. "He'll have to know," he said, "but later will be soon enough."

"I wish they hadn't invented automobiles."

"Or damage suits," pop said. "I've worried about this every time I heard the boy start his car."

Jimmy was up early the next morning and gone early. He did his homework in the study hall before school took up. That was part of the deal he'd made with pop. He could work at the supermarket, earning money to pay for the car, but if his grades went down—blooie!—no job, the car went into the garage and stayed there. And he was campused—no movies, no dates, until his report card was good again.

He had a little trouble concentrating—the accident, the memory of Mrs. Murphy's bleeding face kept getting in the way. But he got through the school hours somehow. And he went from school to the police station. The law said he had to file a report within twenty-four hours of the accident. A uniformed man gave him a blank and pointed to a desk. Jimmy filled in the spaces of the blank. He drew a diagram—Car A, Car B—showing how the accident had happened, then took the form back to the man at the counter.

"Car A hit Car B." The policeman looked at Jimmy. "Car B is your car. Are you trying to say she ran into you after you passed her?"

Jimmy's face flushed. "Yes, sir."

"Good Lord!" the officer said. "Of all the flimsy alibis I ever heard, that takes the cake!" He threw the form in a box. "Now I've heard everything!"

Jimmy left the counter and the police station, cheeks flaming. He got into his car and fumbled with the keys. Every time, every gosh-darned time! If you were seventeen, you were a slob, a lying slob! The cops, Charlie Stern, pop, Cricket, Mr. Murphy—not one of them would even say "maybe."

"I'll show 'em," he said, "or bust something!"

He stopped at the supermarket and talked to the manager.

"You've got time off coming," the manager said. "Take as much as you need."

Jimmy went back to his car. He drove out Dutch Hill Road to Forty-seventh, parked there and looked around. Houses on one side of the road, brush and trees on the other. Most of the houses close by were big and new, fine lawns and lots of shrubs. But there were old places, weathered and shabby, on the side streets that wandered away toward the hill.

"One of those," Jimmy said.

He left the car. He climbed sun- and rain-warped steps and rang an old-fashioned doorbell. He talked to a woman with gray hair and watery eyes.

"I'm looking for a man who saw an accident last night," he said. "He wears bib overalls and a vest and a shirt with chopped-off sleeves."

"Nobody here like that," the woman said.

"Thanks anyway," Jimmy said.

He knocked on other doors. He talked to an old man, to a girl who wouldn't smile because she had braces on her teeth, to a woman whose hair was redder than any fire engine he had ever seen. He walked up one street and down another. Before he ran out of daylight, he had been to every old house within a quarter of a mile of the scene of the accident.

After dinner he spread a map of the city on the kitchen table and began to pencil out the streets he'd covered. Pop and Cricket came to look over his shoulder and ask what he was doing.

"Keeping track of where I've been," Jimmy said. "That way I don't have to go over the same ground twice."

"You're looking for the witness?" pop said.

"Yes," Jimmy said. "He was on foot. I figure he lives within maybe a mile of where the accident happened."

"That could be." Pop's frown said he was thinking hard. "One thing you'd better face, son. When you find him, he may break your heart. He may not have seen it or he may say you're to blame."

"Then I'll know," Jimmy said.

The next afternoon Jimmy took up the search as soon as school was out. He knocked on fifty or sixty doors, asking the same questions every time. Most of those he talked to were interested; most of them tried to help. Two people were sure they knew the man he was hunting, but both were wrong. One of the men they sent Jimmy to see was confined to a wheel chair, the other had been in Alaska for more than a month.

He used up the afternoon. He was walking back to his car when the bullet-nosed sports job came down the street, Ben Murphy at the wheel. The stocky man parked at the curb, close by.

"Over here," he said. "I want to talk to you."

"Yes, sir," Jimmy said.

"I was rough with you the other night," Murphy said. He wasn't smiling, but there was no anger in his face. "My wife goes downtown to buy a hat; next thing she's in the hospital. I was worried sick about her. Naturally. Since then, I've had time to think. I've known and liked your father for a long time, done a lot of business with him. I don't want him hurt or you hurt."

Jimmy said, "Well, thanks, Mr. Murphy."

"The bills have to be paid—the hospital, the doctors, the garage. Your insurance will take care of them." Murphy's eyes had no part in his brief smile. "This is between friends, boy. Let's keep it that way."

"I don't know what you mean."

"You're a worried guy," Murphy said. "You'd be less than human if you weren't. It could be unpleasant—complaints, litigation, your driver's license gone." He smiled again. "I see your car out here every time I go by. You're scrambling around trying to find something—somebody to get you off the hook. Right?"

"The witness," Jimmy said.

"A waste," Murphy said. "Forget it. Nothing's going to happen to you. Go home and rest your feet. The insurance company will pay the bills and everything will be fine." He put the car in gear.

"And be careful, kid. The next guy might not be a friend of your father's."

Jimmy said, "Mr. Murphy, I——"

But the sports car was moving, gravel spurting under the wheels. The taillights flared red, and it was gone around a corner. Jimmy stared after it.

"Fine!" he said. "As long as my insurance company has to pay, it's fine! And what does that do to me?" Jimmy set his jaws. No matter what Mr. Murphy said, he wasn't quitting yet. The man in the bib overalls had to live somewhere. He'd been afoot. He——

"Wait a darned minute!" Jimmy said.

He went back to his car, a new idea in his mind. The house nearest the scene of the accident was new and very big. The woman who answered the door was young, a pretty woman. She listened gravely to Jimmy's description of the witness.

"No," she said. "He doesn't live here."

"What I thought, he might work for you," Jimmy said. "Mowing the lawn, trimming the shrubs. One of the odd-job men that come around. Sometimes they leave a card."

"Sorry," the woman said.

Jimmy tried the house next door, the one next door to that. He found a blond and chunky man who had seen the witness. "Asked me to call an ambulance," he told Jimmy. "A stranger, though. I'd never seen him before. I've never seen him since."

Jimmy found people who'd heard the crash, who'd gone to see what had happened, but none of these remembered a thin gray man who wore overalls and a vest.

"Somebody must know the guy," Jimmy said.

He went on with it, until dusk thickened into dark. He went home to find pop and Cricket talking quietly in the kitchen. They stopped talking when he walked in, looked at him, waiting. He didn't have to tell them he'd had no luck; they saw it in his face.

Cricket was suddenly very busy at the range. Pop crumpled a beer can in his hands.

"Charlie Stern called," he said quietly.

Jimmy said, "I'm fresh out of insurance?"

"That's the size of it," pop said. "Charlie'll try to get you in the assigned-risk pool, but that'll take time."

"And cost more," Jimmy said.

"I can drive you around evenings," pop said.

"No," Jimmy said. "But you gave me an idea."

Two people could cover twice as much ground as one. Ten or twelve could hit every house within a mile in just one afternoon. A lot of kids he knew had cars, not all of them had jobs. Jimmy made a list and got on the telephone. Beans Hall had an appointment with a dentist. Jack Davis had a tennis date.

"I'll skip that," he said. "Ringing doorbells might be fun."

"I'll buy your gas—two gallons," Jimmy said.

He had it organized before he went to bed. Nine cars and twenty kids showed up on Dutch Hill Road at Forty-seventh, the next afternoon. Jimmy spread his map on the hood of Jack Davis' car.

"Each car gets a street," Jimmy said. "Up one side and down the other. Every house—don't miss even one. Then come back and report and get a new assignment."

"What if we find the guy?" Jack Davis said.

Jimmy said, "You get two extra gallons of gas."

He stayed behind as the cars fanned out through the neighborhood. He found a stump beside the road and used it for a desk. Just keeping track of where the kids had been turned out to be a job. Sometimes there were two or three cars lined up, waiting to report. And twenty searchers could have as little luck as one. The kids turned up several people who had seen the man, but none who knew his name or where he lived.

"We'll keep her goin'," Jimmy said.

He was talking to Fats Porter and Bob Hently when he heard

the blaring horn. Busy with the map and pencil, he did not look up. The horn yelled again and again. Fats Porter grunted his disgust, turned away and then turned back.

"Jim," he said, "I think the guy wants you."

Jimmy looked up. The bullet-nosed sports job was back again, parked on the shoulder of the road. Ben Murphy was peering over his shoulder. He hit the horn again, beckoned impatiently.

"I'll be right back," Jimmy said.

There was no smile on Ben Murphy's face. "You!" He thrust the word at Jimmy with a lifted chin. "I told you to go home and rest your feet!" he said. "Didn't you hear me, kid?"

"Yes," Jimmy said. "I heard you."

"So now you brought your gang!" Murphy's voice was harsh. His big hands gripped the wheel so tightly the cords of his wrists stood out like iron wire. "I was nice to you. Let it alone, let the insurance company pay the bills—that's all I asked. But no! You want to mess it up, shove it into court, make it tough for me to collect!"

"It wasn't my fault," Jimmy said.

"I'm giving you one more chance!" Murphy said. "Keep on and you'll get it—in the neck! You and your old man. I'll take care of you first. My wife will sign a complaint, criminal negligence, reckless driving. You'll be looking at a judge before you know it. You'll lose your license, get slapped with a fine and maybe a jail sentence. And that's only the beginning! We'll sue your father for a hundred thousand dollars for what you did to my wife's face!"

Jimmy said, "You can't——"

"The hell I can't!" Murphy said. "You're a minor; he's responsible for what you do. I'll sue and I'll win and I'll clean him out—every last dime, house, car, everything. He'll be the rest of his life paying off the judgment, and that's a promise, kid!" His lips flattened. "Go home and stay there, or you and your father will be in more trouble than you ever dreamed about!"

"Yes, sir," Jimmy said.

He watched the sports car roar away and then went back to the stump he'd used for a desk. He picked up the map and folded it carefully. He looked at his friends, eyes dull.

"You can take off," he said. "We're all through."

He found pop working in the garden, stripped to the waist. Pop wouldn't use a power cultivator. "These mitts of mine like the feel of an idiot-stick," he'd said. The truth was that pop liked hard work. One look at Jimmy's face was enough to bring him out of the garden.

"You found your witness," he said.

"No. And I guess I'm not going to. Mr. Murphy said he was going to sue you if I kept trying to cause him trouble." Jimmy swallowed. "Can he do that, pop? I mean, for a lot of money. A hundred thousand—everything you've got?"

"I've been expecting him to," pop said quietly.

Jimmy's voice broke. "Why didn't you tell me? I thought my insurance would be enough. I could have gone on looking and ruined you."

Pop's face was tight with thought, his eyes searching. "When did Murphy make this pitch about cleaning me out?"

"Just a while ago," Jimmy said. "The first time I saw him, he said he wasn't going to sign a complaint. All he wanted was for my insurance company to pay for everything. Great for him, but not for me. I kept on looking. This time he got real mean. Said if I didn't quit trying to get out of paying he'd clean you out."

"He did, did he?" Pop took Jimmy to a set of lawn chairs and made him repeat every word of both conversations he'd had with Murphy. There was anger in pop's face, mixed with deep concern. "Still think you were in the clear on the accident?" he asked.

"I know I was."

"But now you're willing to throw in the sponge?"

"For gosh sakes, pop! If it was just me, I wouldn't care. But it's you and mom now. I can't do anything that would make Mr. Murphy ruin you!"

Pop laid a big hand on Jimmy's arm. "That's a tough thing to say to your old man, lad. You'd give up fighting for something you feel is right to protect me. Am I so helpless?"

"Pop, I didn't mean——"

The big hand tightened on Jimmy's arm. "Don't ever quit," pop said slowly, "don't ever quit anything you think is right as long as you've got a breath left in your body. Every man's got a light that guides him. Turn it off for me, for anybody, and you'll get lost in the dark."

"You want me to go on?"

Pop nodded. "Come hell or high water. And if you want help, I'll bear a hand."

Jimmy got up from the chair, excitement growing in him. "I could use some help, pop. There are places me and the kids couldn't look because we're minors. I thought a man like him might spend a lot of time in taverns and bars. They won't let me in alone, but if you were with me they might."

"What do you mean, might?" Pop stood up, six feet tall, one hundred and ninety pounds of hard bone and muscle. He swelled his chest for Jimmy. "Who's going to argue?"

Jimmy grinned, delighted. "Nobody!"

"So, O.K.," pop said. "Get the wagon out."

Jimmy watched him cross the yard toward the house, so proud he could hardly stand it. "What a guy to have for a pop!" he said. "A one-man army!" He ran for the garage and backed the station wagon into the drive. Pop came out of the house presently, wearing slacks and a sports shirt, and got behind the wheel.

"You're the skipper," he said. "Where to?"

"He was walking," Jimmy said. "He could have been on his way to a place or on his way home from one. We could start where I had the accident and hunt in one direction. If we don't have any luck, we can come back and hunt the other way."

"Will do!" Pop put the car on the road.

They began their search at a crossroads a half mile from the scene of the accident. There were two stores here—a service station and a tavern. The men in the tavern swung around to stare at Jimmy, the bartender came down the bar to wave him away. Then pop came through the door.

"Hold fast," pop said. "This is my son."

The bartender looked at the spread of pop's shoulders, at the size of his arms, at the thick brows that were down in a scowl.

"Yes, sir," he said. "What can we do for you?"

Pop said, "Take it, Jimmy."

"I'm looking for a man who saw an accident," Jimmy said.

He got to look in the face of every man there, and no one protested. They listened to his description, they tried very hard to place the man, and all of them were genuinely sorry when they could not be of help.

"I'll ask around," the bartender said. "Come back in a day or two if you don't have any luck."

"Thank you all," Jimmy said.

The next place was another tavern, and the scene was repeated. It was followed by four more taverns, three cheap bars and a package store where wine was sold. They didn't find their man, but it was not because of resistance. The round-faced, man-tall boy and the quiet, big-shouldered man were a team no one cared to deny. When they had covered every place within a reasonable walking distance in one direction, pop turned the car and they began to hunt in the other.

"Still with me?" pop asked.

"We'll find him," Jimmy said. "We can't miss."

They found him in a dingy, hole-in-the-wall joint. He was drinking wine with a beer chaser in a booth toward the back. Jimmy almost missed him because he was wearing a suit instead of overalls and a vest. A thin wisp of a man, older than his fifty years, unshaven. He had a weak mouth and blurred eyes.

"Do you remember me?" Jimmy asked.

"Maybe I do," the man said. "And maybe I don't."

Pop came up behind Jimmy. He put a big hand on the table. "Make up your mind," he said quietly.

The blurred eyes looked at the hand for a long moment. "Yeah," the man said then. "I remember you, kid."

Jimmy's knees almost folded under him. After all the hours of searching—finally! He tried to swallow and found his throat too dry. "Did you see the accident happen?"

"I was there, wasn't I? I saw it."

"Whose fault was it?" Jimmy asked. "Mine or hers?"

The man rubbed his stubbled chin. He took a drink of wine and a swallow of beer. Then he grinned at Jimmy. "Yours, kid," he said. "You cut in on her and ran her off the road."

The color drained from Jimmy's face, the strength drained from his legs. Pop put a hand on his shoulder and turned him. Jimmy started a protest, but the hurt and deep sympathy in his father's face told him the case was closed. He pulled free of his father's hand and went out and got into the car. In a few moments, pop came out and got in beside him.

"Tough," pop said gently. "I'm sorry, lad."

Jimmy didn't answer.

Pop fumbled with the car keys. "It was a chance we both knew you were taking. So you lost. But I'm still damned proud of you. You gave it a good fight."

Jimmy turned a quivering face toward his father. "I wasn't taking a chance," he said. "I knew if I found the guy, if he'd seen the accident, he'd clear me. Why? Because I know I didn't cut back too fast!"

"He saw the accident. He said——"

"Pop! He lied!"

Pop stared at Jimmy. Then, suddenly, he swore. "What in hell is the matter with me?" he asked. "I can believe a booze-brain or I can believe my son. Who do I believe? The booze-brain. I ought to have my rump kicked!" He slapped the door of the station wagon open. "Be right back!" he said.

He was gone five minutes—an eternity for Jimmy. And when he came back, he was grinning. "You're the champ," he said.

Jimmy's face began to light. "Pop, did he really——"

"He sure did," pop said. "I offered him twenty-five bucks to see the accident our way. He said no. I said fifty bucks and he said no. I said a hundred, and he said yes."

"No, pop!" Jimmy's voice was agonized.

Pop grinned. "Easy does it, boy. All I wanted was to find out if he was for sale. He was. So I put my fist under his nose and asked if maybe he hadn't sold out to Murphy first. Turns out he had. For fifty bucks."

"Murphy paid him?"

"This is a wino," pop said. "His brains are pulp. He'd sell his soul for the price of a few bottles, and he can't think farther ahead than a few. He saw Mrs. Murphy run into you after you'd passed her—the accident was her fault. You're a kid, driving a heap. You couldn't pay him anything to testify. But a man who owned the car Mrs. Murphy was driving could afford to pay him not to testify. He got Murphy's name and address from the newspaper account of the accident, went around to Murphy and made his pitch—pay up or he'd look you up. Murphy paid."

"But that makes Mr. Murphy a crook!"

"So it does," pop agreed.

"Why—why would he do it?"

"It's a chance to clip your insurance company for your public liability—ten thousand bucks—and for a bandit like Murphy that's important. Sure, he's got insurance of his own. One-hundred-dollar deductible and maybe seven-fifty medical, about a tenth of what's going to be needed. And without that witness, he's got grounds for a lawsuit against you and your insurance company—his wife's beautiful face has been smashed. What's the value on that? Ten thousand? Fifty thousand? All this he gets for just fifty bucks."

"No wonder he was afraid I'd find the witness."

"Yeah," pop said. "No wonder." He put the car in gear.

"Wait a minute, pop," Jimmy said. He was staring through the windshield. "Now we've got to think about something else—something that's been driving me nuts. She ran into me. We can prove that now. But how? And why? Stop and think about it. The only way—she'd have to do it deliberately."

"Her foot could slip off the brake——"

"And jam the gas down? And hold it down that long?"

"For the love of Mike!" pop said. "She wasn't mad at you. She couldn't gain anything by running into you. She could get herself in a bad smash-up, and she did! Jimmy, lad, it just doesn't make sense!"

"Maybe it does." Jimmy turned his head slowly to look at his father. "Remember the tangle I had with the guy who smelled like a brewery? He had a beat-up fender; he got a brand-new fender out of the accident. Maybe Mrs. Murphy wanted to hit me just a little, to cover up a bent fender or something like that. But she hit me a lot and went out of control."

"The Murphys can afford to fix their own fenders."

"You've got to run into something to bend a fender," Jimmy said. "Can they afford to fix what Mrs. Murphy hit before she ran into me?" He looked at his father. "I may be wrong, but I've got to talk to the cops. Right now. Will you take me downtown?"

"When you tell me what's in your head," pop said.

They walked into the police station together, faces grave with concern. There was doubt in their minds, but their responsibility was clear to them, and responsibility can sometimes be an enormous burden. Jimmy talked to the lieutenant in charge of traffic.

"I went by that hit-and-run accident on Lake Boulevard, just after it happened," he said. "It scared me pretty bad. I've been thinking about it a lot, watching the papers. But I've never seen where you found the driver."

"We haven't found him." The lieutenant was a thin, sharp-nosed, dour man. Light glinted on his rimless glasses. "But I'd give my right arm to find him. The old woman he left in the gutter will live, but she'll never walk again."

Jimmy swallowed. "Could the driver have been a woman?"

The lieutenant, looking at Jimmy's pale face, wondered if the boy was going to be sick. "It could have been a woman," he said slowly. "All we've got is a description of the car—a big, late-model sedan."

Jimmy turned his stricken eyes to pop, asking for help, for guidance. But what help could there be? And what guidance, except to point the way straight forward? Pop put a big hand on Jimmy's shoulder.

"I don't know for sure," Jimmy said. "I'm not accusing anybody, see? But I've got to tell you what happened. After I passed the accident on Lake Boulevard, I went out Dutch Hill Road—that's the way I go home. There was a woman driving real slow out there. I passed her. And after I passed her, she speeded up and ran into me."

The lieutenant tipped his head. "She ran into you? After you passed her?"

"We've got a witness," pop said.

"All right. Go on, son."

"The woman, Mrs. Murphy, had been downtown buying a hat —her husband told me that. She'd go home by way of Lake Boulevard. Everybody does who lives out our way. It's quickest by fifteen minutes. So she had to go past the place where the woman was hit. If she'd stopped to think what she could do or drove real slow, I'd have caught up with her where I did." Jimmy's eyes were miserable. "Why would anybody run into a guy on purpose?"

"You tell me," the lieutenant said.

"To cover up something like a bent fender?"

"Or a cracked headlight," the lieutenant said softly, "or a dented hood. Because every car that's gone into any garage with that kind of damage has been reported to us and we've checked it out. Mrs. Murphy's car was checked out, the damage charged to you. You'd better tell me the name of your witness, son."

Patrolman Sam Riggio came to the Franklin home early the next evening. There was no need for him to do it. But he, too, was a man with a sense of responsibility. He made his partner, Mark Bradford, go to the door with him. Bradford was the man who resented teen-age drivers, sometimes to the point of hate. Riggio was smiling when pop opened the door.

"We'd like to talk to Jimmy."

Pop led them into the living room. Jimmy was playing cribbage with Cricket. He stumbled to his feet awkwardly at the sight of the police officers, his round face twisting in a worried frown.

Cricket said, "Oh, my goodness!" and flew around the room, picking up papers and straightening cushions.

"We've come with an apology," Riggio told Jimmy. "We didn't call you a liar, but we refused to believe you, and that adds up to the same thing."

Bradford stepped forward. "You've got a right to chew us out," he said, "but I've got to tell you there's not much left to chew. The lieutenant got to us first. We jumped to a wrong conclusion, we let a hit-and-run driver get away. The lieutenant takes a dim view of that kind of work. We're lucky to be alive."

Jimmy said, "Did—did Mrs. Murphy do it?"

Riggio nodded. "Once we'd talked to your witness, it was easy going. We went from him to Murphy to ask Murphy why he'd paid the fifty dollars, and from there to Mrs. Murphy to ask why she'd run into you on purpose, since it had to be that way. She's not a tough criminal with a thought-out plan. She's a frightened woman with an enormous burden of guilt. She wanted to be rid of it. She gave us a confession."

Pop was frowning. "Did Murphy know about the hit-and-run when he paid the wino the fifty bucks?"

"No," Riggio said. "And neither did the wino. When the wino showed up at Murphy's front door with an offer to get lost and keep his mouth shut for fifty dollars, Murphy grabbed it like a shot.

It was small money, money he could throw away or deny he'd ever spent. And it cleared his wife of the blame of hitting Jimmy."

"It also paved the way to a damage suit," pop said, "against Jimmy, his insurance company and me. A damage suit that could go fifty or a hundred thousand. A bargain for fifty bucks."

"Not such a bargain." Riggio smiled. "When he'd thought about it awhile, Murphy saw that his wife must have run into Jimmy on purpose. He asked her why, she told him, and then he had a can of beans he was afraid to open. What could he do about the wino? He couldn't go to him with more money and a ticket out of the state. The wino would want to know why—all he'd asked for, all he'd wanted, was fifty bucks. And if the wino found out why, he could blackmail Murphy for the rest of his life."

"But leave it alone," pop said, "and it was a million to one the wino would never put the two accidents together. The police didn't and their brains aren't pulp."

"That was his choice," Riggio agreed. "A Hobson's choice, and Murphy made the wrong pick. He calls it bad luck. I call it the kind of thing that happens to a man with larceny in his heart."

Cricket said, "He should have gone to the police and admitted his wife was the hit-and-run driver."

"And face criminal action and a lawsuit that could bankrupt him?" pop asked. "Not Murphy!"

When the police had gone, pop put his arm around Jimmy's shoulders and grinned proudly at Cricket. "This is my boy," he said. "His guts and good sense saved me a lousy fortune."

Cricket knew her son well, knew why there was no light in the boy's eyes, why he tried to pull away from his father.

"Mrs. Murphy will be all right, sonny," she said. "I've talked to her doctor. It isn't so bad as they first thought. There may not even be noticeable scars. She'll be pretty again."

Jimmy turned to her, doubting. "Mom, honest?"

"I promise."

"That's—that's wonderful." Now Jimmy's face began to glow. "If you could have seen her the way I did. I thought—well, I was afraid to think! Holy cow!" He caught his mother's face suddenly between his hands and kissed her. "You're the most!" he said to her, and went quickly away.

Pop stared after him. "After what she did to the old lady, after what she tried to do to him, he's worried about her face! How do you like a dope like that?"

Softly, Cricket said, "Only very, very much."